John Courage

A novel

Based on a true story

Mimi Tashjian

John Courage Copyright © 2016 by Mimi Tashjian

Cover & Interior Design by Scribe Freelance | www.scribefreelance.com

Cover photography and design: Kathy Russell and Jenn Mendez

Photograph of the author: Kathy Russell

ISBN: 978-0-9968179-0-5

Printed in the United States of America by Ingram Content Group

John
Courage

For Martha —
Happy reading;
Happy riding!
XO
[signature]

For my mother, who took me for my first ride,
and for my father, who suggested it.

For Scott and Ken, who have kept me in the
saddle for more than twenty years.

For DL, Charlie and Brooke,
the reason I breathe everyday.

For Michael.

And all along I believed I would find you
Time has brought your heart to me
I have loved you for a thousand years
I'll love you for a thousand more

—CHRISTINA PERRI

PART I

1

Just like almost every day for as long as she could remember, Josie Parker anxiously awaited the bell signifying the end of the school day at Middletown High. No sooner would she hear the sound than she would be out the door ahead of most of her classmates, and running across the campus, past the soccer field, around the tennis courts and through the faculty parking lot, she'd come to a stop at the otherwise empty bike rack.

Jumping on her rickety Schwinn and thinking, *I'm too old to have a bike like this*, she pumped the pedals as fast as she could that June afternoon and raced the half-mile distance along the rolling asphalt hills of Cooper Road, slowing down only to negotiate a safe turn into the worn-down gravel driveway that led to her family's home alongside Barrett Park and the Navesink Creek, in the vast, hill-laden horse country of Monmouth County, New Jersey.

Sweeping through the back door, Josie called out, knowing her mother was somewhere in the house.

"Hey Mama, seven days until I am officially a senior!" she proudly pronounced at the top of her lungs.

Book bag tossed to rest on the kitchen table, Josie ran up the back stairs to her room and shed her school clothes as she sat on the toilet. Jumping up, she stepped into the jeans she'd hung yesterday on the back of the bathroom door, then found a fresh, no-longer-good-enough-for-school blouse in the painted chest of drawers stationed across from her antique mahogany bed. She pulled the blouse over her head, grabbed her windproof jacket from the bedpost and headed back downstairs to the kitchen of the clapboard-sided, three-bedroom colonial she had lived in since the day she was born. She sat at the small, round table just long enough to gulp down the Hawaiian Punch and graham crackers set out for her as she slipped her legs into the tall, black rubber riding boots that waited by her chair. Her mother silently braided Josie's blond locks. Not much was spoken between them that day, but not for any reason of ill intent or dismay. Josie and her mother were very close.

It was a beautiful spring day in 1974. The air was crisp and the sky was clear; Josie was, as usual, in a hurry to get to the barn. Her mother was well aware. This was the daily routine in the Parker household.

"Two hours, Josie!" her mother hollered, smiling and wiping her hands on her apron as Josie ran out the back door. "Two hours!" she yelled again as she followed her girl and stood on the back steps. "Dinner is at six and you need to be CLEAN!"

Dorie Parker and her husband, Frank, knew their daughter's passion all too well. They would never discourage it, for they knew the goodness that came from it. Dorie herself had grown up obsessed with horses, and she had passed this love on to her daughter, who at the age of three had experienced her first pony ride. Now, at sixteen, Josie wished for nothing more than to be able to spend every minute of every day at Hidden Green Farm, located across Barrett Park and over the creek, just minutes from the Parkers' house. Dorie understood from her own experiences that the lessons of life learned, and the knowledge gained at the barn, trumped anything she had ever learned in a classroom. As much as she appreciated the importance of education, she wanted more than anything to give Josie the gift of a lifelong relationship with horses. Watching her daughter run through the backyard toward the park gave Dorie a sense of satisfaction and comfort at the same time. She cherished her only child, Josie-Rose Caldwell Parker.

Josie was a tad more than average height for her age, and she didn't really have the body of a rider. Her torso was long, so she would never quite look well-suited on the smaller horses at the barn. She'd often acknowledged to herself that she was just a little envious of the girls who were "all legs," and wished hers were longer and that her hips were a bit narrower. Her waist-length, strawberry blond hair had just the right amount of natural wave to give her a feminine quality no matter how "tom-boyed up" she was. She preferred to wear it in braids, and she loved when her mother would pull and twist it into perfect form while Josie sat at the kitchen table. Her wide, sun-kissed face was a happy one, her brown eyes always bright and inquisitive. Her button nose, covered in barely noticeable freckles, sat perched over her perfectly pink lips which, when Josie was born, resembled the shape of a miniature rose bud. Thus, her name, Josie-Rose. Dorie's mother, Josephine Caldwell, approved, especially of the family middle name. As did Frank Parker, whom would forever after call his daughter Rosebud, a nickname Josie detested but tolerated because he was her dad.

More than just about anything, Josie loved horses, and to know the love of horses is to know it is all-consuming. She read about them, watched television shows about them, made them the focus of any school project she could—whether it be science, English, or history. She dreamed about being a member of an Olympic show jumping team, like Mary Chapot, or becoming a leading hunter trainer, like Charlie Weaver, or a famous equitation coach, like George Morris. She dreamed about becoming a renowned veterinarian, about running the best show barn in the Northeast. Any one of those futures would suit Josie Parker just fine.

Josie ran as fast as she could manage in her loose, clunky boots—into Barrett Park, past the wood and steel picnic tables, the tall, industrial strength swings, the painted, plastic rocking animals on the big fat coils, the spinning wheel. *Yuck, I hate that thing*, she reminded herself as she passed it. *That one always makes me sick.*

Past the monkey bars she tossed a quick glance at the baseball diamond, where at this time of year, twice a week, the Parson Prep School varsity team would be practicing or playing games. Most days she waved behind her as she hurried along, no time to waste on boys. In the boys versus horses battle, horses usually won; Josie understood horses. But some days, if the timing was right, she would make an exceptional pause to watch her friend Cleve Gregory, especially if he was up at bat.

"Hey batta, batta!" she would holler, laughing. "Hey batta, batta, come on batta!" Then she would shrug her shoulders as if to say, "Sorry," and turn to continue her trek. On those days Cleve followed her with envious eyes as he headed back to the bench, so much would he rather be dashing to catch up to her. For he too had the passion and would prefer to spend every minute at the barn, mucking stalls, feeding, watering, grooming, sweeping, cleaning tack. But twice a week he made the compromise his dad had insisted of him and played ball. It was a small price to pay if it meant he could have all weekend at the barn.

Cleve was in the same grade as Josie yet almost a year older. At three or four inches taller, he had an imposing presence; one might even say a movie star quality. His skin was darker than hers, and his sweeping, thick, dark brown hair fell perfectly across his forehead. He couldn't help but catch everyone's attention.

Cleve and Josie had been friends for what seemed like forever. Their bond was over horses; horses did that to people. Cleve hung out at Hidden Green as often as Josie, except for the baseball days. Aside from a few years of lessons as a child, he'd had no real training, but he was naturally athletic and had great instinct when it came to knowing what it took to make horses perform well. He rode on occasion but mostly executed odd jobs around the farm, for which he was paid a nominal amount of money every few weeks. Truth was, he would work for free just so he could be there, but the extra pocket money sure came in handy. He was hoping he'd soon have enough to make an offer on a beat-up Chevy truck he'd seen down at Diller's Used Autos. A guy needed his own wheels; cliché but true.

Josie's own secret was that she thought Cleve was incredibly irresistible. She liked him much more than just as a friend but hadn't told anyone, not even Tessa, her best girlfriend; although, truth be told, Tessa was keenly aware of the chemistry between Josie and Cleve. Lately, Josie found herself cognizant of Cleve in a way that was different from the way she was aware of any other guy. His back was broad and his plaid, man-tailored shirts fell without flaw from his shoulders to his narrow waist. His jeans fit impeccably, and she couldn't help but notice they were just tight enough in all the right places. Sometimes when she thought about it, she shivered. His lips were created with perfection, just the right amount of puffy, and when he spoke, those perfect lips moved slowly, softly. She felt herself blush every time they spoke face-to-face and she despised that about herself. When they did talk, his voice was always gentle. The way he stared into her eyes made her uncomfortable in a weird way that felt really good. *He'd be perfect in a Marlboro ad,* she'd often think. *He's such a perfect cowboy.*

Josie moved quickly across the park that day, darting through the huge maple and ash trees and flitting down the worn-in, overgrown path to the Navesink Creek. At certain times of the year there were special "goings on" in that little stretch of Mother Nature's growth and Josie felt privileged to experience them. Rarely could she keep herself from stopping, if only for a few seconds, to marvel in all of its beauty.

In early spring, robins' or cardinals' nests in the viburnum bushes, full of chirping, hungry chicks, might catch her eye. In June, the creek turtles would dig along the sandy bank, making their nests. In July, the wild raspberries were ripe for picking and Josie would sometimes bring a small bucket from home to collect some of the faceted red jewels for dessert. In October, if she were very lucky, she might glimpse the sly red fox scooting into the underbrush, hoping to escape notice.

Not so this day. Josie scampered on. She climbed up the bank on the far side, followed the path through the mess of overgrown brush, and pulled herself up and over the three-rail fence that circled the main riding ring at Hidden Green Farm. She stopped to take a breath and to admire this place she loved so much. Then she hopped off the fence and cantered through the ring pretending to be on horseback, imaginary reins and crop in hand, jumping the cross rail fences, trotting the cavalletti poles.

"Cluck, cluck, let's go," she said and snapped her tongue, her arms moving forward and back in rhythm. "Whoa now, whoa." Josie knew this was all quite juvenile, and she always hoped that no one would see her, but she'd been doing it for so long now that it had almost become a ritual.

It was Wednesday, and on Wednesdays twice a month, the blacksmith William Fells came to the barn. Josie loved the smell of the burning hooves; she loved the clank-clank-clank sound of the farrier's hammer against his andiron. She treasured the horseshoe nail rings William would sometimes make for her and the other girls at the barn; she had quite a collection of them at home. If she didn't dally, she could usually get there in time to watch him shoe his last horse or two of the day.

She entered the barn and yelled ahead, "Hey William, you still got a few?"

2

The main barn was old and in great disrepair, but it was still beautiful. The architecture was English Tudor, faded mustard-color stucco with lots of wooden beam trim and a red asphalt roof, overgrown with ivy. There was an old metal silo just out the back door to the right, which nowadays was used to store farm equipment.

Mike O'Hara rented Hidden Green from the Jordans, a rarely observed family of four who lived in the dramatic, antebellum farmhouse at the far end of the long, fence-lined dirt drive that came down from Cooper Road. No one in the Jordan family had anything to do with the animals that inhabited the farm, or for that matter, the people connected to those animals. It puzzled Josie that she had never seen anyone come or go from the big white estate. *I'd love to live that close to the barn,* she thought, *to be able to hear the horses whinnying and snorting, to smell the hay first thing every morning. How amazing would it be to look out my window and see all my mares grazing in the pasture? I wonder why they own a place like this if they're not into horses.*

"This place is just real estate to the Jordans, Josie," Mr. O'Hara had explained to her a while back. "Someday they will tear it down and put up a bunch of houses around a cul-de-sac," he'd said with a hint of cynicism.

Driving in from Cooper Road, the gelding pasture along the right was spotted with trees and a few natural jumps; it doubled as an outside course to practice on before going to competitions. That time of year, slender, green spears of grass were well on their way to poking up through the dirt. The wooded property that paralleled the gelding pasture on the other side of the driveway had been sold off years before. Eventually the long drive opened to the courtyard, where mothers would park and wait while their children took their riding lessons.

The entrance to the main barn was lackluster; nothing more than a small, unremarkable Dutch door that hung loosely on its rusted iron hinges. For the better part of every weekday, activity on this side of the barn was limited, but at lesson time the courtyard was always abuzz with cars pulling in and out, children coming and going, mothers chatting. Few parents ever actually ventured to the ring to watch; here in the courtyard they enjoyed their own social gathering until a dozen or so young equestrians came piling out that vapid barn door with smiles on their dirty faces, exhausted and happy.

Beyond the courtyard, at the very end of the drive and just around to the right, was the cottage that had originally been built for the barn help. This is where Mike O'Hara lived. One of a few other small structures adjacent to the main barn was the standing stall shed, which housed the Hidden Green Riding School horses. Inside this utilitarian building, two long rows of divided spaces—'slots' of sorts, each no wider than four or five feet—provided only enough room for horses to stand facing one direction. Because there were no stall doors to confine them, it was necessary to tether them by the halter to a hook in the wall, with just enough slack to let them reach their grain and water buckets, and if agile enough, to lie down. Although far from luxury accommodation, every school horse at Hidden Green had a roof over its head at night and just the right amount of protection needed from the elements.

The private boarders and Mr. O'Hara's own horses lived in the big stalls of the main barn. Although now quite worn, they were originally crafted with beautiful iron and brass trimmings, forged hayracks, and Dutch-style doors that allowed the horses some freedom from the limits of their containment. There were fourteen stalls in the main barn, all painted white with black trim, and when you became a private boarder, it was a right of passage to be designated a stall here. There were far too many cobwebs and broken glass windowpanes, and the brass knobs everywhere needed polishing, but the barn still maintained a regal quality.

Mr. O'Hara employed two strong workers, Jeb and Sancho, to muck stalls, sweep the barn, manage the cobwebs, feed and water the horses, clear the paddocks and pastures of manure, mow, and execute all the other day-to-day responsibilities of maintaining a riding school and private show stable. They came and went religiously and never spoke much; when they did it was in broken English. But each exhibited a loyal and devoted connection to the horses they cared for. The boarded horses were groomed every day, a luxury not afforded the school horses unless they were on the schedule to be used in a lesson. In addition to Jeb and Sancho, Luka was responsible for grounds maintenance and general carpentry around the farm, and then there was Cleve.

Mr. O'Hara also "employed" several of the private boarders, who arrived every day after school (except Mondays when the barn was officially closed) in time to groom and saddle up the school horses that would be ridden in the day's group lesson. Rather than wages, their "compensation" was a free lesson twice each week and the opportunity for extra rides on any of the unassigned school horses. Perhaps the biggest benefit was that their parents were given a break on the cost of the private board. This barter system was appreciated by all; this was not a rich kids' barn.

On weekends, most of the barn chores belonged to this group of working boarders, and to Cleve and Josie too. Cleve kept mostly to himself, but Tessa, Libby O, Suzanna, Josie, Joni, Lyssa, and Rachel were a tight bunch. They felt very special and very privileged, though they were, with one or two exceptions, quite the opposite. Their bond was their mutual obsession with all things equine, and they shared the same desire—to spend as much time as possible at Hidden Green Farm.

From the first ride she could remember, Josie felt so right in a saddle. She was rarely intimidated by any horse. Rather, she was curious and motivated to figure out what inspired their idiosyncrasies; to understand why they exhibited behaviors that sometimes made them seem afraid, belligerent, or mean. She believed there was no bad horse. *They have different personalities, just like people,* she had written in her journal. She felt compelled to visit each new horse in its stall, to bring them treats to make them feel at home. She would walk them around the farm to ease their fear of being in a new place. She'd sit on the fence at the in-gate of the paddock when they were turned out for the first time, to be sure they didn't run too hard, or put themselves at risk. She owned an innate trust for horses and consequently they always seemed to reciprocate.

Mike O'Hara was keenly aware of Josie's maturity and level of interest in the well-being of the horses. He knew she had an exceptionally natural manner that almost every horse responded to with immediate positivity. He knew that when it came to horses, Josie had a heart the size of his six-horse van. He understood that to her, horses were less a possession and more living, breathing beings with souls and emotional needs, and he knew that this would keep horses in her life forever. Teaching her was never a chore; he knew she really listened and cherished every bit of wisdom he had to share.

"Josie, look here, what do you make of this?" Mike might ask when he discovered something amiss with one of the school horses or ponies. "Looks like a popped splint to me, what do you think?" He wasn't really looking for an answer, it was just his subtle way of imparting knowledge.

Her response was always sincere and inquisitive, never simply a respectful accommodation.

"So how do we treat that? Can he still be ridden? Will it go away or will it always look like that now? What makes that happen?" She always had a million questions.

Josie understood the conformation of a horse. She studied the legs of the school horses when she groomed them and noticed the variations. She'd visually follow the line of a horse's back, from the withers at the base of the mane to the top of the tail, and knew how everything should line up in order to please judges at the shows. She would watch when they were being ridden and instinctively could recognize the ones who moved correctly. Josie was never shy to report to Mr. O'Hara something that seemed wrong, and on many occasions she'd identified signs and symptoms in need of veterinary attention.

"You cost me a fortune in vet bills, Josie Parker," Mr. O'Hara would tease. She'd listen and observe intently as the veterinarian conducted examinations and would silently (most of the time) make her own assessment. She was always quite proud when she would come up with the same diagnosis as the vet.

"Hey Doc Thurman, don't you think it looks like the left hind on

Leo?" or "Hey Doc Thurman, if you do a flexion test won't we see if it's his stifle?"

"Hey Josie," Doc Thurman would respond in a calm, low voice, "how about you let me be the veterinarian here, huh?" He would smile and tell her, "Run to my truck and get me the radiograph box, you can help me with the X-rays."

Before he'd have the chance to look over at her, she would already be in a full-speed gallop to his truck.

3

"Hey William! Who's still on the list today?" Josie called out again to the farrier as she walked up the aisle, instinctively peering into each stall, checking legs, buckets, hay nets. "Hey, Shaka, hey buddy. Looks like you could use a new salt lick." She spoke to every horse as though they understood her perfectly.

The sliding doors adjacent to the wash stall were open, William's truck was backed up to the edge of the barn, and Clown, a big red Morgan with a black mane and tail, was standing quietly on the cross ties. Josie came to a stop, watching, listening. William, draped in his farrier's apron, stood bent over holding Clown's rear right leg between his knees. He was working the long rasp back and forth across the front edge of the well-behaved horse's hoof. It made the most unusual sound. *Schweep-schweep-schweep.* William looked up and wiped his sleeve across his face, then continued filing.

"Check that forge again," he called to his assistant who was positioned at the truck, working by the small furnace used to bend and mold the horseshoes. "Hey Josie, just finishing up Clown. Had to put some bar shoes on this guy this month. His old ones are there on the truck. If you want one, help yourself."

"You know I do. Thanks, William." She gave Clown a scratch under his forelock, and pulled a sugar cube from her pocket. "Here you go, pal."

Along with her horseshoe nail rings, Josie had a collection of old steel shoes in a basket beside her bed at home. She was sure that one of these days she would think of something to do with all of them. She grabbed a couple from the truck.

As Josie trotted off, William looked up and smiled, thinking, *I'll be darned if that girl doesn't turn out to be a blacksmith some day.*

The boarders' equipment, commonly referred to as tack, was kept in a room separate from the one that stored the riding school supplies. Saddles and bridles were lined up along the walls, resting on racks that had been specially made to hold them. Fancy show trunks, custom made in the barn colors of hunter green and gray, were lined up under the rows of saddles, and below the bridles were the everyday tack boxes that Mike O'Hara had constructed of plywood, then painted black. Each box had been assigned to a boarder, and Mike had assigned one to Josie too. The tack room was considered the chapel of the barn. It was a sacred place and Josie felt energized every time she walked in. She kept her own saddle here. She had saved her allowance and any spare change she could find, in a jar on her bedside table for nearly a year. When she had half what was needed to buy a second-hand saddle her mama made up the difference as an early birthday gift, and thus Josie had acquired her first official piece of tack. The little brass plate tapped into the back of the seat, engraved in simple block letters, JOSIE PARKER, gave her an incredible sense of pride every time she walked into the tack room and saw her saddle sitting up on its mantle.

In Josie's tack box, like most others, there were chaps, a hard hat, a crop and spurs, riding gloves, and grooming essentials—a curry comb and a brush, a hoof pick and a mane comb, scissors, braiding thread and big, wide-eyed braiding needles. There was also a natural sponge and a scraper for bathing, and of course saddle soap, Lexol, and a can of NeverDull polish—necessities for cleaning tack. She had an old rain jacket that smelled of mildew and a box of Domino sugar cubes. Josie had everything that might be needed, except for one thing. She didn't have her own horse. She dreamed that one day there would be enough saved in that jar on her bedside table to buy one, but she also knew that dream was not likely to come true. *Never mind*, she would think. *All of the horses at Hidden Green are like my own, and maybe someday...*

She blew an air kiss toward the horseshoes William had given her, imploring luck, and tossed them in her box. As she turned to walk back out into the barn, Cleve Gregory came through the tack room door with command.

"Hey Jos'," Cleve said not as though surprised to see her, but as though he'd actually planned to meet her there. He stood so close that for a nanosecond their chests were actually touching. She was uncomfortable, but in a way that made her desperate to stay right there pressed up against him. But she wasn't quite confident enough to handle whatever might happen next so she stepped back. Cleve stepped forward, playfully taunting her. That little shiver ran through her. They both smiled, she shyly, he with total conviction. Then he moved across the room and fidgeted with a bridle.

"Hey. No baseball today?" she asked awkwardly. She knew the answer but it was the first thing she could think of to say. Cleve grinned and torqued his head.

"C'mon, you know I don't play on Wednesdays." He turned away from the bridles and walked back to her. "Have you got one to ride later? Let's do a little training. We can use the small ring. I heard the other girls talking about riding in the big field today. We can have the ring to ourselves."

"OK, yeah," she said as she lifted her tack box lid and pretended she was looking for something. "I'm not sure who I am riding. Maybe Puff. Maybe Jackson. I haven't checked the work board yet to see who is on the lesson list." She kept looking down into her box. She was so nervous being around him and she hated herself for that, yet she loved the indescribable sensation she felt—as though he could flip the switch on some kind of stirring deep in her core. All he had to do was look at her. Josie Parker was beginning to understand what that inner commotion was all about.

Cleve sat down on the tack box next to hers. He reached up and twirled one of her braids in his hand. He was not nervous, not ever, not at all.

"Yeah, well be sure you check out the stitches Doc Thurman put in Tether's left hock. They're amazing." He tilted his head in a way that forced her to look right into his eyes. "You have pretty hair Josie Parker." He let go of her braid.

"You're nuts, Cleve, quit it. Stop teasing me." She scrunched up her nose and lips in a crazy contortion to disguise her embarrassment. "C'mon, let's get to work."

He rubbed his hand up and down her arm as he stood up, nodding in agreement.

Yes, for sure, the bond between Cleve and Josie was a strong one.

He knew it and she knew it, but aside from Tessa, no one else had seemed to notice. The infatuation was becoming more of a real "thing" all the time, and that was why, she figured, she always became so shy in his company. Other girls might have been able to put it out there, but Josie was innocent. This thing with Cleve was definitely going somewhere and she found herself in unfamiliar territory. Still, she was intrigued by its temptation. Serious consultation with Tessa, two best friends getting to the heart of the situation, would be required on the phone that night.

Josie closed her box and walked toward the tack room door. Cleve followed closely behind. As she reached for the knob she felt his hands on her waist. He spun her slowly around, gently pressed her back against the door, and leaned his body into hers, an inch shy of contact.

"Hey," he said sweetly. "I'm not teasing you. You do have beautiful hair. And the freckles aren't bad, either. I'll see you out in the ring."

The two stood motionless for what seemed an eternity to Josie. She was trapped in the amazing sienna pools of his stare. She thought for sure he was going to kiss her, and she knew for sure her heart was about to explode in her chest. *Kiss me*, she thought. *Kiss me.* She held her breath.

He broke the silence instead. "Here, let me get that for you." Cleve took his hands from her waist and reached for the door, but left his stare upon her, unrelenting. Josie turned to break free as her anticipation quickly faded and her inner chaos deflated with an obvious exhale. She was left impetuously yearning for another moment like this.

Simultaneously, Tessa Jensen abruptly pushed through from the other side of the tack room door.

"Hey, let's go you two. We've got seven horses to tack up," she scolded as she moved past them, heading for her own tack box. She inconspicuously gave Josie a wink and a poke in the side. Tessa was no dummy; she knew what was going down between these two there in the tack room.

The moment was over. Cleve and Josie, busted, headed as though strangers silently down the aisle toward the work board.

Cleve wasn't quite sure what it was that attracted him to Josie. He just knew that he liked being around her more and more lately. He knew that she loved being around horses as much as he did and he found that to be very cool. Every girl at the barn considered Cleve a stud; even beyond Hidden Green he had plenty of girls chasing after him. But it was different with Josie. He thought the freckles across her nose were really pretty, and he liked that she got really shy and girlish when he stood close to her. She never chased after him, and that made it comfortable to be her best friend. But at the same time he wanted her to chase, just a little bit anyway. This confused his guy brain. He was fairly confident that she liked him as much as he liked her, but a guy could never be too sure. He never called her on the phone, although lately he'd actually considered it. He knew that a call was pretty much a girl's first sign that a guy was really into her. Tons of annoying, stalker girls called him a lot. But truthfully, every time the Gregory phone rang in the evening, Cleve would secretly hope it might be Josie. It never was, and though disappointed, he instinctively knew she wasn't the kind of girl who would call a boy. He liked that about her, too.

Mostly he liked when he would catch her looking up from a chore to see if he was looking her way. Whenever this happened, which seemed to be often these days, he silently implored her to hold his gaze. They carried on like this, knowing, but not quite going, there.

4

Josie jumped in to help with grooming and tacking up the lesson horses for the afternoon class. She checked the work board to see who was on the list that day.

"I've got Leo," she said out loud to no one special, and put a check after his name.

"OK, I will get Ham and Eggs," one of the other girls offered. Ham and Eggs were the two adorable paint ponies who shared a stall at the far end of the standing stall shed.

Cleve looked at the day's chores listed on the board and headed for the silo. William the blacksmith was closing up his truck and lesson kids were arriving for the four o'clock class. The barn was buzzing now.

After the last lesson rider was mounted, the boarders tacked up their own horses and headed to the smaller ring alongside the main one behind the barn. Unless it was one of the two days a week reserved for them to have their own group lesson with Mike, they would exercise their horses on their own, practicing diligently to stay prepared for any upcoming competitions.

Josie hopped on the pretty bay mare named Puff who was one of the more difficult school horses. Puff was known for dragging her mount to the jump. "Charging," Mr. O'Hara called it. Almost everyone who rode her would just pull back hard on the reins, afraid of being run away with. Josie knew this just made things worse and it certainly had left a lot of riders with blisters on their fingers.

Mr. O'Hara never really rode any of the school horses himself, unless there was a serious problem, so Josie would pretend she was the assistant trainer. She was always up for a challenge and Mike was happy to let her work on the ones that needed some attention.

"Whoa girl, easy does it, whoa Puff." Gently she stopped the mare and coaxed her back a few steps, then required her to stand quietly at the end of the ring for a minute or two.

"Hey, wanna go out to the field?" Tessa, mounted on Opie, trotted up and slowed to a walk alongside Josie and Puff. "Suzanna said she would go, and Joni too."

"No, I think I'm gonna stay right here and work on Puff. She is really dragging to the jumps. The lesson kids are all afraid of her. Cleve is gonna help me."

"Oh I see," Tessa teased. "Okee dokee. Well, have a nice date." She giggled and turned to head out of the little ring. "Let's go, you guys," she called to the other riders. "Have fun, you two," she teased, passing Cleve as he walked out into the ring. Josie shot her friend a dirty look.

The riding school lesson was going on in the main ring, and Josie and Cleve smiled at each other with raised eyebrows as they silently acknowledged to one another how funny it sounded. Cleve did a little silent imitation of Mr. O'Hara. Josie giggled.

Mr. O'Hara called out to his lesson group from the center of the ring. "All walk! Reverse and continue at the walk!" His voice was deep and commanding. "Sitting ter-rot! Sitting trot please! Susan, lower your hands, and thumbs to the sky!" he instructed. "Now pick up the canter please! All canter!" Josie and Cleve both laughed out loud and then turned to the matter at hand, Puff.

"Want me to lower the height a little so you can try trotting in and cantering out?" Cleve asked, already making his move toward the first jump.

"OK, sure. But I think I should trot in and then slow to a trot in the middle too, so make them pretty low." Up on Puff she felt completely confident in Cleve's presence. They were at their best doing this stuff together and it was clear they both loved it. "Actually Cleve, make the second jump in the line a little higher than the first. It'll set her back a little. Could you also put a ground rail out on the backside? Please?" She emphasized the "please" to let him know she wasn't trying to be bossy. He looked up at her and smiled.

"You got it, boss," he responded.

"I shouldn't have to touch the reins," she added. "Maybe put a ground rail in front of the first jump too. Thanks."

This was when Cleve liked hanging around Josie the most. He

recognized how smart she was and that made her even more attractive.

"Good idea. We'll get the poor thing really confused," he joked. He lifted a spare rail from the side of the ring and carried it over, placing it a half stride in front of the first jump. Josie trotted Puff through the center of the ring and began the exercise.

Instead of pulling on the reins when Puff got quick, Josie patted and talked to her. After a few times through the routine, the mare figured out that no one was fighting her and that if she didn't fight either, it didn't require so much energy to clear the hurdles. *Gosh if I could do this with her everyday for a week, she'd be all set,* Josie thought as she gave Puff a final gesture of "job well done," loosened her girth, and walked around the ring to let the mare cool out.

"That really makes such a difference in her," Josie said looking over to Cleve.

Cleve nodded in agreement as he reset the jumps to how they'd been before they started, a cardinal rule of the barn, then headed in for evening feed and water. Josie dismounted and walked silently alongside him, leading a tired Puff.

This is so perfect, she thought to herself.

This is so perfect, he thought to himself.

Josie hoped she would dream that night about how it would be if every day were like this with Cleve. *It would just be incredible,* she thought.

Man, it would be so cool if every day was like this with her, Cleve thought as he finished up the day's chores.

Her work with Puff had not gone unnoticed, nor had Cleve's contribution. Mike O'Hara had seen the whole exercise as he watched discreetly from the lesson ring, in between instructions to his pupils. He knew that even at sixteen, Josie Parker was a natural, and a valuable asset to Hidden Green Farm. He knew she really made a difference with his school horses. He also knew that he would lose her to college all too soon.

At a quarter past five Josie locked her tack box and headed for the back door toward home. Cleve's voice came out of nowhere.

Walking up behind her, he asked, "See ya Saturday? Baseball tomorrow and I'm not sure about Friday." He wrapped an arm playfully around her neck and rocked her back and forth. Josie laughed and wriggled her way out of his grasp, turning to look at his handsome face. He continued poking at her, and she played along, trying to dodge his every move.

"You know where to find me." She responded platonically. *God, why is it so hard to just talk to him like a normal person!* She scolded herself. *Saturday is three whole days away. Why couldn't I just have said, "Hey, so why don't you call me tonight?"* Although she was secretly happy to know he was looking forward to seeing her on Saturday, she couldn't help but wonder, *What's he up to on Friday?*

"OK, great. See ya then." He twirled her braid in his hand then headed toward the front of the barn. "That was great today. Totally great."

"See ya. Yeah, it was. Great, I mean," Josie replied. *Why does he twirl my hair like that?* She fingered the braid herself, then headed out across the main ring and looked back at the barn as she made her way over the fence, pausing to pluck a daisy from the unruly patch meandering through the rails. *God, I love this place so much.* She ran on towards home, Clown's horseshoes banging against one another in her hand. *I hope these days never end.* She air-kissed the horseshoes and ran on.

"Hey, I'm home," Josie called out as she burst through the back door. She laid the horseshoes on the kitchen counter and handed the daisy to her favorite mama in the world. No sooner had she done this than Dorie Parker picked up the shoes and moved them, without a word uttered, to the bench under the phone. She reached into the cupboard for a small glass bottle to use as a makeshift vase and filled it with water, then she snipped the bottom of the daisy with scissors before sliding the stem down into the narrow neck.

"Hey kid, you about ready? Dinner is hot on the stove. Why don't you just do a quick wash-up and change your shirt, OK?" Dorie put the daisy in the center of the table.

"Yup, sure. But Mom," Josie hollered from the powder room, "you have to see the stitches Doc Thurman put in Tether this morning. I can't believe I missed him doing them. Darn school gets so in the way of all the good stuff." She ran upstairs and returned a minute later, clean blouse, wet hands and face.

Josie kissed her dad on the cheek and sat down next to him at the kitchen table. Mama served up the food and joined them. Josie knew her mama would oblige her. She'd probably go to the barn the next morning to see what Josie had told her about. Unlike most of the other moms Josie knew, Dorie Parker loved any excuse to be in that barn.

The reminiscence of its smells, sights and sounds took her back to a time of wonder in her own life, and for a nanosecond she envisioned herself as a sixteen-year-old girl with a straw hat perched over her pair of braids, leading her favorite mare to the barn from the pasture. It was a time she cherished in the very same way Josie now cherished every new experience at Hidden Green.

One of the dogs nudged her, impatient for table scraps, and Dorie popped back into the present. She rose to clear the dishes.

By the time dinner was finished most nights, Josie was typically so tired she couldn't make it through dessert at the kitchen table. She would excuse herself, go up for a shower, attempt homework, talk to Tessa on the phone awhile, nibble at the piece of cake or cookies Mama would bring up to her, and often wake up bent over her desk with her face in a book, her dad gently shaking her shoulder.

"Hey, Rosebud, dream girl. Let's go, lights out."

"OK, thanks Dad. Love you. Good night. Tell Mama good night too."

She'd drag herself across the room, pull back her covers, and slide into bed with a moan, "*Aaahhhhh.*" Then she'd close her eyes to dream about what was to come the next day at the barn. "Move over Ralphie," she would no doubt have to complain to the mutt, one of two who slept with her almost every night. "You're like an elephant in this bed!"

5

On Saturday mornings, unless they were headed to a horse show, Cleve Gregory would usually ride his bike to Josie's house. He lived quite far away, in a neighborhood on the other side of Cooper Road, and although the barn was actually closer than Josie's house, he liked leaving his bike at her garage and walking through Barrett Park with her to Hidden Green. He'd been doing this for a long while. He had a driver's license but he rarely had a shot at using his mother's car, and anyway, he was reluctant to change the routine.

"Hey Mrs. Parker, how are you? Where's Josie?" he'd ask, pressing his nose up tight to the backdoor screen until Dorie would invite him in. "Is she ready? Lotta work to do today. Don't want to be late." As if she ever would be late.

"She'll be right down, Cleve. C'mon in and have some breakfast. Bacon and eggs? French toast?" This was part of the routine too. Every time Dorie asked, Cleve accepted, yet she never once felt like he expected the offer. *Funny kid,* she thought. *His hair's too long and he's a bit shy, but he's a hard worker and he sure seems to like my girl.*

Dorie listened from her position at the kitchen sink while Cleve and Josie talked about the coming day at the barn.

"Doc Thurman is coming today to check on that abscess Romeo has, and I think he's gonna vet that new black horse Mr. O'Hara got in. Something tells me that one is for Tessa, but no one is talking," Cleve said.

Josie rambled on exuberantly as the two downed the French toast, bacon, and orange juice Dorie Parker quietly put in front of them. Cleve was mesmerized by the joyful animation of Josie's face, her freckles frolicking across her cheeks when she'd laugh aloud, like flirty stones skimming across the surface of a pond, at the hand of a small boy standing near the water's edge.

Cleve had thought before what he was thinking now, that Josie always looked particularly beautiful on Saturday mornings. There was something electrifying about her face. It was fresh, ready, curious. Her eyes had a quiet yet hungry sparkle; her energy was light, it floated around her and permeated the room. He adored her poised, girlish demeanor; different from her more frenetic manner when she was working at the barn during the week. He was envious, in the most admirable of ways, of her obvious inner peace and how she wore that peace on her sleeve, somehow unknowingly infusing those in her midst with a sense of harmony and balance. Cleve liked just being around her. He needed her balance, craved her harmony, and on Saturday mornings, he could count on finding it there in the kitchen of the Parkers' house.

Outwardly, no one would likely notice the personal struggle that Cleve was enduring; he did his very best to conceal the suffocatingly real and painful details of his unraveling family life at home on Laukner Lane. He wanted Josie Parker to know nothing of the muddled mess he faced everyday at the hands of narcissistic parents who could see the world through their eyes only.

He folded his napkin and finished his juice as he waxed poetic to himself that Josie somehow took him seriously when no one else did; she seemed to understand his journey. He figured though that she could never possibly understand the constant battle he fought defending his own principles against the expectations of parents who believed the rest of society would measure their value as great if they produced the perfect Ivy League specimen. Having already failed miserably with their eldest son, Cleve was now their singular target. Josie's life, on the contrary, seemed so perfect.

Cleve snapped out of his own heaviness and pushed up from the table, carrying the remains of breakfast to the sink. Now it was Josie's gaze that followed him. His jeans were perfectly wrapped around his hindquarters as he skimmed across the kitchen and navigated around Mama, trying to win the contest of who would do the dishes. When he turned in defeat, Josie thought perhaps she noticed just a faint glimmer of something that resembled enduring sadness in his usually confident eyes. He blinked and the essence of it was gone; she figured herself wrong in her judgment. She too extricated herself from her daydreaming and stood up, moving to the mudroom to retrieve a windbreaker.

Josie wondered lightheartedly if Cleve ever bothered to brush his hair on the weekends. Every Saturday it looked the same.

"One of these days a robin is going to set up house in the back of your head, Cleve," she teased as she followed him through the Parkers' back door.

"Shut up," he replied playfully, a touch embarrassed. But then again, not really.

This particular Saturday morning, just as they entered the wooded path that led down to the creek, Cleve reached ahead and put his hand on Josie's shoulder. Josie felt his hand and it gave her a chill. It made her nervous. Well maybe not nervous exactly, but his touch stirred within her an unfamiliar, good kind of feeling..

"Hey wait a minute, stop here. I have something for us." He fumbled in his shirt pocket, and pulled out something that looked like a lumpy cigarette. He hesitated for a second, half-wondering why he was even doing this. He'd have bet his truck money on her reaction; he was just about positive she would completely freak out. Not because it was pot, but because it was Saturday, the best day of the week at the barn. But he was compelled for some reason to enter into the challenge, almost against his own will. Perhaps she would surprise him; perhaps she would save him. Perhaps, without realizing it, that was his notable motive. And perhaps it was a subliminal way for him to begin to let her in on his secret strife.

"Is that a cigarette? That's gross, and it'll kill you," Josie said emphatically and made a face like someone might if they had just smelled stinky cheese. "Why would you smoke, Cleve? Especially when you work at a barn. As in, fire? Straw? That's just dumb. And gross. And dumb."

"It's a joint, Josie. I got it from my brother. Pot. Home grown. C'mon let's smoke it. I smoked some with him yesterday and being high is fun. It's not dangerous. Smoke it with me Jos'. It's cool, no harm done. C'mon, wanna give it a try?" he asked, hopeful yet at the same time figuring she would say no.

"No way, Cleve. Are you nuts? Not dangerous? Really?" She was mad. "First of all, I've seen your brother high...hanging around my school. He looks like a loser stoner. In fact it seems like he's always high. And his friends look like losers too." *And going nowhere fast,* she wanted to say, but didn't. "Second of all, I'm riding today, why would I want to be high? I'm not doing it...that's just dumb. And it is too dangerous. And stupid. I'm not going down that path, Cleve, and you shouldn't either. I'm going down this path," she pointed ahead. "Right now. What the hell is wrong with you?"

Josie stormed ahead. What a total waste of time. She had to water and muck ten stalls before she could ride that day. Which meant, as it was, she already wouldn't be tacking up until long after lunch. Clearly there was a part of Cleve Gregory she didn't know. *So that's why he didn't come to the barn yesterday,* she figured. But it had never occurred to her to think beyond what she felt was obvious.

Cleve stuffed the joint back into his shirt and jogged after her, catching up.

"OK, fine," he offered in an out-of-breath, dejected voice. "Fine. Just forget I even had the idea." He circled around her. "Sorry," he offered. *Stupid girl,* he thought defensively, but at the same time he was embarrassed and uncomfortable. *It's just a joint,* he told himself. Josie ignored him and ran ahead. He shrugged his shoulders, flung his bangs off his forehead and headed for the back barn. *Screw her, stupid girl,* he thought again.

It hadn't occurred to Josie that Cleve may have simply been using the pot as a vehicle to start a conversation that was difficult for him to initiate. It hadn't occurred to Cleve that he might have been grasping at straws (or joints, as it may be) to get her to notice that something was askew. He only knew that he had screwed up and now she was mad. He needed her balance. He needed her harmony. If he didn't have that, what would he have?

Josie thought Saturdays were the best day of the week at Hidden Green. Everyone got there early. There were no lesson kids; it was just the private boarders, Libby O., Cleve, and Josie.

Libby O. was Mr. O'Hara's daughter, and why everyone called her Libby O., as opposed to just Libby, was a mystery. She had five ponies and was a great rider. She was small, so even though she was Josie's age, she could still ride in the pony divisions at shows. She was often champion, sometimes both champion *and* reserve champion. No one at Hidden Green was jealous—well, maybe just a little envious. She was Mike O'Hara's daughter after all. At the shows she was kind of a celebrity. Everyone knew who she was and knew her ponies as well; all were named after counties in Ireland.

Libby O. lived on the weekends with her dad in the cottage behind the barn. She lived during the week with her mom in the nearby town of Fairhaven. Her mother didn't care for horses at all, and had been divorced from Mike O'Hara for many years. Nevertheless, Libby O.'s parents still got along quite well. Libby O. and Josie were pretty good friends at the barn, but their relationship was tricky, and Josie always felt like they were somehow in competition. Over what, she wasn't quite sure, but it had never really been that big of a deal. Sometimes Josie's mama would let her stay the night with Libby O. at the cottage. Tessa would stay, as well, and they would have so much fun listening to Mr. O'Hara tell stories of days, and horses, gone by. Mike O'Hara had been in the horse business for a long, long time.

Tessa Jensen was one of those girls who were "all legs." Even though they were exactly the same height, her waist was a good four inches above Josie's. Josie thought Tessa was the prettiest girl at Hidden Green; her stunning auburn hair and her sharp features qualified her to go head-to-head with some of the models Josie had admired in *Seventeen* magazine.

"You should be a model, Tessa," Josie had suggested once to her pal. "You'd be perfect. Just as good as Patti Hansen or Lisa Taylor."

"Ha-ha, I will leave that job to my mother, thank you very much." Tessa's mother was beautiful as well, and had enjoyed a moderately successful career as a local runway model. She drove Tessa crazy.

Tessa owned a horse called Opening Night. He was a sway-backed chestnut and he could be a big spook. But Opie could jump really high, so Tessa was practicing to be able to compete in the junior jumpers with him. For now she was showing him in the equitation classes, where the jumps were lower but the courses were still very challenging. Mr. O'Hara was on the lookout for a junior hunter for Tessa, too. Maybe the black horse Doc Thurman was vetting was, in fact, for Tessa. The good news for her was that her mother loved horses. The bad news was that her mother lived vicariously through her when it came to horses, so she was always pushing hard at Tessa to do more, more, more.

"She should be your mother," Tessa would often tease Josie. "I don't want a lot of horses. Just Opie, he's plenty."

Wouldn't trade my mama for all the tea in China, but I sure would love a barn full of my own horses, Josie daydreamed.

Tessa loved Opie, but before she got him she had always hoped that her mother would buy her Rex, one of the popular school horses. It had really caught her off guard the day Mr. O'Hara announced that the parents of one of the riding school students had purchased Rex as a birthday present for their daughter. Tessa was furious; her mother had known how much she longed to own Rex, and could easily have afforded to buy him. Tessa interpreted the event as a huge plot against her.

"YOU probably bought him for that girl, just so I couldn't have him. YOU don't think he's good enough, but I think he is. Why does everything always have to be about YOU, Mom?" Tessa had shouted at her mother that day after Mr. O'Hara's announcement.

Sadly, her mother had responded by spontaneously smacking Tessa across the face. Right there in the barn. Josie wouldn't have believed it if she hadn't seen it with her own two eyes. Tessa was Josie's best girlfriend in the world and she felt her pain.

"She's just a selfish bitch," Tessa had told Josie on the phone later that night. Josie couldn't imagine ever feeling like that about Mama.

"Don't worry, Tessa. You're gonna get a great new horse and you will love him. One thing you can count on is that your mother will always buy you horses and she will only settle for the best!"

This was true and admittedly Josie was just a little jealous knowing that Tessa would have a barn full of horses if it were up to her mother. What Josie would give for just one! But she loved her best friend, and she knew Tessa would always be a part of her life, with or without horses. And even though on occasion Libby O. could do a good job of causing trouble, Josie felt that the three girls were a tailor-made trio.

"Triangle friendships are never easy Jos'," Mama once told her, "especially with girls. Just hang back and let the chips fall where they may. Always remember this: keep your friends close, your enemies closer. Just be you. Be gracious, be kind, and treat others the way you'd like to be treated. But be careful. Libby O. is no doubt a little jealous of the connection you and Tessa share." *Mama's a genius*, Josie thought at the time. *She always gets it right.*

Suzanna was, by virtue of being the oldest, in charge. She had graduated from high school a year ago and her parents were allowing her to take some time to ride before matriculating to college. At least that was what Suzanna told everyone, but Josie had always wondered if perhaps Suzanna had just not been able to get in anywhere. She was quite the tomboy; she had a deep voice and never seemed interested in boys. She was physically strong and wasn't afraid of anything or anyone. You could say she was actually a little bit mean. Not a bully, just kind of a know-it-all. She went to every show that Mr. O'Hara went to, and she did well. She was super competitive, and fortunately no one else at the barn yet rode in the junior jumper division. Her best friends, Joni and Rachel, competed in the hunters and the equitation. They were a tight clique. Suzanna was responsible for a lot on the weekends and she took her task very seriously. She would write assignments and instructions for the day on the big chalkboard hanging in the main barn.

It seemed to Josie that Suzanna always assigned the easy chores to Rachel and Joni. It really wasn't fair that the younger girls had to muck the hardest stalls. Suzanna, of course, didn't see it that way. She believed in "seniority." This Saturday proved no exception.

"We always get stuck with the damn standing stall barn. And again we have to wash all the water buckets! Isn't this like the third weekend in a row?'" Tessa complained to Josie. "We're never gonna get to ride!"

"It's kind of obvious what is going on here. All they have to do is muck the main barn and clean the school tack," Libby O. added as she approached her two friends who were standing by the silo. "I should tell my dad how messed up this is."

"Well today we get the pleasure of pulling manes, too," Josie chimed in. "I think like five of them. I'm not even sure I know what I'm doing when it comes to pulling manes, but I'll do three, you guys get the others. I wouldn't bother telling your dad anything, Lib', you'll just piss them off and they'll do something ridiculous to us next weekend, like make us move the entire manure pile." Josie laughed and then all three of them broke into giggles, which caused Joni and Rachel, who were setting jumps in the main ring, to look up. They shrugged their shoulders at one another and returned to their task.

Yes, it was Saturday, and everyone knew there was a long day of hard work ahead. Josie pushed her wheelbarrow toward the back barn and grabbed a pitchfork from the silo. She started in Westover's stall since he was already out in the paddock. As tedious and disgusting a job as this was, Josie really didn't mind mucking. She could learn so much from being this intimate with the horses—she could see who drank plenty of water and who didn't drink enough; who had runny, stinky droppings, a sign of a temperature or something else awry; and who had made marks on the sides of the stall from kicking or chew marks along the edges from a nasty habit called cribbing. She always checked their legs, their eyes, their ears and noses.

She picked through Westover's stall, lifting the piles of excrement and tossing them into the wheelbarrow, followed by the straw that was pungent, wet and rancid. Then, grasping the handles of her full and heavy cart, she began her trek to the manure pile. Rolling the wheelbarrow up the wooden planks that formed a roadway through the pile to the day's dumping site was always a challenge. The last thing Josie wanted was to go off the edge of the planks. The manure pile was foul. Just the thought of falling in freaked her out. Dumping the manure was the worst chore at Hidden Green as far as she was concerned.

"Easy up that ramp, Parker," Cleve yelled over to her from the equipment shed. "I saw a new family of rats in there this morning! A big, healthy mama scurrying around looking for food. Nice and wet and smelly in there, girl. Don't fall in!"

Josie shot Cleve a dirty look and focused back on her balance. As she backed the wheelbarrow down the ramp, Cleve headed in her direction. He playfully blocked her from taking her last steps.

"Hey," he pleaded, stepping out of the way to allow her off the ramp. "Hey, I'm sorry about this morning. It was a bad move. You're right. I was a jerk. Temporary insanity. Friends?" He twirled her right braid.

"Sure. And yeah, you were a jerk. Now get out of my way." Josie smiled and pushed on the wheelbarrow handles. Their arms brushed as she passed him and her heartbeat hastened. Halfway to the hayloft drop, she wanted to stop and turn back. For just a second she fantasized about him kissing her right then and there; she so wanted it to happen. Josie looked over her shoulder at him. Cleve saw her do it and knew he had missed his moment. He turned back, jogging across the farmyard, coming to a standstill just behind her. He grabbed her arm with playful intention. She set the wheelbarrow down, raised her chin and leaned her shoulders back on him. She closed her eyes, wanting to secure this moment in her memory like a photograph to a scrapbook, to be saved in eternity.

"Jos'." He touched her shoulder now, maneuvering her to face him, and with his eyes alone he told her, once again, that he was sincere in his apology for his earlier behavior. He surveyed the farmyard with discretion; no one was in sight.

She looked at his perfect lips and then into his captivating eyes. She reached to push away the lock of hair crossing his forehead.

"I'm going to kiss you now," he said, practically in a whisper, virtually putting his heart in his hand and offering it to her.

She didn't shy away. She was ready.

He wanted to be right with her and he was desperate for her balance. He knew he would find it in her kiss. The world with her in it was all he wanted, and this moment was all of that.

"Then do it," she responded demurely, but with a newfound confidence. She waited for him to bring his lips to hers.

From across the farmyard someone hollered.

"Hey Josie, what do you want from the deli? Same as usual? No mayo, right?" Libby O. had just interrupted what surely would have been the singular most incredible moment to-date in the insignificant love life of Josie-Rose Caldwell Parker.

Cleve released his grasp, immediately as disappointed as Josie. He offered a quick smile and a wink, then left her standing alone at the hayloft drop as he meandered back in the direction of his chores. He kept his back to Libby O., staring straight ahead and moving slowly, implying no hurry, insinuating no guilt of any wrongdoing, and, most importantly, attempting to shelter the undeniable proof that he was physically, quite physically, a slayed man when it came to Josie Parker. He had played his card and been thwarted, but he could live with this temporary postponement knowing he and the strawberry-blond girl with the best freckles were both on the same page. So could Josie.

She bent her knees to grasp the handles of her wheelbarrow and headed for fresh straw.

"Thanks Libby O., that's just perfect," Josie called back to her friend, who was still standing in the same spot, quite paralyzed, with her mouth wide open. *So is the sandwich order,* Josie joked to herself. She would rather it not have been Libby O. who had seen her "almost tryst." She would probably run right to Tessa—if not desperate to find out if Tessa knew something she didn't, then definitely to spill the beans. This would put Tessa on the spot and Josie felt badly about that. Libby O. might even be really mean and spill it to Joni or Rachel. She sometimes did things like that, thinking it made her appear cool, without first considering what the consequences might be. Plus, she always seemed jealous and resentful of anyone who had a boyfriend. Josie figured this was because Libby O. had never really had a boyfriend of her own. *Do I have a boyfriend of my own?* she mused.

Josie returned to the barn and spread lime across the dirt floor to diminish the sharp, vinegary smell of horse pee. She used the cutters from her back pocket to pop the wires that held the fresh bale of hay together, and spread it around the stall. She pulled out the few pieces stuck in her braids and moved her wheelbarrow to the next stall in the row. She walked back and grabbed the pitchfork. *Damn it,* she said to herself. Her adrenaline was fully engaged, powering its way through her body; she felt fluttery inside. Waiting for the next encounter would be torture. *When?* she wondered, *when? Not soon enough,* she conceded.

Always around noon, one of the girls who had a car, usually Joni or Lyssa, would drive to the Middletown Deli to pick up lunch. That day Libby O. had clearly been elected to collect the orders.

Josie's usual was sliced turkey and cheese on a hard roll, lettuce, tomato, no mayo. Salt, pepper, and a little oil and vinegar. A can of Coke was her standard, along with a package of peanut butter nabs or those Hostess marshmallow Sno Balls, or a pack of Drake's Ring Dings. Money was strictly budgeted in the Parker household, but Josie's mom gave her lunch money every Saturday and Sunday. Money Josie did not have to pay back from her allowance.

When Lyssa returned with the sandwiches, the girls gathered to eat. It was a glorious spring day and the picnic tables under the trees out by the ring were the perfect spot for lunch. Josie collected her goods and sat down next to Tessa at one of the tables.

Before anyone joined them she whispered to her friend, "Did Libby O. say anything to you about Cleve?"

"What are you talking about? No. Why? What?" Tessa was dying to know why Josie had asked her that.

Right then Libby O. and Lyssa sat down at the table. Libby O. wouldn't even look in Josie's direction. *What the hell is the big deal? Josie thought to herself. Nothing really happened! What is her problem?*

Tessa kicked Josie under the table and whispered, "What's her problem?"

Josie shook her head. "Not now. Later. Later." She handed Lyssa a five-dollar bill. "Thanks," she said.

Josie loved being a part of this ritual. Loved it. Even though she felt a little bit awkward because of her inability to reciprocate, she never tired of listening to all the girls talk about their own horses. Oh, Josie had plenty of stories about the Hidden Green horses, but she knew the girls wouldn't really be interested. So here under the trees, she was content to mostly just sit and listen.

Joni's horse, Consider This (also known as Joey), was a bay thoroughbred that had been retired from the racetrack because he just wasn't fast enough. Josie found that amusing because Joey usually ran away with Joni. As a result, Joey was bridled with a fierce bit that worked by pinching the sides of a horse's mouth. Joni and Rachel, sitting with

Suzanna at the other table, were discussing Joey's running away again. Josie listened.

"He's so soft and quiet in the corners, until we turn to the first jump. Then he just sets his sights and drags me. He puts his head so high in the air I can't control him," Joni said to Rachel. *Probably because she pulls so hard against that awful bit. Must hurt like hell,* Josie thought. "Even the twisted wire bit isn't working and now the corners of his mouth are raw from it," Joni continued.

Josie spoke up. "Joni, if you don't mind me saying this, why don't you try some draw reins and a lighter bit?" Joni was a little surprised by Josie's interjection, and she responded with a rather mighty display of attitude.

"I was thinking that a Pelham might be a good bit to try," she raised her brows glibly as she looked in Rachel's direction, as though not even acknowledging Josie's suggestion.

"I guess," Josie continued anyway. "It's just that the draw reins would help bring his head down and then he wouldn't fight so hard against the bit. You could try a snaffle bit, which won't hurt his mouth so much. All the judges at the horse shows are looking for them these days." Josie looked down at the hollowed out lines in the picnic table wood. "Just sayin'." She popped the top on her soda, feeling very relieved that, for whatever reason, Libby O. had seemingly not said anything to anyone about Cleve.

Joni didn't respond again. Instead she looked over at Rachel and Suzanna, a little embarrassed that a barn rat, a girl who didn't even have her own horse, was giving her advice. Spontaneously the three older girls began to giggle and, changing the subject, Rachel called out to Libby O.

"Hey Libby O., word around Red Bank Catholic High last week was that you've been telling everyone Cleve Gregory is your boyfriend. Since he goes to Parson Prep and you go to RBC, how can that be unless he's your boyfriend here at the barn? How else, where else, would you see him? C'mon, fess up. What's going on with you two?" Rachel continued poking insinuation at Libby O.

"What!?" The word came out of Josie's mouth before she'd had the consciousness to stifle it. Everyone looked over at her questioningly, wondering what investment she had in this bit of idle gossip. She looked down. Quickly all attention turned back to the perpetrator.

Josie's ears started to ring and she felt like she was going to faint. Or be sick. Or cry. Or die. She wasn't sure which, but she prayed that whatever was to happen next would be far less painful than what she was suffering right now.

Libby O. appeared genuinely mortified. She glared in Josie's direction. The sweat that had instantly begun to bead on her forehead, cheeks and upper lip made it appear as though guilt was practically melting from her face.

Please don't say anything, Josie prayed. *Please. Nothing. Nothing about Cleve and me. Nothing about Cleve and you. Please. Oh, please.* If she could have raised her hands to her ears without selling herself out, she would have. She looked beyond the group of girls, searching discreetly for a sign of Cleve. Nowhere in sight. She wasn't quite sure if she was relieved or disappointed.

Libby O., thank God, responded only by telling Rachel to mind her own business, then ran off from the table without denying or confirming the rumor. Suzanna, Joni, and Rachel giggled in their own small huddle, seemingly proud of themselves for inflicting humiliation on someone outside of their clique.

"Is that true?" Tessa leaned over to Josie and asked in a whisper. "Is that what you were asking me about before? Stop. I totally know Cleve is crazy for you, Josie. Come on, that's obvious. I don't get this rumor stuff. But I will get to the bottom of it. Libby O. can be a bitch, but I have a feeling she was just making up a story to appear cool at school. I'm sure she figured none of us would ever hear about it, so there'd be no harm done. I don't think she'd do anything to hurt you, and I can't imagine Cleve has even the slightest interest in her. Just goes to show how fast a lie catches up to you. She's probably so embarrassed right now. And those girls are mean-spirited bitches for sure." She gestured in the direction of the others. "Joni and Rachel love stirring the pot. I will go find Lib' and find out if there really is anything going on."

"No Tessa, stay out of it, please. Don't make it any worse for me than it already is." Josie spoke with such sharpness in her voice that Tessa was left with no option but to respect her friend.

Josie was completely bewildered. *Libby O. and Cleve? At the barn?*

How? Where? Ugh. I'm going to be sick.

She thought she was pretty tuned in to Cleve, but was he playing her? *He would never,* she told herself. *No, there is something not right about all this.* Suddenly she was angry. But she kept her fury to herself. She was jealous and agitated by the thought of him playing Libby O. against her. She couldn't help but feel this was somehow all conjecture. *Something doesn't feel right. I don't think it's true,* she thought. *It can't be. Who has any proof? He wouldn't do it.* But Josie just wasn't sure. She was sure that she didn't want to share Cleve. Especially after what had almost happened between them earlier that day. Her head was spinning.

Who does Cleve really want? The thought was so painful.

6

Libby O. didn't show up at the barn on Tuesday or Wednesday. Josie tried calling her, but her mother said she was sick and wasn't taking calls. Josie avoided Cleve as best she could; it felt like he was keeping his distance too, which suited her just fine for now. She needed to sort things out. She was mortified and hurt. By whom she wasn't really sure, and this made the whole ordeal even more confusing. *This is really screwed up,* she thought.

On Wednesday night she called Tessa to discuss the situation. Her emotions were all over the place.

"I'm really confused, I thought there was something going on between us, and now I just don't know. And I think he knows I'm upset and is avoiding me," Josie lamented. "I mean, he almost kissed me in the tack room last week. He all but kissed me at the hayloft drop. If it hadn't been for that damn girl—and now she won't even take my call."

"I'm not sure what to say. And by the way, Libby O. wouldn't take my call either. I think she's just embarrassed," Tessa offered. Josie didn't hear a word of it.

"But Tessa, he twirls my braids whenever he's near me. That has to mean something. I mean he fucking twirls my braids. That *has* to mean something!"

"You are making absolutely no sense, Josie. Your braids have nothing to do with it. And I'm sure he's not avoiding you. Libby O. has just been telling tales about herself at RBC, and she got caught, or she's spread a rumor because she is jealous about you and Cleve, and she got caught, or—well, I'm just not going to believe that Cleve would try to use you in any way. No way. And if he is, you know, an asshole gigolo, I can't believe he would do it with two girls from the same barn. I mean there are a million girls out there who would sleep with Cleve Gregory!" Tessa's love of drama had gotten the best of her. She put her hand over her mouth.

Removing it, she offered an immediate apology, "Sorry Jos'. I didn't mean it like that. I didn't mean anything by that. I'm the ass. I'm sorry. I know this just sucks. Just go ask him. Just walk up to him and put him right on the spot."

"I was really angry about the joint, though," Josie speculated. "Maybe that was some kind of test. Maybe he thinks I'm too nerdy and straight. But I don't think Libby O. would be into that, either."

"Well, now who's being dramatic? A test? I'm sorry, Josie, but boys just don't have that kind of aptitude." The two friends laughed.

"I just don't get it," a profoundly sad Josie repeated.

"Yeah, I just don't think—I mean, do you think they are possibly doing stuff? You know, like, stuff?" Tessa asked her friend. "I mean, sometimes guys like certain girls for one reason, and certain girls for a different reason. I'm not saying Libby O. is a slut, don't get me wrong. I don't think that about her. I don't think she gets high or does drugs, either. I'm sort of shocked to know that Cleve smokes pot. Actually, maybe I'm not. Everyone smokes pot except you. Ugh, sorry again. Foot in mouth."

"Tessa! You are *not* helping!"

"OK, but seriously Jos', what would you do if he wanted you to, you know, touch him. You know what I mean. If he, like, pushed his hand down there while you were making out?"

"How would I know the answer to that, Tessa? Seriously. I can't believe you are asking me that. That's not what this conversation is about." This was not something Josie wanted to discuss right now. Again, her best friend was not helping.

"First of all," she continued, "we've never done anything at all. I told you, he only *almost* kissed me in the tack room. He didn't get the chance to kiss me at the hayloft drop. Secondly, you know full well I'm such a nerd about all that stuff, and I think he knows that too. Half the girls at school *are* having out-and-out sex, giving blowjobs left and right, taking acid and tripping. I'm just trying to figure out if the guy I thought was almost my boyfriend has another girlfriend!" The two girls cracked up laughing at the ridiculousness of the conversation and said good night.

Josie was unable to think about anything else. On Thursday

afternoon, she finished up her chores, rode two horses without concentrating on them at all, and decided that she was going to say something to Cleve. She couldn't stand it any longer. She didn't even know if he was at the barn. She put her equipment away and walked out of the tack room on a mission to find him. He appeared as if on cue.

"Hey Jos'." His typical greeting.

"Oh, hey, what's going on?" She hadn't planned on the confrontation happening this quickly and was caught off guard. She tried to act nonchalant but here he was, chest-to-chest with her again. *Why does this keep happening?* She backed up, just like she had during their last meeting in almost the very same spot. Josie was, as before, nervous. She didn't have the confidence now that she'd had on Saturday. She tried to gather her words.

Cleve interjected before she could get a word out.

"Horse show this Saturday, we gonna groom?" he asked enthusiastically.

As if we're a team, she thought to herself. *Like you care if I go.* She snapped back to reality when Cleve leaned in, his cheek very close to hers.

"Earth to Josie Parker. Hey, you gonna go?" She felt his lips brush against her ear. Those perfectly puffy lips. She felt his warm breath on her skin as he whispered, "I like it when we groom together." *Damn it don't let him play you, Josie Parker,* she scolded herself.

"Yeah, of course I'm going. Why wouldn't I?" she replied curtly, smirking defensively. She used her best tomboy body language. She didn't want him to see her vulnerability.

"Whoa, easy daisy! Don't bite! Get the twitch, man!" Cleve threw his hands up and took a step back. After short contemplation he got serious. "Jos' are you OK?" he asked with real sincerity. "You mad at me or something? You're practically foaming at the mouth. A little colicky today? Actually you've been a little weird all week. Avoiding me?"

"No, no," she quickly backed down. "Sorry, I was thinking about something else." *Like you and Libby O. together,* the thought raced through her mind. She faked a smile. "Sorry about that. Didn't mean to snap."

"OK, no problem. See you tomorrow. Saturday too. Good night."

He headed down the barn aisle, completely aware that Josie wasn't moving an inch. He knew something was on her mind. In fact, he knew exactly what was on her mind. With just a slight turn of his head he hollered over his shoulder, teasing, "Good night, Cruella de Vil!" He laughed out loud as he pushed open the back door.

"OK, see ya. Yeah, thanks a lot for that compliment! Funny, Cleve," she teased back, doing her best to not sound deflated, forcing a smile. Then suddenly she remembered she had planned to ask him about the rumor. Spontaneously she called out in an effort to catch him before he was gone. "Hey Cleve?" Her voice was not fierce or anxious, but loud enough for him to hear, and pleading, in the hope he would acknowledge her.

Thank God, he said to himself, then out loud, "Yeah?" He quickly turned to look back, relieved the conversation wasn't over. He knew what was in her head, and he wanted to clear the air as much as he figured she did. He had missed her all week. It had been weird not feeling what he thought had become a mutual attachment. A mutual affection. A budding romance. She'd given him no chance to continue on from where they'd left off.

"Never mind, see ya tomorrow." Once again she was paralyzed with insecurity. *It just can't be true. I can feel our connection, even right now.* But she didn't have the guts to ask him. *I need to know, damn it. I need to know.* Josie stared down at the ground, defeated, fighting tears. She didn't have the guts.

Then, a split second later, the sound of Cleve's paddock boots tapping across the barn floor unexpectedly startled her. She looked up and watched as he moved back to her. *God, he's so handsome,* she thought.

"Josie. Listen," he said. He stood directly in front of her, just inches away, and she felt that damn chill run up her spine. "It's all good, Jos'. Don't believe every rumor you hear. Jealous, gossipy girls are the worst." He gently put his hands on her cheeks, lifting her face. "Don't believe everything you hear. Girl talk is cheap. And cruel. And a serious turn-off. Trust me, it's all good, real good." He tilted his head to the side, shrugged his shoulders, raised his eyebrows, and turned up one side of his mouth. He stood like that long enough to sense that Josie was OK.

She smiled at him. He yanked both of her braids just forcefully enough that she winced and offered a sincere, "Ouch." Cleve saluted her, then turned like a soldier, headed back from whence he came, and hollered, "Good night Cru- elllllaaaaaa!" In a flash, he was gone.

How did he know? How did he know? I'm an idiot, a fool. But I'm a much happier fool right now than I was last Saturday.

Josie promised herself, writing in her journal that night, that she was going to believe in Cleve. Now that she was sure he was into her too, she wasn't about to let anyone else have him. She also promised herself that she would take the high road, and make amends with Libby O. as soon as she showed back up at the barn, regardless of what Libby's motive may have been. She turned on her stereo before she climbed into bed. Jim Croce serenaded her until the day faded.

If I could save time in a bottle, the first thing that I'd like to do, is to save every day 'til eternity passes, and then, I would spend them with you.

7

Friday came. Tack got cleaned. Boots got polished. Manes and tails got braided. Bandages were rolled up in anticipation of early morning leg wrapping. The cabinet in the van was packed with saddles and bridles, hay, and buckets full of grooming supplies. Lightweight blankets were put on the horses going to the show to help keep them clean through the night, and each one got a small dose of muscle relaxant with their evening feed.

Josie could feel Cleve watching her all afternoon. It felt good and every once in awhile she would look up and make a face at him, silently begging the question, "What?" Then he'd just smile and go back to his work.

The girls who were showing took their spurs, helmets, gloves, and crops home with them to ensure all their personal articles actually made it to the show. Mr. O'Hara had blown a gasket at the last show when Libby O. had no hardhat or spurs because her show trunk had somehow been left behind.

"OK, everyone here no later than five fifteen tomorrow morning. Van rolls out at five forty-five sharp," he announced at the "pre-show" meeting held in the tack room. "Suzanna, your dad can pull his trailer right up behind the van tonight if he wants." Suzanna's dad always transported her horse to the shows in the two-horse trailer he owned. "Jeb and Sancho will have everyone fed, wrapped, and ready. Josie, you know you are the loading champ, be here on time." He smiled in her direction, then winked.

As if I'm ever late, she thought and smiled at the floor. Josie had a knack for loading the horses and the spooky ones somehow trusted her more than even Mr. O'Hara, who would often lose his patience and hand the bad loaders off to her or Cleve. Josie had every intention of being there early.

The excitement was so great that no one even flinched at the mention of this ridiculously early hour. The girls all filtered out, chattering on the way to their cars. Josie hung behind until everyone was gone. She loved the barn at the end of a long day, after the sun had gone down and the animals were all fed and watered and settling in.

She turned off the barn lights and listened to the sounds of the horses nuzzling their hay. She heard John Henry let out a long groan as he lay down in his straw bedding. She smiled and turned to walk out to Mama's car. She was starving and exhausted, but most of all she was secretly happy to know that Cleve Gregory was hers, even if everyone else might think he was Libby O.'s. She actually liked it that way. She closed her eyes and dozed as the car rumbled home.

Later, she sat curled up on the big, corduroy couch in the TV room, hanging out with her dad, who dozed in his recliner while Mama cleaned up the kitchen. The TV screen flickered as Josie wrote her day's journal entry. *I sort of wish I had a horse to show tomorrow. Then again, I'm probably better on the ground. No matter, I will be there with Cleve.*

Frank Parker's own snoring popped him awake. He looked over and noticed the coy smile on his girl's face. He could tell she was unaware there was anyone else in the universe right now. He read her mind. *Must be that Gregory boy,* he mused. He pushed up into a straight position in the recliner and reached for the day's newspaper. He slapped it open loudly to jog her brain back into the here and now.

"Rosebud, get yourself up those stairs, four thirty is gonna be here before you know it. Have fun tomorrow. They're lucky to have you." As always, he was proud of her dedication.

She picked up Ralphie, kissed her dad good night, and headed up the stairs to her room. Snuff followed behind. "Night, Mama," she called out.

On the weekends that Mr. O'Hara took the private boarders to local shows, Josie and Cleve would go along as grooms. Jeb and Sancho, who would only travel to groom during the indoor series, would stay behind to handle all the responsibilities at the barn. And rain or shine, in the morning's dark chill, at some moment close to 5:45 a.m. the Hidden Green van would pull out of the long driveway and onto Cooper Road, bound for a day of hard work, competition, and with a little luck, a few tri-color championship ribbons to bring home. Going along as a groom was a lot more fun than being left behind at the barn.

Some of the girls would have their mothers drive them directly from home to the show. The older clique would usually have a sleepover at Suzanna's or Rachel's because they each lived fairly close to the barn. Sometimes Tessa and Josie would stay overnight at the cottage with Libby O. This was usually fun but not so great if the show was on a Sunday. Mr. O'Hara would make the girls get up extra early to go to church at 5:00 a.m. in Red Bank. Pretty funny considering Tessa was Jewish. Didn't matter to Mr. O'Hara.

"You sleep here, you go to Mass. That's the deal," he'd say.

Tessa never seemed to mind, and more than once Josie teased, "You're more Catholic than Jewish ya know." The three girls would line up like zombies in the pew, sleeping in the car to and from the church.

Lyssa had an awesome navy blue Volkswagen Beetle and she would usually volunteer to swing by the barn to pick up anyone who needed a lift. It was considered a huge coup to get to ride with her, but Josie preferred to ride in the van with the horses. Besides, she would get car sick if she had to ride in the backseat of a car, and getting the front seat in the VW was *never* going to happen; she just wasn't cool enough to merit a front seat score. Cleve would usually ride shotgun in the van cab with Mr. O'Hara, but if Libby O. grabbed that spot then Cleve was relegated to the back. Josie liked that just fine, too.

Show days were incredibly long but Josie always looked forward to them, especially this one. She knew that she and Cleve would be together all day, side by side, working as a team, and she couldn't wait.

8

State Spring Horse Show was not far from Hidden Green. After about forty minutes of travel, Mr. O'Hara pulled the six-horse van into the designated parking area, Suzanne's dad pulling the trailer in alongside. The show grounds were bustling with horses, riders, parents, trainers, grooms, and lots of vans and cars. The sun was just coming up; not quite six thirty and the air still held a chill.

State Spring was a one-day local show, but was considered an important one. Exhibitors competed for points that would help qualify them for the series of indoor shows in the fall, including the biggest coup, a spot in the order of go at Madison Square Garden, where the National Horse Show was held every November.

The pulse this early in the morning was surprisingly vibrant, no sleepy heads to be found. Everyone was busy readying themselves for their first class; the show would start promptly at eight o'clock. There were two proper riding rings and a large field with jumps spread around it. This was known as an outside course. Ponies showed in one ring, equitation and high jumpers in the other. All the "over fences" hunter classes, as well as those that just required working at the walk, trot and canter, (otherwise known as the under saddle), were held on the outside course. If an exhibitor arrived early enough they were permitted to school, which means practice, in any of the rings.

Josie and Cleve quickly organized the Hidden Green setup. Time was of the essence. Tack trunks came off the van, water buckets were filled, and hay nets were thrown under the truck to get them out of the way for the time being. Horses were bridled in the van then walked down the ramp. Each owner held their own horse while Cleve and Josie brushed them down, pulled straw from their tails and checked that braids were undisturbed, mouths were not green from the hay. Saddles were thrown over backs, girths tightened. A little hoof polish applied, a small blanket, known as a cooler, thrown over the hindquarters, and finally a pat on the neck and each horse was ready for the task ahead. Riders were given a quick leg up onto their mounts and one by one headed in the direction of the equitation ring where Mr. O'Hara was waiting.

"Wait, Tessa." Josie instructed, "Take this crop with you for now, but put some spurs on later, instead." Tessa always appreciated Josie's recommendations. "Just in case he needs to be reminded who's boss," Josie said laughingly.

Libby O. walked off without a cooler on her pony's hind end.

"Hey, hold on a sec'," Cleve called after her. "Let me get a cooler for you."

Josie kept a close eye on the transaction, admonishing herself for still being a bit skeptical. She was embarrassed when Cleve looked over and caught her suspicious eye. He frowned at her and she quickly looked away.

Up at the ring, Mr. O'Hara watched each of his students work their mounts on the flat, schooled them over some practice jumps, and offered last minute instructions. At about seven fifteen he reported back to Josie and Cleve.

"Flammie needs fifteen on the lunge line, Opie needs some draw reins now and a little tap right before he goes in, and Joni is going to gallop Joey on the outside course for fifteen minutes...he's pretty wild, as usual."

"The ponies are fine," he continued, "Libby can just get on each of them a little early and canter around a bit. Suzanna is all set. The bad news is that Reinoud is limping, so Lyssa will have to scratch. Josie, find a minute to stop into the show office and put in a call to Doc Thurman. He might be coming here today and could take a look." He lit a cigarette and headed back up to the rings, stopping to chat along the way, tipping his straw hat to friends and fellow trainers. Everyone knew one another; the horse world was a well-oiled if not somewhat incestuous subculture.

Even with everything under control, there was no time to spare; it was full tilt until the first horse went into the ring at eight o'clock. Mr. O'Hara worked his way back and forth between the rings and the outside course all day, coaching his team of riders, looking for acquisition prospects, rarely coming back to the van.

Josie and Cleve had a short breather once all the girls were up and schooling. The two of them sat on a tack trunk, leg pressed against leg, her foot looped over his. Already starving from the activity of the early morning, they inhaled the breakfast sandwiches one of the mothers had bought for them at the horse show cantina.

"This is the best," Cleve offered in between bites. Josie wasn't quite sure whether he meant the sandwich or the horse show or maybe something else. She knew what she hoped he'd meant but she didn't want to seem presumptuous.

"Yeah, it's pretty great," she said. "I hope they're all good today. It would be cool to go home with a few tri-colors. Not to mention some good points."

This wasn't the conversation he was hoping for either, but he went with it too.

"Well, maybe Tessa will win both the big equitation classes," he said. "I'm pretty sure George Morris is bringing a few of his students. I know Armand is here. He and Leslie are the ones to beat. Maybe Alan. Well, we'll see. It could go either way today."

Josie jumped up and off the trunk.

"C'mon, we better get going. My money is on Tessa winning both." She crumpled up the foil her sandwich had been wrapped in and pitched it almost six feet into the trash bin. She poked two fingers up into the air, then raised her fists high like a strongman at a carnival. Cleve laughed at her cartoon-like animation. She grabbed the shovel and manure tub and headed up the ramp to muck the van stalls before the horses returned.

"Hey, Josie." Cleve called after her.

"Yeah?" She looked back at him and saw the strangest look on his face. His expression was pained, almost. *What exactly is it that he wants to say?* Now it was Cleve who seemed to be the one frozen with fear. This allowed Josie one of those uncharacteristically confident moments that were becoming more frequent.

She smiled and pushed her braids back over her shoulders.

"Let's go!" she said with enthusiasm, freeing Cleve from the awkward place in which he seemed pathetically stuck. She turned her attention back to the ramp and smiled, thinking to herself, *This is so good. This is so good.*

The day marched on. Josie and Cleve didn't stop. Rubbing, brushing, watering, painting hooves. In between classes they untacked and loaded horses into the van or trailer to rest. They traded off going to the rings to help Mr. O'Hara, and to put a towel to boots and flanks and necks right before a rider was to enter the ring. Shiny boots were mandatory for HGF exhibitors.

"Don't ever let me see one of my riders go in the ring with dull boots. Presentation is half the battle." Mr. O'Hara's stern voice had intimidated more than a few grooms over time. Josie and Cleve needed no reminder; they prided themselves in perfectly turned out horses and riders.

They carried coolers and exhibitor numbers, spurs, crops, hoof dressing, and hoof picks up to the ring. Josie studied the course diagrams posted at the in-gates, in case at the last minute Mr. O'Hara wasn't sure of the route a rider had to take. They clapped and whistled and "woo-hooted" when one of Hidden Green's riders put in a good round. They grabbed cheeseburgers and hose-water lemonades for lunch when they found a quiet moment.

Beyond their brief conversation over bacon, egg and cheese sandwiches at the crack of dawn, Josie and Cleve barely said a word to one another all day, unless it was about the horses. Still, they were both immensely aware of the electricity in the air. The chemistry between them that day had taken them to a whole new level. Although physically they had not yet really connected, they both felt the same undeniably powerful draw. Josie worked hard to contain her glee, and to keep her focus on the reason she was at the show. She wondered if anyone else had noticed. Not that she really cared.

By two o'clock they were both exhausted. There was a break in the day and Josie needed to pee.

"I'll be right back. Bathroom break," she said to Cleve. "Can you get Opie down from the van? The equitation Medal class is about to start. Tessa must be around here somewhere."

"Yeah, I know. If you see her, let her know she goes fifteenth in the order," Cleve responded.

Josie planned to make the visit to the port-o-john a quick one. *There is no way I'm sitting on the seat*, she thought as she approached the lineup of six or seven green huts. She reached for one of the doors with the little green and white "VACANT" sign exposed, but her attention was completely sidetracked by the sight of Tessa walking out from behind the row. Alan Harmon, one of the best equitation riders in the country, followed rather sheepishly behind. Josie was stunned. Tessa was equally thrown by bumping into Josie; this was clearly meant to be a covert endeavor. It was not a good moment for any of them.

What the hell is she doing? Josie wondered, embarrassed for herself in this moment, but more embarrassed for her friend. Tessa had been having a great horse show. She had won her first class and the Medal class was about to begin. *What is she doing with Alan Harmon? She knows he's been dating Susie Kurtz since last fall. And really? Behind the toilets? Yuck.*

"Tess', you OK?" Josie asked, starting toward her friend, dumbfounded. Alan said nothing—not hello, not goodbye. He couldn't, wouldn't make eye contact with Josie. The tall, undeniably handsome boy stood there only long enough to push his long blond locks off his forehead and behind his ear, then quickly disappeared. Josie shot him a fierce glare as she continued over to her friend. She grabbed Tessa by the arm.

"You're hurting me," Tessa complained, looking down at Josie's grip on her.

"You're damn right I am. Are you fucking crazy?" she asked her best pal. "What were you doing back there with him, Tess? Alan? Really? You know he goes out with Susie. I don't get you. The Medal is about to start and you are primed to win. C'mon, that was stupid. God, Tessa, your mother would kill you."

"My mother's too fucking busy trying to seduce the judges," Tessa defiantly lashed out. "She makes me sick. Fuck her, fuck this whole thing. I swear Josie she makes me hate it. She *makes* me hate it. I hate it all. At least Alan just wants to have some fun. I really wanna just have some fun. I am sick to death of the pressure she puts on me." Tessa stormed off toward the HGF van before Josie could even retort.

"Wow," she said aloud to no one as she stepped back toward a vacant port-o-john, "that is messed up." She shook her head and thought, *This is going to entail a long phone conversation.*

When Josie arrived back at the van, Tessa wouldn't look at her. She acted like she was actually mad at Josie and maneuvered around her, doing her best to stay at arm's length from her friend. *She's not pulling that bullshit,* Josie thought to herself, walking directly over to Cleve and taking Opie's reins.

"I got this," she said indignantly. "I've got Opie, thanks." Cleve didn't know what was going on, but he could tell by Josie's stern, serious tone that there was something up between the two girls. He wanted nothing to do with a catfight. He handed over the reins, throwing his arms up in surrender, and backed off. Josie winked at him and led the horse over to Tessa.

"Look, whatever is up with you, I'm on your side. You never told me you liked Alan Harmon. If you really like him, that's fine. Just don't sell yourself short to get back at your mother. It's your reputation at stake Tessa, not hers. Don't let her influence who you are. You are too good for that. And don't let Alan Harmon psych you out. You're competition in the ring that he'd rather not have."

"She's a bitch, Josie. Did you see her at the ring? Standing right next to the judge's box, talking to Ted Snyder in between rounds? It's fucking humiliating. It's always, *always* all about her. She didn't even have anything nice to say to me when I won the damn class. I won the damn class fair and square. 'Your reins were a little long and your pace was so inconsistent when you rode Armand's horse in the test.' That's all she could say. Can you fucking believe that? I hate it. I hate her. I just hate her."

"I know, I know. She's unbelievable. But you don't hate riding. You love riding and you love horses, Tessa, and you are the most amazing rider I know. Now get on this horse, forget your stupid mother, and ride your ass off and win the Medal for yourself, not for anybody else. And let me tell you one other thing girlfriend, you don't need Alan Harmon to make you feel good about yourself. You've got yours truly, me, and I've got your back. *Forever.* Now get on and ride, girl, ride."

The two friends hugged. Tessa slid her number over her jacket collar, Josie gave her a leg up onto Opie, and together they headed for the ring.

"Your mother *is* a selfish bitch," Josie mumbled as she walked just a few paces behind her friend.

The afternoon progressed and Tessa wound up second in the Medal. Alan Harmon's horse stopped three times at the combination jump and he was disqualified. Josie was secretly thrilled. As for the rest of the Hidden Green group, it had been a winning day. Suzanna's jumper, Ransom, won his second class, executing the fastest round with no rails down. Joey dragged Joni around the outside course in their first two classes. But by the third class he was tired and she wound up with first and second place finishes, and won the under saddle, good enough to be champion in the junior hunter division. Of course Libby O. dominated the pony classes, and Rachel got low ribbons with Flammie in every one of her four classes. Reinoud, except for a hand walk around the show grounds, stayed in the trailer all day because he was lame. Lyssa, though disappointed, got to hang out with all her pals from other show barns. The last class had finished and the show was coming to an end.

Tack trunks, buckets, coolers and hay nets were loaded into the van along with some very worn-out horses. Cleve swept the ramp and he and Mr. O'Hara raised it up and pushed it under the truck body. The dust trailed behind as a very content team HGF followed the long line of vans exiting the show. Lyssa and Tessa, who refused to ride home with her mother, rode in the navy VW. Joni, Rachel, and their moms, and Suzanna with her dad navigating their trailer, all headed back to Hidden Green.

9

Libby O. had decided to ride shotgun in the cab with her dad, so Cleve and Josie were packed, like saddles, up in the cabinet of the six-horse van. Nestled in with all the equipment, they were arm-to-arm, leg-to-leg. The success of the Hidden Green exhibitors was a triumph they could call their own as well. Their muscles were sore from all their hard work, they were dirty and smelly, and they were tired, really tired. There was no conversation. They'd been up since well before five o'clock and they were talked out, walked out and hungry.

Cleve felt himself falling in and out of sleep, his head cocked to one side and his eyes heavy, but he was keenly aware of Josie's arm pressed against his. Through the dim light he looked at their legs, stretched out in front of them. He let his foot fall to the side, which caused his thigh to rest against hers. As Josie drifted off, her head tilted to lie on Cleve's shoulder. Cleve quite liked this and he rode along thinking about how great they worked together. They'd had such a great day. He was even crazier for her now. Cleve smiled a sleepy smile, and leaned his head back against the wall. He'd heard about the stupid rumor Rachel had tried to set on fire. He also knew that there was no way, *no way*, that would ever turn to truth. This was the girl for him, this girl pressed right up close against him in the cabinet of the van. She was kind, gentle, and compassionate, and her beauty overwhelmed him. It was so natural. He knew she was shy, and naïve. He knew that rumor was what had made her act so weird during the past week, and he liked the way she'd handled it. He closed his eyes and dozed. *She's far from Cruella de Vil*, he thought. *She's fuckin' awesome.*

Without warning the van hit a huge bump in the road and shook them both out of their own thoughts. Josie realized she had her head on Cleve's shoulder and was a tad embarrassed. She didn't want anything to spoil how good things were between them. She thought perhaps she should inconspicuously try to move, but the warm, comfortable feeling of his shoulder made her hesitate. She stayed like she was, hoping maybe he was asleep and wouldn't notice. As she closed her eyes and began dozing off again, she heard Cleve's voice.

"You asleep?" he asked quietly. Immediately Josie became aware of her pounding heart.

"No. Well, kind of. I'm so tired. What a great day though, huh?" she mumbled.

Who knows if it was the rumbling feeling that the van gave their bodies, or the closeness they couldn't escape in the cabinet, but somehow Cleve and Josie realized that they were both thinking the same thing. This was the moment. Cleve shifted his weight and leaned his face down toward Josie's. She didn't shy away. She turned her face to his and he put his hand gently on her cheek. She closed her eyes and exhaled. He took in her breath and they kissed. Maybe not Cleve's first kiss, and that didn't matter, but definitely Josie's first kiss of any consequence. They kissed slowly, five, maybe six times. There was nothing awkward about it. Josie felt weakened by the way her lips fit perfectly against Cleve's. There, in the cabinet of the Hidden Green Farm six-horse van, surrounded by saddles and show coolers and grooming buckets, she couldn't imagine anything being more romantic.

At that very moment Josie Parker fell head over heels in love with a boy for the first time. She kept her eyes open now, and as Cleve kissed her again she felt the taste buds of his tongue press against hers, just for a second. Their eyes locked, and using no words, so much was communicated between them. She hoped he didn't feel her shiver. Of course he did, and it made him pull her closer. They remained still, nose tilted against nose for just a few more seconds. Cleve kissed her one more time, his lips softly encompassing hers for the most incredible few seconds of her life to date, and then slowly he pulled away. She rested her head on his chest, which raised and lowered with each heavy breath he took. She could hear his heart pounding, just the same as hers. He kept his arm across her body and his leg pressed up against hers, and they rode the rest of the way in silence, neither one wanting the trip home to end. Josie was clear now about Cleve. She trusted his love, she wouldn't question it, and she knew he wouldn't give her any reason to. Cleve thought about how fortunate he was to have a girl like her. She was genuine and good, and she gave his heart and his brain repose, something he couldn't seem to find anywhere else in his life. What a very good ending this was to what had already been a very good day.

The van pulled into the courtyard at Hidden Green at about nine o'clock. Cars lined up in the courtyard alongside the barn, and the girls jumped out to help unload. Josie's dad was there waiting; she waved to him, signaling she would be out in a bit. He waved back, peering above his reading glasses, then continued with his crossword puzzle. He was in no hurry; he knew she would be the last one out.

In time the barn lights went out and Josie and all the others filtered into the waiting cars. As her dad navigated up the long driveway, Josie spotted Cleve walking along the edge of the gelding pasture.

"Dad, wait, there's Cleve walking home. Can we give him a ride, Dad? Please?" Frank Parker slowed the car and rolled down the window.

"Hey kiddo, jump in, we'll drop you home." The brakes squeaked just a little as he stopped the car.

"Hey, thanks Mr. Parker, you're savin' me. I'm dead tired." Cleve opened the door and slid into the back seat, behind Frank Parker, next to Josie. *This is kind of awkward,* she thought. She glanced up at the rearview mirror. Her dad seemed to be watching the road. As they turned onto Cooper Road and headed in the direction of the Gregory house, Cleve reached across the darkness and took Josie's hand in his. She hoped the car ride would last forever. She wrapped her hand tightly around his and closed her eyes. *An even better ending to this day,* she thought. *Maybe I'm already dreaming.*

Frank Parker glanced in his rearview mirror. He knew exactly what was going on. He thought it was perfect. He thought Cleve Gregory was a good, hard-working kid. He and Josie shared a great passion. *Just like Dorie and me,* he thought. He reminisced about how special young love was and couldn't wait to tell his wife that Rosebud had herself her first real boyfriend.

As if she didn't already know.

10

Dorie Parker was reading on the porch Sunday morning after breakfast, and as she watched Josie clip down the steps she called out in her usual fashion.

"Be home in time for dinner—in time and CLEAN!" As always, she smiled. She was proud of the dedication this young girl had. She felt greatly responsible for that. Dorie was happy with the news that Frank had shared about Josie and Cleve. *Nothing like a barn romance,* she mused. *Love and horses, how much better can it get?* She laughed out loud. *She's having the time of her life,* she thought. She turned back to her book, and then looked up again when she heard Josie's voice.

"I know Mama, I know!" Josie yelled back as she trotted away. She was almost to the edge of the yard when a strange feeling came over her that stopped her in her tracks. Josie spun around and returned to the porch. "You know I'll be home on time. You know how much I love the barn. You know how much I love you too, Mama." Josie wrapped herself around her mama and hugged her hard.

Oh boy, butterflies and rainbows for this girl, Dorie thought, smiling. *My girl has fallen hard.* Dorie squeezed her precious only child and scolded her.

"Go. Go to what you love. Love what you go to. Don't have it any other way. Don't ever compromise on doing what makes you happy. Ever. Not ever in your whole life. It keeps your heart big and full. Go on, git. I'll see you later." She affectionately swatted her daughter on the backside. "Wait! I forgot there's a bag of carrots in the fridge for you."

Josie ran back in for the carrots and then was on her way. "Love you, Mama! Love you! I'll see you later."

It brought tears to Dorie's eyes to see her daughter in love. *I love you too, my only child, my beautiful Josie-Rose.*

Josie arrived at Hidden Green in time to pitch in with the morning chores. Everyone was moving about the barn methodically. There would be no riding, instead the horses would rest and get some extra time out in the pasture.

She wondered what it would be like between her and Cleve today. She was so anxious to see him. He was hers. Hers and she knew it. Today, she felt sure, everyone else would know it too.

Just as she was filling up the hayrack in John Henry's stall, from the standing stall shed came a shrill scream that stopped everyone in the middle of whatever task he or she was performing. Mike O'Hara headed immediately toward the direction of the scream and all the girls, including Josie, followed him, inquisitive and fearful at the same time.

Tessa was standing in front of Gladys's stall, where the gray mare appeared to be lying down. Her legs were collapsed underneath her, and she leaned a bit to one side. Her back was crunched up against the plywood wall of her stall and in a "fool the eye" way, one could almost believe she was still breathing. She wasn't. Tessa was shaking and her face was ashen. Tears were rolling down her cheeks.

"She's dead, Mr. O'Hara, she's dead. She won't move! She's dead." Tessa shook her head and bawled. All the other girls recoiled and began to whisper amongst themselves.

"What happened?" Joni finally asked, almost shouting in fear. No one had an answer.

Josie walked silently up to Gladys and gave her a stroke on the neck. Her body was still warm, so she couldn't have died that long ago. Her eyes were open, which made Josie sadder than any other part of this experience. She knew Gladys had died from colic. Josie wasn't afraid. She was curious. She looked up expecting to see Cleve. *Where is he?*

"I'll have to get the tractor so we can drag her out to the mares' pasture to bury her," Mike O'Hara said quietly, examining the mare. He put a cigarette in his mouth and walked out of the barn, his eyes staring at the ground. This was not the first time Mike O'Hara had lost a horse to colic, and though he would rather have been there to attend to her when her intestines were twisting, the reality was, he hadn't been. He couldn't have afforded colic surgery for her anyway, but perhaps Gladys could have been saved by taking away her hay and water, and by walking her so she couldn't lay down; lying down always made colic worse.

Josie thought to herself, *I wonder what it would be like to feel really sick to your stomach and not be able to throw up. Throwing up is gross but it almost always makes me feel better. Poor horse. I wish horses could throw up.*

Mike O'Hara backed the tractor into the standing stall shed and he, Sancho, and Jeb secured some ropes to Gladys's legs. *Where the heck is Cleve?* Josie wondered. For the next hour they pulled and pushed, backed the tractor up, drove the tractor forward, and finally poor, dead Gladys emerged from the barn. She was dragged to the middle of the mares' pasture where Mr. O'Hara had excavated a horse-sized grave, and off she went to greener pastures.

The girls all sat around the picnic tables eating the sandwiches Suzanna had brought back from the deli. Preoccupied, they cleaned their bridles, dirty from the show the day before. There was little eye contact; no one wanted to acknowledge the events of the morning. Rather, they went about their tasks, talking occasionally about mostly trivial matters. The atmosphere was somber. They were all mourning the loss of Gladys.

Someday I will be in charge of a barn where horses will not die from colic, Josie promised herself. Then, once again, she thought, *Where on earth is Cleve?*

Despite all the drama of the morning, Josie could not stop thinking about what had happened in the van cabinet. And now Cleve was nowhere to be found. She understood the meaning of mortified for the first time in her life, because she was. This was worse than the Libby O. nightmare. *He played me,* she figured. *He probably wants to avoid seeing me now. He probably regrets what happened and doesn't know how to face me.* She had really looked forward to being around him today. She had dreamed all night about how it was finally going to become clear to everyone that she was Cleve Gregory's girlfriend. Instead she felt defeated, used, and alone.

Part of Josie wondered if Cleve was all right, and part of her was more than just a little curious; it just wasn't like him to not show up. So with as much self-confidence as she could muster, which wasn't much at all, she left the barn shortly after lunch. Telling no one that she was leaving, let alone where she was going, she headed in the direction of Cleve Gregory's house, not exactly sure what her intentions were, not exactly sure what she might find. She hoped it wouldn't make things worse, but she was willing to take the chance.

It was a long walk to the Gregorys'. She wished she'd had her bike. It took her almost an hour. When she saw his house in the distance, she almost changed her mind. *No, damn it, I didn't walk all the way here for nothing. But I'm never telling anyone I did this. Not even Tessa. Never,* she promised herself. She walked up the front path of the Gregorys' house and pushed the doorbell.

"Hey, Josie, what're you doing here?" Cleve's brother Hap asked as he opened the door, unfazed by the highly unusual presence of Josie Parker standing on the front stoop.

Josie's first thought was, *You're drunk Hap. Or high. Or both. You're gross. Sunday afternoon and this is all you have to do?*

Clearly Mr. and Mrs. Gregory were not around. Hap was nineteen, and it was common knowledge that he was always getting into trouble. He had graduated but not gone away to college, and he seemed to spend all his time hanging around guys who were still in high school. Creepy guys. As far as she knew, Hap had no job and was just living off the Gregorys, and probably selling pot. He didn't like horses; it seemed he didn't like much of anything except hanging out with his dirtball friends.

"Cleve's out back." He smirked, detecting her objection to his being high, and pointed for her to run around the side of the house, which was certainly more acceptable to her than the idea of having to go past him. "Guess you don't want a beer," he teased after her. Josie gave him her best evil eye and headed to the back yard.

"Hey," she called out, forcing a smile as she approached Cleve. He didn't respond. She instantly felt like she was imposing. *Oh well, no turning back now.*

Cleve was sprawled out on his back in a hammock swinging between two trees. A leaning picnic table and a poorly tended perennial garden were the only other elements that adorned the small backyard, which was enclosed by a privacy fence badly in need of repair. Josie was surprised at such neglect. The Gregorys, she'd thought, were fairly well off. Up the deck steps, music was blaring out of the open sliding glass doors.

"Hey, you didn't come to the barn today, everything OK?" she called, still from a distance. She did notice that he seemed to have on the same clothes he'd had on at the show yesterday. "Are you sick?"

"Just busy doin' other stuff," he said. "Just dealing with some stuff here." He rolled on his side to look at her for a second and then rolled back. "What's going on?" Josie was almost sure he was high. Or drunk. His face looked puffy and his eyes were like slits. She tried to ignore it but suddenly there was a huge lump in her throat and she felt like she was suffocating.

"Gladys colicked this morning. She's dead. Mr. O'Hara and Sancho and Jeb buried her in the mares' pasture. It took all of us and the tractor to get her out of the standing stall shed." Josie sucked in air as though she'd just surfaced from being held too long underwater. She exhaled.

"Wow," he responded, dull and uninterested.

"Wow? That's all you have to say? Wow?" The pitch of her voice went way up and she lost her composure. "She's dead, Cleve! A horse is dead! What is wrong with you?" Josie felt tears welling in her eyes. The lump in her throat disappeared and she found her anger. "Is this where you've been all day? Getting high and spacing out on the hammock? We needed you at the barn! God, Cleve. Are you proud of yourself here, hanging out with your loser brother, wasting an entire day, while horses are dying?" Josie knew she was becoming quite theatrical, but she couldn't believe this was the same guy she'd just spent the best day of her life with.

"God, you asshole!" she continued. "I can't believe you, Cleve!" She was losing control of her emotions; the one-sided confrontation had become a catharsis and she couldn't stop herself. She burst into tears. She was freshly in love with this boy. This made her even angrier. He was spoiling her love. He chose to stay home and get stoned with his brother rather than spend the day at the barn with the horses and with her, not even twenty-four hours after such an amazing day and that ride home in the van. She waited, holding herself together with every ounce of strength she had, giving him the chance to defend himself, to explain, to react in some way. She got nothing.

"You're not who I thought you were, Cleve. I thought last night in the van meant something. I thought—" Josie stopped herself mid-sentence. Coming here had been a huge, spontaneous mistake. She pivoted and ran. Two strikes today. First Gladys, and now Cleve. He could barely lift his head from the hammock to look at her, and he was no doubt stoned. She was heartbroken. Heartsick. Her first meaningful kiss on Saturday; her first break-up on Sunday. *He's not the guy I thought he was. Damn him. Damn you, Cleve Gregory. I hope I never see you again. This has been the worst day. I've gone from the best day to the worst day in less than twenty-four hours. The worst day. And a dead horse, too.*

Cleve raised his head and pushed his exhausted body up from the hammock in time to catch a glimpse of Josie's back just as she rounded the side of the house.

"Wait, Jos', wait, it's not what you think. Josie, Josie." He cleared his muddled throat and tried to find a voice loud enough that she might hear him and come back. His attempt was futile. "I'm not high. I'm not stoned," he said out loud to himself, looking down at the ground now, sitting at the edge of the hammock. "Wait," he tried again in a vain attempt. "Ah, shit, Josie." She was gone.

He needed to explain. He couldn't blame her for what she was thinking. He had already planted the "loser seed" when he'd pulled the joint out that day. And yet it was so far from the truth. Last night, home had presented a crippling welcome to Cleve. Life defining. Quite possibly the worst night of his life to date. She had no idea that the night that was supposed to have ended on such a high for both of them, had actually ended terribly for him. How would she know? She couldn't possibly know what had happened after Frank Parker had deposited him curbside in front of the house on Laukner Lane. He had never shared with her what had been going on in his life beyond the fence line of Hidden Green Farm. He really hadn't had the chance. And now she was gone.

The one pure, wholesome ally that he had—the one person who gave him, without even knowing, the inspiration, the ambition, the motivation to believe in his own dreams—was gone. And it was his own fault that he'd lost her. Lost her balance, her infectious harmony. There had been no one left for him to have faith in besides her, and now this amazing girl believed he had stolen from her, stolen her heart, for all the wrong reasons. She had given him that heart, so cautiously, so genuinely, entrusting him with its care. And in her eyes, in just one day, he had let her down.

He knew Josie saw it all so differently than how it really was. If he hadn't been so physically exhausted, so humiliated, so emotionally spent right then, he would have run after her. He knew he should have. He should have found the strength. *If I were a better man*, the stricken seventeen-year-old thought, *I would have. No wonder she thinks I'm a loser. Actions speak louder than words.* He'd lain there on the hammock.

"I should run after her. I should, damn it, I should," he said out loud, trying to convince himself to get up and go after her. But his emotional defeat was too deep; he was in no position to try to explain anything. He was trying to figure it all out himself. He looked to the side of the house where she'd exited, willing her to come back. To save him. Nothing happened. He hurled a beer bottle across the yard, smashing it into the fence. He threw his hands up over his head and let out a deep, loud, wounded growl. Tomorrow would be too late. He headed into the house. She would be home soon. He would not let this day close out without at least explaining to her that his ability to even function right now was compromised, and not because he was stoned or drunk; he would assure her that his words were his truth. He hoped she'd hear him out.

Josie ran the entire four miles home. She ran as hard as she could, in an effort to keep herself from completely unraveling. She had no idea that still to come was the real reason this was to be the worst day of her life.

11

Josie was relieved to be home after her incredibly long and disturbing trek to and from the Gregorys. She saw Aunt Gayle's car in the driveway as she came across the yard. *Hmmmm,* she thought. *I didn't know she was coming for dinner.* As she pushed through the back door she was overcome with all the mixed emotions of the day. She just wanted to bury her face in her pillow and not think about anything. Not dinner, not homework, not her journal, not Gladys, not Cleve Gregory. Josie hurried past the kitchen. She had no interest in food, no interest in talking. She went by so quickly that she didn't even notice her dad and his sister, Gayle, sitting at the kitchen table, or that Mama wasn't in her usual Sunday afternoon spot, in front of the stove.

Josie had no time to answer the knock on her door before her dad entered her room; she really didn't want company right now. Snuff and Ralphie ran in ahead of him, heads down, tails between their legs as though guilty of some bad behavior. Snuff jumped up on the bed and pressed in next to Josie. Josie rolled over and pushed herself up to sit against the headboard.

"Ugh, not now, Snuff. Can you guys just leave me be?"

"Josie," Frank Parker began as he walked across the room and sat down on the edge of her bed. "Where have you been?" he asked in a gentle tone. "We've been trying to find you. This has not been a very good day." He slid his hands slowly back and forth on his thighs, searching for courage. Looking down at his only child, he took in a big breath and attempted to go on. Josie interrupted him.

"I know Dad, I know, everything went wrong today. Gladys colicked and, and..." She didn't know how to continue. *How could I possibly explain about Cleve?* she wondered to herself. *Mama would get it, but...*

"Josie, Josie." He pulled her into his chest to hug her and she accepted his arms freely. She loved her dad so much. No other dad she knew would understand what she was feeling right now. In fact, Josie thought, *How does he know what I've been through today?* This caused her to push back, feeling a sudden sense of apprehension and uncertainty. She looked up at her dad's distressed face.

The truth was Frank Parker hadn't heard a word of what Josie had just said. He gave no resistance as she retracted from his embrace, and instead took her hands in his. He paused there for a second, then slowly raised his hands to brace her above the elbows. He looked deeply into her eyes.

"Josie, something happened to Mama today," he said, as firmly and strongly as his voice would allow. "Something bad." He adjusted how he was sitting on her bed to steady himself. "We called the barn a thousand times but no one answered. We sent someone there to get you and you had gone. No one was sure where you were. It wouldn't have mattered. Everything happened so fast." Frank Parker took a breath and looked down at the well-worn rug on the floor of his daughter's room.

"What are you talking about, Dad? You aren't making any sense. What are you talking about? Why is Aunt Gayle here, anyway?" Josie began to sense that maybe she would rather not hear any more of what her dad had to say. Frank Parker continued, his words a maelstrom of sentences borne of someone very emotionally wrought.

"Mama got really sick today, Rosebud. Something happened. We don't know for sure exactly what. She collapsed in the front hall. I called an ambulance. I couldn't help her. They couldn't help her. She's gone, Josie. I'm so sorry, Rosebud. I'm so sorry, but Mama is gone."

"What?" She looked up at her dad as she pushed away from his grasp. "What? she asked again. "What are you talking about? Where is she, Dad? What do you mean she is gone? Gone to the hospital? Take me there then." She asked the question, but she knew precisely what her father was doing his best to convey. Mama was not at the hospital. "Mama!" she hollered towards the upstairs hall, jumping up from her bed. "Mama! Mama, answer me! Dad, where is she? We can help her, we can help her, I know we can." Josie couldn't make sense of anything. There was a terrible, invasive ringing in her ears. She needed to help Mama. She couldn't help Mama. She was incredibly confused. She felt as though she was outside of herself, outside of her room, outside of the universe, looking in from a very dark place.

"She's gone from us, Rosebud. I'm sorry. I'm so sorry. It was so fast. There was nothing anyone could do. She was gone in an instant. I'm so sorry. She loved you so much. She would never have wanted to leave you this way." The tears ran silently down his face. Ralphie tried to console him, wagging his tail, pushing in to his lap. Snuff spun in a circle and lay down again, sinking into the depression Josie had made in her pillow.

Josie's vision blurred. She thought she was going to fall over. Her dad was right there to steady her.

"Got you baby girl, I've got you." Frank Parker wrapped his arms around his precious child. Josie couldn't feel anything, she couldn't see anything. *Wake up,* she thought, *wake up!* This had to be a nightmare. The day had been a bad one to start. This *had* to be a dream. She felt the room going black. She held on somehow. "Mama!" she yelled as loud as she could. "Mama, where are you? No Dad, no! No, no, no."

Frank Parker clung to his Rosebud while she sobbed and screamed, writhed and shook her fists, until she finally burst free and ran down the stairs and out the back door. Frank Parker had no strength to run after her. He sat down at the top of the staircase, put his face to his hands, and began to sob himself. He sobbed for the loss of his wife, for the loss of his daughter's mama, and at the thought of Josie spending the rest of her life without a mother. Without Dorie Parker. His beautiful partner. Josie did not deserve that. Dorie did not deserve that. And Frank felt very alone.

Josie ran as hard and fast as she could until she thought she would collapse. Across the back yard and into Barrett Park, she ran as the sky grew dark and the world spiraled around her. She stopped at the spinning wheel and yelled into the universe.

"I hate this fucking ride!" she screamed at the top of her lungs. She grabbed one of the handles and holding tight to it, she began to run, building up the speed of the ride that always made her feel sick. When the wheel was turning as fast as she could make it go, she jumped on and laid down, looking up as storm clouds moved across the early evening sky, closing in around her. She thought of what her mama had said to her just that very morning.

"Go to what you love. Don't have it any other way."

The tears streamed down her cheeks in silence. As the wheel spun around she closed her eyes and imagined herself galloping through the woods on a beautiful chestnut horse. She could feel the wind blowing across her face as they raced out into the center of an open field. The horse came to a halt and raised his head. She looked up to the sky and the force of the wind became unendurable. The field began to spin circles around them. The horse screamed and Josie buried her head in his neck in an attempt to ward off the dizziness that was now consuming her. *I'm going to be sick,* she thought. She forced her eyes open, extricating herself from the dream, as the spinning wheel slowed to a stop.

She lay there, on her side, knees pulled up to her chest, sobbing, for quite some time, until the sun was almost down and she heard thunder nearby. She lay silently for a bit more time. Then numbly, as though outside of herself again, she stood up and started back home from Barrett Park.

The rain began to fall. How had this day even happened? Josie trudged towards home, her very confused mind caught between the real and the imaginary. How could she wake up from this nightmare? Yesterday had been so perfect. She decided quite simply that she just wouldn't let go of yesterday, that's all. Yesterday Josie knew her mama would be with her always. Yesterday Josie knew that Cleve was hers.

No, she thought, *nothing can take either one of them away, if I just hold on to yesterday.* It was her own protective hoodwink.

Of course the beguiling notion made sense only fleetingly, and as she reached the backyard, reality confronted her again. She climbed the back steps with the help of the railing, feeling the weight of the world upon her. She opened the screen door. Her Dad would need her now.

12

Josie had never worn a black dress before. She didn't even own one. Her Aunt Gayle suggested that perhaps they would find one in Mama's closet that would work.

"That would be repulsive, Aunt Gayle." Josie was not about to wear her dead mother's clothes. So on Wednesday afternoon Aunt Gayle took Josie to Bamberger's Department Store at the nearby shopping mall, to look for something appropriate for a daughter to wear to her mother's funeral.

Aunt Gayle drove in circles looking for a parking spot. Josie stared out the window blindly. She was in the midst of yet another out-of-body experience. The last few days had seemed completely obscure, and it was easier for her to just float along in a haze. *This isn't real,* she thought. *I am going to wake up from this dream and it will be last Sunday and I will be getting home from the barn. Gladys will not be dead, Mama will not be dead and Cleve will not be so... stupid.*

The car passed the pizza parlor at the end of the long row of stores. Josie's focus was drawn to the shop. At that very moment Hap Gregory walked out the front door, and as if things were not already as bad as they could possibly be, the next person to emerge was Cleve. Suddenly, everything preternaturally went into slow motion. Cleve and a short, plump girl with bleached blond hair, a black leather jacket, and lots of dark eye makeup came out of the pizza shop. Josie knew who she was. Cara DeSoto. Everyone knew who she was and many of the boys at Parson Prep apparently knew her "quite well." It was no secret that she was easy. His arm was around her neck and he seemed to be steadying himself against her. As if on cue, Cleve looked up and his eyes locked with Josie Parker's, just for a second, a mere second, but in that time so much was communicated between them. She hadn't seen or heard from him since she'd left his backyard. *Now,* she thought, *what difference does it make? What difference does any of it make? Mama is dead. So what if he's with some loose piece of change.*

"You are not who I thought you were Cleve Gregory." Josie's sad eyes spoke without sound. "I thought you loved horses the way that I do, and I also thought, well, I thought you loved me."

"You don't understand, Josie Parker," Cleve's guilt-filled eyes responded silently back to Josie's. "You have everything so together and I can't hold a candle to you. You're so—you're so above me. This is not where I want to be, not who I want to be. It's just that everything is out of control. I'm just trying to hang on."

Of course one head did not know what the other head was thinking, and it was not a good moment for either of them.

Cleve looked down at the pavement and turned back to the pack, and Josie, already numb, looked away and realized that Aunt Gayle had found a parking space.

"OK, let's go find a dress for you, sweetheart," Aunt Gayle said gently as she pushed the car's gearshift into park.

Josie prayed they would not bump into anyone she knew inside the God forsaken mall. Especially Cleve. She momentarily found anger. *And fuck you Cleve Gregory, you probably don't even know my mother is dead.*

Unfortunately, as soon as they walked into the building she saw him in the distance. He was sitting on a ledge that surrounded the fountain positioned at the mall's axis, and Cara DeSoto looked like she was sucking his neck. Josie felt sick. She wanted to walk right up and confront him. *This is better than Saturday? This is better than me? What are you doing, Cleve? What is this about? It's not who you are. It's not, it's just not. I know this is not what you are about. What are you doing?* A hundred thoughts raced through her mind.

This time it was Josie who didn't have the emotional strength. She had just lost her mother for God's sake, and besides, Aunt Gayle was with her and that would be completely embarrassing. She almost wished that Cleve would see her; she was curious, just a little, to know what he would do if he knew she saw what was going on. Cleve didn't see her, but Cara DeSoto did. She looked over Cleve's shoulder as she wrapped her arms around him and caught Josie's stare. She glared back at Josie, as though to say, *I've got him and you don't. You are nothing. Just some puny little "Rebecca of Sunnybrook Farm" nerd. You don't have what he's looking for, you won't give him what I will.*

"That's a lie," Josie said out loud, her voice serving to snap her out of her fantasy.

Aunt Gayle heard her, and taking notice of Cleve, and then the devastation in Josie's eyes, she took her niece's arm and suggested they take a look for a dress in Bamberger's. Josie turned her attention back to the mission at hand, but in her already broken heart she felt the undeniable, sickening pain that comes with losing your first love.

These days were completely a blur. Josie and her dad were never alone and rarely had a moment to talk privately. There really wasn't much to talk about anyway. Frank Parker physically embraced his only child every time their paths crossed in the house, but mostly he was on the phone or talking with Aunt Gayle, or feigning interest in conversation with any one of the endless number of visitors who stopped by the Parker home to pay their respects. Overwhelming amounts of flower arrangements and food arrived at the house every day. Josie found this odd.

People bring all this food, but when your mother dies you sure don't have much of an appetite. They bring all these flowers that are going to die, just like Mama. I don't understand that. Flowers are not going to make me happy again.

Tessa and Libby O. came to stay overnight for a couple of days and the three pals spent the time up in Josie's room, listening to records, braiding one another's hair, reading old *Chronicle of the Horse* magazines that Tessa brought over, and playing board games. Josie had no interest in going to the barn, she had no interest in anything really. But her girlfriends provided a welcome distraction to the overwhelming sadness hovering over the Parker household.

"I heard Cleve Gregory was at the mall, making out with that loser Cara DeSoto. She's such a slut. She always has hickeys and she's always high," Libby O. volunteered for no apparent reason. "That girl has a different boyfriend every week. What would Cleve want with her? Something's not right about that. Besides, we know he only has eyes for you, Jos'."

"I heard he was with her too," Tessa jumped in. She glanced in Josie's direction. "I also heard the police were at his house Saturday night. Must've been some party," she said.

"I saw him there. At the mall. With her," Josie stuttered to her friends, ignoring the comment about the police. "He's been hanging around his stupid brother, that's why. He's such a loser." She shook her head in dismay. She was lying. She didn't think Cleve was a loser. Her mouth and throat felt so dry.

"He's so different when he's at the barn." Tessa said. "But he hasn't been there all week."

"He hasn't been there since the show," Libby O. offered. "My dad says he might have to fire him. Apparently he showed up for work seemingly high a couple of weeks back. What an idiot."

The look on Josie's face compelled Tessa to change the subject. "Hey," she said, gesturing toward the stereo and motioning to Libby O, "skip that record and play some Harry Chapin."

"It was rainin' hard in Frisco, I needed one more fare to make my night." Tessa sang into an imaginary microphone until she and Libby O. buckled over in giggles. Josie sat at her desk, silent, and wrote in her journal.

Last week was the most amazing week. I thought I saw a glimpse of what my future would be. Mama was supposed to be in it. Mama wasn't supposed to have a fucking aneurysm. Cleve was supposed to be in it. He wasn't supposed to be an immature jerk caving to his brother's dumb behavior and gross friends. I wasn't supposed to be a stupid girl. I'm a stupid girl. I ruined everything by imagining things would be wonderful. I'm not even twenty years old and I've lost my mother. I'm almost twenty years old and I've never even had a real boyfriend. I'm not ever gonna be part of the "it" crowd, I really am a little bit "Rebecca of Sunnybrook Farm." And that's why Cleve is probably sorry he ever kissed me. And I love him. It's probably my fault that he won't ever come back to the barn. Probably, probably, probably. His loss. My loss. Mama. She drew a little heart in her journal. Then she connected another one to the first. *Two hearts lost,* she thought. And one completely broken.

"Two Hearts," she whispered. *Great name for a horse. Or a barn.*

She put down her pen and turned to listen to the music. Writing things down always helped Josie Parker feel better. Unburdened.

Liberated. She knew she was going to hurt for a long time. But right now she would lean on her friends who were there to help her through. She walked over to her bed and climbed in between them.

"She was gonna be an actress, and I was gonna learn to fly, she took off to find the footlights, I took off to find the sky." The three friends sat braiding one another's hair, singing Harry Chapin until they collapsed, all snuggled on Josie's bed with Ralphie and Snuff, and closed their eyes for the night.

Friday morning came and the rain had finally cleared. Josie opened her eyes and lay motionless, staring at the ceiling. Tessa and Libby O. were still sleeping. Josie wished she could have slept right through until tomorrow. That would mean, in a way, that this day would never have happened. Instead, she threw back the covers and moved quietly into her bathroom.

Staring at herself in the mirror while she brushed her teeth, she assessed that she was prettier than Cara DeSoto. *In a natural way*, she said to herself. *I would never bleach my hair and I would never, ever wear all that eye makeup.* She pulled her pajama top over her head and looked at her bare breasts. *They're too small,* she thought. *I look like a boy from the neck down. Why would any boy, why would Cleve, have any interest in me? Mama? Who will have the answers for me now, Mama?*

She wrapped her bathrobe around her and walked back into her room. The girls were up. Tessa's nanny was picking them up at eight thirty so that they could go home to get ready and then attend the funeral with their parents.

"I love you guys, thanks. Thanks so much. See you later, unfortunately." Josie hugged her pals and they were gone. She pulled on some underwear from her top dresser drawer and turned to pull the tags off the horrid black dress she swore she would throw away the following day.

Josie, her dad, Aunt Gayle, and Josie's grandmother drove to the funeral parlor where the procession of black cars would commence. The hearse, which would carry Josie's mama to the church and then on to the cemetery, would lead off, with the rest of the family following behind in a limousine. Josie was in a fog, numb and merely putting one foot in front of the other.

Once inside, the director led the family into a small room. At the far end was the casket, open and luring. Josie's dad and Aunt Gayle lumbered slowly toward the horrible box. It was so quiet in the room. The silence almost made Josie want to scream. Agitated, she turned to leave. As if he could read her mind, the director stepped directly in front of her, blocking her exit.

"Wouldn't you like to see your mother, Josie?" he asked.

This guy is creepy for sure, she thought to herself.

Josie shook her head no, and stared toward the far end of the room, where Aunt Gayle and her dad appeared to be praying over Mama's box. *Creepy*, she thought again, and then, *that is not Mama in that box.*

"Are you sure? I think it would be a good idea. You can say good-bye to her. If you want to." The director was trying, gently, to coax her into spending one last moment with her mother. "Some people regret it if they don't." He backed away and disappeared, leaving Josie standing alone.

If for no other reason than being shamed into it, Josie mechanically made her way toward the horrible box. Her dad and Aunt Gayle had now settled in the front row of folding wood chairs lined up facing the casket, and they were silent as Josie approached her mother.

Oddly, Josie felt like a tiny child. The room seemed to grow to enormous proportion around her. She took a deep breath, pulled back her shoulders, and looked down into the horrible box. The body lying there in the box resembled Mama, but it wasn't her. There was so much powdery makeup on the face that Josie couldn't even see skin, and the makeup effused a really disgusting smell. The hair was very badly styled, not like Mama's. *She doesn't brush it that way. She doesn't brush it that way at all.* The body was clothed in Mama's dress, but still, it wasn't Mama. The lipstick wasn't Mama's color. *It's not even close.*

Josie stared into the horrible box and realized she didn't feel any sadder, hovering over the dead stranger. It didn't make her feel any worse, and she was almost relieved. She didn't feel anything, really.

Although, she supposed, in some way it reinforced her belief that Mama was not there at all. She was not in that body, not in that box. Mama was floating, somewhere in the universe, perhaps somewhere far away and lovely, or perhaps right here in the funeral parlor. She wasn't wearing the dress, or the lipstick that Aunt Gayle chose to have her buried in. She was a beautiful, winsome, floating spirit, and yes, Josie did sense that spirit right there beside her. Mama may well have been in the room, but she was definitely not in that box. Josie knew right then that Mama would not ever really leave. She would always be with Josie, just embodied in a different way. Josie touched the horrible box gently; she genuflected and walked away. She walked arm-in-arm with her dad, Aunt Gayle and Grandmother Caldwell following behind, out to the black limousine just behind the ominous-looking hearse.

"Wait here with Aunt Gayle, Rosebud. I will be right back." Her dad walked over reluctantly to watch the horrible box being lifted into the hearse. The procession soon made its way out onto the main road, in the direction of St. Michael's Church.

The morning remained devoid of sentiment for Josie, despite going through all the motions of the funeral. As she walked down the church aisle behind the horrible box, she looked left and right into the pews and saw so many familiar faces, such sadness in them all. She took her seat in the front pew along with her dad, Aunt Gayle, and Grandmother Caldwell. At the appropriate time she walked up to the church pulpit and read the psalm someone had decided she should read.

She wanted to say to everyone, "Don't be sad. Mama isn't really gone, she's just floating." But she knew that would be terribly disrespectful to her dad and grandmother. She listened to her dad offer the eulogy but absorbed very little of what he said. She sang along to Amazing Grace and Eagle's Wings, but she was in the midst of a complete out-of-body experience. She felt relieved when she finally placed her long-stemmed rose on the casket at the cemetery, just before the funeral director announced that everyone was invited back to the Parkers' home for lunch. As she climbed back into the black limo, she knew that she would not return to this place. She promised herself that she would find another way to keep Mama's memory alive. She wasn't sure how, but she would figure it out.

13

Back at the Parker home, there were so many people that Josie felt almost like a stranger in unfamiliar territory. She filtered through room after room, nodding her head to acknowledge each gesture of condolence. In the dining room she picked up a mini quiche from a shiny silver serving tray, took a bite, and discreetly put the unfinished piece down on a back corner of the English mahogany sideboard. She still had no appetite.

When it seemed as though everyone of any consequence to her had finally disappeared, Josie found her dad and excused herself. She moved insipidly toward the stair hall, with the intention of going up to her room. Her hand was on the banister and she couldn't wait to put her head on her pillow. It may have only been two o'clock, but she was exhausted. She wanted everyone to be gone.

She started up the stairs and looked back, just for a second, to make sure the dogs were following her. She thought it quite likely that she was hallucinating when at that very moment, Cleve and his mother walked through the front door. Immediately she was angry. *How dare he? No Cara DeSoto today? Jerk,* she thought, defensively. A big jerk, a big jerk whom she happened to love.

Mrs. Gregory awkwardly embraced Josie. She seemed so rigid, even her clothing—stiff, dull, her skirt three inches too long. She was so thin. Her eyes looked tired and sad. She hadn't known Dorie Parker well enough for that sadness to come from Dorie's death, and Josie couldn't help but wonder what it was. She'd seen that same sadness in Cleve's eyes before.

"I'm so sorry, sweetheart. Your mother was wonderful and taken from us way too soon. I'm sorry, dear. I'm so sorry." She hugged Josie again. "Let me go find your dad." She gesticulated to Cleve, as if to say, *Keep that poor girl company*, then proceeded down the hall towards the living room.

Josie stood frozen, staring at Cleve, who stared back in silence.

After what felt like an eternity, she sat down, slowly, on the second or third stair. He moved to the stairs and sat down next to her. Her insides were shaking.

"Hey," Cleve said quietly, leaning forward, hands clasped, elbows resting on his knees. Staring straight ahead at the front door, he asked, "Hey Jos', how are you doing? You doing okay?" She hardly heard what he said, but she was keenly aware of the length of his arm pressing against hers.

"Pretty good," she responded generically. "I'm pretty good. Thanks for asking. Thanks for coming by. Thanks." Josie nodded her head in acknowledgement of what she had just said. They sat in silence for a long while. She had never felt so awkward. Cleve knew she was uncomfortable. With intention, he moved his thigh to connect it with hers. She shivered. *Damn it.* He shifted again to put his arm across the front of her, reaching for her far shoulder, shifting her body while he shifted his own. The two were now facing one another as they sat on the stairs. He lifted her chin to engage her.

"Look, Josie, the other day at the mall...I'm sorry about that. It, well, I'm not gonna tell you it wasn't what it looked like. I wish you hadn't seen any of it. There is nothing between Cara DeSoto and me. She's a distraction, that's it. I'm sorry about last week in my backyard too. I was an ass, and I'd like to explain, when it's a better time. Now isn't the time. I'm really sorry about your mama, Jos'. I know how close you two were and she was so great. I liked her so much. She made me so many great breakfasts." He turned the corners of his mouth upward, just slightly, hoping to invoke some sign of possible forgiveness from her. Nothing.

He sat quietly for a bit more time, then stood up and turned to face her. Josie looked quizzically up at him. His brown locks fell perfectly across his forehead today, nothing new except that the rest of his hair was actually brushed. His khakis were fresh; his belt displayed his grandfather's monogram, engraved on the small silver buckle. His tie was tied an inch or so too short.

Josie pondered this epitome of handsomeness standing in front of her now. She adored his tweed blazer with the turned-up collar, and the slightly rumpled, blue-checked Brooks Brothers shirt underneath it. She wanted to be angry with him. She wanted to hate him at this very moment, but she couldn't. She was madly, totally in love with him. He spoke again.

"Hey, I called here a million times after you left my house Sunday. Understandably no one answered the phone. I just want you to know."

A few tears welled in her sad brown eyes and rolled down her cheeks. He leaned in and wiped away one and then another. Cleve looked deeply into Josie Parker's eyes. When he knew he had her full attention, he resumed talking.

"Listen, this is your mama's day, not mine. I am so sorry you've lost her and it's not my intention to be disrespectful to her in any way, but this may be my only chance to make sure you understand there is something I am very *not* sorry about. I'm *not* sorry about our van ride home last weekend, Jos'. Everything felt amazingly right between us that entire day, especially the ride home. The truth is I've felt super connected to you for a long time now and have just been afraid to tell you, too afraid to let anybody know. It always seems like once other people know too much, things have a way of getting screwed up. I liked keeping it a secret. I know that wasn't fair to you. But I kind of felt like on some level you knew, and that you felt the same way."

He paused, not because he was embarrassed to talk to her this way, but because he knew he needed to tell her so much and that he had to do it quickly, and he wasn't sure how. Josie sat motionless, acutely focused on Cleve.

"Listen," he continued. "There's a lot of shit—sorry —going on in my house that's really messed up, Josie. I'm just gonna leave it at that, but trust me, it's messed up, and it's messing me up. I won't be going back to work at the barn. I'm not just gonna bail, I'm gonna tell Mike O'Hara on Tuesday." He paused again, in a valiant effort to find the guts to keep going. "Please don't give up on me." He looked straight into her eyes. "I love you, Josie Parker. I may be a screwed up seventeen-year-old guy, but of that I am sure. I love you. I've never known a girl like you; no one will ever compare to you." And there, it had been said.

He leaned in and affectionately put one hand around the nape of her neck, pulling her face close to his. He leaned in closer and whispered in her ear, then pressed his lips against her forehead, keeping them there for several seconds. He stood up straight and quietly implored her, "Please, remember what I just told you. I meant every word. I'll see ya, Jos'."

He turned, put his hands in his pockets, and hesitated for just a second or two. He'd walked through that door in front of him a half hour ago, an off balance, beaten down, seventeen-year-old boy. Now, as he used all of his strength to push his broad shoulders back, he walked out that door, an ambitious young man with conviction. He had only Josie Parker to thank for that. He refrained from looking back as he crossed the threshold onto the porch, but it wrecked him not to. He was almost desperate to see her face for just a minute more. Then he heard her voice.

"Fairy tales aren't real, Cleve. You can't expect me to believe you," she said as she stood up and walked toward him. "They're stories for books; they don't really come true."

He turned back to the gift of her freckles, the waves of her strawberry blond hair, the sadness of her weary but beautiful eyes. He touched her arm and smiled.

"Wanna bet?" He pulled her in to his chest and squeezed her tightly in his arms, perhaps unknowingly attempting to absorb as much of her balance as he could. He let go of her and headed off, calling from the sidewalk, "And who said anything about fairy tales anyway? This is life!" He was gone.

Josie was paralyzed. She managed to sit down on the front steps to think about what had just happened. She closed her eyes and felt his arm against hers, his thigh pressing on her thigh, his lips on her forehead. She would not easily forget what he said to her today. Josie Parker believed in Cleve Gregory and he certainly seemed devout about what he had whispered in her ear. At the same time there was no telling if she might ever see him again. She knew he was on his way somewhere, though she didn't know exactly where. Neither did he.

Josie sat motionless except for the spontaneous smile that now appeared on her face. She smiled, ever so briefly, for the first time in over a week. She remained on the front steps for a long time, holding onto the sound of Cleve's whispered words. In the midst of all the sadness, there was one good thing. Cleve Gregory loved her. And she was proud of him. She knew he would become a strong, credible man. She just knew. She really hoped she would see him again.

"No one will ever compare to you," he'd said. He was her very first love. He had not stolen her heart. He had shown her heart how to have a stronger beat.

The dogs came bounding out onto the porch and Josie pushed herself up off the steps. She realized she was starving after all.

It wasn't until Josie climbed into her bed that night that she began to feel incapable of holding off the profound sadness that had been hovering around her for days. She'd done a heroine's job of keeping tears at bay, but now she was so utterly weary that she was losing her power over them.

Frank Parker came in and sat on the edge of his daughter's bed. He brushed the hair off her forehead and kissed it.

Wow, she thought. *Kissed on the forehead twice today. Each time by a man I love. Well at least this day is ending better than it began.* Her eyes were welling up. She wanted to be strong for her dad. He would miss Mama so much. They were practically attached at the hip. As she squeezed her lids tightly down, she had a brief vision of her parents, long ago, holding hands in Barrett Park, watching her climb and run and slide.

"Sleep tight, my sweet girl." He brushed her hair back again. "It's been a tough, tough week. I know you are more than exhausted. You've handled everything so bravely. Mama would be proud."

"Good night, Dad." She squeezed his hand. "Tomorrow will be better." As though the adult, Josie patted her dad on his thigh.

He stood up and walked across the room. Without looking back he said, "Ah, Rosebud. I hope so. I sure hope so. I love you, sweetheart." She knew he was crying. She knew she would cry now, too.

"Love you too, Dad."

When the door closed behind him, the moment hit. It didn't happen fast, but her tears could be denied no longer. They were ready and they were necessary. She pulled her quilt tight around her and hugged it. Snuff and Ralphie jumped up and pressed themselves against her in an act of compassion, as dogs so often do when they sense pain or despair. Perhaps it was the security of her blankets around her. Maybe it was the love and devotion of those dogs. Maybe it was the end of an exhausting process of doing everything they had to do to get Mama to "a better place." Then again, maybe it was that even though Josie firmly believed Mama would always be with her, reality was sinking in; she would never see her again, never hug her again, never hear her yell out the back door,

"Two hours Josie Parker!"

Whatever the catalyst was, Josie Parker cried. Josie Parker cried for the loss of her mother. She cried for her father's pain and she cried for herself. She cried for the love she felt in her heart for Cleve Gregory, and she cried for his struggle too, whatever it was that was going to keep him from her.

Josie Parker cried so hard that she had no recollection of when her crying gave way to sleep and when the darkness gave way to sunlight.

14

Summer's warm and comfortable embrace seemed clipped short for Josie. The days ran one into the other and she hardly noticed the passing of time until suddenly there was only a week left before her senior year would begin. Her focus at the barn had grown even stronger. There had been enough death this year, and she was determined to keep every horse at Hidden Green healthy and happy. She got to the barn early every morning. She paid attention to everything going on. She helped anyone who would permit it. The blacksmith, the veterinarian, the hay and feed guys, Mike O'Hara. She absorbed everything she could. And at the end of every day, she rolled into her bed and stared out her window to the stars.

"Good night, Mama," she spoke out loud in the direction of the brightest twinkle she could find. Every night. And every night she couldn't keep herself from thinking about Cleve. He had not returned to Hidden Green. Josie knew he had told Mike O'Hara he was quitting; Tessa had seen him shaking Mike's hand at the door of Mike's cottage on the Tuesday morning after Mama's funeral. No one ever talked about why he stopped showing up. No one at the barn talked about him at all. He had not reached out to Josie since the day of the funeral and she didn't feel it was her privilege to reach out to him. Tessa tried her best to refrain from mentioning his name, but every once in a while she couldn't help but ask Josie if she'd heard from him. The answer was always the same.

"No, nothing. It haunts me. I never even see any of the Gregorys around town, which I suppose is a good thing. I would feel awkward asking about him. One of these days I just have to stop thinking about him, Tess'. Stop living in the fairy tale. I just keep letting myself think that I will hear from him, even though I know I won't."

"Would you ever go over to his house?" Tessa queried during one of their nightly phone conversations.

"No way, Tessa. Cleve told me he had complicated stuff going on at his house. Whatever it was, he was very upset by it, maybe even embarrassed. Maybe his brother is really messed up. I don't know. If he wanted me to know, he would have found the time to tell me. He doesn't want me to know. And he doesn't want to be around me. Who knows why?" she asked rhetorically. "Who knows." She shook her head. "I'm pretty sure it's not because of Cara DeSoto, though."

"Yeah, well if it is then screw that, screw him," Tessa offered back. "But Jos', let's just drive by his house. If we take my mother's car we won't be obvious. I will drive and you can check it out. We can even disguise ourselves. My mother has wigs. And scarves. We will wear lipstick and look ridiculous. We will be private investigators," she giggled. "Don't you just want to drive by?"

Josie knew better than to think that would be a justifiable thing to do. *It's completely wrong*, she thought. But now Tessa had really piqued her curiosity. Josie asked herself, *What harm could there be in a simple, quick drive-by?*

"Yeah, actually, I guess I do," she admitted, but she immediately regretted her admission. The romantic Josie remembered the words he'd whispered in her ear that day sitting on the front hall stairs, words she'd never shared with anyone else. Words she held locked in her heart and that gave her the confidence to hold on. She wasn't even sure what she was holding on to. Hope, she supposed. She didn't want to do anything that might spoil her hope. As long as she had that, she knew she still had some small part of Cleve. Her inner struggle was constant but in a way it had come to represent possibility. Too much information could ruin everything. The romantic in Josie let her believe that he would find her when the time was right. The sensible Josie reminded herself, *Fairy tales don't come true. He felt sorry for you because your mother had just died, for God's sake.* Between Mama and Cleve, some nights her heart ached so much that she wondered if she would ever be able to feel joy again.

They met at Josie's house after school the following Monday. Tessa drove her mother's brown station wagon over to the Parkers', arriving armed with two blond wigs, two pairs of big, dark Jackie O sunglasses, two of her mother's silk Hermès scarves and a tube of bright pink lipstick. The partners in spy planned the drive-by for just after sundown, figuring they were less likely to be noticed and also might have a better chance of seeing into the windows of the Gregorys' house. Josie had to admit there was a certain cool-feeling, nervous adrenaline rush that this whole undertaking gave her, and Tessa was so into it that the excitement was contagious.

"You're like one of those women on *Charlie's Angels*, Tessa! You are a one-woman militia. I think you are more curious than I am."

"C'mon, girlfriend, you know you are dying to know what's going on over there. I mean, it's been months. And we know from Libby O.'s friend at Parson Prep that Cleve hasn't even shown up there. School's been back in session for what, like three weeks now? Where could he be going to school if it's not PP, Middletown, or Red Bank Catholic? I mean, it's senior year!"

The Parker dogs growled and barked nervously when they saw Tessa and Josie come down the stairs, not recognizing the two girls in their wigs, glasses, and scarves. Tessa paused to admire herself in the mudroom mirror.

"I wish I had a camera, we look hysterical," she complimented her work. "No one would ever believe we would do this. I mean, look at us Josie, you and me, the two biggest geeks on earth!"

"Let's get out of here before my dad gets home and sees us, I'm not exactly sure how I would even begin to explain this weirdness!" Josie pushed her friend hurriedly toward the back door, giggling nervously.

"We could always just say it's an experiment or some kind of school project. OK, OK, I'm going." Tessa moved away from the mirror.

"An experiment that could land us both in the loony bin, or jail!" Josie exclaimed. The two girls laughed heartily, loving the glamour as much as the drama, as they safety belted themselves into the station wagon. With Tessa behind the wheel, they pulled out of the Parkers' driveway onto Cooper Road.

"I hope we don't pass my dad," Josie moaned.

"Don't worry," Tessa said, laughing. "He wouldn't recognize us!"

Tessa made the turn onto Cleve's street, and Josie was struck with a momentary stab of fear. *What if he is out in the front yard?*

"No," she said. "Tessa, we can't do this, someone is going to see us. This is not right. You've got to turn around."

"No one is going to see us dummy, and if they did, no one would know it was us. If anything they would think I am my mother, only because of the car. But she never drives this car, anyway. By the way, Josie Parker, there is no law that prohibits us from driving down Laukner Lane if we damn well want to. OK, pay attention, there's the house, I don't want to go too slow, so focus. Take off the sunglasses now, it's dark enough anyway."

Josie took off the glasses and pulled at the silk scarf to cover more of her forehead. She flipped the sun visor down and slumped lower into the passenger seat. She squinted to see into the Gregorys' driveway as they got closer, looking for a car. She couldn't believe she was doing this. The large house was dark, making it difficult to see anything, even the front yard. There didn't appear to be a single light on, inside or out. Not even a porch light, though it was still early in the evening. Not one sign of life that Josie could see.

"I can't really see anything yet. Wait, what is that? There, in the front yard, along the walkway? Do you see what I mean? Tessa!" Josie yelled in a whisper.

"No, I don't. I'm driving, jerk! Looks like a sign, a real estate sign or something."

Josie had already figured that out. No car in the driveway, no lights on inside or out. A FOR SALE sign propped boldly in the front yard. Another sign stuck across it that said UNDER CONTRACT. Cleve Gregory was gone, really gone. It would seem the entire Gregory family was gone. He wasn't just not around, he was *gone* gone. And without a word from him.

Now Josie's hope was gone, too. Tessa was heartbroken for her friend. They drove back to the Parkers' house in silence, peeling their disguises off as they cruised along, bringing their adventure to a close and their curiosities into reality.

In late September, a gentleman arrived at Hidden Green as a new boarder. He brought with him—in a fancy, private two-horse trailer—a big chestnut horse with a white face and four knee-high white stockings. This handsome gelding intrigued Josie; there was something exceptional about him.

The gentleman, Mr. Bonington, was a polo player and a foxhunter. He was a tall man, really tall, with broad shoulders, a bald head, and a prominent chest. He wasn't long on smiles or pleasantries. He paraded himself pretentiously, boasting custom made, cordovan field boots, canary britches, and shirts with his monogram embroidered on the cuff or breast pocket. He rarely spoke to anyone except to bark out a command or a reprimand.

"This stall needs more straw in it, now man," he directed Jeb one afternoon. No "please" or "thank you," or "would you mind?" Just a "do it now" tone.

No one at the barn cared for Mr. Bonington, but the big chestnut horse was a different story. He was full of personality. Josie fell for him instantly. Lars was Mr. Bonington's foxhunter, and boarding him at Hidden Green would make it convenient to hunt with the famed Monmouth County Hounds, who set off each week from mid-November until March just a few miles down the road. Fox hunting had become quite popular and there were a number of new boarders who hunted through the winter months. Mr. O'Hara was even thinking about starting his own hunt, and one of Cleve's summer projects, long since abandoned, had been to convert the small outbuilding adjacent to the manure pile into a kennel so that some hounds could be maintained.

In no time flat, Lars and Josie were an alliance. Any time Lars was on the board to be prepared for his owner, Josie would put her name down to get him tacked up. If by chance Mr. Bonington arrived at the farm while Josie was still grooming Lars, he never spoke to her. Rather, he would stand and watch, impatiently waiting for her to pick Lars' feet, comb his mane over, and shake the straw out of his tail. She secretly loved dragging out the whole process just so she could antagonize this loathsome man.

Once Lars' bridle was on and the girth tightened, Mr. Bonington would nod a condescending indication of thanks, then reach for the reins. And every time, Lars would recoil. Mr. Bonington, in retort, would yank on the reins, pulling down harshly on the fierce Pelham bit in Lars' mouth.

It was clear that Mr. Bonington was no animal lover. Lars had a job to do and beyond that the man had no affection for this kind and gentle gelding. He also had no idea that Josie would secretly have apples and sugar and kisses ready and waiting after the ride was over and Lars had been rubbed down and put away. Unknowingly, Lars was just the panacea Josie's wounded heart needed.

Josie watched one Saturday afternoon as Mr. Bonington and Lars headed for the trail that led from the far end of the back paddock, through the woods, to a big open field down the road from Hidden Green. The property belonged to the Jordan family and Mr. O'Hara maintained it. He had installed some natural jumps there, mimicking what would be found in real hunt country. It was a total rush to take the right horse out to gallop around that field, to fly over the elements. Josie didn't get the opportunity to ride there too often, but when she did she felt as free as a girl could feel on a horse.

Mr. Bonington's stirrups were always too long and it made him look like he was trying to ride western style. He had the fanciest chaps she'd ever seen and he carried an exceptionally long whip. *Really? Is that whip really necessary?* Josie wondered what for. Today, Lars sidestepped across the paddock. The few times she'd ridden him he'd been calm and relaxed. She cringed as Mr. Bonington dug his spurs into Lars' side, causing the already nervous horse to lunge forward. The man's balance was awful, and he yanked on the reins incessantly. Horse and rider disappeared into the woods at a swift canter, Lars already breaking a sweat on his neck and between his hind legs. Josie shook her head with disdain as she turned back to her chores.

She navigated her way up the plank ramp in the manure pile and dumped her wheelbarrow. As she turned to maneuver her way back down, she caught sight of something moving along the edge of the woods near the entrance to the trail. Curious, she looked up and was surprised to see Lars, trotting across the back pasture in the direction of the barn, reins caught around his leg, stirrups flapping wildly. No Mr. Bonington anywhere in sight. She carefully backed the wheelbarrow down the last stretch of the ramp, parked it, and nonchalantly but hurriedly walked toward Lars, who'd paused by the picnic tables. He bent his wet, foaming neck to eat some grass.

"Easy boy, here ya go." She stopped a few feet shy of him and gave him a chance to know she was there, to inhale her trustworthy smell. He raised his head, snorted, and high stepped across the yard to the other side. "Whoa boy, easy now. Easy." Josie wondered what had happened. "Hey now, hey now." She eased her way slowly toward Lars and pulled some sugar from her pocket. "C'mon now, here ya go." She extended her arm, two small white cubes balanced on the flat surface of her palm. Lars raised his head from the grass and stretched his neck toward her. His nostrils widened and he snorted, then shook his entire front end. Josie wasn't sure what would happen next. She stayed absolutely still, talking quietly to him until finally he took one step closer to her, then another, and when his nose reached Josie's hand his top lip swiveled the sugar into his mouth. He nodded his head up and down as he focused on the sweet treat and Josie slowly reached out with her other hand. Patting his neck, she lifted Lars' leg and unlooped the tangled reins. "Easy, Lars. Here we go, OK. It's OK."

She gave him a gentle pat on the neck and another sugar cube. He was drenched and puffing hard. As she led him toward the back door of the barn, she looked discreetly over her shoulder just in time to see Mr. Bonington emerge from the trail, mud caked on his fancy chaps, anger plastered on his face. Josie chuckled to herself.

She hooked Lars up to the cross ties at the wash stall and began to remove his tack. The clack, clack, clack of boots across the cobblestone let her know that Mr. Bonington had reached the barn. He walked straight past Lars and Josie without so much as a word, pausing only to flail his whip at the horse's face. Lars recoiled nervously.

"He's fine, Mr. Bonington," Josie offered even though it was apparent that Mr. Bonington couldn't care any less. "Are you OK?" she asked politely. No response.

Obviously embarrassed, Mr. Bonington continued through the

barn and out the front door. *You nasty fucking bastard,* thought Josie. *You prick.*

That was the last anyone at Hidden Green ever saw of him. He never even came back for Lars. Mr. Bonington wouldn't be missed. Of course no one was happier about this than Josie Parker.

The days of winter arrived. The barn was cold and most nights Josie, Jeb, and Sancho put extra blankets on all the horses. Steam rose off the manure pile as though it were a brewing volcano. The rats scurried quickly through the soiled straw, digging tunnels into the warmth, and the plank ramp was icy and slippery. Josie's toes were always frozen. Her clunky rubber boots were certainly not warm and they were getting quite snug. For Christmas she might have asked for new boots, but she was not interested in celebrating Christmas without Mama around.

Lars had been relegated to school horse status, but because he was so big he remained in his stall in the main barn. Mr. O'Hara had "inherited" him after the sweet gelding had left his owner in the mud. It came to light that Mr. Bonington had thought Lars was a hopeless, restless horse—never quite trustworthy—and he was happy to unload him. Money was no object and it suited him just fine to "donate" the horse to Hidden Green.

Josie found Lars to be quite the opposite. She spent all her free time grooming him, feeding him endless amounts of treats, trimming his ears and whiskers, and straightening his blankets at night before she headed home. As Christmas approached she even pushed the edge of protocol and hung a stocking on his stall door, something typically reserved for the horses who had private owners. She knew he didn't belong to her, but it seemed as though he belonged to no one, so she silently adopted him.

As it would happen, he was considered too unreliable to be a school horse; he was so big and a spooky jumper, and it was a liability for Mr. O'Hara to let any novice ride him. None of the boarders wanted to be bothered so Josie took him on. This suited her just fine. Soon she knew every inch of his conformation. She knew every spot he liked to have scratched, and lately he'd taken to nickering as soon she walked into the barn. Despite his being a spook, she loved riding him, which she did every day.

Some evenings, curled up on the couch at home, Josie drew sketches of Lars. Her dad listened intently as she'd tell him about the lessons Mr. O'Hara gave her and about the practice drills she would create and execute. Frank Parker was well aware that this horse was solely responsible for resolving Josie's grief. He made a mental note to find time soon to visit Hidden Green to see what was so special about the gelding, and truthfully, to thank him.

Now and then Josie would think about Cleve. Sometimes she imagined him showing up at the barn to help her set small courses in the ring. He would help her when Lars was afraid. He would take a hand on the reins and walk alongside, patting Lars' neck and talking to him in a soft but firm voice, "Easy boy, here you go, easy now." Someday she hoped to have the chance to tell Cleve all about Lars. For now she'd have to settle for telling him in her dreams.

15

Snow came early, and by Thanksgiving there were several inches covering the ground. Jeb plowed the ring so the girls could still get the horses out for some exercise, but lessons were cancelled until there was a good melt.

On the Friday after Thanksgiving, Josie got to the barn early, pulled Lars from his stall, and hooked him up to the crossties. This would be a quiet day at Hidden Green. She and Tessa had agreed to get there at the same time so they could take Lars and Opie on a trail ride out to the big field. It would be so pretty to ride through the woods. It was a cold day and the horses would have to work hard to move their legs through the snow, but it was good for them and a rare treat.

When Tessa arrived she went directly to the chalkboard and wrote, *Gone out to the field. 10:30. Josie and Tessa.* This was a mandatory rule at Hidden Green so that riders' whereabouts were accounted for. She pulled Opie out of his stall and gave him a quick grooming. The girls put on their chaps and helmets, zipped up their ski jackets, and pulled on their gloves.

Josie and Lars led the way. Lars was definitely the braver of the two geldings. Josie had never known him to actually be afraid, just a little intimidated by some of the more elaborate jumps in the ring. She had never figured out what happened that day he dumped Mr. Bonington, so she always paid close attention to his body language when she rode him out in the field. Tessa and Opie followed close behind. The two friends crossed through the back pasture; Josie leaned over and opened the gate at the far end and they followed the trail into the woods.

"It's not too deep in here, let's trot," Josie called back to Tessa.

"OK, go ahead." Tessa shortened her grip on her reins. The horses trotted along, bending and bowing at trees that resembled zombies, birds that darted about. A huge red fox jumped off a snow-covered, felled tree, and Lars raised his head high, stopping dead in his tracks. He let out a fierce snort.

Josie squeezed her legs against the saddle. "You're just a chicken shit, Lars."

The girls laughed and they continued on.

Once they emerged on the other side of the woods, the girls paused to let the horses take in the enormity of the blanketed field. Except for the silver beeches, which held their leaves until spring, the large trees of the surrounding woods were barren and their branches reached out hauntingly. Squirrel and hawk nests were exposed. Tiny footprints offered evidence that wild things existed by night, but were now hiding. The jumps, although mostly covered with white drifts, pushed up through the snow.

"Let's go!" Josie gave Lars a squeeze and picked up the canter, then squeezed a little more and Lars began to gallop. Tessa followed behind, not so closely that Opie would think it was a race, but near enough that he would have confidence knowing he had a comrade out there with him.

Josie loved the sense of emancipation. She listened to Lars' heavy breathing and to the sound of his legs rising up and reaching out to get through the snow. *Whoomph, whoomph, whoomph.* Even though it was so cold out here in the field, Lars broke a sweat from his hard work. Josie trusted this horse completely. She loosened her hold on the reins enough to let him stretch his neck and gallop freely. She kept just a light feel of his mouth for balance and held on with her legs, pushing her heels firmly down in her stirrups. Lars never once lost his footing. She leaned her chest close in against his mane and felt his entire body stretching out long, all four feet flying through the air, reaching out for the ground and the next stride. She took the reins in one hand and patted his neck a few times with the other. *This horse is so solid,* she thought as they galloped on. *This is what riding is all about.*

The girls traversed the entire perimeter of the field and when they reached the opening back into the woods, they slowed to the walk. Neither horses nor riders were cold now. The steam rose off the horses' necks and flanks.

As they circled the field again, this time at the walk, they talked girl talk. They hadn't talked about Cleve in a long while; Tessa carried guilt on her shoulders like the weight of the world. She regretted ever suggesting the drive-by that day.

"Where the hell do you think they went, the Gregorys?" Tessa inquisitively brought the subject up.

"No idea, Tess'. I honestly have no idea. I just wasn't in a place to ask him for information. I couldn't. Too much happened at the same time. The good, the bad, and the ugly. I swear, I couldn't have made that week up if I'd tried. I mean really, who has that happen to them? My mother dies the day after I fall in love for the first time and then my boyfriend vanishes into thin air." Josie made air quotation marks with her fingers when she spoke the word, boyfriend. She sort of laughed. "That's my story of life and love so far." She looked ahead. The girls and their horses walked along in silence for a while, then Josie spoke again.

"Anyway, Cleve and I are not about now. It's really hard for me to explain, but I get it. I have to just believe that he was mine for the time he was supposed to be mine. Kind of like this horse. I get him when I get him. That's it. There's other stuff to worry about. Like school, like the barn. Like getting my dad through these holidays. I'm OK. Really. This is now, who knows what the future might bring. All I have when it comes to Cleve, is maybe. That's all I ever really had when it came to Cleve, ya know? If I never hear from him again, you may have to figure out how to rescue me from my misery. But today, I'm OK." She laughed. "Thanks in great part to that awesome gallop we just had! Thanks to this dude right here." Josie bent forward and patted Lars on both sides of his sweaty neck.

"Are you ever going to tell me what he whispered in your ear that day after your mother's funeral? I mean, come on, tell me," Tessa pleaded.

"Nope. If I told you, you would just laugh and say exactly what I said, that fairy tales don't come true. And you'd be right. And then my dream would be ruined. Maybe hope is gone, but a girl can have a dream, can't she?" Josie smiled at her best friend.

Tessa respected her friend, and she knew she'd already caused her enough hurt. But she let out a loud "AARRRRGGGGGHHHHHH," to voice her frustration at not knowing what the secret was. "Let's walk one more lap around the field. Now I have to tell *you* something."

"OK, what's up?" Josie asked her friend.

"Well, I will never say to you that fairy tales don't come true, because I think they just might. Alan Harmon has been calling me. I went to a movie with him last Saturday night. I've been kind of afraid to tell you because of, you know, what you saw at the State Spring Show, and I know you've been hurting over Cleve. I wanted to be sensitive about that. I went out with Alan a couple of times during the summer, but he was still dating Susie. I didn't tell you because you would have bitched me out. I knew it wasn't right anyway. I told him I wouldn't do it that way, that Susie is a decent girl and I wouldn't want someone doing that to me. I made it clear that if he wanted to go out with me, he had to break up with her first. So...he did! Ironically, she was very cool about it. Turns out she has a thing for Armand anyway." Tessa was getting cold and fidgety. She wasn't sure how her pal would react. She apprehensively pulled at the zipper on her jacket.

"Oh my God, Tessa, I'm in shock! I mean, good for you! I didn't think you really liked Alan. I thought you were just trying to antagonize your mother that day at the show. Wow, that's awesome. He really is such a nice guy. So great looking, too! I just didn't want him to take advantage of you. Tell me more, damn it! Wow, I can't believe you've been holding out on me!"

"He's really nice Jos' and he really likes me. We have so much fun talking on the phone and he doesn't live too far away, really. I snuck out with him when we were at the Medal finals at Harrisburg; my mother didn't even know and, well, I spent two nights in his room!"

"Oh my God, Tessa! You are crazy!" Josie was surprised by her friend's uncharacteristic move. "And? And? C'mon, I need details!"

"I'm gonna do it again when we go to the National in New York next week. He's so cool. He was like, 'Tessa, no pressure. Whatever you want to do.' About, you know..." She whispered the word and looked around, as though it would become public knowledge should any of the trees or birds hear her. "He's gonna turn professional after the Garden, and work for George Morris or maybe Ronnie Mutch."

"Tessa, I don't know what to say. I'm really and truly shocked. You bitch! You kept it from me all this time? I hate you! But I'm so happy for you! It sounds like I'm gonna be the only nerd left in this town. Go girl, you go girl." Josie shook her head, a little disappointed that her friend had kept this a secret for so long. Then again she loved her friend for not putting it in her face. It would have stung for sure.

The two girls laughed at the nerd comment. Josie reached out to hold her friend's hand, just for a second. Tessa and Josie would always have each other's backs, men in their lives or not, and they both knew it. They made the turn into the woods and headed back to the barn. Josie felt her own sweat, now cold against her body. She was invigorated from the ride and the conversation. For the first time in a long while, Josie felt her joy.

16

Tradition held that Aunt Gayle hosted Christmas Day dinner at her house in nearby Shrewsbury, but this year Frank Parker had something different in mind. Josie would rather have skipped the holidays altogether, but her dad insisted they invite Aunt Gayle and Grandmother Caldwell, known also as Grancy, to spend the night of Christmas Eve, and to stay for Christmas Day dinner at the Parker home. Josie lobbied in weak protest.

"Your mama would be disappointed to know that we skipped Christmas because of her. Besides, Rosebud, I have some very special gifts for you this year."

"No, Dad, you can't. Really, this is not a year for presents. There is nothing I want. I have nothing for you. Nothing for Aunt Gayle. The idea of presents seems so shallow. I didn't think it would be right. It just won't be right."

"Holidays are for family gatherings, Jos'. That's the way we've always done it. We're not gonna fall apart now. We are going to show gratitude for all the goodness we have." Frank Parker looked serious. "Besides, Grancy and I could use the moral support, and it gives Aunt Gayle a year off if we do it here. She can take charge of the kitchen and we can help her cook. C'mon kid, dig deep and find a little Christmas spirit. It's gonna be a good one, I'm tellin' ya."

"OK, OK, I'm in," Josie replied without giving her objection much more thought, and gave her dad a hug. *Well, I guess I better find some time to go shopping*; she made a mental note.

On Christmas Eve the snow fell silently through the night sky, gently but with enough measure that the trees and ground were soon thinly blanketed in white, evoking an ethereal ambience that provided the holiday with the spiritual aura it deserved. Frank, Aunt Gayle, Grandmother Caldwell, and Josie sat serenely at the dinner table. Snuff and Ralphie snuggled nearby. There wasn't much conversation, but it wasn't a solemn affair. Josie was happy. It had been a good day.

Just before dinner the four of them had decorated the tree that Frank and Josie had cut down earlier in the week and propped in the living room near the fireplace. With a roaring fire ablaze, the whole scene made for a pretty picture. As Josie unwrapped the tissue from each of the ornaments, she reflected, and then shared her memories out loud.

"I made this macaroni bell in second grade. It was one of Mama's favorites," she said to Grancy as she proudly held the foil-and-noodle concoction up in the air. "Every year we expect the macaroni will be completely disintegrated, but it's still going strong. And this one, this is my very favorite. You are my favorite," Josie whispered to the red glass cardinal as she clipped it to one of the Fraser fir's more prominent branches.

"It's a beautiful tree," Grancy pronounced as she worked at setting up the nativity scene in between the red poinsettia plants on the hunt board. Aunt Gayle wrapped the felt tree skirt, the one Mama had made years back, around the tree stand and Frank climbed the step stool and placed the tin foil star at the top.

Every year he made a tree topper from cardboard and tin foil, his sole contribution to the event. Except for this year, as he took on what had traditionally been Mama's job of dressing the tree with lights. When all seemed perfect, the four family members stood back and admired their work. The atmosphere was not laden with sadness, rather they all seemed unburdened to have completed the day's holiday tasks in cheerful form, proud of their accomplishments.

"Mama would approve," Josie was the first to remark.

"Yes, she certainly would," Frank Parker agreed, smiling at his daughter's fortitude, but feeling grief at the reminder of Dorie's absence.

There seemed to be, all of a sudden, an awkward silence in the room as they stood collectively, pretending they were still admiring the tree, yet each knowing what, or rather whom, the other was really thinking about. Aunt Gayle fidgeted with the poinsettia leaves. Grandmother Caldwell was unable to say anything. The tears welling in her eyes were not from anguish, but from the pride she felt seeing the lovely young lady whom her daughter, Dorie Parker, had raised. She saw so much of Dorie in Josie, especially tonight. She did her best to shield her tears behind her spectacles and managed a small but ardent smile as she looked up at the bright, shining colored lights on the tree. Josie, sensing the momentary melancholy, walked over and gave her grandmother a hug.

"We did good, huh, Grancy? Mama taught us well, although Dad, you sure had a rough time with those lights. Took you three times as long as it ever took Mama! I heard you cussing!"

The heaviness lifted and Grancy found her voice.

"Dorie was a royal pain in the ass about those lights. They had to be just a certain way. From the time she was a teenager, no one was allowed to put lights on the Christmas tree but her. Looks pretty good to me, Frank, with one little exception." She pointed to the top of the tree. "That one blue one up there, it's about half an inch too far left."

They all looked at Grancy, wondering if she could possibly be serious. She quickly broke into a smile and offered a nod and a wink in Josie's direction. Gayle and Josie burst into laughter as they all goaded Frank about the sounds they'd heard coming from the living room earlier that afternoon, shortly after he'd announced he was 'going in to do the lights.'

"C'mon you wise guys, let's eat. My lasagna's going to turn to ice," Aunt Gayle had scolded, and they wound up where they now sat, full to the brim and grateful for what had been such a wonderful day.

Simultaneously the group rose from the dining room table to move into the living room.

"Thanks, Gayle. That was a great lasagna, as always," Frank Parker complimented his sister.

"Thanks, Aunt Gayle—and thanks for showing me how to make it." Josie was genuinely thrilled that she now knew how to make that delicious tomato sauce. As Aunt Gayle carried dishes toward the kitchen, Grancy spoke up.

"Frank, what do you say we give Josie her gift tonight? I can't wait until tomorrow morning. It's so special and the waiting is more than I can take." It wasn't really a request and Frank Parker knew he had no choice. But he agreed with Grandmother Caldwell anyway.

"Sounds like a plan, Josephine. I believe this is it right here." Frank Parker reached down under the low branches and stood back up holding a box the size of, *Hmmmmm, a riding helmet,* Josie mused. It was beautifully wrapped in silver paper with red and green ribbon. *Aunt Gayle definitely did the wrapping,* Josie thought to herself. *No way could Dad do it like that.*

There weren't many presents under the tree. *The requisite annual new nightgown from Aunt Gayle,* Josie figured as she eyeballed what was there, *along with a crisp fifty-dollar bill in the envelope affixed to the top of the box.* And most likely Gayle would give her brother Frank some kind of tool. Every single year Grancy gave Frank Parker a new scarf and gloves, and even though they weren't really relatives, she always had something for Gayle too. Mama would always give Grancy suggestions for things Josie might like, so Josie could always count on that gift being something she would love. She wondered how that would go this year, but she didn't really care. She was truly grateful that they were all there together, and the warmth she felt left her believing that Mama's spirit was right there in the room with them as well.

Frank Parker handed the square box to Josie. *Much heavier than a hard hat. Smaller too, and there's stuff moving around inside. Hmmmm.* Josie was truly puzzled. She sat down on the couch next to her grandmother and opened the envelope attached to the package. Snuff jumped up on the couch and curled into Josie's hip. Silently, she read the letter written by her father's hand.

Merry Christmas, Rosebud. This will not be a particularly easy day for any of us, and I hope you know how proud I am of the way you have conducted yourself throughout the holiday season this year. Of course it goes without saying that I am always proud of you. You remind me so much of your mother and watching you navigate your way through life keeps her memory alive for me. I met her when she was just a year younger than you are now, and I knew I loved her the moment I saw her. I miss her every day, and what a blessing it is to be able to see little glimpses of her through your actions. I'm so grateful for that. I never thought she would leave this world ahead of me; somehow you enable me to believe she is not that far away.

Mama loved you more deeply than words could ever describe and I don't think it's necessary for me to even try. I know you felt her love every single day. I'm confident you will always feel it. She told me so often that she couldn't imagine a more wonderful daughter, and she felt great pride knowing that you were so naturally inclined to show compassion for all that surrounds you. Your passion for horses mimicked her own ardor; it allowed her to vicariously relive many equine adventures of her own younger days. She, too, saw so much of herself in you.

She respected you for the friends you've chosen, the dedication you exhibit, and the enthusiasm you have for all of life. She loved that the two of you shared everything, everyday. She was your mama, but you gave her so much.

This first Christmas without her, I am going to share with you the only thing of significance I have to give you that will help you keep Mama close, and which will enable her, in spirit, to continue to share her life, which was all too short, with you.

Josie looked up at her dad, who was staring back at her, smiling. He nodded for her to continue reading.

This gift is from Mama; Grancy and I have been charged with delivering it to you. The contents now belong to you, and only you, to do with them whatever you would like. What you find in this box I hope will remind you of what an elegant, beautiful woman Mama was. Each piece will provide a special memory for you, for each piece has its own special story to tell. Most importantly, someday, some way, the contents of the box will be ready and waiting to have a profound impact on your own story; a story I reckon is as yet unwritten.

I implore you to allow this gift from Mama to create magic in your own life. What do I mean by that? Don't worry, Rosebud. When the time is right, everything will become apparent. Don't cling to the past, but cherish the memories it has given you. Look forward to what is yet unknown. Continue being just who you are. Live with the grace, devotion, and integrity your mama imparted. She left us way too soon, but she left us with so much love to hold in our hearts. She lives on for all of us, in you. Merry Christmas, Rosebud. I love you very much. Dad.

Josie returned the letter to the envelope and set it on the couch next to Snuff. She felt as though she had just somehow officially become an adult. The baton had been passed from Josie Parker, girl, to Josie Parker, young woman. From this point forward her own story, her very own story, would begin to unfold.

Slowly and meticulously, she removed the bow and the silver paper. Josie wanted to savor this moment for as long as she could, yet she was also desperate to know just how the first chapter of her story would begin. That chapter was, metaphorically, right in front of her. *What the heck is in here?* The wrapping paper fell to the floor.

Josie recognized the box right away. It was sterling silver, not new by any means but brightly polished and very sophisticated. It was intricately engraved with swirls and curlicues. Mama's monogram graced the top and a beautiful silk tassel hung from the tiny key that inhabited the keyhole on the front side. The two small, delicate hinges at the back were themselves intricacies of a fine hand. The box was a work of art; it had been paramount to her childhood and Josie couldn't believe that she had forgotten all about it. As a little girl she had often looked up at it sitting on Mama's dresser. She knew there were beautiful trinkets in the box. Sometimes, when Mama was readying to go out on a Saturday night, or maybe to a wedding, Josie would sit on the bed and help her choose which pieces to wear. Mama would twist the beautiful colored stones onto her ear lobes, push the latches together to hold cloud-colored pearls around her neck, stand patiently to allow Dad to hook the German crystal bracelet around her wrist. Back then, Josie thought her mama could have been Cinderella, she was so beautiful.

Now the box was hers. She ran her hands across it. She held it on each side, squeezing it gently, mentally preparing herself to reveal what Dad may have left inside. Not that it even mattered. She looked up at Frank Parker and with hardly any sound, she whispered the words, "Thank you, Dad." She looked at her grandmother and said nothing, but reached a hand over and gave her forearm a gentle squeeze. This was a moment Josie-Rose Caldwell Parker would never forget. A rite of passage. Her mama's jewels were now hers. The pieces in the vintage silver box were her tangible connection to the person she loved most in the universe. She took a breath, twisted the tiny key, and lifted the top.

Josie was overwhelmed, and Frank, Gayle, and Grancy knew that she needed some time alone to take it all in. They graciously relinquished the room to her; Gayle off to tidy up the kitchen, and Grancy and Dad retiring to the family room for a little port wine and some Christmas cookies.

Every gem Josie could remember was in the silver box. Her dad had given her every piece and he was right, each one would have its own story to provide Josie with a memory of Mama. She closed the silver box, turned the tiny key, and held it on her lap. Josie remained there on the couch for a very long time. She reread the letter her dad had written and thought to herself how selfish it had been for her to not want to celebrate Christmas. She was glad he had insisted that they would. She tilted her head back and shut her eyes, just to rest for a minute, and the balance of the evening passed.

"Let's go, Rosebud, it's almost midnight. Merry Christmas!" Frank Parker nudged his daughter, who had fallen sound asleep on the couch. "Tomorrow is another day, and we all could use some shut-eye. This was a good day and tomorrow will be even better. What time should we head over to Hidden Green?"

She stirred and took a deep breath. "I think we should go at ten," she yawned. "I'm sleeping in. What do you think?"

"Ten sounds like a plan. Aunt Gayle of course will join us; it's too tough for Grancy."

"That would be great, Dad. It's so special there on Christmas. I can't wait." She stood up from the couch, walked over to her dad, and hugged him tightly. "Dad, thank you so much. This is the greatest gift in the world. Thank you, thank you, thank you. Other than Mama coming back, nothing could top this. Nothing."

Oh you just wait, Frank Parker mused to himself.

"C'mon, let's go to bed," he said. "I'll turn out the tree lights and check the fireplace. You let the mutts out back for a minute."

Josie climbed under her covers on the snowy Christmas Eve and combed through the box of jewelry. She sifted through the beautiful pieces and admired them, one by one. She laid them out in a pattern on her blanket and remembered Mama wearing so many of them. She closed her eyes and envisioned the pretty dresses Mama wore, her smile, her beauty, and even the sound of her voice, although remembering the sound of her voice was becoming more and more difficult. She carefully returned each piece to the velvet interior, hesitating with the piece she had years ago dubbed the jewel of the jewel box. The large sapphire and diamond ring set in platinum was an heirloom that had been in Dorie Parker's family for five generations. Mama wore it mostly on special occasions. She had always let Josie try it on, and Josie had known that someday the ring would be hers.

"It just keeps travelling through the generations, Josie. Someday it will find a way to serve a purpose greater than just making a finger look pretty, but for now, we will just keep passing it along. It's the Caldwell family time capsule. You will be the keeper of the ring when my days are done." Josie tried it on tonight just to be sure her finger had not grown too big to fit into the delicate, sparkling circle of Caldwell history. As Josie pressed her arm away from her body and tipped her hand to admire the ring, she thought about her dad's written words, *Allow these pieces to create magic in your own life.*

She returned the ring to the silver box, closed the lid, turned the tiny key, and put the box on her bedside table. She turned off her light, laid her head back onto her pillow, and thought, *Someday has come way too soon. I'd take Mama over that ring any day.* To affirm the gift was not given in vain, she promised herself right then and there that she would create magic in her own life. She wasn't sure how or when or what that even meant, really. But she promised herself.

Rolling to her side, she pulled up her blankets and threw an arm over Ralphie, who was already nestled in. *Merry Christmas, Mama. Love you.* As she thought the words, *love you,* her mind rendered its last thought of the day. *I wonder what Cleve is doing tonight? Merry Christmas, Cleve. Wherever you are, Merry Christmas.*

17

G rancy stood up from the breakfast table.

"I will clear the kitchen, she pronounced. "You all go on, have fun. Merry Christmas! Go on, get going."

As the dogs spun circles at the back door, Aunt Gayle, Frank Parker and Josie pulled on boots, jackets, mittens, hats and scarves.

"I've got the sugar and the carrots," Josie called out. "Dad, you have to haul the apple basket, it's too heavy for me. C'mon you guys, let's go!"

"Hey, bossy boots, did you forget I've done this now for about the last five years? I know my job." Frank Parker chuckled at his daughter's anxious outburst. "I will be right out." He trotted up the stairs to grab his camera, hid it under his jacket, lifted the apple basket, and caught up with the girls.

Aunt Gayle pulled the door open, and the dogs trampled out and flew off the back porch. They knew exactly what was going on, and there was snow to be sniffed.

It had become an annual event in the Parker household; on December 25, just after breakfast, Dorie, Frank and Josie would bundle up, take the dogs, and follow Josie's path through Barrett Park, over the creek and the post and rail fence to Hidden Green.

The barn, officially closed for the day, always had an especially intimate feeling on Christmas morning. Because no one else was there, the sounds of the barn were amplified and they were sounds Josie cherished. The horses moving about, nickering, foot stomping, noses rattling grain buckets, tails whishing across the stall boards, the doves cooing up in the hayloft.

The Parker family would move from one stall to the next, handing out treats to warm noses, whispering "Merry Christmas" as they worked their way from barn to barn. It was a very personal undertaking that they all looked forward to. This year would be different; it would behold the added character of being conducted in Mama's memory.

There was no reason to switch the lights on in the main barn this morning. The sun was shining through every stall window, and the reflection from the snow cast an exceptionally beautiful glow. Some of the stall doors were adorned with stockings, some with wreaths. Of course Josie's first inclination was to head directly to Lars' stall. Frank and Gayle followed closely behind.

When she looked down the barn aisle, Josie could see from a distance that something other than the stocking she'd put up was attached to Lars' stall door. A little stitch of panic ran through her. Frank Parker gave an elbow and a nod to his sister, smiled, and picked up a brisk step to keep pace with his daughter who was now hustling down the aisle. He discreetly pulled out his camera.

"What is this?" Josie asked aloud. Even though she could clearly see the huge red ribbon tied across the bars of Lars' stall door, she was confused. She stepped back a few feet, puzzled, looking through the bars to be sure Lars was in there; it was then that she noticed the big gift tag that had been crafted out of a piece of shirt cardboard. For some reason it reminded her of her dad's tin foil tree star. She stepped forward now, closer, almost afraid to know what it said. Completely mystified, she read the tag:

MERRY CHRISTMAS, JOSIE! PLEASE TAKE GOOD CARE OF ME. I'M YOURS, ALL YOURS, UNTIL NEXT SEPTEMBER. NOW WHERE ARE MY TREATS? LOVE, LARS (and Dad).

Josie noticed that a stall nameplate had been mounted to Lars' door. It was identical to all of the private boarder stall plates—shiny green with white lettering. She read it to herself, in complete disbelief. Across the first line of the stall plate, in bold capital letters, was the name LARS. On the second line, in smaller letters—Josie Parker. *This is not really happening,* she said to herself. Just as protection, in case this was a dream, she pinched her arm. She felt the pinch.

"No dream," she said out loud to no one.

Josie looked back at her dad and Aunt Gayle, who had both stopped a few paces away to give Josie the space to take this all in.

"Dad, what is this? I don't get it. What does this mean? What does this mean?" Josie was desperate for a rational explanation. This wasn't rational. She thought she knew exactly what it meant but she was afraid to be wrong. Her father could not afford to buy her a horse. Her heart was pounding and her head felt dizzy. She waited, anxiously, for Frank Parker to provide an explanation.

And so it was on that Christmas Day, Lars became Josie's. Some stealth planning had gone into the whole event. It had been Mike O'Hara's idea. He had made Frank Parker an offer that was hard to refuse. If Josie continued to work at the barn on the weekends and took care of Lars everyday, and if Frank would handle the veterinary and farrier bills, as well as any other out-of-pocket expenses, then Mr. O'Hara would give the Parkers full room and board free of charge, and Lars would officially be Josie's until she left for college the following September. Josie knew even this would be a stretch on the Parker family budget.

"No, Dad, I can't let you do this. It's too expen—"

Frank Parker cut his daughter off right there.

"Hey Rosebud, tell you what," he said calmly, quietly. "You worry about Lars. I'll worry about the rest. I got this. Mike and I are all good. This horse is yours, and yours alone until September." He moved to the stall door as Josie opened it. With tears pouring down her face, she threw her arms around the big chestnut horse's neck. As though he knew exactly what was going on, Lars wrapped his head down and around her, instinctively hugging her right back. Frank Parker snapped a picture. At the sound of the shutter's click, Lars raised his head high and lifted his upper lip, and it seemed he was smiling for the camera. The Parker family burst into laughter. Frank took another photo of his girl and her horse. *That's gonna be a good one,* he thought to himself.

Aunt Gayle offered a carrot to Lars. Josie turned to her dad and embraced him with all her might. She had no words. Even if she knew what she might say to him, she was unable to speak. Mama's jewel box had already been enough.

As the three stood silently in Lars' stall, Josie patted her horse. *My horse,* she thought to herself. She had her first horse! Her very own horse! Well, for nine months anyway. She supposed it was akin to a lease, which a lot of people were doing these days. She couldn't believe it. The thought had never even entered her mind.

This horse is the best thing that has ever *happened to me. It's already happening. This is magic. He is the first chapter of my own story,* she wrote in her journal that night. She couldn't wait to get to the barn the next day. And she had the whole week off from school! Right away she would start teaching him everything she knew so that he would become the most prized school horse Hidden Green would ever have. He would have a perfect lead change, a flawless half pass. Her dream of having a horse of her own had come true. The next nine months would prove to be life defining for Josie Parker, and for Lars as well.

18

For Cleve Gregory, the holiday season had not been nearly as poignant as it had been for Josie Parker. He'd spent Thanksgiving, along with his now emotionally tortured mother, at the home of some friends they'd made since their move from New Jersey.

Within a week of Dorie Parker's funeral, Lila Gregory had packed herself, her sons, and the family dog into her station wagon, navigating the six-hour drive from Middletown, New Jersey to her parents' farm in Warrenton, Virginia. On that fateful Saturday night when Frank Parker had dropped Cleve at home after the horse show, John Gregory had announced that he was divorcing Lila as quickly as possible. His paramour was already several months pregnant with their child and he had every intention of moving in with her, permanently and immediately. Lila had done her best, for the sake of her children, to tolerate plenty of deceit in her marriage over the years. The final blow was the news of her husband fathering a child with another woman. When Cleve walked in the back door, the verbal war between his parents had been in full tilt.

On the following Tuesday, John Gregory had his pronouncement presented in writing. Two shabbily dressed, unshaven, cunning men—one with a camera—served Lila with divorce papers as she walked out of the grocery store.

"Lila Gregory?" the man without the camera asked as he approached her.

"Yes?" she responded, caught off guard, as had been the man's practiced plan. He shoved something at her so aggressively that she had no choice but to grab hold of it.

"Don't try to pretend you didn't receive these papers because your photograph is being taken right now. Your husband says he will see you in court. Have a nice day now, ma'am." The two men had appeared and disappeared so fast it was as though they'd flown in and out like bees, rendering their sting swiftly. Lila hadn't even known what had happened, until her entire body started shaking from the shock of being accosted and the realization of what she was holding.

Lila Gregory was devastated, humiliated, and scorned. For two full days she remained prisoner to the anguish of that moment, struggling to shake from her mind the faces of those two ogres. When finally her humiliation turned to anger, she couldn't get away from that house, that town, that life fast enough. Operating in the core of an adrenaline rush borne completely of emotion and confusion, she vacated the house on Laukner Lane, leaving behind unmade beds, winter coats, and eggs and milk in the fridge, not even bothering to check for the day's mail. The house that had been her home for almost twenty years meant nothing to her now. It had been a shill. She drove, staring aimlessly out the front windshield, no faster than the speed limit, Hap in the front seat and Cleve stretched across the back. Lila never once looked back, not even in the rearview mirror. At the stop sign at the end of Laukner Lane, she made a left turn toward what would become the rest of her life.

Hap Gregory nearly lost what was left of his ravaged mind. The disintegration of his family, despite the realization that it had been held together with not much more than Band-Aids and lies, put his already degenerating brain over the edge. He slammed his fist into the door of the car probably a hundred times as they made their way down I-95, and swore that he would kill his father for doing what he'd done. He lit up a joint more than once, openly and defiantly, as the car rolled along. His mother didn't even bother to comment. Lila Gregory was paralyzed.

The horrific event as a whole didn't really matter much to Cleve. As far as he was concerned, his father had shown his true colors. He was a liar, a cheat, and a thief. And Cleve didn't care. This whole fucked-up situation was almost a gift, an opportunity. He'd had every intention of leaving town anyway; this just gave him a free ride. Now he could save the money he had been planning to spend on a used pickup truck, and he could use it to find a place to live on his own. Somewhere, once he set foot on Virginia soil, he would find a way to get started living his life, his way, following his passion, rather than a life other people thought he should live. There was only one important fragment that would remain unresolved. His relationship with Josie. *I'm not there to help her through her darkest days, and I didn't have a chance to explain anything. She'll hate me for sure, in no time,* he thought as he stared out the window of the station wagon, watching the tiles in the Baltimore Harbor Tunnel whiz past. He felt like a coward, having left with no real explanation, offering only a vague, immature promise to the one person who made him feel like he could conquer every obstacle in his path; the one girl he wanted to feel his own flesh pressed against in the early hours of each morning. The girl who deserved more than a simple, "I'll find you when I deserve to have you."

John Gregory quickly seized the opportunity to manipulate the entire situation, claiming to a judge that the intention of Lila's actions was abandonment. Somehow he had managed to secure a court order that allowed him to put the house on the market by the following week, at a price that was sure to have it under contract quickly. He never thought for a second about how this might affect his sons. He thought only about himself.

There ended the history of the Gregory family of Middletown, New Jersey. Poof. Eradicated from Laukner Lane as though none of them had ever existed, as though all that they had experienced there—childbirth, new sofas, new cars, birthdays, holidays, saving wounded birds, burying a family dog, work promotions, cookouts, graduations, athletic awards, the small fire in the basement that could have burned the house down, lost teeth, anniversaries, puberty and adolescence, leaks in the roof, and favorite Christmas decorations—as though all those milestones of a family's existence had never really happened at all. The house was sold and with it, any recognition of a life built within it. A vast collection of memories floated off in the wake created by the actions of a very selfish man.

Of course Cleve knew there were always the proverbial three sides to every story, but his father could have handled things so differently; with kindness, humility, and his own share of sacrifice, sparing the heartbreak and irreparable implosion of the lives of those who'd loved him most. In his quest to find what he thought would make him happier, regardless of the cost to others, he had pushed his oldest son into the dark abyss of drugs and his ex-wife into the bottomless bottle of vodka, and Cleve would just as soon see him rot in hell.

Were it not for his mother's continuing descent into the oblivion of depression and alcohol, Cleve could have easily banished his father's existence completely from his mind. But her drinking kept the memory of the man—and the wreckage he had caused—very much alive. As a result, greatly in part to save himself, Cleve saw less and less of her, unable to watch her self-destruction. And quite honestly he had to admit that he was somewhat bitter at her for her weakness and resignation. She was still young and beautiful, but her self-confidence had been stolen and her heart had been spoiled. The ensuing disease ran through her body like maggots over roadkill. Cleve blamed and hated his father for this brutal transgression of his mom.

But for Cleve, the greatest curse was his loss of Josie Parker. So often he would picture her face—smiling and liberated when they were working together at Hidden Green; tortured and trapped in profound sadness, sitting on her staircase the day of her mother's funeral. He knew intellectually that he was not solely responsible for her devastation, but the knowledge that he'd played a part in causing one tear to roll down her freckled cheek plagued him in the lonely darkness, and often in the brightness of day. He was convinced that he had relinquished his right to seek her out, to ask her forgiveness now. What an idiot he would seem. She had every right to have struck a match to her memory of him, and truly, he wished for her that she should never have to feel the gut-wrenching pain of missing someone the way he did her.

On Christmas morning, Cleve woke up alone in the small loft space the Randolph family had provided him, above the equipment garage at Creek's Bend Farm in Keswick, Virginia. Cleve had been working for the Randolph family's hunter operation for more than a few months. It was just the job he had searched for, and being able to live there on the property allowed Cleve to fully immerse himself in a world that spared him the memories he had fought hard to leave behind when he, his mother and brother had deserted Middletown.

19

Peter Randolph IV was a true Virginia gentleman, cut from the cloth of a well-respected "first family of Virginia." He'd been around horses all his life. His father, Peter III, had owned many stakes-winning steeplechasers, had been master for the hounds in Charlottesville, and had managed the family investment in several of the leading thoroughbred race tracks in the Southeast, not the least impressive of which was Churchill Downs.

At the young age of thirty-five, Peter IV's inheritance had left him not only with a vast fortune, but perhaps more importantly to him, the notable two-hundred-fifty-acre farm on which he'd been raised. He'd become proprietor of the main house, an enormous, white, federal style mansion with black shutters and deep, wrap-around porches, which he had restored to perfection fifteen years ago when his parents and only sibling had been killed in a tragic accident. His father had piloted the family's small plane straight into the depths of the Chesapeake Bay while joy-flying during a summer vacation on the Rappahannock River. Peter IV had been away at summer school at the time, his lack of scholastic aptitude the single reason he had not met with the same premature demise as his father, his mother Kendall, and his younger sister Jane. His father's sister had finished his rearing and arranged for him to attend Washington and Lee University.

Despite his lack of devotion to the classroom, Peter was a student of observation of the world. He listened, he watched, he read voraciously; everything from the *Farmer's Almanac* to Charles Dickens to *The Chronicle of the Horse* and *The Wall Street Journal*. It was his good fortune that the Randolph family name carried great influence at several of the prestigious Virginia schools of higher education, and as such he matriculated to graduate school at the University of Virginia. There, he read his way through three years of law books, following which he immersed himself in the operations of the legacy he had been left.

Peter lived at Creek's Bend Farm along with his wife Mary-Lyle, also a descendant of one of the South's most revered families, and also a graduate of one of the South's most prestigious colleges, Sweetbriar College for Women. As was considered proper and customary for children of the southern elite, their three sons spent the better part of each year at boarding school in northern Virginia and summered for eight weeks at a camp in South Carolina. Mary-Lyle busied herself with the Junior League and the Keswick Garden Club, and of course she and her husband were perpetually asked to serve on dozens of charity boards from Alexandria to Richmond to Roanoke. Having exchanged vows hardly a month after Mary-Lyle's graduation from Sweetbriar, their marriage had matured into one of respect and partnership, a relationship of devotion and tolerance, and neither imagined that life could be any finer than it was. One truth held to be self-evident—discretion was an art form in southern families.

Now at fifty, Peter had—aside from sitting on the boards of several of the family companies—retired from the business world. He was enjoying tremendous personal reward in developing winning show hunters, bred from his own stock of mares and stallions, and in overseeing the harvest of the red and white grapes he grew at the farm; his vineyards received widespread accolades for the incredible cuvée they produced under the label of Creek's Bend.

Cleve Gregory's timing could not have been more perfect, and Peter Randolph had quickly become a huge fan of the young, ambitious boy from north of the Mason-Dixon line. Cleve's instinct with horses, particularly as a ground trainer, reminded Peter of himself as a younger man. He actually admired Cleve's impressive intelligence and worldliness, which he surmised came from genuine curiosity, a love of the written word, bullish ambition, and the kind of passion that draws the line between real horsemen and those who are just playing in the game. Although there was an element of mystery to Cleve Gregory that he couldn't quite put a finger on yet, the patriarch had enthusiastically knighted himself Cleve's mentor, feeling a gentleman's sense of responsibility for this doppelganger who happened into the Creek's

Bend fold.

"You know mah family trail leads straight back ta' Thomas Jefferson, Cleve. If y'all ever decide you want to give college a try, I am quite sure a call from me to the president of the university would get you a front row seat in their commerce school. How y'all doin' with the high school night school thing? On track to be finished by June?"

And so it was that Cleve Gregory was able to apply to the University of Virginia, and by December he'd been accepted. He would begin the following September, and the kind and generous Peter Randolph IV would continue to employ and house him. He had even arranged for Cleve to have a full scholarship, if he was willing to help out with coaching the riding team at the university. A far cry from Middletown, New Jersey in such a short amount of time, this was an offer Cleve could not afford to refuse.

In the meanwhile, he worked tirelessly for Peter, offering his own knowledge when appropriate, and devouring all there was to learn during his tenure as foreman of the farm. Two of the most highly regarded young hunter riders in the country, Charlie Weaver and Martha Sifton, worked exclusively for Peter Randolph. For the likes of Cleve Gregory, this was akin to a Catholic priest receiving private lessons from the Pope himself.

Cleve thought of Josie often, very often. He thought of her when Charlie would impart some of his expertise regarding an unruly three-year-old colt, or when Martha would show up at the barn with her long blond hair in braids. He wanted so often to call Josie, to share what he knew would fascinate her. He knew he could talk to her for hours and never even be close to telling her all he had to tell. And he would never even be close to bored, or uninterested, in anything she might care to share with him.

He thought about her when he would dare to entertain a date in Charlottesville; a date with some perfectly beautiful, southern darling who'd no doubt affect the ingénue, but who was really quite savvy, employing the skills her southern mama had no doubt taught her, on the lookout for a potential handsome husband, even if she were only the age of a college co-ed. Fathers found pride in marrying off their daughters quickly in the South, and smart, attractive young men, of manners born and bred, with a substantive knowledge of horses and politics were a sought-after commodity in Virginia.

Despite a promise made to himself that he would never date a girl with strawberry blond hair or freckles, Cleve Gregory was never at a loss for the company of a beautiful girl. He was never at a loss for invitations to the best social events of the season in Keswick, Charlottesville, Warrenton and Middleburg, despite the shortcoming of hailing from the North. His association with Peter Randolph IV had elevated his social status to just shy of that of General Robert E. Lee himself. And although he spent countless hours in the company of perfectly sparkling young ladies, he could never quite shake the pull of his first love. That was when he missed Josie the most. He satisfied the needs that his masculinity wouldn't allow him to ignore, but he never felt the emotional desire to pursue more than just a few dates with the same girl. This left him unfulfilled and sometimes wallowing in self-pity.

Here it was, Christmas Day. He was alone. Creek's Bend was officially closed so that all the farm and vineyard staff could enjoy some family time. He'd had enough family time at Thanksgiving. He had already made his morning rounds to check the horses, and he was back on his couch, daydreaming. He wondered what she was doing. He thought he might have a shot at it being interpreted as a gesture of holiday spirit if he were to give her a call. *She might not even take my call. Would her father even allow her to take my call?* It had been months, tortuous months for him. *Have they been for her?*

He closed his eyes and let his imagination picture her at Hidden Green, tacking up one of the school horses, getting help from his replacement; no doubt some tall, blond guy with a rugged, chiseled face, flawed denim jeans belted with a rodeo buckle, a plaid flannel shirt tucked in, and beaten-up cowboy boots. Cleve felt jealousy surge through his veins. He opened his eyes and reached for the phone. He knew her telephone number by heart. He lifted the receiver. He stared at the numbers on the dial. *What if she won't talk to me? Then I won't have hope any more. At least right now I have hope, and I can hold onto the idea that she might talk to me when the day comes that I do call. I'm not ready to know that she has given up on me, and I'm not in a position to fulfill my promise.* He convinced himself to put the phone down.

He reached to the table in front of the couch and picked up the book of poetry Peter and Mary-Lyle had given him for Christmas. The cover itself was a thing of beauty. Italian marbled paper with a blue parchment square, printed with gold lettering, affixed on the top half of the book:

COLLECTED WORKS
COMPILED BY PETER RANDOLPH IV
for
CLEVE J. GREGORY

He opened it, leafing mindlessly through at first. Noticing that a page had been dog-eared, he wondered if it had been a gesture of purpose. He gathered that it had been when he discovered the folded loose-leaf sheet that had been inserted precisely at the dog-eared page. He unfolded it and read the handwritten words.

Change the "he" to "she." Merry Christmas. Regards, Mary-Lyle and Peter.

Cleve was incredibly moved by this act of kindness. Quite taken aback actually. This family had done so much for him in the short time he'd shared affiliation with them. He felt as though Peter Randolph had amazing insight into who Cleve was, who he wanted to be, and importantly, how he could achieve his goals.

Before endeavoring to read the poem now staring up at him, he contemplated all that had happened in these last several months and acknowledged just how fortunate he was to be working at Creek's Bend. He stood up and walked to the window, looking out across the farm's amazing acreage. For just a few more minutes he reminisced about the freckle-faced girl he knew he would love forever. He knew too that it was time to really take hold of all that was in front of him, to make the most of opportunity. He was suddenly even more anxious to move forward from his turbulent past. He turned from the window and clapped his hands together once, a symbolic gesture to dissipate any negative energy in the room.

"It's Christmas for crying out loud." He sat back down and reached for the book. "Merry Christmas, Josie Parker. Wherever you are, Merry Christmas."

He reminded himself to change the "he" to "she" and read the poem by David Harkins.

SHE IS GONE

You can shed tears that she is gone
Or you can smile because she has lived.

You can close your eyes and pray that she will come back
Or you can open your eyes and see all she's left.

Your heart can be empty because you can't see her
Or you can be full of the love you shared.

You can turn your back on tomorrow and live yesterday
Or you can be happy for tomorrow because of yesterday.

You can remember her and only that she's gone
Or you can cherish her memory and let it live on.

You can cry and close your mind,
Be empty and turn your back

Or you can do what she would want:
Smile, open your eyes, love and go on.

20

Josie spent every waking moment possible focused on making life better for Lars and making him a better horse. She read every noteworthy horsemanship book she could get her hands on and she used allowance money to subscribe to *The Chronicle of the Horse*, the "bible" of the horse show world. Though she would never be able to afford to take him to a show, she was confident that if they'd been able to compete, they would have always come home champions.

The other girls at the barn, not just Tessa, but Joni and Rachel and even Suzanna once in a while, were actually starting to seek out her advice if they were struggling with their own horses' behaviors. Joni had even asked her to ride Joey a few times.

It wasn't long before every professional that came to Hidden Green wanted to steal Josie away. Doc Thurman, William Fells, and other trainers who came with clients to try horses. They all knew that this young girl was about to graduate from high school and that she had a special talent with horses and horse care. Someone like her, at such a young age, was not easy to find. They all offered her jobs, and Josie discussed each offer with her dad, but ultimately she was committed to sticking with her plan to go to college.

"I've always thought I wanted to do something professional in the horse world, Dad, but I'm sure I don't have enough talent to be a pro rider. I think I could teach, and I know I could run a barn, but maybe I need to try something else for a while, huh?"

"Horses will always be a part of you, part of who you are, part of your story," her dad advised. "Your relationship with them and with the friends you've made at the barn will last a lifetime. It will all remain. You can step out and step back in at any time. You can always come back," he said. "You've taken care of horses all your life, Rosebud. You are a natural caregiver. Maybe you should consider becoming a doctor, or a nurse, or a veterinarian."

Frank Parker wanted his only child to be able to support herself. He knew she was compassionate, smart, and ambitious. He also knew that for the better part of her years she'd had one focus—horses. He knew the horse world could be a carnival existence and that Josie needed more exposure to the great wide world beyond New Jersey.

By the first of April she had been accepted, with offers of scholarship, to several four-year colleges, all of which had highly regarded nursing degree programs. By the fifteenth of April she had committed to one of the top nursing programs in New York City. It had been quite a while since she'd thought about Cleve Gregory and what he'd whispered in her ear that day at Mama's funeral. *Fairy tales don't come true, Josie,* she reminded herself as she contemplated the next chapter of her story.

Graduation from Middletown High School was no big deal to Josie. She hadn't even gone to the prom. Her friends who mattered were all from the barn and a bunch of different schools. Libby O. was graduating from Red Bank Catholic and going to work for her dad, and Tessa was graduating from Ocean Township but she still had one more year to ride as a junior, so her mother wasn't letting her go to college yet. She hadn't even applied anywhere.

"I'm fine with that," she told Josie. "More time with Alan."

Suzanna had taken her gap year and was apparently going to take another, and Joni and Rachel had already been commuting to college in Philadelphia, so they could continue to ride.

There was really only one reason Josie was excited about graduation; it represented the beginning of summer and that meant she could spend every day for the next two months at the barn. She would leave in late August for nursing school and she planned to make the most of her time left with Lars. A deal was a deal and she was truly grateful for what she had been given; she never kidded herself about it. She assumed that once she was gone, Lars would be relegated to the school horse lineup, and although this made her lose sleep some nights, she resigned herself to at least being able to visit him, and maybe catch a ride when she would come home for holidays and semester breaks. Josie continued to focus on her goal of teaching Lars as much as she could.

On the last day of July Mr. O'Hara called her into his office, a small room in his cottage filled with memorabilia of a thousand years: trophies, loving cups, engraved silver trays in need of some polishing. A pair of custom, tall black riding boots stood in a corner. Photo after photo, all black and white, all framed, boasted beautifully turned-out horses jumping over fences, with show-dressed riders atop, some of them actually him in his younger years. His desk was a mess, full of piles of lesson schedules and boarder's bills, hay and straw company invoices, farrier lists, a full ashtray, and a riding crop.

"Josie Parker, you are really something special, you know that?" Mr. O'Hara asked, not really expecting her to answer. He extinguished his Marlboro and continued. "It's hard to believe you are leaving soon. Everyone I know wants to steal you away from Hidden Green. I'm proud of you, that you chose to go to college. I know you will make a great nurse, but the horse world will suffer a great void without you in it, at least this horse world will." He paused, then smiled and added, "Lars will miss you most of all." He lit another cigarette and leaned back hard in his chair. "You've brought that horse a long way," he said. "He's become an extremely valuable gelding, thanks to you." *Hmmmm,* she wondered. *What exactly does that mean?*

"Thanks, Mr. O'Hara. You have no idea how much I'm gonna miss Hidden Green. All the horses, all the good times, all my friends. I've been so lucky. Having Lars as my own has been incredible. I could never thank you enough. I'm really glad you are happy with how he's come along."

She choked a little on her words, and looked out the window to the standing stall shed. She really would miss this run-down old place, but it made her proud to know that because of her efforts, Lars was going to be the best lesson horse Hidden Green had ever had.

"So," he continued. "I wanted to tell you that I have, uh," he hesitated, "I have found a new home for Lars."

Josie was certain she had misunderstood what Mike O'Hara had just said, so she continued to listen.

"He will be here 'til you leave for school. Sometime around Labor Day he will move over to Jack Berardi's place in Navesink. Jack's been looking for a new horse to fox hunt with the Monmouth County Hunt and he thinks Lars can fit that bill. He needs a big, solid horse." Mike O'Hara didn't dare look directly at Josie as he dropped this bomb. Rather, he looked over and past her, squinting, pretending to look at something far into the next room. He knew this news was going to crush her.

Josie discreetly grabbed the sides of the chair she was sitting in to brace herself from falling. Tunnel vision came over her, along with a ringing in her ears and that out-of-body sensation she had not experienced in a long time.

"Oh. I see. OK," was all Josie could manage to get out. She fought against the lump in her throat. *Really?* she thought. *Really? What am I supposed to say? He isn't asking my permission. He isn't even asking me what I think about the idea. He doesn't have to. Lars is his horse after all. He's just been mine to borrow.* This was a fait accompli for Lars. *Poor horse*, she thought, *poor me*. She fought hard to keep the tears away. She had no right to cry. This horse had been a loaner. His fate, sadly, was not hers to decide. Yet his fate, it seemed all too apparent, was all her fault. She had made Lars a talented, trustworthy performer and Mike O'Hara saw profit in her hard work. She was angry, and she was profoundly sad.

Adding insult to injury was that Mr. Berardi's barn had always frightened Josie. She'd never been there, but she'd heard Doc Thurman talk plenty about the ailments and injuries horses suffered all too often at Jack and Jill Farm (yes, Jack Berardi's wife's name was really Jill). The kind of injuries horses suffer when they were ridden too hard and not physically strong enough, or ridden in poor footing, like out in a hunt field, or just plain not properly cared for.

"I've taught him so much, Mr. O'Hara. He would make a really fantastic school horse for you. I think he could even win in the Big Eq'. Are you sure? You wouldn't just lease him to someone here? I don't think he was the best foxhunter for Mr. Bonington. I mean, Mr. Berardi's barn..." She stopped herself. It just wasn't her argument to make. She knew she had no right. In that moment her heart was breaking, but what could she do? It was futile for her to argue. Mr. O'Hara had a good sale in front of him, and she had to face it. That's what he was in the horse business for. She thanked him for everything once again and left the office.

Oddly, that night, for the first time in as long as she could remember, Josie dreamed about Cleve Gregory. Cleve was driving a pickup truck and Josie was sitting next to him. They were hauling Lars in a two-horse trailer, driving in the middle of the night along a road she didn't recognize.

"Where are we going, Cleve? Where will we keep him?" Josie asked in her dream, as she looked over at the most handsome guy she'd ever known.

"We'll figure it out, Jos', at least we know he is safe now. He will be with us and we will give him a good life. We will have a good life, you, me and Lars." Cleve reached out a hand to her but she couldn't feel his touch.

Suddenly, still dreaming, Josie found herself standing in the middle of the same road, but now alone in the dark. Looking ahead she saw the taillights of the two-horse trailer getting smaller and smaller. She could barely make out Lars' hind end and tail. She felt frightened and abandoned.

"Wait," she screamed. "Wait, you forgot me! Cleve! Lars! Wait for me!" She woke up in a sweat, confused and exhausted, her alarm buzzing.

The dreaded day inevitability had arrived; Josie had to say good-bye to the barn. After hugging everyone that was there, promising not to stay away too long, she ventured into Lars' stall for the last time.

"Lars, Jack and Jill Farm isn't that far away," she whispered to the chestnut horse she loved so much, as she wiped away tears. "I will visit you every time I come home, and I will come home a lot," she rationalized. "I will keep a close eye on you and you will be fine." She filled his grain bin with an entire bag of snapped carrots, then walked around him just to be sure everything was in order. She hugged his neck, closed the stall door, pulled the stall plate out of its holder, and quickly left the barn through the back door. If she'd stayed a minute longer she knew she would have fallen apart completely.

Tears poured silently over her cheeks as she walked home through the park one last time, clutching the stall plate that boasted Lars' and her names. Josie thought to herself, *I don't think I could ever do this again, it's way too hard to let go. I let myself get too attached, knowing I would have to give him back. Too hard,* she thought, *especially when you have no control over an animal's destiny.* Anger and resentment filled her as she contemplated why, other than for great profit, Mr. O'Hara hadn't kept Lars. She ultimately reminded herself that horses were how he made his living and in her core, she couldn't stay mad at him. He wasn't a bad man; he was just a businessman.

Josie walked into the house and searched for her dad. He hugged his only girl; he knew it had been a rough day for her.

"I can't believe it's all over, Dad. This is so surreal."

"Like I told you, Rosebud," he tried to reassure her, "none of it is going anywhere. It will be like this whenever you come back. Believe me. New York City isn't the other side of the universe, you know." But Josie knew herself well. She was not going to be a commuter student. She was going to be a committed student. Life as it had existed for her at Hidden Green Farm was over. New York and nursing school were looming on her horizon.

PART II

21

Six or so years later...

It was early summer and Josie had come home to New Jersey for the weekend. Frank Parker had remarried just a little more than two years after Mama had died, and although Josie was inclined to not like the idea, Marlene was perfectly acceptable. Pretty, actually. Kind and devoted to Josie's dad. She seemed to give him joy. She made it obvious that she adored Josie, and the feeling had grown to be mutual. Josie appreciated that Marlene acknowledged Dorie Parker in a heartfelt way at every holiday, and never imposed herself in any way as Josie's "mother."

"I never had the pleasure of meeting your mother, but she had the good sense to choose your dad, and she raised a beautiful young woman," Marlene told Josie the day her dad had introduced them. Josie was appreciative of this; it enabled her to feel comfortable enough to talk about Mama anytime. Still, she had not been home for ages.

Josie had graduated from nursing school just a little more than two years earlier. Right away she joined a company that placed nurses in short-term assignments around the country with hospitals that were in need of supplementary help. She'd worked in San Francisco, Denver, Boston, Atlanta, and most recently in New York City. She wanted some time at home before she made any decisions about where she might accept her next tour of duty. She was content with what she did for a living, but lately some unfinished business had been nagging at her, and she was compelled to go home to face the demons she'd left behind. The few moments of her chance providence a month or so ago were branded in her mind like a tattoo. She thought about that twist of fate almost every day. She thought about it now.

Josie had left the hospital at the end of a long overnight shift. As she negotiated her way down Lexington Avenue towards the subway entrance, she felt the warmth of what promised to be a perfect spring day pass across her tired face. It rejuvenated her just enough that she thought perhaps she would treat herself to a proper breakfast at the Greek diner just down the street before rattling home to her apartment in SoHo.

She preferred downtown city life. The groove was a little more relaxed, the rent was cheaper, and the population much more eclectic than the Upper East Side.

I wonder, she thought as she dodged and weaved through the commuter crowd this morning, *why so many people who work all the way down on Wall Street come all the way up here to live?*

She supposed it was because everything was fancier uptown. The buildings of the Upper East Side projected a far more majestic quality than the lofts and industrial spaces of lower Manhattan; the flagship designer stores along Madison, and the legendary lunch spots tucked in nearby were places to see and be seen. The most prestigious hotels and museums were uptown, and then of course there was the view of Central Park, which came, at a very high price, with ownership of the co-ops along Fifth Avenue. Everything uptown seemed just a little bigger, a little better, a little more blue-blood, and for those who had been fortunate enough to benefit from the recent red hot flush of the stock market, bigger was definitely better. Although Josie's salary was impressive, it didn't compare to what the Wall Streeters made, and it hadn't elevated her to a rank that included entitlement to travel the city by private car, or even by taxi. So at the end of most of her shifts, she would pop in the earphones of her music player and hope that she might grab a prized seat on the Lex-line route, where she could close her eyes and drift for the fifteen or twenty minute ride from 68th Street to the Spring Street stop.

She waited for the light to change at the corner of Lexington and 70th Street. *Now that's just the kind of guy I'm talking about,* she mused to herself as she watched the athletic-looking stud, with broad shoulders and fantastic hair, raise his arm in an attempt to hail a cab just across the intersection. *He and his gray suit are probably hustling to get to the bottom of the island in time for the morning stock exchange bell.* She was oddly consumed with watching this particular banker, leather briefcase and folded newspaper in one hand, flagging one of the coveted yellow sedans buzzing down Lexington with the other. She was so mesmerized that when the light changed and the pedestrian sign bid permission to cross, she didn't even notice. Movers and shakers on either side left her behind, with dozens more headed toward her at the same time. Oblivious, she stood motionless, evoking numerous dirty looks and a few catcalls.

Maybe it was the conspicuous obstacle she had made of herself, holding steady there in her hospital scrubs, or maybe it was just serendipity. But when the dapper corporate cutie angled his torso to open the door of his cab, he turned his head in her direction just enough to engage in eye contact with her, though for no more than a mere second or so. No sooner had it happened than Josie watched the taxi door close, the left-hand blinker light up, and the yellow sedan pull away. She felt a vaguely familiar shiver travel the highway of her nervous system, from her ankles to the back of her neck, and she snapped back into consciousness only to realize that she had completely missed her opportunity to cross the street. The light was red again. A new crowd waited on each corner, and when the sign finally bid passage, this time Josie was the first one off the curb. The diner was just half a block down, and she was starving now.

As she made her way through the pretzeled foot traffic, she gave her shoulder bag a protective squeeze and looked up and ahead towards the diner. *Wait. What the hell,* she said to herself, swearing that the guy in the gray suit jogging up the block in her direction was the same guy she had seen pull away in that cab minutes ago. Then, before she could blink her eyes, there came the revelation. The hair, the eyes, the shiver. It all added up to only one possibility. *It couldn't be,* she thought, perplexed as all hell. *But why else would this guy be jogging up the sidewalk directly towards me right now?*

"God, I knew it was you," the out-of-breath banker confirmed. "I knew it the instant I saw you. Who knows what compelled me to look in your direction, but I knew it was you right away. Man! I knew it!"

He had stopped firmly, a foot or two away, and was bent over, hands on his knees, still clutching his briefcase and paper, and trying to catch his breath. "And I prayed you'd still be here on the sidewalk," he huffed, tilting his face to look up at her. "I thought surely I would miss you and never be certain it was you. But it is you. It is."

He stood up straight now, glancing to the left and to the right, as though wondering if anyone noticed them in the midst of this definitely awkward, completely random, chance meeting after almost seven years. He spoke again, still a little winded.

"The cabbie thought I was nuts, I had to argue and give him ten dollars to make him stop just half a block from where he picked me up." He took another breath, composing himself now. He pushed his hair off his forehead. Josie looked shyly away and then back. "But I had to know. I can't believe it's really you, Jos', wow. Look at you." She looked, frankly, a little shell-shocked. He ducked his body down a little now, in case she needed a better view of his face. She didn't.

He made no move to embrace her. The space between made them each uncomfortable, but neither knew how to diffuse the weird energy. She stood in front of him, both hands tightly clutching her shoulder bag, doing all she could to discreetly steady her nerves.

"Wow, Cleve," she said, almost whispering. She couldn't believe she was saying his name, let alone standing in front of him. She half giggled, half broke into tears, stretching her eyelids to prevent it from happening, and echoed his sentiment. "Wow, how could this ever happen? I had no idea you were in New York. I would never in a million years have ever thought that you might be here." She shook her head, mouth wide open with elation, and asked, "What *are* you doing here, anyway? Look at you, the epitome of preppy-dom. You look like some kind of trader or something." She smiled and hoped her tone had not come across as sarcastic. She was, however, still in a bit of shock.

"And you," he threw it right back at her, "you look like you could be a nurse or something." He winked, not exactly answering her query. "You look great," he said flatly, and, tilting his head to see from another angle, "different." He found himself wanting to reach out to touch her face, but restrained himself.

Different? What was that supposed to mean? Josie pondered, trying to interpret his comments. *He means I really don't look great and I'm not like how he might have remembered me.* Cleve broke the strained pause in the conversation.

"Man, how are you? I mean, you sure look like a nurse in that outfit. Are you good? Do you love it?" he asked sincerely if not hurriedly.

"I'm great. Yeah, yeah, it's a good career. Interesting for sure," she responded, maybe not quite as sincerely or hurriedly. "Yeah, I'm good. How about you? Wall Street, huh?" She shook her head in disbelief.

"Yup, oh man, it's a long story. But I'm great too. Yeah. All good. New York is one crazy place, huh? I mean look what happens here…two old friends meet completely out of the blue." Now there was a really awkward pause.

Two old friends. She almost cringed, but she smiled anyway and extended an offer, pointing at the door of the Greek diner.

"Hey, I'm heading in here for a quick breakfast, just pulled an all-nighter at Lenox Hill Hospital. Want to join me?"

"Ya know," he said, the crystal clear beginning of his decline of the invite, "I'd love to, really, but I'm super late now." He pointed over his shoulder and gesticulated in an effort to explain that he'd been on his way when fate caught him off guard. "If I miss my morning meeting I'm screwed. Sorry. Man, I'd love to catch up though. Can I call you later, organize something for later this week maybe?"

He seemed sincere. Of course he was sincere. *It is Cleve after all, right?* Josie thought to herself, *right?*

"Sure, here." She fumbled through her bag. "Here is my card, I will write my home number on the back. I'm working just up at Lenox Hill right now; I sort of move around a lot." *OK, enough information Josie,* she scolded herself. *Zip it now and just smile. The rest is up to him.*

"OK, great, thanks, perfect. I will call you later. Tonight. I promise. Wow, I can't believe this. See ya, Jos'." He was walking away now, back to cab-hailing position, talking over his shoulder as he moved away. No embrace, no kiss on the cheek, no anything.

"Bye. OK, yeah, sure. Bye," she said and turned into the diner.

Josie Parker stared at her telephone all evening but when it rang later that night, she couldn't bring herself to answer it. She wanted to hold onto the memory of a very different Cleve Gregory than the one she'd bumped into on the sidewalk, and answering the phone was too risky. She cried herself to sleep that night, and for several nights after that.

22

By the time she pulled into the driveway, it was late. She parked her beat-up Volvo wagon in front of the garage doors, grabbed her stuff, and walked up the porch steps to the back door. The house was quiet; Marlene and Frank had gone to sleep. Only the dogs greeted her, along with a note on the kitchen table. She propped her backpack on the mudroom bench and put her duffle on the floor. She bent over to rub the dogs.

"Hey you guys. Come here Snuff, hey Ralphie, hey guys," she whispered. The wagging tails banging against the wall and their soft squealing noises caused a bit of a racket. She noticed how old and stiff Snuff was getting. "Shhh, shhh, OK, OK," she said, trying to get them to settle down. She knelt all the way down and gave them hugs, which they reciprocated with lots of very wet kisses. The big welcome from them felt, well, like she was home. It felt good.

She read the note.

Some leftovers from dinner in the fridge if you are interested. See you in the morning. Supposed to be a beautiful day. We're glad you are home, Josie. XO, Mar.

There was a heart drawn at the bottom. She loved it when people drew little doodles. She drew them in her journal all the time. She unwrapped the cotton scarf from around her neck and tossed it, along with her tan trench coat, over a chair at the table. She checked the cookie cabinet, grabbed a few fudge stripes, and poured herself a glass of milk. Josie took a big gulp and looked around the room.

"Nice to be home," she said out loud, in an admission to herself. She refilled the glass and put the milk bottle back in the fridge. Just for a second she had a vision of Mama braiding her hair while she sipped her Hawaiian Punch. A tiny shiver ran up her back.

Marlene had changed a few things in the house but Josie didn't really notice; to her everything was just the way it had always been. This was home. *San Fran, Atlanta, New York City, you can have 'em,* she discerned. *Glad to have been there but this is the best place.*

She turned and, balancing the milk and cookies in one hand, threw her backpack over her shoulder and flipped the switch to turn out the lantern hanging over the kitchen table. The duffle was full of laundry, so she left it behind.

"You can stay right there," she instructed it. *Home feels so good,* she thought. *Why have I stayed away for so long?*

Josie headed up the stairs, dogs following behind. Marlene had thoughtfully left the bedside light on and Josie's room was warm and inviting, as though happy to see her. She loved her room, despite that it reeked of the prehistoric remains of a teenage girl's existence. Still, the room held so many memories, so many souvenirs of a wonderfully happy childhood. As she crossed the threshold she held her breath, like Alice through the looking glass. *I really need to get rid of some of this stuff,* she mused as she looked across to the Ricky Nelson poster on the wall, the orange lava lamp on her desk, the paper flowers arranged in the stretched-out, glass soda bottle. She picked a few pieces of colored wax off the drip candle propped in the old raffia-cloaked wine bottle.

The bed boasted some new pillows and sheets, but Josie's snuggly, old tattered quilt was perfectly folded against the footboard. And there, on her bedside table, was her favorite photo of herself with her mama. Her dad had snapped it one morning years ago. Dorie Parker in her famous apron and Josie dressed in her signature jeans, blouse and rubber boots, about to dash to the barn. She must've been about fifteen.

"Hey hold on a minute, Rosebud," he'd yelled into the kitchen from his den that morning way back when. "I got this new camera and I need some models to practice on." He must have taken twenty pictures of his two gals standing there on the porch. When she moved away to nursing school, Josie thought about taking the photograph with her, but it seemed wrong to take it away from its spot in her room. So she'd grabbed one of the nineteen or so others to keep in her wallet. This was her favorite, it caught Mama just right.

"Hey, Mama," she whispered and lightly connected her fingers with the corner of the picture frame. She closed her eyes and felt Mama's touch, just for an instant.

Josie put her bag down, and began to undress. She pulled a flannel nightgown over her head and stared at herself in her mirror. "Not half bad, Josie Parker," she said out loud. *Not half great either—you're no Michelle Pfeiffer but you're OK.* Truthfully, she was a beautiful young woman. Long and lean, perfect in a pair of jeans, a white man-tailored shirt, and a leather Gucci belt. She rarely braided her hair anymore, but just for fun, standing there in front of the mirror, she grabbed three locks from over her shoulder and twisted and turned them into a shoulder-length plait. She did the same on the other side and stared into the mirror for a few seconds more, then realizing how silly she looked, released them both and shook her hair back into place. For an instant she swore that she'd seen Mama standing right behind her.

As she climbed in under the new sheets and her old quilt, the dogs jumped up and straddled her, something she spontaneously realized how much she'd missed, and which made her feel really loved. She picked up that favorite photo and stared at it for a minute. "Love you, Mama," she whispered. She placed it back and opened the drawer of the bedside table.

"Ah," she sighed. There it was, that beautiful sterling silver box. That precious little key with the silk tassel attached to it. Josie took the box from the drawer and opened it. The soft, aubergine velvet lining was worn down in a few places, but it was beautiful in its age. She'd left it there for safe keeping when she'd moved to New York for school, but every time she did visit home, she would go through the box, performing the same ritual.

She gave Snuff a push to move him over and laid each shiny piece out on her quilt. The strand of pearls first. *I think those actually might be fun to wear,* she thought for the first time. *Tomorrow I will try them on.* She laid them on her bedside table. She revered the brooches: one, a cluster of emeralds and diamonds; another, a coral and gold piece that looked like a bouquet of flowers; one with rubies and diamonds that resembled a firework bursting in the sky.

"That one was made by Schlumberger," Mama had told her. "Dad got it for me from Tiffany & Company in New York."

Gold clip-on earrings, shaped like knots. The twist-on pair with all the colored stones; Josie closed her eyes and envisioned Mama securing them in place on her ear lobes. There were several bangles of silver and gold, one that resembled a piece of rattan that had been dipped in sterling. The German crystal bracelet, with alternating horse and fox heads connected by little gold snaffle bits, was one of Josie's favorites. She lifted it up, laid it across her wrist, raised her eyebrows in affirmation that she might like to wear this too, and laid it on the table alongside the pearls.

There was, of course, the ring. She put on the Caldwell family ring. It still fit. Thank goodness. She flopped back on the pillows, closed her eyes, folded her other hand over the sapphire and diamonds, and thought of her mama. Almost always the vision was the same; Dorie standing on the back porch wiping her hands on her apron, calling out to Josie.

"You need to be on time and clean!"

She sat up, smiling as she took the ring off, and carefully placed everything except the pearls and German bracelet back in the box. She returned the box to the drawer, scrunched down under the covers next to Snuff, turned off the light, and slept until the morning sun came through her window and across her face.

The familiar aroma of breakfast filtered up the stairs and into Josie's room. *Who needs an alarm when there is bacon and toast in the kitchen?* she mused dreamily. She popped out of bed and pulled on some jeans, a polo shirt, and running shoes. With a baseball hat and a sweatshirt in hand, she headed down the stairs, dogs thundering behind.

Although it was clearly Marlene's back she saw as she walked into the kitchen, in her mind she heard Mama's voice bidding a welcome home and good morning salutation.

"I'll be back in a bit," she said as she gave Marlene a quick hug. *Got some demons to face this morning.* She pulled the sweatshirt over her head, grabbed a few pieces of bacon and a slice of rye toast, and was out the back door.

"Hey, how about some juice?" Marlene called after her, but Josie was gone. Marlene picked up the forgotten baseball hat from the kitchen table and hooked it over a rung on one of the chairs.

Josie retraced the path she had run so many times. This day however, she walked, contemplating how many less strides it now took to cover the same ground she had crossed over and over since childhood. She passed the awful spinning wheel in Barrett Park, and readily found strength to smile up at the sky and wink. No words were necessary. She felt no pain or sorrow. She was in a good place with Mama. In her core Josie felt she had grown and matured into a woman with so many of Mama's qualities that she swore some days she could feel two hearts beating in her chest. This essence of Dorie Parker's spirit raised Josie Parker up; it couldn't bring her down. And Mama's light, which she had often prayed for in the last dozen years, had always been there to guide her. She walked on.

She glanced quickly, almost sheepishly, at the baseball diamond, and tried her best to keep walking. She couldn't. *Cleve,* she reflected. This was the most important demon to contest. She stopped in her tracks and turned to squarely confront home plate. She had to put together some kind of deal with herself here, she decided, and she had to do it right now.

She allowed herself to think about the seventeen-year-old boy who had made her feel so yearningly weak. She pictured herself waving as he walked back to the team bench. *That Cleve,* she thought. Her memory took her back to the day Cleve had helped her school Puff in the Hidden Green ring, long ago. *That Cleve, the one I thought was so much like me. How did we ever turn out to be so different? Time to let you go. Time to let him go.* She looked across the field.

"Hey batta, batta." She spoke the words only to feel them roll off her tongue.

She leaned against a tall oak and reminisced about being sixteen and in love with Cleve Gregory. She closed her eyes and listened to the sounds around her. She never took the time to "smell the roses" in the city, whatever city it may have happened to be. This revelation affected Josie more than she thought it would have. She walked on a little further through the park and stopped to sit on a felled tree. She contemplated her career. Six days a week, she went to work, then went home. Once in a while, she went to work and then went out with friends, or on a date, or to a movie or a show. On days off she played the tourist, went to the grocery store, window-shopped. She read a lot. Too much. Her life was, well, benign.

Yet here, after just a few moments in Barrett Park she felt like she was smack in the middle of a movie set, an epic romance being filmed. She felt the presence of everything around her. That's what it was…she actually *felt something*. And, her feelings were real. She loved being right here, right now. And, she figured, when you are in love your feelings are the most vulnerable. Everything is magnified, everything is in front of you for the purpose of being absorbed. Josie Parker felt like she hadn't felt in a long time. She felt like herself.

She smiled now and reckoned that her romantic nature would render her always in love with *that* Cleve. She surely hadn't found anyone else who could eradicate his touch from her memory. No one else had been able to erase the belief she still held that life with *that* Cleve had promised a world full of all that really mattered, and perhaps so much more. Sadly, the boy she used to yell "Hey batta, batta" to was only a sweet memory. Josie acknowledged to herself that her need to come to this resolution was what had really brought her home to Middletown, New Jersey that weekend. She had to let go of the fairy tale Cleve.

He lost that bet, she thought. She sat for a few more minutes and stared out across the park. Tears welled in her eyes but none actually rolled down her cheeks.

"I will love you always, Cleve Gregory."

And with conviction, or so she thought, Josie Parker closed that chapter of her life.

She stood and continued on through the park. Today she had to jump the creek; she didn't have any muck boots on. She was anxious to get to the barn, prepared to face another demon. But at the same time she wanted to take in every memory that lingered here on the path to

Hidden Green. Successfully navigating her way through the brush, Josie climbed up onto the fence that circled the main ring, her heart racing. She paused and sat there for a few minutes, taking in the entire vista. Remembering.

Josie had gone to visit Lars at Jack and Jill Farm, as she'd promised him she would, when she arrived home from school for Thanksgiving holiday her freshman year. What an incredible relief it was to find his physical condition as outstanding as it had been when she'd had him as her own. She shared with her dad that she was worried about how he would hold up through fox hunting season, which was about to begin, but she was so happy to see that he seemed to be faring well thus far. Josie promised Lars she would return the following February or March to check in on him.

Unfortunately, contrary to what Mike O'Hara and Jack Berardi had hoped would be the case, Lars fell short in his new role. He was not a horse that was confident when asked to run at a flat-out pace through unfamiliar woodlands, up and down steep rocky ravines, around blind corners, or across creeks and gravel roads.

Sadly, before Josie was able to make another visit, Mr. Berardi, seemingly as spontaneous as Mr. Bonington, had made the decision that Lars was not worth his keep. Midway through hunt season, just months after he'd acquired the big chestnut horse, and without communicating his intention to Mike O'Hara (who would gladly have taken the horse back), Lars had been sent to the RichRanch Horse Auction in Pennsylvania, never to return to Jack and Jill Farm. Just like that, Jack Berardi had wiped himself clean of the horse.

By the time Josie became aware of Lars' tragic fate, it was too late to try to track him down. There wasn't anything she could have done anyway. *Mr. Bonington could have told them that he was no foxhunter,* Josie reminisced as she sat there on the fence. *I tried to tell them.* She had worked long and hard to develop Lars into the perfect horse for young, novice students of equitation or the hunter ring. Nothing could describe the pain and anguish Josie suffered over the discovery of his destiny. For weeks afterward, she'd awakened many nights in a sweat, having envisioned poor Lars, his body skeletal from starvation, his neck rubbed raw from being tethered too tightly in a dark, dirty holding pen, where he stood awaiting his fate. A fate that had little chance of a happy ending. Slaughter—that was Josie's worst nightmare. Death from starvation and neglect a close second. To ease her torment, she tried to convince herself that he had likely been sold to someone who had a riding school, kind of like the one at Hidden Green. At least then his life would had been spared. Perhaps someone might care for him the way that she had.

Jack Berardi's actions had a profoundly negative impression on young, passionate Josie Parker. She hadn't gone back to Hidden Green during visits home since. She hadn't walked into a barn again. Not until something larger than life had tugged on her heartstrings and told her it was time to go back. And now, here she was. She was ready, she knew.

She opened the barn door. The first thing to impress her as she stepped over the threshold she'd run through so many times in her life, was the smell. She stood there and inhaled. Exhaled. Inhaled again. The hay, the manure, the leather, the horses. The horses. The horses. Josie couldn't believe how long it had been. This world had been such an important part of her life. A stone's throw from her folks' back porch yet she hadn't been to Hidden Green in over six years.

She supposed that she understood things a lot differently now. And she supposed that she had just simply needed to leave; not necessarily the horses, but all of the sadness that had rained down upon her in such a small period of time, the loss of Lars serving as the final blow. Now she had found her way back. The circle was complete. There was no need to waste time rehashing the past. This morning was her epiphany; she had almost known it was coming. Especially after her fateful meeting with Cleve. It seemed as though time had given her perspective. Nursing had been a fine, respectable career, but nursing didn't lure her out of bed every morning the way the barn had when she was a teen. She surmised that perhaps she had not had demons to conquer, just life experiences to learn from. And so it was that Josie learned. *This is who I am, this is where I am supposed to be.*

Josie Parker was back now, surrounded by the things that mattered;

the things that mattered to her, anyway. Not more than three minutes at the barn had passed and she knew that she would never, could never, leave again. Except maybe to pack up her belongings in New York. She stepped all the way in and closed the barn door behind her. Her heart was big and full.

CLOVER FIELD FARM

23

Addie Crawford had been riding since the age of seven. It all started when her mother, a rider herself many years before, had taken her to a small riding barn just a few miles from their house in Colts Neck, New Jersey, to feed carrots to the horses.

As luck would have it the barn manager offered to give Addie a ride around the ring on Captain, a retired show horse whose job had become one of keeping young children safe while they were learning to walk, trot and canter.

"Please, Mommy, please," Addie begged until Pamela Crawford acquiesced. The barn manager led Captain six times around the ring, and it was a fait accompli from there.

"We offer beginner's lessons here if your daughter would be interested," the barn manager offered to Pamela. "There are a few school ponies I think would be just fine for her. If you are interested we could set something up for—"

"Tomorrow, Mommy, tomorrow!" Addie jumped up and down and screamed at her mother.

"Well, I guess you have the answer." Pamela smiled at the woman who led Captain into his stall. As the woman untacked the horse, Addie fed him a carrot and patted his soft, pink nose. The barn manager slid the stall door closed and looked at Addie.

"Come on, I'll introduce you and your mommy to Snowflake and Stuart Little, it looks like you will be learning to ride both of them!"

Six years and several snarky, naughty ponies later, Addie was ready to venture into the highly competitive divisions of the "A-rated" horse show circuit. She had long since left the humble beginner's barn where she had learned all the basics and the last four years she'd been riding at Clover Field Farm, one of the top show barns in the Northeast. Her trainer, Kenna Mahon, had found a great new prospect for her in Europe, and the horse would arrive at Clover Field very soon. Kenna had produced more than a few national champions in the equitation, hunter, and jumper divisions. Riding with her was expensive, intense, and demanding, and it was also an absolute privilege. She was the best at her craft; she took on only truly talented students and she had seen talent in Addie Crawford.

Addie was excited. She had only seen the new horse on a videotape, which had been air expressed to her parents by Kenna, who'd flown over to Germany to try him a month earlier. Increasingly, American riding trainers were importing European high-jump sport horses and retraining them to compete as show hunters, the beauty pageant of the equestrian world. Addie thought this horse was the fanciest she'd ever seen. He was a beautiful bay horse with a bold white blaze and three short white socks.

The "A" show circuit was made up of the crème de la crème. The circuit required a yearlong commitment to be competitive, and included traveling to a series of horse shows all over the map. The most qualified riders of all ages (often from the wealthiest families in the world) and the most beautiful, talented horses would all travel to Wellington, Florida every winter to compete for three months at the Winter Equestrian Festival, also known as WEF. All but a handful of the horses from Clover Field were shipped there in December and stayed until April each year.

Addie had been showing at WEF for a while, her first few seasons just during school holiday breaks. But last year she had stepped up from the children's divisions to begin competing in the junior hunters, junior jumpers, and the Big Eq', as the highly competitive equitation Medal and the Maclay classes were otherwise known. She had quickly become a force to reckon with. She had several horses, two of them great hunters that had won plenty with her, but one was now lame and would be out for at least a year.

Addie was grateful that her folks had agreed to buy this new horse. This would likely be her last full year of campaigning, and she had her sights set on winning the junior hunter championships at all three of the "indoor series" shows—the Pennsylvania National in Harrisburg, the International in Washington DC, and the National, held at Madison Square Garden in New York City. She would be heading off to college the following fall, and even though many of her peers would take a gap year, her dad had made it clear that she could go hard now, but when college time rolled around, with the exception of one last tour of the indoor series, that was it for the horses. Addie was okay with this.

Tall and lean, Addie Crawford was striking to say the least. She had the body of an athlete. She was competitive, smart, and disciplined. She hadn't really yet discovered boys, although they had discovered her. She had a contagious smile and her personality drew everyone in, in a flash. This year, from late January until the end of March, she would fly to Wellington every Thursday and return on Sunday nights or Monday mornings. It had been difficult for her parents to gain permission from the headmistress of Addie's prep school, Morningstar Academy. She had not been thrilled with the idea of Addie missing two or three days of classes each week, especially in her senior year. But Pamela Crawford argued that her daughter was an excellent student, took plenty of AP classes, could be privately tutored on the show grounds, and perhaps most pertinent, all of her college applications were complete and ready to be submitted. Ultimately the headmistress gave her blessing, with the caveat that Addie had to maintain or improve her grade point average, and that she would endeavor to miss as little school as possible during the rest of the school year. Pamela Crawford knew this would not be a problem for her ambitious daughter.

Most of Kenna's students boarded several horses each at Clover Field. At this level of competition it was customary to have at least one horse for the equitation, one or two for the jumpers, and one or two for the hunters. Addie's parents had bought and sold several horses for their daughter, but this was the first one that was to come from Europe. Most of her others had been talented yet safe veterans of the Clover Field program. Addie was enthusiastically challenged by the prospect of making this new horse famous all by herself, along with Kenna's coaching of course.

"Equitation is what really teaches you to ride," Kenna preached to her students all the time. She firmly believed this, having won the National Medal and Maclay equitation championships herself during her junior years. Addie didn't love the equitation, but did it at Kenna's insistence. She loved riding the hunters, and this new horse showed all the promise of becoming famous.

It was September, the time of year when horses often rediscover the playfulness they lack during the warm days of summer. Addie was already qualified for the Medal and the Maclay finals, and for the indoor series with her other hunter, Classified. Soon she would have her beautiful new bay, with a few months of time left to practice at home before starting off the WEF circuit with him as part of her string.

Addie's parents were financially able to provide whatever Kenna thought Addie would need to ride at this competitive level. Addie rarely took any of this for granted. She cherished every one of the horses she owned, and coddled them with carrots, Rice Krispies treats, and peppermints. It was clear they all loved her. She paid attention to everything and had learned a lot about horsemanship and horse care. The competition bar was set very high at the barn and although all the junior riders were friendly to one another, they were all serious competitors. Addie's attitude was as kind as her heart was big. She wanted to win for sure, but if she couldn't, she always hoped one of her barn mates would. Not everyone at Clover Field could be defined by these same good intentions, however, and for Josie Parker it was refreshing to know someone was in it for more than just the tri-color ribbon.

Josie had been managing Kenna's barn operation since a few months after that fateful spring weekend when she had decided to put nursing on the back burner, and she had never second guessed herself. She'd had no argument about the decision from anyone who knew her, namely her dad, and she was happier now than she had ever thought she could be. She loved everything about the Clover Field operation. She had great respect for her friend and boss, Kenna; and she saw a lot of herself in this pip of a girl, Addie Crawford.

The new horse would arrive at quarantine Friday and Addie couldn't wait. She'd already bought him a new halter, sporting a shiny brass nameplate that she'd had engraved with the name from his German passport, Grande Mont. Her tack trunk was loaded with horse treats, and in her nervous excitement she'd cleaned her saddle herself, not something boarders typically did at Clover Field. Most of the young riders showed up, got on, rode, got off, and left. Horsemanship had deferred to the reality that most riders of Addie's generation were over-programmed. The opportunity to hang out at the barn all weekend had taken a back seat to other sports or social commitments. Only the riders who were considered working students spent the lion's share portion of their days at Clover Field. Addie Crawford was the exception. She had the passion that was all too familiar to Josie Parker, and she shadowed Josie every chance she got, asking questions, offering to help, suggesting options. Josie and Addie had quickly developed a sisterly closeness.

New horses came to the barn frequently and new owners all reacted differently, but like Josie, Addie and her mother Pamela were very personal and intimate with their animals. Josie had a soft spot for these two; she adored the dynamic that existed between them. Josie was constantly reminded of moments she'd shared with her mama when she was just a little younger than Addie, and vicariously she lived some moments that she might have had if her mama had not been taken from her that awful day. These memories sometimes made Josie sad, but mostly she was grateful for the opportunities to pay silent tribute to all that her mama had done for her, and it only enhanced her developing friendship with the Crawfords.

Pamela Crawford, like Dorie Parker, had ridden horses when she was a young girl, and although she had stopped for almost twenty years, she couldn't resist the urge to be back in the saddle. She had been taking some lessons from the assistant trainer at the barn during the past year. About six months earlier, she had purchased one of the horses Kenna had for sale at the barn, and Pamela was planning to show her in the adult hunter division in Florida during the coming season. *This is a special mother-daughter deal,* Josie thought, and she was just a tiny bit envious.

24

Friday morning Josie's phone rang at 5:00 a.m. *Oh shit,* she thought, *this won't be good.* She was typically at the barn by six or six thirty at the latest every morning, and unless something was wrong, most things could wait until she got there.

"OK, what's going on?" No hello was required at five in the morning.

Kenna's voice was garbled, but awake and serious. She was clearly upset.

"The Crawford's horse didn't make it. It freaked out going up the ramp at the Frankfurt airport, flipped over the panel, and collapsed. Never recovered consciousness. They put it down at the airport and Margrethe called me at one o'clock last night. Can you believe it? Ugh. I feel so damn bad. Damn it, Josie, why the Crawfords' horse? Damn it."

"What the fuck are you telling me, Kenna? Grande Mont? No way. What? Oh man, this is really bad. I know how bad this is, believe me." Josie was shocked. She knew all too well about losing a horse, and the memory of it swept through her. She clenched her jaw and squeezed her eyes shut to stop her mind from racing back to the awful day she'd found out about what had ultimately happened to Lars, and snapped herself back into the present. *Damn it, Addie was so excited.*

"OK, so what are we supposed to do?" Josie asked.

"Listen, not to seem insensitive but the seller has another horse she is willing to send as soon as she can get all the paperwork done and organize a flight. A few weeks at most. I didn't see it when I was there, but Margrethe says it's very cool. Good breeding. Sound. Talented. Great mover, amazing jumper. No performance holes. Just not great in the stall. Not great to work around. We can have it for the same money, and if the Crawfords don't want it, the seller will leave it with me anyway, through Florida, to sell. Margrethe can also send me video of some others. What do you think Pamela will say?" Kenna knew Josie and Pamela were becoming friends and she hoped Josie would break this news to the Crawfords. Kenna abhorred confrontation and never wanted to deliver bad news, especially when it involved the health of a horse.

Kenna rambled on, "We can look for something else but you know as well as I do that getting the money thing figured out will be a bitch. Margrethe says it's not the best-looking horse and a little tough to work around, but it's the under saddle winner and brave. I'd hate to lose a lot of time. I really wanted Addie to get to practice at home for awhile before we head south."

"Holy shit, Kens', I just don't understand this! Oh man, Addie's gonna freak! She is going to be so upset. OK listen, they are coming to the barn this morning. I will tell them right away. Kens'," she said emphatically, "I will tell them. When do you need to let Germany know about sending the other horse? I mean, I will talk to Pam about it. I'm not sure what she will say."

"OK, you tell them. Just see how it goes. I will tell Margrethe we will give her some idea in a day or two, and to start on the vetting anyway. I love the Crawfords. Damn it. Poor Addie, she was so psyched. OK. I'll be at the barn before ten, see you then."

Josie kept an eye out for Pamela's car and walked straight out to the courtyard to meet her when she saw her pulling in. Fortunately she arrived alone. Addie would get there later that morning, after taking a test at school.

"Hey," Josie offered, still unsure of just how she was going to broach the subject.

"Hey! Good morning, any word yet? Is he at quarantine?" Pamela asked as she zipped up her fleece vest. Dressed in britches and boots, she was planning to have a ride before Addie arrived.

"Actually we did get a call, yes. Not the best news I'm sorry to say. Something has happened, Pam, and I've got the unpleasant task of telling you. It's not a great situation."

"Oh my God, what?" Pamela Crawford couldn't imagine what words could possibly come out of Josie Parker's mouth next.

"I'm so sorry, it's terrible news actually." Josie stared down at the ground. She took a big breath and continued. "Grande Mont flipped at the airport and we're not quite sure what happened next, but he didn't make it." Josie fumbled through it as best she could.

"What do you mean he didn't make it? Didn't fly? So what does that mean? When will he get here? Shoot, Addie is going to be so disappointed."

"No, actually. No, Pammy, he didn't make it at all. He died. They euthanized him there at the airport."

"Oh no! Oh my God. Oh, I can't believe it. This is horrible. Horrible! Poor animal. What the hell happened? What do we do now?" She stood in disbelief, her hand over her open mouth, thinking about how sad this was for the horse and how crushed Addie was going to be. She also was thinking about the money her husband had wired to Germany just a few days earlier. "I mean that was a lot of money we wired over there. God, the poor animal. Poor Ads." Pamela's emotions were all over the place.

"I'm not quite sure, Pam, we don't really have all the answers yet. We do know that Grande Mont will not be coming. Don't worry about the money. Margrethe is certainly willing to make right on the whole thing, and so is Kenna. In fact, honestly, Margrethe would like to put another horse for Addie on a flight as soon as possible. She says she does know of another one that could do the job just fine. A replacement." *Should I be getting into this already?* Josie wasn't sure. *Well, I guess I'm into it now.* "We could at least get a video quickly."

"Josie, I'm quite blown away right now, I'm not sure I'm able to digest anything. Maybe I should just ride, or at least try to, and then let's talk in a while. What time is Kenna getting here? And oh gosh, Addie. Addie is not going to take this well at all. She's already attached to the damn thing, watches the video over and over every night."

Believe me I understand more than you could imagine, thought Josie. "I know. Listen, don't think I'm heartless because I brought up the replacement. We are all on the same page here and just want to make this work out for Addie. Kenna will be here any minute. She was on her way awhile ago. I think she may have stopped at the quarantine to tell James. You go have a ride. Good idea. Let me get Sadie tacked up for you. I'll send Kenna out to the ring to talk to you the minute she is here. She is really upset about this too, especially for Addie."

Two hours later, Addie drove into Clover Field and parked next to her mother's car. Kenna and Pamela met her at the barn entrance and the three headed to Kenna's office. Josie saw them and made her way there. The three of them had agreed not to tell Addie of Grande Mont's fate. Better that she should only have to bear the disappointment of the horse being too lame to make the trip worthwhile.

"Margrethe felt he just wouldn't hold up in Florida, Addie. I guess it was a bad injury. Honestly, can you imagine how disappointing it would be to have that horse arrive and be crippled before WEF even got started?" Kenna made the whole thing sound completely logical.

Quite surprisingly, Addie took the whole event in stride. Her concern was for the health and comfort of the broken horse and she found consolation in the notion that Margrethe could send a replacement by the end of October. Better yet that it had all the attributes required of a winner. Addie was practical. Compassionate but practical.

"No video, let's just go with it," Addie suggested.

Josie almost envied the young girl's mature ability to take most of the emotion out of it. Better that she had never gotten to know the horse, she thought. Certainly better that she doesn't know what really happened.

Once Kenna assured her that she had no need to worry about Grande Mont, Addie set her sights ahead. This wasn't going to be a total loss. This was just going to be a horse of a different color. Thanks in most part to Addie, the day did not end nearly as badly as it had started.

25

On the Tuesday afternoon that the plain chestnut horse arrived from quarantine, Kenna, Addie, Pamela, and most of the other Clover Field clients were checked in at the New York Hilton and totally focused on the National Horse Show. Only Josie and a few of the guys were there to give him the official welcome. There was a lot less fanfare over the delivery of this gelding. Addie was neither bitter nor indifferent about the last-minute switch; she just thought she would take a little less invested approach this time. Besides, she was totally in National Horse Show mode. It was the beginning of November and except for the National, the indoor series was over. Kenna 's students had done well, one winning the Medal final at Harrisburg, and another coming in second.

Ramon, considered the most knowledgeable and able groom at Clover Field, led the gelding out of the van, down the ramp, and towards the barn. The chestnut's head was high as the sky and he pranced sideways, snorting and rattling and causing as much commotion as he possibly could.

"Ha! Making a grand entrance I see!" Josie used a strong, deep voice to address the horse, already attempting to let him know who the boss was.

Ramon, under his breath accused the horse, "Loco, todos, muy loco." He kept a hold on the lead shank just at the halter and kept his own shoulder aligned with the shoulder of the horse. This was the safest method of walking a frisky animal, and Ramon had the sense to handle the horse using every precaution. He'd seen too many of his friends wind up with serious injuries. It was never worth being casual around a horse. Especially a horse you didn't know, like this rather homely-looking gelding that had been sent as the replacement.

"Ramon, what do you think," Josie said, a statement rather than a question. "Let's put him in the stall at the far end of aisle one. That way he'll be able to see what's going on outside, plus it's a quiet end of the barn. Make sure he has water and a flake or two in his hayrack. Throw a sheet over him now and a blanket later. It's chilly, and since he's nervous we might as well keep him a little extra warm, don't you think?" Josie wasn't really looking for an answer, she just didn't want to come across as bossy. She headed for the office with the horse's arrival paperwork.

Awhile later, she walked down the barn aisle and noticed three of the grooms standing outside the new gelding's stall.

"Hey, como esta? What's going on? Everything OK here?" she directed her questions to the guys.

Ramon replied, "This horse es loco, Miss Josie, crazy! I'm no go in that stall, he bite me, I know it. Look, his ears flat. He show me his teeth! Este caballo es tan loco! Peligroso tambien!" Ramon always spoke two languages when he was nervous. "Look at him! He crazy!"

Josie opened the stall door. The chestnut horse, full of courage and attitude, lunged forward at Josie with his ears back and his teeth bared. "Whoa!" She recoiled quickly. "Hey, hey you brat, who do you think you are?" She threw her hands up and in his direction, and now it was he who recoiled. The stand-off had begun. "Listen, you. You want some food tonight, you better be a gentleman." She watched as he backed away and noticed that something seemed rigid, awkward about his hind end. "OK guys, let's just let him hang out for a little while. He's fine. I'll keep an eye on him. Thanks."

Backing up had definitely been problematic for him. Josie had not seen anything like it before. *Is it nervousness? Muscular? Or maybe neurological? What the hell is that? Oh wonderful, problems already. Well I'm gonna get right to the bottom of this.* Josie went into the office to call her go-to guy, Doc Thurman. Doc was not Clover Field's regular vet, so she rarely saw him in person, but Josie had stayed in fairly close touch with him since her days at Hidden Green. She never hesitated to call him for a consultation if she had a veterinary quagmire. He was always happy to comply, always gratis. He adored Josie Parker. Everyone in the equine world adored her. She had become the "it" girl, although she had no idea.

"Sounds like it could be something called shivers," Doc Thurman responded after listening patiently as Josie described the gelding's behavior. "Let me do a little more homework and I will call you back tomorrow. Actually, I'm gonna be just down the road at Colonial Farm around eleven. I could stop by after I finish there. It would be a treat to see you anyway," he offered.

"Really? That would be awesome! Would love to see you. Gosh, Doc, what's it been? A year at least, maybe longer?" Josie was selfishly thrilled at the prospect of seeing Doc Thurman. She was also thrilled at the prospect of having him look at this funny little horse that she couldn't quite seem to figure out.

"Great," Doc said. "I will see you around lunchtime then. Now that I think about it, I've got a little surprise for you anyway."

"No, no, I hate surprises, Doc!" But it was too late, Doc Thurman had already hung up the phone. *Ugh. What surprise? I hate surprises, damn it.*

She hung up the phone in Kenna's office and began her regular end of day rounds. In customary fashion, she poked her head in every stall, making sure there was enough water, hay, straw, and shavings, so that horses could lay down and be comfortable at night. She checked that blankets were snug, and that halters were off and hanging on the front of stall doors.

She stopped last at the stall that was now home to the sort of funny-looking, plain chestnut horse whose name was apparently John Courage. That's what his passport said. John Courage. Josie liked the name. A lot. She had no idea what it meant exactly, but she liked it. *He looks like a Johnnie,* she thought as she stared in at him. Addie would be back in a week, and of course it would be her decision to keep or change the name. Meanwhile, all names aside, there was plenty of time to bond with her latest charge.

Josie rolled back the heavy door and took a step into the chestnut's stall. He reeled around from his hayrack, ears flat back, teeth and nostrils flared. This time Josie held her ground. She threw her hands up and surprised him, but she spoke with a gentle voice.

"Hey, whoa, I don't think so, fella." Josie was letting him know, once again, who the boss was going to be, employing a more sensitive tactic than earlier in the day. She took a step forward and the horse whipped right back at her again. *Well that worked like a charm,* she thought sarcastically. "Hey, hey, here now, I've had just about enough of your bad manners." Josie took a large, aggressive step towards him and grabbed hold of the horse's blanket just at the shoulder. She held on as tightly as she could and rattled the blanket back and forth, with authority. "Enough of that mean spirit, you brat. Who do you think you are dealing with?" *Don't bite the crap out of me either,* she said to herself.

The chestnut horse was completely caught off guard by her gutsy move. His defenses mellowed almost immediately. His ears came up and he looked around at Josie as if to say, *Wow, you got me.*

Josie commanded him back and he moved away. Again she noticed that it was tough for him to back up. She stood motionless for a few seconds and then pulled a molasses horse treat out of her pocket.

"C'mon over here you brat." She held out the treat and the chestnut horse slowly came forward. From as great a distance as he could manage, he stretched his neck out to reach her hand and twisted the treat into his mouth. Josie stepped forward discreetly and rubbed him on the neck. He accepted her affection. She scratched him on the forehead then moved back toward the door. She held out another treat as she slid down along the stall boards until she was squatting. John Courage took another curious step closer to Josie, and then another. He stuck his head and neck out again, sniffing for more molasses treats. She sat down cross-legged in the straw.

"Oh, you like these, don't you fella? Here you go. Here you go, Johnnie." She spoke quietly now, vying for his trust. She fed him several more and allowed him to push his nose against her face, her shoulder, her knee. She stayed there on the ground, in his stall, for quite a long while. Eventually, the horse became less curious with Josie and went about just being a horse, pushing straw around, nuzzling the ground for bits of hay and grain. In time, he circled and groaned and knelt down on his knees then laid the rest of his body down in the straw. He curled his nose in and closed his eyes. Josie waited a few minutes and rose as slowly and quietly as she could. She knew if she startled him that he would jump back up. Getting up and down was not the easiest move for a thousand-pound animal. *Goodnight my new friend, John Courage. Nice to meet you, and what a great name you have.*

Josie latched the stall door and took one more lap around the barn. Walking out to her truck, she reflected on her days at Hidden Green. She remembered when Gladys had died how she'd promised herself that someday, when she had her own barn, she would protect her charges as best she could. *Well, this may be as close as I ever get to my own place, so I better get it right,* she thought.

Josie navigated the roads to home. She drove in silence, no radio tonight. She thought about Cleve Gregory for the first time in a long while. She supposed he came to mind because she was going to see Doc tomorrow, which caused her to reminisce. She hadn't thought of Cleve in terms of "what if" or "when" since her day of reckoning in Barrett Park. Their spontaneous, fleeting meet-up in New York had moved her past those schoolgirl dreams. Yet tonight those dreams stirred in her core. They took her to a very pleasant place. She actually sighed out loud.

She giggled, remembering how chivalrous the words were that he had whispered in her ear the day of Mama's funeral. She smiled now thinking that she had believed him. Tonight, more than nine years since that day, she could honestly say that the love she'd felt for Cleve had been her greatest love; since him, nothing else had really mattered. *Funny how you can't predict your future, no matter how logically you might try.* Now Cleve was a hot-stuff Wall Streeter, and he thought she was traveling the country being Nurse Josie. She was happy for him, he'd seemed proud of what he was doing. And she was happy for her, for she was certainly proud of the road she'd taken. She wondered for a few minutes, whether he'd ever given thought to even visiting his hometown again. She felt a twinge of jealousy, resigning herself to the likelihood that by now he'd found someone to help erase any memories of those Hidden Green days that he might have held as precious.

"Life is not a fairy tale, Josie, don't go down that path again," she said out loud, the same words she'd said to herself so often. *I know better now,* she thought. *But what great dreams it has made for.* She smiled again.

Josie turned up the heat, turned on the radio, and told herself, *Enough now.* Shorty, her new terrier, and Ralphie were curled up and asleep on the front seat. She gave them each a rub and pushed her thoughts ahead to tomorrow.

Surprise, huh? I hate surprises.

26

The night was cold and it was late. Josie walked up her front steps and grabbed an armful of logs from the stack of wood on the porch. She swung the screen door back with her foot. The dogs ran ahead through the tiny entry parlor and positioned themselves by their food bowls, fidgeting impatiently.

Once the fire was lit, Josie picked up their bowls and set them on the kitchen counter. She threw her hat and gloves into the basket she kept near the front door and hung her jacket.

"Come here, let's take off your coats," she called to the dogs.

From the refrigerator Josie grabbed the leftovers of the night before. She divided what there was of the meatloaf and mashed potatoes between the two bowls, piled some kibble on top, and set them down for the pups. She headed to her bedroom, undressed, and took a long, hot, steamy shower, returning to the kitchen to figure out what there was for her to eat.

"Looks like it's a bowl of cereal for me," she said, looking over at the dogs. "You guys get meatloaf and mashed, and I'm eating Frosted Mini-Wheats!" She set her bowl down on the family room coffee table, stoked the fire, and headed for the couch. "Oops, almost forgot the wine," she said to Ralphie. She danced a little jig and sang, "Gotta get the wi-ine!"

Josie loved decorating and often, like tonight, she would close out her day with a pile of *House & Garden* magazines in front of her, curled up in a pair of sweatpants under her flannel nightgown, a glass of red wine within reach and a warm, crackling fire. Oh, and two dogs wedged against her, of course.

The small cottage had belonged to her since about a year after she began working at Clover Field. Grandmother Caldwell had left her just a little bit more than enough money to buy it without having to apply for a mortgage. The price had been affordable since it wasn't the kind of place that would appeal to many buyers. She hired some of the grooms from the barn to paint inside and out, and a carpenter to put in some new kitchen cabinets and fresh bathroom tile and fixtures, and to replace some of the railing that had rotted out on the front porch. Soon, she figured, she'd have to replace the roof.

"Savings account back to zero again," she moaned to her dad when he came to see the place after she deemed it "house tour ready."

"Real estate is a great place to save your money, Rosebud. Something tells me you will do just fine with this investment. You've already made it beautiful." Her dad was still her biggest fan. The two of them made a point of getting together at least once a month for dinner. He only lived twenty minutes away and they spoke often by phone. Frank Parker had never second-guessed his daughter's decision to abandon nursing for horses. He knew even before she'd asked for his advice that she'd wind up back with her true passion, whether he'd given his blessing or not. Her happiness mattered more to him than anything. Sadly, he had lost Marlene to breast cancer, so Rosebud was all he had.

The cottage was by no means sophisticated, but it suited Josie just fine. She'd spent all her spare time for about a month just arranging and rearranging her furniture and belongings, until finally she was satisfied that she had it right.

There were just two bedrooms in the cottage, Josie's on the first floor and a small, dormered guest room upstairs. Fortunately each had its own bathroom. Every once in awhile Josie would have an overnight guest, usually one of the junior riders from the barn whose parents were going away, and once or twice a year, Tessa—still her best friend— would come to spend a long weekend. Tessa now lived in Florida, having surprised everyone (except Josie, who had been privy to the plan) by running off with Alan Harmon the day she'd turned eighteen. More surprised than anyone, Tessa's mother had been mortified. She tried for a long time to force them to split up and she had stooped to some low tactics. True love prevailed however, and Alan and Tessa were married a year after the brilliant run-away, in a small ceremony that included Alan's parents, Tessa's dad, Josie, and Alan's best friend Armand. Soon after that they moved to Wellington. They managed, with some inheritance money, to buy a small farm, and together they'd built one of the most successful local show barn businesses in the area; Alan riding and teaching, Tessa responsible for the billing, the bookkeeping, and organizing the show schedules. They were incredibly, enviably happy and Josie truly loved them both. She stayed with them whenever she was in Wellington and they were, the three of them, very, very close. Josie loved having company at the cottage, and so did Shorty, who always managed to finagle his way into snuggling with the guests.

One special possession had taken its place on Josie's bedside table the day she moved into the cottage. Mama's jewelry box. Not much had changed for Josie regarding Mama since her death. Josie missed her every day, like crazy. She kept her favorite photo of the two of them on the mantel over the small bedroom fireplace, and now alongside it was a prize picture of Dorie and Frank Parker, on their honeymoon in Cape Cod. Somewhere at her dad's house she'd come across another great photo—her mama as a little girl, sitting on a fuzzy black pony. Written in pencil on the back were the words, *Fury, Dorie, age ten.* Anyone might have easily mistaken Dorie for Josie, excepting for the fashion. It was uncanny how much they looked alike. Josie cherished that photo too, and had added it to her mantel-top collection.

The jewelry box still held all but one piece of the jewelry that had been in it the day her dad gave it to her. Josie had worn only a few pieces: the pearls, the German crystal bracelet, and an old Timex watch. She wasn't much of a jewelry girl—too risky to wear anything valuable to the barn, and she rarely went anywhere that required the kind of dressing up that called for the likes of the jewels in that box. On days she deemed special, she'd make an exception and pop on the beautiful emerald-and-diamond studs, saying a little prayer as she tightened them in her ears. *Please don't let me lose these, Mama. Shine your light on me today and keep them with me.* They always made her feel extra feminine.

She conducted inventory of the box every few weeks, especially when she felt the need for some spiritual connection. Tonight was one of those nights. For some reason Josie was a little melancholy. As always, she let each piece tell her a story.

Mama, I remember you at the Thanksgiving table in these pearls, she thought as she slid the beautiful strand through her hands. *I remember the Christmas Dad gave you this pin; your eyes grew as big as the moon when you saw the Tiffany box,* she thought as she held the ruby Schlumberger pin up to the light. Josie took the sapphire and diamond ring out of its little flannel pouch, still the most special piece of all, and wore it, as usual, while she perused the other pieces. Before putting it back, she held it up to the light.

"You are going to be the story of my life," she said to the ring. "Whatever that means." She thought about her dad's words, *Someday it will all become apparent.*

She never shared this ritual with anyone, not even her dad. Well, actually, she had shared it with Tessa. But Tessa was Tessa. When she would make her annual visit to the cottage, Tessa loved sitting on the bed and sifting through all the trinkets just as much as Josie did. So when their daughter Rosie was born, and Alan and Tessa asked Josie to be godmother, Josie decided it was absolutely appropriate to share a piece of jewelry from the box. Along with a small, heart-shaped gold locket engraved with Dorie Parker's initials, Josie had sent a note that read:

> *You are family to me, Rosilyn Jane Harmon, and so I want to share some Parker family magic with you. Wear this little charm in good health, and may its karma someday bring love to your heart, the kind of love your parents share. Xox, Auntie J.*

Like Frank Parker had told her they would, these pieces kept her close to the most influential person in her life. The person who'd made her feel more loved than anyone ever had. She closed her eyes, leaned against her headboard and silently prayed. *I miss you so much, Mama. Please shine your light on me and Dad and everyone at Clover Field. I love you and think about you every day. Please shine your light on that new chestnut gelding at the barn, too. I don't think he's gonna be easy. But he's special. I just know he is special.*

Josie closed the box, twisted the little key, and put the key in the drawer of her bedside table. She switched off the light, Shorty's cue to burrow under the covers and nestle at the bottom of the bed. *How does he breathe down there?* Josie wondered.

Her last thoughts of the day were about the chestnut gelding, John Courage, and about the surprise Doc Thurman had mentioned on the phone. *What the hell is the surprise? Damn it. I hate surprises. Surprises always have consequences.*

Ralphie jumped up on the bed, circled the extra pillow a few times, and curled into a ball. The three friends slept.

27

The sun's rays filtered into the open space between the curtains and Josie woke with a start. Immediately her brain started to stir. This was going to be one crazy day. Doc Thurman would be there at some point early in the afternoon, so exciting! She thought about how long it had been since they were last together. William, the blacksmith, would be there at ten, and there was a long list for him. She would have to be sure he made time to check the chestnut horse; his feet definitely needed attention. She would mention the backing up thing to William. He might have some advice to share. It was thirty degrees outside according to the thermometer suctioned to the outside of her bathroom window. Josie dressed accordingly and put the dogs in their jackets. She threw on her own coat and hat, picked up a mug of coffee, and opened the door. The dogs bolted ahead.

Her property was almost three acres in size, and it backed up to conservation land, which made the space seem vast. An old post and rail fence, creating a boundary from nothing, really, ran along one side of the area she and her dad had turned into a real backyard. No one else lived within miles. In the summer, the array of color and texture found in the perennial garden Josie had planted was akin to a patchwork quilt. Frank Parker would spend hours photographing hummingbirds here, the beautiful little neon-green wonders who frequented the bee balm blooms. He tended regularly to the vegetable garden that he and Aunt Gayle had created as a birthday gift to Josie the previous year. The gardens provided solace for Josie's dad, a great distraction from the sometimes overwhelming sadness he had to battle on occasion these days. Losing two wives in such a short time had not been easy for him to endure.

About fifty yards or so from the back door stood an old four-stall barn that had been neglected for a long time. Two paddocks ran from the small structure all the way to the front edge of her property, alongside the cottage. Looking over that way, she thought to herself,

Someday, if there is a horse in my paddock, he will be the first thing I see when I look out my bedroom window in the morning. She flashed back to the Jordan family's big white antebellum farmhouse with the red door. *That would be like a childhood dream come true,* she mused. The barn had electricity, and the stalls were a good size. She figured when she had some spare money that she and her dad could put on a new roof and replace the stall boards and doors, if for no other reason than to make it look better.

At the far back edge of the yard was Josie's pride and joy, her chicken coop. She'd purchased a pre-fab one from the feed and supply store, and carved out a spot to give a home to eleven hens and a very boisterous cock. Again she'd hired a few of the guys from the barn to build a serious fence around the coop, protecting the chickens from varmints while giving the birds space to roam. Every morning she collected the production from the day before, and every day she would show up at Clover Field with a large basket of very fresh eggs for all. Today Josie's yard looked brown and sad and cold; she hadn't yet removed the plant stakes that had held up the lilies, the hollyhock, or the clematis. In the vegetable garden there were the very frozen remains of some cauliflower heads and squash lying in the dirt. The chicken coop, however, was very productive.

"Nice job, chickadees! No one at Clover Field will miss breakfast this week!" Josie hollered as she gathered the eggs, swept out the coop, spread a few handfuls of food, and turned to look for the dogs.

"Here! C'mon, let's go you guys. Lots to accomplish today! Here!" The dogs bolted out of the woods, tails wagging. Ralphie ran towards the back door while Shorty stopped to shoot an evil eye in the direction of the chickens.

"Shorty! Don't even think about it! Here!" Josie reprimanded. Shorty loved to torture the chickens, barking fiercely in their direction, but truth be told he was scared to death of them, especially since the rooster had chased him last summer. "Shorty, let's go! Here!" she called again, and after a lap around the coop he made his way toward the back door of the cottage.

"Let's give him a little bit of Ace to keep him calm and put him in the small paddock out front," Josie suggested to Ramon as she stared into the chestnut horse's stall. "Keep an eye on him, and bring him in when William gets here, OK?" Josie slid the stall door open and he swung around defensively.

"Hey, John Courage, good morning to you too. Looks like you got out of bed on the wrong side. They weren't kidding when they said you were tough. Hey, let's be friends Johnnie, whaddyasay?" Josie reached out a hand holding a carrot. He stretched out his neck and snapped off a piece. Josie slid a halter over his head and led him out to a grooming stall. "Let's get you ready to go out and play," she said sweetly to him. He listened to every word. "You're a smart one, aren't you? I see those ears moving back and forth, you get every word I'm saying." She threw a turnout blanket over his back.

Ramon led the gelding out to the small front paddock and let him loose. Josie watched from the courtyard. He spun, let out a huge buck, galloped forward across the paddock, spun again, and headed back to the gate. He raised his head and snorted, spinning again. He repeated these clever dance moves a few more times, then settled down and lowered his head to the ground, pushing the dirt around and looking for a few bits of frozen grass on the cold November morning.

"He's good," Josie hollered out to the paddock. "Leave him there a bit. Thanks." Ramon waved in acknowledgement and headed back to the barn.

Hmmmmm, you've got a pretty good spin there, John Courage, Josie thought as she turned to head back to the barn. *We'll figure you out, my friend. Yes, we will.*

William waved as his truck passed Josie. *Good, he's here early. That will let me fit Johnnie into the lineup.* She wanted to try to get on him today too. She didn't ride that often these days, but she was curious to see what this cocky character was all about.

The morning rolled along and just as she found herself thinking that Doc Thurman ought to arrive at any minute, Josie noticed his vet truck pulling into the Clover Field courtyard. She hesitated inside the tack room, listening for paddock boots, and could swear she heard two sets.

"Hey, I left the hoof testers in the rig and we're gonna want them." Josie heard Doc say. "You mind running back out?" The second set of paddock boots motored back out of the barn. "Josie around?" Doc asked someone. As she walked out to greet him he was shaking Ramon's hand. He turned to her and smiled.

"Right here, Doc." She walked to him with purpose and gave him a big hug. "Wow, it's been too long. I'm so glad to see you!" she said sincerely, her smile so wide it almost hurt.

"Josie Parker. Lucky me to get a call from a girl as pretty as you. So good to see you, kid. I still can't get over that you found your way back to this crazy horse world. Gosh, feels like I haven't seen you in an age. Show me watcha got that's so special you needed me. As I recall, you always seemed to have all the answers yourself when you were a kid," he teased.

"Thanks so much for coming, Doc. You know how much I respect your opinion. The one I called you about is a total brat to deal with in the stall, you will hate me for it. But I do think he is special, despite his weird issue. C'mon, I will show you what I'm talking about. It's so great to see you, Doc."

"OK, hold on a sec', my vet tech just ran back to the rig to grab some equipment." Doc Thurman stood in place, looking into a random stall.

"Vet tech, huh? I figured that's who the extra set of footsteps belonged to. Wow, getting high and mighty, aren't you? Business must be good," she teased. "That's actually cool. I thought about maybe doing that myself before this Clover Field job came along. Let's see who my competition is," she quipped.

"Funny you should say that, Miss Parker. Very funny, indeed. Here he comes now. Oh, and about that surprise I promised." Doc Thurman nodded in the direction of the vet tech.

28

Josie knew who the tech was the minute she turned her focus to watch him travel back across the courtyard from the rig. She knew by the walk, like she'd seen it yesterday. She knew by the way he was dressed, the plaid flannel shirt, the jeans that fit perfectly. But most of all she knew by the way his hair swept perfectly across his forehead. What she didn't know was what to do. And she was totally confused. *What the hell happened to Wall Street?*

As he walked closer and his lips began—slowly, like they always did—to part into a smile, Josie stood, frozen. She wanted to tuck her shirt back into her jeans, but that would look ridiculous. She wanted to push her hair back over her shoulders, but that would look *obvious*. She wanted to run to the tack room to check her face in the mirror. Not happening. He stepped into the barn and took Josie's breath away. Cleve. *That* Cleve. *What are you doing here*? She wanted to know everything. Every single thing. Right now. But right now she also thought it best to just breathe.

"Wow," was all she could muster up. "Wow. You sure got me, Doc," she said, never taking her eyes off of Cleve. His amazing, deep set yellow-brown eyes stared back into hers and their chance, flawed reunion in New York vanished. It was as though they were standing outside the tack room at Hidden Green the day she had worried that he was more into Libby O. than he was her.

"Cruella de Vil," he said with sweetness in his voice, and she knew right away that he was thinking of that same day too. "Wow, it's great to see you. I can't actually believe this. You threw in the scrubs?" Cleve turned to Doc Thurman, pushed his shoulder to throw him off balance, and said, "Man, you got me too, Doc, I had no idea." He looked down at the rubber aisle matting, then up at Josie. "I honestly figured you were taking care of old folks, emptying bed pans at some hospital in, like, Alaska," he said. "Should've known you couldn't stay away from what you loved so much. Trust me I know how hard that is." He looked straight into her eyes, as though trying to let her know what the last nine years had really been like for him. He smiled at her now; he couldn't believe he was standing in front of Josie Parker. Josie Parker couldn't believe she was standing face to face with the boy who had vanished from her life the day of her mother's funeral. Doc Thurman couldn't understand why these two old friends didn't give one another a hug.

Now it was her turn to look down at the matting. For a second she felt the heat rise into her face and she was angry, so angry. This moment brought back memories she'd rather not have today. Quickly though, she remembered that there were other people here and she needed to get a grip. She closed her eyes for a second, took a deep breath and raised her focus up, turning to Doc Thurman. She leaned her head back and smiled at him, hoping he might rescue them all from this moment. He sensed an awkwardness he had not anticipated. *Clearly there is more between these two than I ever knew about,* he silently observed.

"OK, well, so much for surprises!" Doc said. "You two can catch up on your own time, we've got work to do." He winked at Josie, and swung his head in the direction of the wash stall. "Let's go have a look at this horse you think is so special."

"The shivers is a neurological issue, Josie," Doc Thurman tried his best to explain. "It's not really anything to worry about, and it's not a progressive kind of thing. If the horse were going to do the equitation, where backing up comes into play, it could be a problem. In the hunters, he should be fine. You'll learn as you get to know him when he's uncomfortable, and obviously you'll try to avoid those situations. Other than that, just go about business as usual." Doc and Cleve watched the horse move in both directions, first across the asphalt, then on the lunge line. "Let's have you get up on him and see how he moves about. You been on him at all yet?" Doc asked.

"No, and I can't wait!" Josie quickly put on her helmet, chaps, and a pair of small nubbed spurs.

Ramon threw some tack on the chestnut gelding and gave Josie a leg up right there in the barn. She took hold of the reins, put her feet into the stirrups, gave a gentle squeeze, and walked in the direction of the indoor ring. Doc, Cleve, Gregory, and Ramon, carrying a flannel cooler, followed her out.

The horse felt fantastic underneath her. His walk was proud; he reached out heartily with each leg, keeping not a lazy pace, but not a nervous one either. Josie could already tell he had a positive self-confidence out here under tack. *So different than how he is in the stall,* she surmised. Leaving the reins loose, she circled the ring at the walk a few times, then cutting through the center, letting him have a look at the jumps that were set up, giving him a chance to observe all of the new surroundings.

Josie picked up the trot, shortening her grip on the reins, letting him know it was time to pay attention to her commands. She could tell from the length of his stride that he moved beautifully; she felt like she was floating across the ground. Without much coaxing or effort, his head naturally lowered. She eased up on the reins and he stretched his neck out in front of her. *Very cool,* she thought, *he has just come from Europe and already has the natural inclination to move like a hunter.*

"You are a quick study, fella." She slowed to a walk and gave him a pat on the neck. As she passed the watchers near the barn entrance, she said, "No wonder he didn't make it as a jumper over there, he clearly wants to be a hunter!" They all knew exactly what she meant. Beautiful, graceful, relaxed, and elongated carriage: all qualities required of a winning show hunter. *Not bad so far for a replacement, John Courage.* Josie picked up the canter, circling the ring five or six times in each direction and executing a few flying lead changes through the center, then released the reins as she came to a walk, letting the horse catch his breath. She lowered the zipper on her ski coat.

Ramon put the cooler that he'd been holding up on the ledge by the ring entrance.

"He's a nice one, Miss Josie, much better here than in the stall. Loco caballo, totalmente. But he's a winner, I keep good care of that one." He smiled at her and headed back to his other horses.

Cleve and Doc Thurman walked out into the middle of the indoor ring.

"Cleve, how about we take the top rail down off the jumps on that one side of the ring," Doc instructed, pointing. "Meanwhile, Josie, let's see him trot some small circles. Has he been medicated today?"

"We gave him a swipe of Ace before we turned him out. But that was at, like, eight thirty this morning."

"OK, that's fine. Go ahead."

As she trotted towards the barn-end of the ring so that Doc could see him move in a small circle, Josie felt the horse suck back for what seemed no more than half a second. The next thing she knew, she was on the ground. The cooler Ramon had set on the ledge proved the perfect excuse for John Courage to play chicken, and he'd spun on his hind end so fast that Josie hadn't even seen it coming. He stood over her, looking down as if to say, *Gotcha, didn't I? You should've hung on tighter.*

Josie stood and dusted herself off, a little embarrassed that she had been spit into the dirt in front of Cleve and Doc. The two came jogging over to her as she gently took the reins and spoke to the horse.

"You trickster, you caught me off guard," she chuckled. "I should have known you were a good spinner after your antics in the paddock this morning."

Ramon, hearing the commotion, came running to the ring.

"Miss Josie, you OK? I'm so sorry, the cooler, I'm so sorry."

"No worse for the wear, Ramon, it's fine. Let's just leave it there. Just as well that we learn this stuff before Addie gets on him. Now we know. I'll no doubt have a good bruise on my butt by tonight, but I'm fine. No worries." She gave a quick glance in Cleve's direction. "I'm fine, really. No worse for the wear."

Ramon gave her a leg back up and she walked back toward the cooler. John Courage bowed and pricked his ears, and Josie gave him a hefty kick forward.

"Enough," she said in a stern voice. "Enough." She walked past it several more times until he seemed unimpressed, then she patted him on the neck and said, "OK, back to business."

She cantered the horse over a dozen or so cross rails while Cleve organized the jumps.

"Super mover," Doc offered. "I don't see anything to be concerned about so far. Would love to see his scope. What's his name, anyway?" he asked.

"John Courage, whatever that means," she answered.

"John Courage was actually the founder of an English brewery in the 1700s," Cleve offered. "Funny name for a horse, but really cool. John Courage. I like it."

Josie and Doc simultaneously raised their eyebrows and looked at Cleve, mutually impressed that he had come up with such random knowledge.

"Hey, I know stuff." He winked at Josie. "It's a really good beer, what can I say?" He laughed, defending himself.

"Bar trivia, fantastic. OK, let's see John Courage get himself over some oxers." Doc pointed to the jumps.

Josie picked up the canter. As she passed through the middle of the ring she looked over to her old friends and said, "Thanks again, Doc. You're the best."

Josie cantered back and forth over a low jump a few times and then began to execute a course. The first jump was set about three feet high with lots of colored flowers at its base. The gelding popped right over, unimpressed with what might have seemed spooky to some horses. She continued cantering and realized they were getting to the next jump quite easily, so she sat up straighter in the saddle, let her fingers take a little more feel of the reins, and whispered, "Whoa, Johnnie."

The red horse ticked one of his ears back for just a second, listening to her command, clearly understanding what Josie was asking of him. They came out of the line perfectly.

"Nice," Doc Thurman called out. "Really nice. Beautiful arc, super with his front legs, and nice and square with his hindquarters. Landed on the correct lead every time. Bring him over to me. I think you guys got a good one here, Josie. Let's just see him back up."

Josie pulled the horse to a halt right next to Doc. She added gentle pressure as she pulled firmly back on the reins. His hind legs seemed rigid and almost spastic.

"OK, that's good. Listen, I think this *is* the shivers. A mild case. He was fine when we did the flexion tests of his muscles, he has no atrophy in his hind end, and he's not gonna be an eq' horse. Just be sure William and Ramon are well aware of the situation. That will make life easier all the way around. He's about ten or eleven, right?"

Josie nodded.

"Yeah, just keep and eye out for any obvious changes and give me or Jesse Block a call if you are concerned. Jesse is Kenna's vet, right? The horse is fine. He'll be fine, Jos'."

"Thanks, Doc. Thanks so much." Josie was truly grateful.

"Cleve can hang here with you a bit. I'm sure you wanna jump around a little more since you're on. I'm gonna borrow Kenna's office and make a few phone calls." Doc knew exactly what he was doing. They were two of his favorite people in the business. *How cool would it be if that chemistry got stirred up again?* he asked himself as he walked out of the ring.

29

Neither Josie nor Cleve felt comfortable with the idea of small talk right now. They were both equally shell-shocked by what Doc Thurman had pulled off today, and neither quite had a grip on the situation. Ironically, Doc Thurman had no idea what he had really pulled off. Simultaneously, silently, Josie and Cleve asked themselves, *just who exactly was that I bumped into in New York three years ago*?

Somehow it felt like their short, youthful, life-defining love affair had happened a million years ago. Then again, it felt like it had happened yesterday. One thing was absolute: there were two heads spinning in the Clover Field indoor ring on this cold, winter afternoon. Wisely, they each focused on the task at hand rather than the obvious and intimidating reality that there were already sparks re-igniting.

"Hey, do you want to do a little course with him? This is the first you've jumped him, right?" Cleve asked as Josie walked around the center of the ring, letting the gelding have a break.

"Yeah, he feels amazing. Let's see what we've got. Want to make the jumps on the diagonal a few inches higher for me? Maybe up to, like, three-six?"

"Yup, you got it. Just watch out for that spin," Cleve reminded her as he walked over and adjusted the jump height.

Josie and John Courage executed the course, jumping the fences in various patterns, at different paces. The horse stayed balanced and confident. He seemed to like the security of Josie keeping a light connection against him with her legs, and she would be sure to pass that knowledge along to Kenna. But Josie knew he was going to be a winner for Addie Crawford.

"Woo!" Cleve hollered as Josie headed for the outside line, completing her course.

"Nice, huh?" Josie said, out of breath, as she walked over to Cleve after letting the horse trot around the ring once on a loose rein. "He's gonna be so perfect for the girl that bought him. I'm really happy for her.

He's adorable."

Here came the awkwardness again. Neither one of them knew where to take the conversation from here, so Cleve went about resetting the jumps while Josie cautiously grabbed the cooler and draped it over Johnnie's hind quarters. She walked the chestnut around the indoor ring a few more times. They both headed to the barn at the same time.

"Kind of like old times, right?" She nervously broke the silence as she threw her right leg over the back of the saddle and dismounted. She slid the left stirrup up the leather and turned to walk around Johnnie to the other stirrup, but Cleve was standing smack in front of her, so close their chests were almost touching. *Now this is like old times,* Josie thought to herself as a shiver ran up her spine. *Déjà vu.* Cleve looked, with intention, straight into her eyes.

"Not to be a jerk, but I was thinking more like, it's high time for some new times," he said. "And yes, it is like old times. It's good to see you, Jos'. Good to see you like this. I consider it fate that you called Doc yesterday about this horse." He patted the gelding's neck. "This red horse right here is entirely responsible for us seeing each other today. John Courage. I had no idea you were working here. Doc Thurman never said a word to me. Not a word. I'm not sure he ever would have thought you and I had...well. Who knows, maybe he figured I already knew you were here." He shook his head, smiling. "I would never have thought to look for you at Clover Field Farm."

His words now—*I would never have thought to look for you*—reminded her of what he'd whispered in her ear long ago. She looked at him, puzzled. Cleve knew this wasn't the time or place to get heavy, so he took a few steps back and lightened the air.

"C'mon Cruella, you get this horse put away, I'm gonna find my boss." Josie led the horse into the barn, looking down at the ground but smiling at his Cruella comment. She reflected back again, to the day he'd called her that at Hidden Green, and on the rest of that conversation. She thought about how profoundly her world had revolved around that boy, at that barn, way back then.

And in this moment, very much in the present, Josie Parker realized just how much her world since then had revolved around Cleve Gregory too, despite her thinking she'd long since been over him. Right now she knew that she wasn't over him at all. She wasn't over his hair, his lips, the way he fit in his jeans. He existed. *That* Cleve existed. New York had been an aberration. It wasn't their time then. Now, though nearly ten years had gone by and a chance meeting had almost thrown them off course, she realized she still wanted to be his girl.

Josie handed the chestnut gelding to Ramon and turned towards the tack room. She needed to see how bad she must look. As she stood in front of the mirror, wiping a damp paper towel across her face, she remembered her own words, *Not half bad, Josie Parker. You're no Michelle Pfeiffer, but you're not half bad.* She fluffed up her hair with her hands and walked back out to say good-bye to Doc and Cleve. *OK Parker, let's see where things are gonna go from here*, she silently challenged herself.

"Great to see you, kiddo. Let's not be such strangers, hey? No more of this six, eight months, a year going by." Doc Thurman gave Josie Parker a big, heartfelt hug. The three old friends stood in the barn aisle. "You got a nice horse there. John Courage. Good luck with him. Addie Crawford is a good little rider, I'm sure it will all go well. Say hey to Kens' for me and tell her that if there is anything I can do for her while she's in Wellington, I'm around."

"You're here for the most part, right?" Josie looked up from unzipping her chaps and nodded.

Doc continued, "We'll be here most of the winter, will probably just check in down in Wellie world for a week or two. I've got a few clients going down but most of my work is here." He picked up his backpack, gave Josie another hug and motioned to Cleve that he was heading out. "I'll pull up the truck. See you, kid." He called back over his shoulder, "Ramon, be well buddy."

"I'm right behind you," Cleve called after him.

The two stood facing one another, but both looked down at the ground for what seemed an eternity. Cleve picked up his backpack and threw it over his shoulder. Josie looked up at him. Where the tears in her eyes came from she wasn't quite sure, but they were there and she knew they were about to roll down her face.

"Hey." Cleve spoke quietly now as he looked around to be sure no one else was near. "Look, Josie." He took a step closer and tipped his head down to look at her with total sincerity, hands in his pockets. "I meant what I told you, Josie. I meant every word. You just threw me off course in New York. I thought the girl I was looking for was gone."

"And I thought the same thing about you, Cleve. I thought that gray suit, well, it seemed to suit you." She almost smiled, but couldn't. "That's why I didn't take your call."

Cleve changed the direction of the conversation.

"Wow, it seems like a million years ago that you were sitting on the stairs at your house, that stinkin' day," he said, referring to Dorie Parker's funeral. "A million years. Do you remember me promising you that some day, when I could offer you a better guy, a guy that was worthy of you and all your goodness, a guy that was real, that I would find you, wherever you were? Do you remember that, Jos'? I said, 'I will find you when I'm good enough to keep you.' These last ten years, have you ever thought about that? Do you ever think about it? Did you ever have any faith in what I said that day?"

"Of course I do. Yes, I have. You have no idea how many times I've thought about what you said. Probably a million times, Cleve." *Is he kidding?* Josie looked around. She was a little self-conscious that this conversation was happening in the aisle of the Clover Field barn. *I guess this is what fate is,* she thought to herself. Cleve reached out for her forearm and gave it a little tug to get her attention back.

"Well, I'm that guy now, Jos'. I've worked really hard at life for a long time. The last five or six years especially have been an incredible journey for me and things are solid now. My life has really started to fall into place. The only thing that's been missing is you, Josie Parker. And despite our flawed meeting in the city, I have wanted to see you. I tried to find you even though you didn't take my call. I went to the hospital to look for you. I got nowhere. I even tried to find your dad's number in Middletown. Unlisted. Then I stopped. I took it as an omen, and I haven't been brave enough to look for you since. I guess I've just been afraid that if I did find you, if I showed up on your doorstep somewhere..." He seemed to have difficulty continuing. He took a deep breath and went on. "I've been afraid that if I found you, you really might be someone different than Josie Parker from Hidden Green. If that happened, then I wouldn't even have my dream anymore. At least having the dream, I could concoct the ending I wanted. New York threw me for sure, but I just couldn't believe that was supposed to be it. I knew that I was just a guy in a suit, biding my time there. But I wasn't sure about you... Anyway, I just haven't had the guts to try to find you, not because I'm chicken shit, but because I never wanted to face the possibility of really losing you altogether, and it was looking like that was the case. It's difficult to explain. Man, it's so complicated to love you." Embarrassed by his admission, he took a break. He shifted his backpack. "Well, I have my shit together now and, well, shoot, here you freakin' are. Right here. I had no idea." He squeezed her arm a little harder now and pulled her in close. "Thanks to a little red horse, with a very big name, here you are, back in my life. It's like magic, Josie Parker. Magic. Yup, I'm goin' with magic here, Jos'." He let go of her, realizing the barn was no place to continue this conversation.

Stop crying and pay attention, she reprimanded herself. *Did he just use the word magic?*

Cleve looked down at the ground, and then away, out toward the courtyard, then back at Josie.

"Anyway, I've gotta get goin'," he said. "Can we talk later? Could I take you to dinner, maybe? I mean..."

Josie looked at Cleve and nodded yes before he finished his sentence. She wiped her own tears with her jacket sleeve.

"Yeah." She spoke in barely a whisper. "Yeah, of course. I'd like that a lot. Doc has my house number. Or call me here."

"Could we just go tonight? Is that too much, too soon?" he asked cautiously.

"Yes, yes, definitely," she responded shyly. "I mean no, no it's not too much, and yes, dinner tonight is great." She tried to laugh at the mixed-up conversation. She was incredibly relieved. She didn't want to lose sight of him in this minute, let alone have to wait days to see him again. She couldn't believe this was happening, and she was overwhelmed with emotion.

"OK, great. Then I can just pick you up at seven?" He straightened his posture, feeling more confident now that Josie had agreed. "I have no idea where you live. Are you on the farm, here?"

Josie shook her head no, not quite able to speak, tears rolling down her cheeks again.

"Ugh," she said, trying to force a smile, dabbing at tears. "Sorry. This is embarrassing. Me, crying I mean. I'm really glad to see you Cleve. Seven sounds good." She took a deep breath. "OK. Whew. Sorry." Now it was Josie who looked away, mortified. *Get a grip, Parker.* The tears would not stop.

Cleve touched her gently on the shoulder. "Seven it is." He headed down the aisle.

Josie followed him with her eyes. For some reason the words *Hey batta, batta* popped into her brain and she giggled out loud, once again wiping tears on her sleeve. *Hey batta, batta,* she said to herself, and she found a real smile.

"Hey, Cleve!" she called out just as he was about to walk into the courtyard. Cleve stopped and hesitantly turned back to face her. *Please don't change your mind, Josie, please don't change your mind,* he prayed.

"The old Haskell cottage. You remember where it is?" she called out.

He shrugged his shoulders then nodded affirmatively.

"That's where I live. I bought it a few years ago. That's where you can get me!"

"Oh, right! Yep, I know exactly where it is. OK, see you at seven." Cleve offered a little salute, spun on the heels of his paddock boots, and was gone. He climbed into Doc Thurman's truck and they drove off.

After a few minutes of silence other than the Eagles' song playing softly on the radio, Cleve spoke.

"Thanks, Doc." He looked over at his boss, a man he respected for so many reasons. "I had no idea she was at Clover Field. It was great to see her. It's been a long, long time. Like, ten years, since I've really seen that girl. Can you believe that?"

"Yes, I could see that you were both quite happy to see each other. More to that story than meets the eye, hey Gregory?" Doc Thurman smiled, holding a toothpick with his teeth. "Well, I'm happy about it. She's always been one of my favorites. Not many girls I've come across are as smart and devoted as Josie Parker. And she's got some sass. You'd be lucky to be the one who lassos that girl's heart."

"Don't think I don't know that, Doc. Believe me, I do. I had her heart once and I really blew it. I'll be damned if I blow it again. To be honest, Doc, I've loved that girl for twelve years. I'm gonna do my darndest to get her back, as her mama used to say, 'Come hell or high water'." It surprised Cleve that he was being this candid about his feelings, but Doc Thurman had become not only a mentor, but also a treasured friend. Doc, not unlike Peter Randolph, had given Cleve great opportunity and a vote of confidence when he'd hired him as his vet tech.

Doc knew Cleve needed some relief right now, so he threw a little humor into the conversation to lighten up the vibe in the truck. He took the toothpick from his mouth.

"Yeah, well I'm taking full credit for this one, kid. Just call me Doc Thurman, magician. Doc Thurman, matchmaker." He laughed at himself as he rolled down his window, threw out the toothpick, and pulled onto the road. Cleve gave his boss an affectionate elbow to the shoulder.

"Sorry, Doc, but I think that chestnut horse with the shivers gets the credit."

"By the way," Doc said, changing the subject. "I called Betsy over at Marelands and told her we'd be a little late. No worries." The two began discussing the details of their next appointment.

Josie wasn't sure how she was going to make it through the rest of the day, but she did know that right now she was going to bring a pile of molasses horse cookies to the chestnut gelding who had been responsible for the amazing morning. Never in her wildest dreams had Josie thought that Doc Thurman's surprise would be Cleve. Cleve was so right about Johnnie. This horse, whom Josie already knew was so special, had brought them back together.

She opened his stall door, fully expecting his typical greeting, ears flat back, head and neck lunging forward defensively. Instead the horse stood quietly in the middle of his stall and stared at her as if to say, *Hey, what's up?*

"Wow, you are a damn quick learner aren't you, Johnnie? Well, I've got some treats for you here. You sure earned them today. Quite the magician you are, oh yeah." Josie gave him a pat on the neck, fed him the treats, and looked over his legs and face. "All good, huh fella? You and me are gonna be best friends from here on in, aren't we? You are a good luck charm for sure. I can't wait for Addie to meet you. I know you are gonna be a good luck charm for her, too. Let's just leave the spin out of it from here on in, huh?"

Josie turned to walk out of his stall and felt Johnnie's nose push on her back. She turned back to look at him, and he walked forward a couple more steps, then padded his left front foot on the ground.

"Oh man, you do like those molasses treats, don't you? I haven't got any more, sorry fella."

She was compelled to walk to him. He nudged her again, and tucked his head between her torso and her arm, leaving it there for a minute or two. It was a profound act of affection, the likes of which Josie had not seen from any horse since Lars. She was surprised to see it come from this one, who not twenty-four hours ago had behaved wretchedly. She patted his neck and rubbed his forelock.

"You are special, John Courage, you are very special. See ya tomorrow, fella." Josie latched his stall door.

She walked toward the office, wondering what she could do next to make the rest of the hours in this workday fly by. Fortunately, the barn phone rang, Josie's focus shifted to the matters at hand, and before she knew it, she and her two collared companions were on their way to the old Haskell cottage.

30

Josie pulled her favorite white blouse from the closet, the one with two lace panels down the front, which rendered it just a bit more feminine than the others in her closet.

"Thank goodness you don't need an ironing," she said. She laid it on the bed next to a clean pair of jeans and her favorite Gucci belt. She'd splurged on it last year and had no regrets about doing it. Especially tonight; she knew it would look great. Shoes were an issue. *Hmmmmm,* she thought, and decided this necessitated a call to Tessa. She sat down on her bed and picked up the phone.

"Hey there, it's me," Josie said after Tessa answered the phone.

"Hello there!" Tessa said enthusiastically. "I was just thinking about you today. Not sure why but you popped into my head right around noon. Everything OK?" Tessa was always happy to hear from her pal.

"Hey, yup. All good. How are you feeling? You must be close to three months now, right? How's Alan? Is he up here for the National? Did you guys have anyone qualify? And how's my goddaughter?"

"All good down here in sunny Florida, seventy-five and balmy. Your goddaughter is great. She is such a gift. Yes, I'm just about three-and-a-half months. No, Alan didn't go to New York. We just had one kid qualify so Carl Bessette is going to help us out and coach her. Way more cost effective. We had a great Washington though. What's going on with you?" Josie half-heard what Tessa was saying, her mind obsessed with thoughts of Cleve.

"Listen, you are gonna kill me for this because I don't have time to explain all the details right now, but..." Josie took a big breath. She couldn't believe she was about to say what she was about to say.

"Tess', I have a date with Cleve Gregory tonight. He's picking me up in an hour. AAAAAAHHHHHHHHHH! Can you believe it?" she screamed into the phone. "You need to help me pick the right shoes."

"What? No way! Cleve? What rock did he crawl out from under? Sorry, I didn't mean that. Josie, I can't believe it! You told me you were done. Buried the demon. Did he call you? Did you bump into him somewhere? Were you back in the city? Come on girl, 'fess up! You must be freaking out if you are calling me about what shoes to wear! I want details, who cares about shoes!"

"Tess, it's a long story. I'm really excited, and really nervous. Don't be mad, but I have to call you back tomorrow. Anyway, then I will be able to tell you about the date too. Right now you have to help me. White blouse, jeans, my blue and red Gucci belt—you know, my friggin' uniform. What shoes? Maybe my navy Pappagallo flats with the buckle? It's freezing out though so should I just wear my LL Bean bluchers? Boots, maybe? I'm thinkin' boots. My flat suede ones." Innately she knew this call had very little to do with shoes. So did Tessa.

"Well, where are you going? Geez, Josie, I can't believe it! You are killing me, killing me! I need details!!" Tessa wanted to know everything, in that very moment.

"Come on, I promise I will call you first thing tomorrow, before I go to the barn. I don't know where we are going. It doesn't matter. Right now, just tell me what the hell to wear!!"

"OK, the suede boots. Definitely. The Paps are too summery. The other ones you mentioned, too casual. Hair? How are you gonna wear your hair?"

"Just down. I'm about to get in the shower now. I have to hurry though so I have time to blow-dry it. Otherwise it will look flat and gross. OK, I gotta go. You are the best. I'm freaking out. I'll call you tomorrow. I promise. Love you. Kiss my goddaughter. See ya. Where did you say Alan is? Kiss him too."

"You better call me! First thing in the morning, unless he's still there!" Tessa teased her friend. "Oh, and wear your mama's crystal bracelet. And the ring! Promise me you will wear the ring. It's awesome and it will bring you good karma."

"Right, Tessa. I gotta go. Love you, girlfriend. Bye." Josie put the phone back in its cradle and headed for the shower.

At seven fifteen, Josie saw headlights coming up the driveway. The dogs started to bark. She checked herself in the hall mirror for the tenth time and walked into the kitchen. She leaned up against the counter and stood still. *Here goes nothing, Josie Parker,* she said to herself as she crossed her fingers. She felt the family heirloom spin on her right ring finger.

"Shine your light, Mama, shine your light on me tonight," she said out loud. She counted to ten.

The front door knocker clacked and when Josie opened the door she found herself staring at, still, the most handsome man she had ever seen. She felt a tremor run through her body and hoped that Cleve had not noticed it. He had, and it gave him the confidence that, until that moment, he wasn't sure he possessed.

"Hey there," he said gently as he stepped across the threshold and stood in the entry hall. He rubbed his bare hands together. "Wow, it's cold out there tonight." The dogs were all over him, tails wagging. "Hey, hey, you guys. Hey Ralphie, how ya doing? And who are you, little jack?"

"We had to put Snuff down—cancer. Shorty's my new guy. Did you find your way here all right? It's different by car. Remember we used to pass by the cottage going through that big field when we rode in the hunter paces?" *Stop rambling, idiot,* she silently scolded herself. She pointed to the back of the cottage.

"Yep, yep. I do." He stood, looking first at her, then glancing into her cottage. "This is nice, Jos'." He nodded in the direction of the family room. "Perfectly Josie, if you don't mind me saying so."

"What exactly does that mean?" She smiled coyly. "Anyway, come on in and see the place. I didn't light a fire because I knew we were heading out."

Josie took Cleve on a quick tour of the house, and the pair exchanged small talk. Josie skipped showing her own room; it just didn't seem appropriate.

"Can I grab you a glass of wine or a beer? I don't have any John Courage," she said with a wink, "but I can offer you a Budweiser."

"No, thanks, I'm good," he said. At the conclusion of the tour, he suggested, "What do you say we get going? I've got a special place to take you for dinner. It'll take us about twenty minutes to get there. Oh yeah, bundle up. I'm tellin' ya it's cold out there."

Cleve helped her into her warmest wool coat. She reached into the basket for a ski hat and some gloves and followed Cleve out the front door, turning back to grab her favorite "stolen" cashmere scarf, one that Aunt Gayle had given to Frank for Christmas one year. She twisted it around her neck as she reassured the downtrodden pups, resigned to the fact that they were not going along.

"I'll be back soon, you guys mind the cottage," she said. "Go on, get in your bed." Reluctantly, the two comrades curled up together, never taking an eye off Josie until the door closed behind her.

"It smells like Chinese food in here, Cleve." Josie peered behind her and noticed the paper grocery bag sitting on the back seat of Cleve's pickup. "Leftovers from lunch?" she joked, admittedly a little perplexed.

"Nope, I told you I have a special place to take you for dinner. I didn't say the food was going to be special, just the place." He smiled. "But it does come from my favorite Chinese takeout place in Lincroft." He leaned in to adjust the radio. He leaned back and looked directly at her, for an instant, capturing her eyes. *He's a man now. A complete man,* she thought. *He's different. And he's amazing.*

"OK, you got me. I'm confused." Josie leaned back against the passenger door and stared at Cleve, waiting for an explanation.

"It's a little surprise. The idea came to me late this afternoon, so it's not going to be perfect, but once I thought about it, I had to go with it. It's gonna make me or break me, I can tell you that. I'm hoping for the former."

"Geez, this day has just been full of surprises." Josie couldn't figure out what Cleve was up to, but it didn't really matter. She was already having a good time.

Cleve drove along the Navesink River Road until they reached the intersection of Cooper Road. He made a left-hand turn.

"Familiar territory," Josie observed. The Parker home was only a mile or so away. Josie smiled and wondered what her dad would think if he knew she was on a date with Cleve Gregory after all these years. She hadn't even bothered to tell him she'd seen Cleve in New York.

They were traveling in the direction of Hidden Green Farm. They rolled along the asphalt hills and eventually passed the big sign indicating the turn-off to Barrett Park. Now the Hidden Green gelding pasture was on their right, and as they approached the entrance to the farm, Cleve put his blinker on.

"What?" Josie still had no clue what was going on. "Why are we stopping here? Wouldn't it make more sense to do this during the daylight?"

"Hold your horses, missy. Just go with me on this," Cleve teased. He pulled up to the barn and parked the car. Josie noticed the old HGF six-horse van parked in the courtyard. She didn't remember Mr. O'Hara ever having left it there. She also noticed that the floodlights mounted to the peak of the barn were on, glaringly, leading her to believe that someone knew she and Cleve would be showing up there tonight. Cleve reached over and grabbed the grocery bag.

"Here, hang onto this. I'll come around and get you. Wait just a second." He reached into the back seat again and retrieved a lantern that Josie had not noticed earlier. He turned it on and got out of the car. Her door opened and, holding the lantern in one hand, Cleve reached out an arm to Josie.

"What is going on?" she demanded.

"I told you, Josie Parker, I have a special place to take you for dinner. Chinese takeout dinner, by lantern light, in the Hidden Green six-horse van. We had some good moments in that van, moments that have kept my dream alive for a long time now."

"Cleve, I don't know what to say." She climbed out of the car. "I'm gonna cry again." She was shaking now, not from the cold, but rather from the incredibly romantic gesture being offered on her behalf.

"No, you're not. Your tears will freeze and then I won't know what to do. Come on, Mike O'Hara left it unlocked for me and promised there would be some old horse coolers inside so we won't freeze to death." He opened one of the van doors and pulled himself, lantern in one hand, up into the van, then turned to help Josie. She gave him the bag of food and then reached her hand up to his. He pulled her up into the van, holding onto her for a few seconds longer than necessary. She was acutely aware of the strength in his grip.

He grabbed a pile of coolers from the cabinet. *That cabinet,* Josie thought. He spread some of them out on the floor of the van, and some over the hay bales Mike O'Hara had left there for them to lean on. He handed one to Josie to put over her shoulders. She noticed the tattered monogram on it.

"This one was Tessa's." She held it up to show him then gave it an affectionate hug, breathing in the past. He hooked the lantern up to one of the crossties and looked at Josie.

"OK, we're all set. May I offer you a seat, mademoiselle?" Cleve gestured towards the floor, suggesting they use the hay bales as a backrest. They sat down together, side by side, and he opened all the little white containers. "Chopsticks?" he offered, smiling.

"Thank you." Josie snapped the little bamboo sticks apart.

"Now, speaking of Tessa, tell me about her and Alan Harmon! Are they really married and living in Wellington?"

Without a hitch, the evening flew by, and if it was cold in that van Josie never felt it. There was never an awkward moment or pause in conversation. As she told him about Tessa, Alan, and baby Rosilyn, Cleve opened a bottle of red wine and poured some into two plastic cups he had brought along. The lantern light gave the van an uncanny romantic charm, and the coolers spread everywhere made it cozy and comfortable. The two shared the food, the wine, and dozens of stories of life that had been written in the last ten years. The saga of Lars was difficult for Josie to tell, for so often back then Cleve had been on her mind and conspicuously absent.

"Sadly, I was never able to track him down. Too much time had gone by. Jack had sent him to that Pennsylvania auction place, far away. I didn't know where to even begin to look. It crippled me. I'm not ashamed to tell you, I didn't set foot in a barn for more than five years after Lars disappeared. I was so angry over yet another loss. He was such a terrific horse, Cleve. We had an amazing bond. You would have seen the talent in him, just the way I did, I know it. And he was only seven years old."

"Well, I sort of know what it's like to not know where to start looking for someone. Funny thing is, and no pun intended, but sometimes you find that what you are looking for is practically right in your own backyard, a whole lot closer than you ever thought it might be. I mean look at us, Jos'. It never would have occurred to me that you were right there in Colts Neck. Never."

She told him about nursing and about finally going back to Hidden Green three-and-a-half years ago, and how William Fells just happened to have been there shoeing on that particular day.

"William told me he knew that Kenna Mahon was looking for a new barn manager and asked me if he could give her my phone number. He told me, 'You don't want to work here, Josie. Mike's become so involved in the damn fox hunting thing that there aren't really any show boarders here any more. The place is getting really run down. There is no riding school at all. I think he auctioned most of the school horses. William told me that Libby O. and Mike had had a big falling out. Not sure over what, but they don't talk to one another any more. When Kenna called me, I told her it would take me awhile to get up to speed, but that after three months if she wasn't pleased with my work, she could give me the boot, no hard feelings. Seemed fair. I've been there ever since."

"And it seems to be a perfect match. You're happy there, I can tell."

31

"OK, Cleve Gregory, enough about me and everyone else we know. Let's hear your story. How did you go from Wall Street suit to Doc Thurman's vet tech? Actually, how did you get to Wall Street?" Josie asked but she wasn't truly sure that she wanted to know. Everything about tonight had been perfect so far. She didn't want anything to rock the boat. Or the van, as it was.

"Well, pass me that bottle of wine then. I'll only drink just enough to give me courage, not so much that I won't be able to escort you home safely, I promise."

"Don't worry, I will keep my eye on you." She smiled.

Cleve took a hefty gulp from his plastic cup and set it down next to an empty food container. He swiped his hair across his forehead. *So sexy,* she thought.

"My life was pretty fucked up when I came to your mama's funeral, Jos'." He paused for a few seconds, trying to remember something. "A wise person, one of the Greeks I think, said, 'Things are not always what they seem; the first appearance deceives many; the intelligence of a few perceives what has carefully been hidden.' I read that in some book at Parson Prep and it was like reading about myself. My life was the perfect illustration of that quote. At the barn, life was great. I had purpose there, I felt like I made a difference. Mike O'Hara was invested in me; he taught me so much about running a farm. You were there, and you found value in what we tried to accomplish with the horses. Man, I loved training horses with you, and ya know, we did a lot for some of those nags." He winked. "Just about everyone else saw me as nothing more than some farm hand who was probably never gonna amount to much. Everybody else being my parents and their snooty friends. I asked my dad once, 'What if I want to be a farmer? What if my goal is not to go to Harvard or Princeton, but to have an amazing farm in Monmouth County that produces livestock and produce?' He waved me off. Waved me off, wouldn't even have a conversation about it. Once I even overheard Joni's ma telling Rachel's that it seemed such a waste for my parents to pay tuition to send me to Parson Prep when all I wanted to do was muck stalls." Cleve rolled his eyes and smirked. He stretched his legs out in front of him then leaned to one side, resting on an elbow. "Can you believe that? They judged me so inaccurately because I liked working at the barn. Did they know that I got straight A's at Parson Prep? That I made National Honor Society? No, they didn't. That probably would have made some difference to them, but none of it made a difference to me. And here's the twist, Jos', here's what messed me up; I worked really hard at what mattered to me and I went home exhausted every night just to be admonished for not being who my parents wanted me to be. The stuff they wanted me to pursue was easy for me, and totally boring. I wanted to be around horses, not on a baseball diamond. I wanted to be around you, not girls who threw themselves at me; you had your shit so much more together than any other girl I knew. And it completely blew my self-confidence that everyone only saw me as a bum because I didn't subscribe to the college prep mantra. It felt like the only people who got me were you and Mike O'Hara. The things that intrigued me, like knowing how to operate farm machinery, or figuring out what makes a horse tick; the things that provoked me, like trying to figure out how to come up with the honorable way to get closer to the coolest girl I'd ever met. Those were the things my parents criticized me for. My father was unrelenting, 'You want to hang out at a barn fixing tractors and broken down thoroughbreds? You'll wind up working at a gas station, or on the backstretch at some race track. You want to chase a girl who probably won't even go to college? That's bum behavior, Cleve, and I won't stand for it.'

"So I started hanging around with bums, my brother and his worthless friends. I hated it, but I felt like I was calling my parents' bluff and there was some redeeming quality in that for a pissed-off, seventeen-year-old guy. I was caught in a crossfire between what I knew was right for me and what my parents thought would make them look good."

Josie sat up and divided the remaining wine into the two plastic cups. "Wow, that's pretty heavy stuff. You don't have to keep going if you don't want to, Cleve. Really."

"It's OK, I want you to know what happened. But I'd rather not have to ever talk about it again after tonight. One of my greatest regrets is that I never found a way to tell you all this back then. It was a really rough time. And believe me, I know you've had some horrible stuff happen, I mean..." He paused and looked at her.

"No, don't worry. You are not being selfish, Cleve. We have a lot of catching up to do, and I want to hear everything." She reached out and touched his arm, encouraging him. "Keep going, please."

Cleve moved to sit next to her. "Man, the day you said to me, 'You're not who I thought you were, Cleve'? Man, that day was the worst. I wanted to say back to you, 'Yes, Josie, yes I am! I'm exactly who you think I am, it's just that no one will let me *be* that guy!' You were the one who understood the real me, the one who made me feel like the things that mattered to me—well, mattered.

"My father made me play baseball—the best way, according to him, to get recruited to the Ivy League schools—and my mother believed that a person's most important attributes were good connections. Listen, I knew they had my best interests in mind, but I just couldn't handle the constant berating for wanting to spend my free time at the barn.

"And here is the icing on the cake, are you ready? You won't believe this, Jos'. I was already about as conflicted as a seventeen-year-old guy could be, and on the same night that you and I rode home together in the van from State Spring, the night that I felt the warmth of your hand in mine in the back seat of your dad's car..." Cleve had tears in his eyes now. "On that very night, I arrived home to the middle of a shouting match going on between my folks, only to find out my father had been cheating on my mother for over two years, and he was going to divorce her. Yup, my fucking hypocrite father. The man who was always preaching about integrity, credibility, hard work, and dedication. And he's a total counterfeit, cheating on my mother. And my mother, always going on and on about how important quality education is, how it defines a person, and how beneficial it would be for my future if I associated with the 'right' people." He stared at the floor of the van and shook his head.

"Cleve." Josie reached out a hand. He pushed his own arm straight out from his body, beckoning quiet.

"I wanted so badly to ask her that night, 'Hey Mom, so how's it working out for you to be married to a guy with an undergraduate degree from Dartmouth, an MBA from Wharton, and a membership to the Rumson Country Club? How's that working out for ya, Mom? Because from where I stand it's not lookin' like it's so great.' But I could never do that to my mom." Again he stared down at the floor.

"Cleve." Josie didn't want him to feel the pain he was clearly experiencing as he relived those moments. "Hey." She tilted her head so that her face was looking up at his, and she smiled. She raised her hand and gently pushed his hair from his forehead.

"No, it's OK, the story is almost over." He got up and moved around for a minute or two, then sat back down next to Josie on the hay bale, elbows on his thighs, hands clasped together. He leaned toward her, as if to assure himself she was listening.

"I'm listening. Every word, I promise. Go ahead." She put a hand gently on his knee, then on his back. She leaned in close, and smiled again.

"So here's the thing. When I didn't show up at the barn the next day, it wasn't because of you. It wasn't because of the van ride home. It wasn't because I was high. It was because of my fucking parents, because of them and their bullshit, phony hype, and I had been up all night. I was crippled with sadness, I was angry, and I was damn confused.

"Then you showed up at the house, and you made it pretty clear that you too, just like everyone else, thought I was a fuck-up. And honestly, Josie, it was a shaker of salt in my already excruciating wound. I don't blame you, of course. You had no idea. But I was so empty at that point I couldn't begin to try to defend myself, and you ran away. Again, I don't blame you. I should have chased after you right then; that was my fatal mistake. And then," he hesitated, "then your mother died. And everything changed. I felt surrounded by loss, just like you. Weird, huh? We were, in a sense, in the same place. The difference was you knew you had to stay and I knew I had to get out of there. So I made a plan. I wasn't going to finish at Parson Prep. The day after your mama's funeral I planned to leave town with the money I had in my pocket and a beat-up truck I was going to buy. But my plan got stymied. Amazingly, it got stymied in my favor.

"My folks' war was just beginning that Saturday night. It continued into the week and by the time Tuesday rolled around, my mother was completely broken. My father was having a kid with another woman. He served my mother with divorce papers in the A&P parking lot. She considered herself road kill. She piled us in the station wagon, and we were gone just days after your mama's funeral."

Josie couldn't believe all of this had happened to Cleve the week Mama had died. She felt terrible, selfish. Really selfish. She had not given him the benefit of the doubt. She had judged him wrongly even after he'd come to her house and asked her not to give up. She listened intently as he continued.

"We moved to Virginia. My mom went to stay with her parents in Warrenton. I moved to Keswick and worked for three years at Peter Randolph's amazing hunter barn. You've heard of him, right? He's got incredible horses, and he is a complete class act. He became a real father figure for me. Saved me, I'd say. What an amazing time that was and we are still so close. Working there was so cool —I mean, Charlie Weaver and Martha Sifton worked for him then too!" He took a deep breath. "I thought of you so often, Josie. There was so much I wanted to share with you." He paused and let the sentence hang. "I worked really hard, saved my money, finished high school with night classes, and thought constantly about what it would take to win your love back—not take your love, but win it. I wanted a shot at you loving me for all the same reasons that I love you."

He seemed almost energized now. This was a part of his story that he was anxious to share, actually proud of. Josie tipped the wine bottle one more time. Empty. Cleve stood up and paced in the van, continuing.

"At Peter's urging, I decided to give college a try. He told me not to worry about what I would do with an education, just to get one first. I got a full scholarship to the University of Virginia, courtesy of the Randolph family. They are Thomas Jefferson's cousins or something like that. I'm not kidding. You know who they are, come on."

He cracked a big smile and Josie was relieved.

"They let me live on the farm rent free while I went to school. I just helped out when I could. My mom—my pitiful, sweet mom—was as invested as she could be. She sent me a little cash every once in a while, which really helped, but she was losing a serious battle against her own demons. She has never been the same, Jos'. My beautiful mom, ravaged by that prick.

"Anyway, after UVA, I went to work in New York for a few years. Wall Street. You know that part." He shook his head and shrugged. "Peter suggested that it would be the experience of a lifetime. Can you believe that? Me, an associate at Randolph Brothers LLC, in the Big Apple. J. Press suits, Hermès ties, the whole nine yards.

"Then, there you were on Lexington Avenue, telling me everything with you was great, so I just figured I would tell you everything was great with me too. And it was. But seeing you that day triggered something in me. It stirred so many feelings in me that I had subconsciously suppressed. I realized, especially after you didn't take my call, that I was avoiding unfinished business, and so were you. It tortured me for many, many nights. So finally, I went to the hospital. To Lenox Hill. I had every intention then of telling you the whole story, telling you how it was that I wound up in that suit, in New York. But you weren't there. You were gone, and no one had any forwarding information. If they did, they didn't want to give it to me and I couldn't blame them. So I stuck out Wall Street for as long as I could. The money was pretty good and I got real lucky. But I knew I didn't want to live in the concrete jungle forever. I missed grass under my boots, the smell of a farm, the sounds in a barn at feed time. Peter Randolph counseled me. He told me that men are motivated to do things for different reasons. He told me that in his experience the most successful men are those who are motivated by passion. And he told me I would never fail if I pursued what I truly loved. So, almost two years ago, I came back here to pursue what I knew mattered most." He took a deep breath. "And that brings us almost to the present."

He stood in the center of the van, arms stretched from side to side, a mile-wide grin on his face. Josie gently clapped her hands and tilted her head back, laughing joyfully.

"Here I am." He put his hands in the front pockets of his jeans. "Veterinary assistant to Doctor Peter Thurman and standing in front of the girl I have loved every day for the last twelve years. Every day, Josie. Even after the day in New York, when I thought maybe I didn't like you so much. That was like bumping into someone else who happened to be named Josie Parker. But once I realized that I had rather misrepresented my real self to you, I hoped maybe you had done the same." He looked into her eyes now, into her soul, into *her*, to be sure she heard those words.

Then, to assuage the heaviness of the moment, he said, "And now here we are in a fifteen-year-old horse van that smells like Chinese take-out!"

"I'm exhausted from all that!" Josie kidded.

The two of them laughed and started to fold up the coolers. They continued to talk, but more now about the minutia of life. As Josie handed him the last folded cooler, Cleve nodded in the direction of the cabinet's open door.

"Hey, what do you think? Should we give it a go?" he teased.

Josie chuckled and without hesitation said, "In your dreams Gregory, in your dreams."

"Oh, trust me, Parker, I've been in there a million times in my dreams."

32

The pickup motored along, and when they were a few miles from the cottage, Cleve reached out slowly and took Josie's hand. His touch was warm and familiar and full of affection, and somehow felt much more significant than the last time he'd done it. They hadn't spoken much since they'd begun the trip back, but truly no words were necessary. Cleve reached to turn up the volume as Phil Collins' voice came through the radio speakers, then took Josie's hand back in his.

How can I just let you walk away, just let you leave without a trace? When I stand here taking every breath with you. You're the only one who really knew me at all...

Cleve looked over at Josie and squeezed her hand a little harder. She reached across with her other hand and wrapped it over his. Only the radio filled the truck with words. She closed her eyes. Here and there Cleve sang along.

But to wait for you is all I can do and it's what I've got to face. Take a good look at me now, 'cause I'll be standing here, and you coming back to me is against all odds. It's the chance I've got to take. So take a look at me now... He pulled the truck to a stop in the driveway and turned off the engine.

They walked up the front path, arms around one another, neither wanting to let go. Each afraid to let the other disappear into the night, in fear of losing—again—something that had finally been found. Josie opened the front door to the cottage, stepped onto the threshold, and turned back. The dogs ran past her, past Cleve, and out into the dark. She followed them with her eyes and, looking up, noticed the snow beginning to fall. She smiled and turned her focus to Cleve.

"It's snowing," she whispered, and stepped back down into the night, so close to him she could feel his breath on her face.

"You're beautiful," he whispered back.

"Thank you, and thank you for tonight. For today too. The whole thing has been surreal. There are no words to describe this."

"No more words, then."

Cleve touched her cheek with his warm hand. He tilted her face up to his and kissed her. She accepted his kiss, parting her lips slowly, and when he offered her the taste buds of his tongue, she shared her own with him. This was not a teenage kiss. This was a kiss that spoke a thousand words. This was a kiss that had begun ten years ago but tonight was very much about the present. Josie felt it throughout her whole body, heart, and soul. It was just one kiss, but it was the only kiss that had ever mattered in Josie Parker's entire life. She knew right then that Cleve Gregory was going to be a part of her story forever. She had no intention of letting him disappear again.

"We've lived in parallel emotions," she said.

Breathing in deeply, Cleve bear-hugged Josie, then kissed her on the forehead.

"With your permission, I will call you tomorrow. This has been a great night. Guys aren't usually much for the word 'magic,' but the whole damn day has been just that." He held both her hands in his for a minute, then let go and backed a few steps down the path, holding her gaze with his until he looked up at the falling snow and, smiling, said, "Remember, we've got John Courage to thank for this. That funny-lookin' chestnut horse with the shivers. He's the magician. Good night, Josie Parker."

"Good night, Cleve Gregory."

Josie stood in the threshold until his truck had turned around and was headed down the driveway. She waved to the fading tail lights. *If this is a dream, it sure is a good one,* she thought to herself.

"Here!" she hollered for the dogs. "Shorty! Ralphie! Here!" They came bounding in, way too cold to defy her command tonight. She leaned her shoulder against the front door to engage the lock, then pressed her back against it and closed her eyes. *This has been an amazing day*, she thought. *I suppose that fairy tales do come true, after all.* Josie looked down at her right hand and spun the sapphire and diamond ring around on her finger. "Thanks, Mama," she said out loud. "Love you."

She tossed her hat and gloves in the basket and hung her coat and scarf, then turned out the lights and shooed the dogs toward her bedroom.

The ringing phone woke Josie from a sound sleep. She had no notion of what time it was, and no reason to feel alarmed. She picked up the receiver.

"This better be good," she said, with no idea of whom she was addressing.

"Well, if you are happy to hear from me, then it's good. Otherwise, I guess I'm pooched. I'm hoping for the former," Cleve said, feeling oddly as though he'd just said something like that to her yesterday.

"Good morning." She felt a smile emerge through her sleepy haze. "What time is it, anyway? I was comatose. The red wine, I think." Josie pulled herself up and sat against her headboard. She couldn't believe she was actually talking to Cleve. The clock said 7:12 a.m. "How are you today? I guess this means yesterday was not a dream after all." For some strange reason she felt compelled to fluff her hair.

"As a friend of mine once said, if I were any better, there would have to be two of me. Not really sure what that means, but it was always worth a laugh on the Randolph Brothers trading floor. I do know what you mean, though. I was afraid to open my eyes this morning too. I'm extremely happy to report that yesterday was *not* a dream. Hey, listen, I have an idea."

"Shoot. I'm all ears. Wait, hold on one second, the dogs are staring me down. Be right back." She put the phone down, threw off the covers, rose from her bed, and walked through the cottage to the back door.

"Wow, it really snowed last night," she said out loud as she opened up the door to let the dogs out.

She came back to the phone and repeated herself. "It really snowed last night. It's beautiful here. Not sure my barn roof can handle the weight of it, though. One of these days the whole thing is bound to cave in."

"Hey, Earth to Josie Parker, I'm trying to ask you out on what will hopefully be our second date. Listen up!" he goaded.

"Sorry, sorry." She giggled.

"Saturday night is the Grand Prix at the National. What do you say we get dressed up real fancy and go to the Garden and watch? I happen to have some credentials for the exhibitors' section. We can go for dinner at Tavern on the Green or even Trader Vic's before. I think I can finagle a reservation somewhere. Might have to be on the early side, I think the class probably starts at seven. Any interest? Wasn't sure how you'd feel about the black tie part."

"Wow, that's a pretty impressive option for a second date. The first one was quite creative too. How are you gonna be able to keep this up, Gregory?" she teased. "Sounds like a great idea. I just have to see what is going on at the barn. What time would we have to head in, like five?"

"Yeah, we could drive, or we could take the train from Red Bank. Either way I would have to get you at your place around four thirty. You game?"

"I'm pretty sure, yes. I mean I would really like to accept, I just need to check the work board, OK? Can you give me a call at Clover Field later? Or tonight?" Josie flashed back to a time at Hidden Green when she'd been too insecure to ask Cleve to give her a call. Here, now, it seemed so natural.

"How about I call you at home tonight? By then I should have a better idea about Trader Vic's or Tavern, and it will give me a chance to check on the train schedule. Is that OK? You gonna be home tonight?"

"You checking up on me, mister? Sounds like you might be trying to figure out how full my dance card is." She was teasing him but she also knew she was right.

"Hey a guy can't be too careful these days. Lots of competition out there, especially over the really cool girls. And if they're cool and pretty too, well then hey, it's like, take a number," he teased right back, laughing. "I'll talk to you later. Get going, you're late for work now."

Josie remembered that the dogs were still outside with no jackets. She also remembered she was supposed to call Tessa first thing this morning. Tessa would have to wait. It would probably torture her, but Josie was truly already late for the barn. Besides, not only was she going to have to reveal every detail of last night, but now she would need some help figuring out Saturday night. She would call Tessa later.

Black tie? What have I got that is fancy enough for Saturday night at the National Horse Show? Maybe one of Mama's dresses, let's hope.

She tried to remember which of Mama's beautiful long dresses she had made the choice to save, thinking that she might have use for them someday. She'd left them at her dad's house until she bought the Haskell cottage. Now they were up in the guest room closet. No time to check now.

She let the dogs in and put some food down for them.

"Sorry guys, I forgot about you! I know it's freezing out there." She picked up the phone and called Clover Field.

"Everything OK there, Ramon?" She listened to the voice on the other end of the line. "OK, no problem. I'm just about to get on my way, see you in a bit. I think I will flat the chestnut horse this morning, so you can go ahead and get him ready, OK? Thanks."

Josie bundled herself and the dogs up, grabbed a couple pieces of toast and a cup of coffee to go, and headed for her truck. *These next few days are going to be slow as molasses,* she thought to herself. As she drove along she thought about what Saturday night would bring.

33

"Your new horse is amazing, Addie! You are going to freak out! When are you coming back to the barn? Tuesday? He is so comfortable and so straight. I've ridden him every day since he arrived and he is super cool." Josie didn't mention the spin. "I'm working on his manners—that may take us some time, but he has incredible personality, and he is quite the cookie monster. He loves those molasses treats. He already expects them whenever I open the stall door. I think he's making friends with Sparks the cat too; I found her asleep twice in his stall. She's his little mascot. He's a funny, funny horse."

Josie was so excited to be at the National Horse Show with Cleve, and she couldn't wait to introduce him to the Crawfords. He looked like Clark Gable in his shawl collar tuxedo and velvet slippers. She wondered where he had ever learned to dress like that.

"You know, Southerners are very proper," he'd told Josie when she complimented him on how well he cleaned up. "I learned some incredible lessons when I worked in Keswick. Ol' Thomas Jefferson's cousins, they took right good care to teach me chivalry and the art of being a gentleman. You can let me know how I'm doin' any time you like." He winked at her and added, in a very southern accent, "Ma'am— or I suppose I should properly say, Miss Josie."

Pamela Crawford extended her hand to Cleve.

"Wow Josie, where exactly did you find this hunk? Have you been hiding him in your barn at home?" Cleve reciprocated the handshake as she continued, "This gal is very special to me, Mr. Gregory. I'm gonna keep a close eye on you. Hard not to keep a close eye on you, actually," she kidded and then winked at Josie, executing a flirtatious little dip in her beaded black gown, tickled by her own pun. She tossed her fur stole over her shoulder.

"Have you met my daughter, Addie?" Cleve responded with a quick gentleman's bow. Addie smiled and nodded, then turned to give a very obvious thumbs-up sign to Josie. All three girls giggled.

"Addie, you look gorgeous. That dress is so cool. I love navy velvet. You had someone in the city do your hair, didn't you? It's awesome." Josie lightly touched Addie's French twist. She loved this kid.

Pamela was especially vibrant and enthusiastic tonight. Addie had done well in all her classes, and although she hadn't won any blue ribbons, she had come quite close a few times and had proven herself to be one of the coming year's "ones to watch." The entire Crawford family was in attendance and Pamela was playing her best "hostess with the mostest," role, even though they were all just sitting in the stands at Madison Square Garden. She invited Josie and Cleve to join them in her private box and they accepted. Cleve excused himself for a few minutes to go say hello to Armand and a few other guys whom he knew from Virginia.

"Hey, I will meet you up there in about fifteen minutes, OK? I just wanna go see some of the old guard. You OK with that, beautiful girl? You *are* beautiful, you know. That dress fits you to perfection," he whispered in her ear.

"So I've been told, by you anyway," she responded coyly, and turned to walk with Pamela.

"You look stunning, Josie! That dress is spectacular! Your figure, my God! That brooch is phenomenal; it's Schlumberger isn't it? His work is so recognizable, so Parisian! Let me just look at you. I've never seen you in anything but barn duds. You are absolutely gorgeous, and not a stitch of makeup! Addie, look at Josie, she is a beauty. Look at this ring, oh my God! Addie, look at this ring. An heirloom, right? It has to be an heirloom." She lifted Josie's right hand to admire the jewel of the jewel box. "Addie, look," she said again.

"It's been handed down for five generations that we know about. I inherited it when my mama died. It's what I have to keep her memory alive," Josie offered, trying to keep the details short. She didn't want to be a bore. "My dad gave me her entire collection of jewelry and told me that someday it would bring my own story to life. I was just about your age when she died, Addie. She was an amazing woman and we were very close. You and your mom remind me so often of what she and I were like, and what she and I might have been like. I'm wearing one of her dresses too. And yes, Pammy, the pin is Schlumberger. It was hers as well."

"Well your mama certainly had style, that is quite evident, and I am sure she passed more than just jewels and clothing on to you. Clearly you embody her spirit, Josie. I mean look at you, your eyes are sparkling tonight. Look at that young man." She nodded down toward the exhibitors' section. Cleve just happened to be looking up at them. Josie blushed. "He is head over heels mad for you. Look, he can't keep his eyes off of you. If I didn't know better, I would guess the two of you are in L-O-V-E. You have a very special way about you, Josie Parker, and I'm betting your mama had a lot to do with that."

"Thanks, Pam." Josie felt tears welling and Pamela seemed to notice. She politely changed the subject.

"So the new horse is great? We are so excited for Tuesday. Aren't you proud of Addie? A call back in the Maclay, and Classified won two thirds and was second in the hack in the large juniors. Come, the Grand Prix is about to start, let's sit." Pamela pointed to her box.

"What did you say his name was?" Addie asked, sliding into the seat next to Josie.

"John Courage," Josie said, crossing two fingers on her right hand. "I've just been calling him Johnnie."

"I like it. John Courage. Whatever it means." Addie shook her head affirmatively.

"John Courage founded a beer company in England in the 1700s," Cleve said as he reappeared and took the seat on the other side of Addie. He winked at Josie as he sat down. "It's pretty good ale if I do say so myself." He gave Addie Crawford a nudge. She smiled a shy, sixteen-year-old Josie Parker kind of smile.

Cleve stood and introduced himself to Pamela's husband Layton upon his late arrival, and the newly acquainted group of friends proceeded to have a wonderful evening watching US Olympian Joe Fargis ride to victory on Touch of Class in the Grand Prix.

They caught the last train back to Red Bank by the skin of their teeth. Josie held Cleve's hand as they whisked down the escalator and ran across the platform in their formal attire, garnering some very strange looks. They leapt into the train car and flopped down onto one of the two-facing-two bench seats.

"Everyone must be at the Studio 54 after party," Cleve kidded Josie. The train was less than half full; not many people headed to the Jersey Shore this late on a Saturday night.

As the train pulled out of the tunnel and into the dark, cold November night, Cleve leaned his head back and took Josie's hand in his, once again. He looked down at the sapphire and diamond jewel on her finger.

"That is a beautiful ring, Jos'. I think I might have seen your mama wearing that a time or two when she used to make breakfast for me on Saturday mornings."

"Wow, yes, it's the same one." She held her hand out in front of her. "My dad gave it to me. I usually never have any place to wear it." As the train rumbled along, stopping at all the stations en route to Red Bank, Josie told Cleve about the silver box, one story that hadn't been told in the van the other night. She told him, as best she could remember, the context of the letter her dad had given her along with the box, and about the heart-shaped locket for her goddaughter.

"That locket is the only piece I've parted with. All the others are waiting to make some magic for me." She winked when she said it.

"Knowing your mama, she's somewhere in the universe lining it all up for you as we speak, Josie Parker." He squeezed her hand, and after they both propped their legs up on the seats facing them, they closed their eyes to sleep. As she dozed off, the gentle back and forth motion of the train car reminded Josie of the van ride home from the horse show years ago. Now, though it had only been four days, Josie had a confident feeling that this time around she and Cleve were, as they say in the equestrian world, "good to go."

Although there had been a few times along the way when Cleve tried to push himself to someone else, it always came back to Josie Parker. Here and now, over ten years later, she was even smarter, even more beautiful, and even more passionate about what she loved in life. Her generosity of spirit was indelibly contagious; anyone who knew her was better because of it. He knew for certain that he was.

Relaxing to the hypnotic motion of the train car, Cleve pondered the possible explanations for just how it came to be that he and Josie were sitting there with one another now. *John Courage? Magic?* He considered the horse and the concept. *Right place, right time? I don't know.* Perhaps it was simple inevitability, but it sure seemed like something more than logic tonight.

The train pulled into the Red Bank station and Josie, as though she somehow instinctively knew they were there, lifted her head from Cleve's shoulder and gathered her things. She smiled at Cleve, but was too groggy to speak. They stood, then moved to the end of the train car. Cleve raised his hand to her face, gently pushing her tousled hair back around her ear.

"I'm going with magic," he said quietly, looking into her sleepy brown eyes.

"Sorry, what did you say?" she asked languidly.

"Nothing." He smiled and helped her onto the platform.

The drive home from Red Bank was quick and quiet; both of them were tired. As they pulled up to the cottage, Josie looked over and could see the fatigue in Cleve's handsome face. They walked hand in hand to the door.

"That was a really great time tonight, wasn't it Jos'? I saw so many old buddies, the jump-off was great, and I really like the Crawfords. I gotta tell ya, I'm smitten with that Addie. She reminds me a little of you. Not nearly as beautiful though. You had the best braids ever." He touched her hair affectionately. "And freckles."

"Hey," she said, "you look so tired and I know you've still got a long drive home. It's well after one o'clock. Don't take this the wrong way, but my second bedroom is all made up. You'll just have to put up with Shorty, he'll be nestled in there with you 'til the sun comes up." She was nervous, having just suggested that he spend the night.

He pulled her body to his and gently rocked her side to side, relinquishing the angst he could sense in her.

"I could make a joke right now about having slept with some dogs in my life, but this is no moment for a joke. So I accept your offer, thanks. I am beat, for sure. As for who nestles in with whom—that, sweet girl, remains to be seen."

He held her firmly in his arms now.

"Josie Parker. Right here in my arms, finally."

He pulled her closer and kissed her. A long, gentle kiss at first, and then another with absolute intention. Josie's knees went weak as their tongues connected perfectly, for just the right amount of time. No more words were exchanged.

Cleve followed Josie into the cottage and the front porch light went dark.

34

Thanksgiving at the Parkers was the best it had been in years. Josie brought Cleve and the dogs to her dad's house for turkey dinner. Everyone was happy; Frank had someone to watch sports with while Josie and Gayle prepared the meal. The dinner conversation took on a new dimension with Cleve there to add stories that hadn't been rehashed every year for the last twenty! Josie told everyone all about Johnnie.

"Something about you and chestnut horses, Rosebud. You seem to be their savior. Those in need find their way to you somehow."

"Well, my track record isn't too good so far, but this one has found his way into a great family. The Crawfords love him. They take great care of their horses, so I think he's gonna be fine."

Frank Parker had kept a warm fire burning all day and into the evening, and after pumpkin pie and coffee, the men moved to the living room to watch some football. An hour or so passed and Josie, who'd been dozing herself, realized her dad was snoring in his favorite chair. She gently tapped Cleve on the arm, signaling that it was time to leave.

"Dad, get some shut-eye. It's been a long, great day." She leaned over her dad and whispered, "Thanks so much for having us. She kissed her dad on his forehead. *How many times has he done that to me over the years?*

Cleve came up behind Josie, put his hands on her shoulders, and leaned in to say good night to Frank. "Good night, sir. Please, don't get up, you've been runnin' around here for us all day. Great day, great food, awesome football. Thanks again."

They each hugged Aunt Gayle and Cleve headed out to warm up the truck.

Aunt Gayle handed Josie some containers of leftovers and said to her only niece, "He is absolutely precious, Josie. He's grown up such a gentleman, so smart and driven by the same things that drive you. How lucky that after all the time that's gone by, you have found one another again. How wonderful that you have childhood history to share, and what a gift it is that he knew your mama." She put her arm around her niece as they walked towards the front door. Josie glanced at the staircase and flashed back, just for a second. "I know I'm not her, but sometimes a girl just needs to talk to her mother. I'd probably be a half-assed substitute, but just know that I am always here. Take your time with that one, he's a keeper." They hugged again.

"Thanks, Aunt Gayle. Love you. Happy Thanksgiving." Josie, Cleve, and the dogs left for home.

Well into December, with Christmas approaching, Josie began to dread that Johnnie would be departing for Wellington soon. Most of the horses had shipped not long after Thanksgiving to enjoy some turnout in South Carolina before arriving in sunny Florida, but the juniors' horses typically stayed north until after the holidays.

Addie Crawford was having a great time getting to know her new horse. She loved riding Johnnie; he was completely uncomplicated for her, and she suited him perfectly. The days Addie couldn't make it to the barn, the ride belonged to Josie. On those days, if his schedule allowed, Cleve would come by the barn.

"I hate to seem cliché, but everything seems to happen for a reason," Kenna said to Josie one afternoon at the barn. "That horse loves two people, you and Addie. She rides that horse better than I can imagine her riding any other. You'd think she's had him for years, and you've prepared him so perfectly. I have high hopes for them in Florida. Too bad he is such a prick in his stall. She loves her animals so much and she's a little afraid of him when she's on the ground, for sure. He's gonna be a pain in the ass for me without you in Florida. He has a great respect for you."

"He and I have, let's say, a mutual understanding." Josie laughed out loud. "I'm not sure he will ever be an easy horse to work around, but I've pretty much got his number and he seems to know that I do. Since the day he got here, Kens', you know I've been so intrigued by him, he's been my pet project. He's really a special animal. He is finicky though, for sure. That shivers thing has to be kept in mind. I've shared a lot with Addie, and Ramon will be just fine handling him. I am sure gonna miss him though."

"Speaking of things happening for a reason," Kenna inquired, "looks to me like you've got a little love connection goin' on, girlfriend, with a pretty cool guy. I like Cleve Gregory a lot. I remember him from back when you and he used to groom for Mike O'Hara's kids at the shows around here. Come to think of it, didn't he work for the Randolphs down in Keswick for awhile?"

"Yeah, we have a pretty cool history with each other. It's been a long road for both of us, but we have a good thing now."

"Well bring him to the Clover Field Christmas party next week. Ask Doc Thurman to come, too. What a great guy he is, always willing to help us out. Hey, about the party..."

Josie and Kenna sat in the farm office and talked for a long while—about the Christmas party, yes, but more about getting organized for the exodus to Wellington, which was less than a month away. Feeling like they were in pretty good shape, as the sun sank low into the wintry sky, they called it a day.

On her way home, Josie detoured to stop at Delicious Orchards on Route 537 to buy a Christmas tree and a wreath for the cottage. She loved choosing her tree here every year. She was particular and D.O. had the best. They also happened to have the best chocolate chip cookies, and she liked giving them as Christmas gifts to the grooms and customers at the barn. She filled her shopping basket with packages of cookies, then headed out to the Christmas Shoppe. This outing could not be rushed, and Josie fretted over picking just the right tree. She wandered up and down the rows of evergreens.

"OK, that's the one." She nodded, pointing to a beautiful, full Fraser fir. "Could you give it a fresh cut please, and put it in the bed of that old blue pickup out front? Thanks. I'm gonna go grab a wreath and settle up. Thanks, here you go." Josie handed a five-dollar tip to the laborer. "Merry Christmas."

As she walked toward the display of wreaths, she noticed quite a commotion near a door that led into one of the greenhouses. A small group of people had gathered around a wire pen that corralled five adorable mixed breed puppies, rolling and wrestling one another. A few young children were on their knees, reaching in to play with the pups, and a man sat on a small stool next to the pen, holding a sixth pup in his lap.

"This one's a bit shy, not so sure about all the wrestling going on in there." The man massaged the little sweetheart with a comforting hand, then lifted him up to Josie, who couldn't resist taking him into her arms.

"Oh my, you are the cutest thing, aren't you? They're for sale?" she asked, wheels starting to spin in her brain. The man nodded as the puppy licked Josie's face, making her laugh. "You certainly make a great sales pitch, little one. How much for this critter right here?" She had decided, before she even asked the price, that a puppy was the perfect Christmas present for Cleve.

Josie navigated her way out of the parking lot with her tree, her wreath, and the new puppy, far more broke than she'd planned to be as a result of this outing. Driving along, she debated with herself whether to name him or to let Cleve have the honor. Shorty and Ralphie were curled up tightly on the back seat, highly insulted by this uninvited intruder.

"Hey you guys, c'mon, no jealousy here. This little fella is for Cleve." Josie glanced in her rearview mirror as she sat at a stoplight. "What should we do about a name for this critter?" she asked, addressing her dogs. A few names came to mind; Josie said them out loud to see if they evoked any reaction from the precious little brown-and-white bundle with the docked tail, who was now fast asleep on her lap. "Christmas?" No reaction. *Too girly anyway,* thought Josie. "Snowball? Snowy?" *Yeah sure,* Josie thought to herself. *Hey Cleve, here's your new dog, Snowball.* She laughed out loud at just how ridiculous that sounded.

She drove along, racking her brain. She looked in the rearview mirror again, this time to check on the tree in the pickup bed. *It's a right nice Fraser fir,* she thought and then burst out loud with, "That's it you guys! That's the name, Fraser! Cleve will love it, I know he will, and he will love you too, Fraser." She rubbed the puppy as he climbed up to lick her face. Shorty growled from the back seat. *I sure hope Dad or Aunt Gayle will take care of this critter for me until it's gift-giving time,* Josie plotted.

35

Clover Field was closed on Christmas Eve and Christmas Day. Only Kenna, Josie, and the guys were at the barn on the twenty-fourth and they all left early. Kenna would cook them all a big turkey dinner at her house on the twenty-fifth. She really considered the guys who worked there her Clover Field family, and she treated them well.

Josie arrived home by three. The cottage looked festive with the tree dressed in colored lights and ornaments she'd been accruing the last few years, many of which came right from nature. Shells collected on day-off trips to the beach in Long Branch, pinecones from the woods behind the house, and blue jay and chicken feathers found on the ground, all thoughtfully placed on branch tips, with shiny silver, red, and green glass balls interspersed—and of course, the macaroni bell and the red glass cardinal. The mantel over the fireplace sported a boxwood garland adorned with white ribbon, dried flowers, and seed pods from the perennial garden, which Josie had spray-painted silver. The Parker family crèche was set up on the front hall table, and the kitchen and dining room tables were decorated with poinsettias and candles. Two Christmas pillows, needlepointed years ago by Mama, were propped in the corners of the couch. Cleve would be arriving soon, and she wanted everything to look just right. She put some Christmas music on and lit some candles.

Fraser was in a crate on the far side of the bed in Josie's room, and she was hoping he would be asleep when Cleve arrived. She wasn't sure how she was going to spring this present, but she was totally confident he would love the pup. For the last couple of weeks Cleve had been talking about dogs a lot. He'd asked Josie what her favorite breeds were, and how many dogs she thought a person could own, and she'd surmised he was contemplating the idea of a pup.

"Are you thinking about getting one?" she'd asked him.

"Not right now I don't think, but who knows. If I came across the right one, maybe. It would be fun to have a puppy around, don't you think Jos'?"

Fraser was sure to be a great surprise.

The knock at the front door followed by Cleve's voice as he entered the cottage got Ralphie and Shorty wound up and barking. Cleve yielded to let them pass him by at the door, and they ran out into the night, wardens of the cottage, not even noticing what he carried in his arms. He snickered at their foolishness.

"Ho, ho, ho, Merry Christmas Eve," he hollered in. "I have a special delivery present for Miss Josie Parker, and since it couldn't be wrapped it really can't wait. Anybody home?"

"Hi there!" Josie called in the direction of the entry hall as she made her way from the family room. "What are you talking a—" she was so caught off guard that she couldn't finish her sentence. "What the—" A small, fuzzy Australian sheep dog puppy with a huge red bow tied around its neck went blasting by her towards the kitchen as Cleve came into view.

"Merry Christmas, beautiful. What do you think? Pretty cute, huh? I figured after all the questions I've been asking you the last few weeks that you probably knew it was coming, but maybe that she's an Aussie makes it a little bit of a surprise, no?" He hugged her and stared into her eyes. "Best Christmas for me in a lot of years, being here with you." Then, letting Josie go and venturing forth he hollered, "Hey where did that varmint go? Here! Here girl. I didn't name her," he called back over his shoulder. "Figured I'd give you the honor. Here! Where are you?"

Josie was stunned. *A little bit of a surprise?* This was a surprise all right and she wasn't quite sure what to do, laugh or cry. This was the epitome of coincidence. She'd thought Cleve had been asking all those questions because he was thinking of getting a dog for himself, when the reality was that he was plotting to get one for her. Cleve's voice interrupted her thoughts.

"Hey, that little vixen headed into your bedroom, OK if I go in there?" he called back as he walked down the hall towards Josie's room.

"Uh, yeah, sure." *Well, here goes nothing,* thought Josie. She couldn't stop herself from breaking into laughter as she followed Cleve down the hall.

"Holy shit, what is this? Who is this? Oh no, what is going on here? You already have a new puppy? You didn't tell me you were getting a new puppy, Jos'. Oh, man." Cleve bent down to open the crate. "Wow, he sure his cute. Hey there little fella." Fraser came tumbling out and the two new pups began a rumble on the bedroom rug.

"I wasn't planning on a new puppy for me, I was planning on a new puppy for you!" Josie put her hands on her head, feigning pain. "I thought all the questions you asked me were because you were gearing up to get yourself a dog. There was a litter at Delicious Orchards when I went for the tree, and I took it as an omen. Say hello to Fraser, *your* new dog. He's a little bit of this and a little bit of that. Merry Christmas, Cleve." Fraser was now tugging on Cleve's jeans at the ankle. "This is exactly why I hate surprises." Josie held one hand still against her forehead.

"Fraser, huh? Hey fella," he bent down and gave the pup a tussle. "Well, I guess our housebreaking work is cut out for us now, isn't it?" Cleve kidded as he stood up and took a step to Josie, lowered her hand from her forehead, and kissed her affectionately. "Merry Christmas, Jos'. C'mon, let's go make the introductions to Ralphie and Shorty and then figure out a name for this token girl."

"I think you just figured out her name," Josie said, quite astonished by the sequence of events. "Token. I like it, what do you think?"

"Token it is." Cleve put his arm over Josie's shoulder and they walked down the hall to let the other dogs in, puppies tumbling in pursuit. "I suppose this gives new meaning to 'the dog days of winter,' doesn't it?" he chuckled.

Josie threw her head back and laughed. *It doesn't get much better than this,* she thought.

THE WINTER
EQUESTRIAN FESTIVAL

36

The Winter Equestrian Festival in Wellington divided the Clover Field horses and clients between Colts Neck and Florida. Fortunately for Josie, her experience and intense work ethic made it easy for her to keep track of pretty much everything going on in both places. She was perfectly content with a quick trip or two to Florida during the circuit, but she really wasn't crazy about long trips on the road. Being able to go home to her own couch, her own kitchen, her own bed every night suited her just fine.

What a WEF circuit it was turning out to be. The Clover Field riders and their horses were winning tri-colors left and right and a number of them, including Addie Crawford and John Courage, were well in the lead for circuit champion honors as March began. Half way through the circuit most of the hunters had earned enough points to be qualified for the coveted Devon Horse Show held in May, and a few of the equitation riders were already well on their way to qualifying for the Medal and Maclay finals.

Addie had really stepped it up and was at the top of her game. She was winning consistently and socially she was having the time of her life. She even had herself a new boyfriend, Jack Sawyer, a tall, red-haired jumper rider from Nimrod Farm in Connecticut, who was so good-looking and perfect that some of her girlfriends swore he was gay. If he was, he didn't know it, or wasn't admitting it yet, and he and Addie were quite inseparable, on and off horses. Pamela Crawford was concerned, of course. She didn't want anything getting in the way of her aspirations for her daughter. But she knew that there was no fighting young love, so she just did her best to keep an eye on her girl, and promised herself she wouldn't intervene unless she deemed it necessary. Addie's riding was important, but so were her grades, and Pamela knew all too well there was nothing like love to distract a girl from her academics.

Addie called Josie every Sunday night to tell her how Johnnie had performed. Three out of three weeks she'd been champion with him.

This week's report was disconcerting.

"He was great on Saturday, first and second over jumps," Addie offered. "Peter was really good on Rain Forest today; they edged us out and wound up champion. Martha was reserve with Movie Star."

"How could that be if you were first and second yesterday?" Josie figured something had gone really wrong. What the hell happened today?"

"I'm not sure." Addie's delivery was so insincere that she knew she had to explain quickly. "Well, to be honest, and please don't tell my mom or Kenna, but I was like, super hungover this morning. I went with Jack to a big party at Cobblestones last night. I snuck in at about two thirty and had to be in the saddle at 8:00 a.m. Johnnie behaved badly in the hack, right in front of the judge. It was like he was annoyed at me or something; we got zip. Forget about the first jump class, I was so hungover I couldn't see straight. Kenna was so pissed off. And in the second class, Josie, he spit me right into the dirt. Spun like a tornado, at a cooler that was hanging over the rail, before I even got to the first jump. Disqualified." Then, as if none of what she had just reported mattered, she blurted out, "But Josie, I had so much fun with Jack. We were dancing all night."

Josie was stunned. That was a lot of information she certainly had not expected to hear. *Out partying all night? Uh-oh,* Josie thought, *she's behaving like a teenager. Can't really blame her, I guess. I mean she is a teenager. She's got that boyfriend now. Her mother would freak out if she knew Addie was out all night.* Josie also knew that Johnnie would take full advantage of a rider that wasn't sharp. It had nothing to do with the cooler; Josie had ridden him enough to know without hesitation that his behavior at the show was completely calculated. It was his way of saying, *Shape up and be in this to win, or don't waste my time.*

Josie knew how smart Johnnie was. She could imagine the look in his eye, the way he'd prick his ears, and the swish of his tail. The "tell-tail sign," she and Ramon called it. You knew trouble was coming when John Courage swished that tail. She wasn't quite sure how to tackle all of this with Addie.

"It's fourth week in, he's probably a little tired, maybe even a little bored," she said. "Does Kenna think you should give him next week off?

A week off might be good." Josie was a little worried anyway about the horse holding up to jumping five weeks in a row. She was quite sure Kenna would give him a break, but she figured it didn't hurt to make the suggestion to Addie.

"Yeah, we gave the jumpers this week off, hunters get week five off, and everyone shows week six."

"As for your eye being off, you're probably tired too, kiddo. You are riding a lot of horses, traveling, and trying to keep up with school and your social life, too. It's a lot to handle. If you don't mind me saying so, keep your focus on why you go there. Everyone is working hard to help you win, Ad'—your folks, Kenna, Ramon, everybody. Partying can really mess that up. I know it's tempting to stay out dancing all night, but dinner and a movie is nice too, and you can get some decent shut-eye. Don't let yourself or your team down. This is your last year, make the most of it. The riding I mean, not the partying." Josie giggled and went on. "Trust me, Johnnie knows when you are off your game, and he will put you in the dirt every time. It's kind of sport for him. He's not really a spook at all. He's brilliant." Josie laughed now, because she knew this was an accurate assessment.

"You're right. You are right," Addie admitted. "I felt awful, in more ways than one, this morning. You said it just right though, and I did, I felt like I let the team down. Kenna knew exactly why I rode like shit and she wasn't happy. She gave Jack such a dirty look when he came to the ring to watch me."

"Hey, Kenna's been down that path. She was a junior, dancing all night at the Polo Pub on Sunday nights back when. Don't beat yourself up too much. Get your priorities in order or I will sick Cleve on you," she said with a giggle. "Now hang up the phone and get some sleep. Call me next Sunday and let me know how the jumpers do. Give Johnnie some molasses treats for me. You should still have plenty in your tack trunk. Maybe, somehow, some way, I will get down there for the last week. Night, night. Love you."

"Night, night. Thanks, Josie. Love you too." Addie hung up.

The phone rang back almost immediately. Josie figured it had to be Addie wanting to tell her something she'd forgotten.

"Yes? What did you forget to tell me?" Josie teased.

"Josie, this is Alan. Clearly you were expecting someone else. It's Alan. Sorry. Sorry to call you so late on a Sunday, but Tessa is in the hospital and I wanted you to know right away."

"Oh my God, Alan, what happened? Is she OK? Is the baby OK?" Josie asked, confused. She was completely caught off guard by this call.

"Everyone is OK for right now, but it's been a rough, scary day. She's in Good Samaritan in West Palm. They say she is in premature labor and the baby is trying to come, way too early. She's barely six months pregnant, you know."

"Right, I know. Oh gosh, Alan, so what do they do? Where are you now? Who has Rosie? Can I talk to Tessa? Sorry, sorry for all the questions. Sorry," Josie apologized frenetically.

"I'm still at Good Sam. Rosie is with one of our customers. She is fine there for a day or two, until things get sorted out. Tessa will be in here for at least three or four days, maybe more. They have her on some medication to make the contractions stop, but it's tricky. It makes her heart race, so they have to watch her closely. I will tell you this, it was really scary this afternoon. She was really brave. The baby can't come yet, Jos', it just can't."

Josie could tell that Alan was very upset and very scared. Tessa was his world. Without her, he'd said many times, he'd be completely lost.

"Right. The baby won't come. Everything will be fine. Sounds like they have her under control. I remember that medication from my nursing days. It's a bit controversial but it helps stop contractions. Listen, I'm gonna ask Cleve if he will watch the dogs and check on the chickens. I'm sure he will. I was thinking about making a trip down there, anyway. I will get on a flight tomorrow and come help you. I'd like to see Tess' and I can watch Rosie for a few days too. Would I be imposing if I did that?"

"Josie, that would be so awesome. I was kind of hoping you might say you'd come. You are Tessa's family, you know that. I can ask my mom to come help if we need her, but I know you can give Tess' the comfort she needs to get through this right now. I know it would help her to see you."

"See you tomorrow, Alan. Give Tess' a kiss for me. Tell her I'm on my way." Josie hung up the phone, and picked it up again. She called the airline, she called Cleve, she called Kenna. She packed a bag.

37

"Hey girlfriend, you doing OK now?" Josie bent over her friend's hospital bed and gave her a soft hug. "You and little number two gave us all a pretty good scare."

"Josie, my best friend in the world. I knew you'd come. I knew it. Alan told me he called you. I didn't want him to. I knew you would be on the first plane you could get." Tessa had tears in her eyes. "My best friend. For so long now."

"Shhhhhh, you're darn right. Hey I'm a nurse, remember? It's in my blood to take care of people, especially my family." She kissed her friend on the forehead and sat down in a chair that she pulled right up next to Tessa's bed.

"People and horses, you mean." Tessa smiled. "I'm fine, really. I just have to stay here a few days for observation, to make sure this horrible, wonderful medicine is doing what it needs to do. I have to stay quiet and calm, my doctor told me, but the contractions have really slowed down and I think I'm OK. My heart is just racing from the meds. Alan's a mess. Funny how much that guy loves me." She smiled, thinking about it.

"Well, here's what I want you to do, Tessa," Josie the nurse delicately instructed her friend. "Close your eyes and go to a peaceful place, a favorite moment in time. I know, I've got it. Listen to me. Listen to Nurse Parker," Josie giggled. "Remember that Thanksgiving a long time ago when we went for a ride in the back field at Hidden Green, in the snow? You on Opie and me on Lars? We had so much fun. It was so beautiful out there that day. Remember the huge red fox that spooked Lars? We galloped around that field and it felt so free, didn't it? Go there now Tess', gallop on Opie in that field; follow me and Lars. Picture yourself leaning down against Opie's neck, listen to his breathing as he gallops along. Listen, can you hear him? Remember how comfortable he was with that big sway back of his? Think about how amazing it feels when you are galloping; when their legs are coiled up and all four of their feet are off the ground; when their legs reach out for the next stride. There's nothing like it, Tess'. It feels so free. Go their now, relax, ride, gallop." She gently pushed the hair from Tessa's forehead, and continued to stroke her friend's face affectionately, until she was confident Tessa was asleep. She motioned to Alan that they should talk outside of the room. They exited the room silently, Josie looking once over her shoulder, feeling a pang of worry at the sight of her best girl friend hooked up to so many monitors.

"What do they say, Alan? Is she confined to bed for the rest of the pregnancy? That's usually the way it works."

"Yes, she will probably get off the medicine but she is on bedrest for the next two months. The baby will be mature enough to be delivered at that point. Our obstetrician has offered to make a house call every week; so kind of her. I didn't think doctors still made house calls." Alan peered back into Tessa's room.

Josie linked her arm into his as they walked the length of the hospital floor to the elevator bank.

"They really don't. You're very lucky. She'll be fine. I know she will," Josie said with completely manufactured credence. "Why don't you go get Rosie and go home? I will stay here for another hour or two and then drive out to your place. Really, go Alan. I got her. I won't let anything happen to either of them. Go."

They hugged and Alan left. Josie sat in silence by her best friend's hospital bed for two more hours. Tessa slept. Josie thought about how long she and Tessa had been friends. More than half their lives, she calculated, and she figured she would never have another friend like this. They knew one another so well. They knew one another's secrets, they had coached and coaxed one another through so many critical moments of their younger years, and here they were tonight. It was as it should be.

"I've got your back, girlfriend, and I know you'd have mine. Love you, Tessa Jensen Harmon," she whispered as she bent to kiss her friend goodnight. As she walked to the door to leave, she heard her friend whisper back.

"Love you, Josie Parker. Thanks, friend."

Josie stayed with the Harmons until Tessa was allowed to go home. She found a babysitter that would come a couple of days each week to help with Rosie, and she told Alan that she would be happy to do the farm billing for him for the next few months. He jumped on the offer.

"The phone bill for these calls is going to put us both in the poor house," Josie pretended to complain to Cleve during one of their nightly conversations. "What's worse is I can't feel your breath move across my face when we talk."

"A bill that is worth every penny," Cleve said. "I miss you Jos'. I miss those freckles. You coming back up, now that Tessa is home and stable? The weather has been amazing. In just the time you've been away little green things are starting to pop up in your garden, looking for you." Cleve feigned desperation. Josie had been gone for over a week. "Even the pups miss you. They are constantly stationed at the top of the driveway, waiting."

"Yes, I have a flight booked for Sunday night. I figure since I'm down here I will go over to the show and check in. It's been torture to be this close to Johnnie and not be able to get over there. Addie should be back down Friday afternoon, so I can probably ride him tomorrow and Friday morning; then she can jump him Friday afternoon. I can watch her show Saturday and Sunday, then catch my flight. Any objection?" Josie asked with sincerity, yet knowing that Cleve would totally understand.

"I wouldn't dare. Just get your butt back here soon, OK?" he responded. "Hey have fun with your chestnut superstar. The one that spins or wins," he chided. "John Courage. He spins or he wins," Cleve repeated, chuckling. "Stay away from coolers hanging over fence rails. I want you back in one piece."

Thursday morning came and Josie was ready to drive over to the horse show. She was excited but also emotional about leaving her friend in her precarious position.

"I have a little good luck charm for you, courtesy of the Dorie Parker magic jewel box. Keep it in your bedside table or pinned to your nightgown, whichever you like. Let it remind you of our Thanksgiving ride years back." She handed Tessa a small, gold galloping horse pin. "It's not real gold, but it was one of Mama's favorites. I hope it brings you good karma these next few months, girlfriend. And remember, any time you feel stressed, close your eyes and go for that wonderful ride." She pinned the small adornment on Tessa's robe.

"Wow," Tessa teased, but with absolute grace and humility. "Does this mean that my daughter and I are now the sole recipients of gifts from that magic box? I am overwhelmed. Really, Josie, it's over the top. I feel the karma already." The two girls laughed quietly.

Josie hugged her pal again. "Watch it you, or I will just take it right back." She winked, gave Tessa the thumbs up, and left before her friend could see the tears in her eyes. Tessa was too busy wiping away her own tears to have noticed Josie's.

38

Kenna had a big hug waiting for Josie when she showed up at the Clover Field set-up at WEF. Six weeks had gone by fast, but everyone who'd been in Wellington for the whole circuit was exhausted, sick of one another and thinking about home. One week left.

"Yay, a fresh face on the scene." Kenna smiled at her pal. "I'm so happy to see you and so happy that you are gonna stay with me the next few days. I'm taking you to Steamers for dinner tonight. We'll go early, lots to talk about. I want to know all about Tessa. I'm sure it's been very stressful. Tomorrow night we're going out with Pamela and Addie. They are so excited you are here. Pam has already made a reservation for dinner somewhere in Palm Beach."

"Sounds good to me, I've had a rough week, I'm ready for some fun." Josie thought about Tessa for a second, then sat down on a show trunk to catch up on what had been going on with the horses.

"I'd rather not have to think about going on from here to the Tampa circuit for more points," Kenna said to Josie. Addie's got to ride well and clinch it this weekend. Peter is right on her ass with Rain Forest, and if Ri-Arm Farm goes to Tampa and we don't, they might just catch her. A lot depends on this week.

"OK, well, I can ride Johnnie today and in the morning if you are OK with that. He's probably a little fresh coming off his week of rest. Where is he, anyway?"

"Down on the end. We had to give him a stall with a view, as you can imagine."

The stabling at the Winter Equestrian Festival was mostly temporary. Aside from a few old, dilapidated polo barns, most of the horses lived in temporary stalls that had been raised under big, open-sided, carnival-style tents. The tents were set up in rows, one after the other, along a dirt road that ran the length of one side of the show ground, just a short distance from the competition rings. With makeshift electricity running through the tents, the grooms and braiders were able to work comfortably at all hours to keep the horses safe, comfortable, and show ready.

Josie felt goose bumps rise on her arms as she walked down the dirt aisle of the Clover Field tent, instinctively looking left and right into each stall she passed, eventually approaching the last stall on the left.

"OK, where's my Johnnie boy?" she called out when she was a stall away.

No sooner had the words left her lips than the chestnut horse raised his head from his pile of hay. With ears pricked forward and his eyes focused in her direction, he nickered and pawed the ground.

Josie opened the stall door. He stepped forward and she extended an arm, molasses treat in hand. He nickered again and moved to her.

"Hey fella, look how nice your manners are today. Hey Johnnie, I've missed you. Hey boy." Josie patted his neck, rubbed her hand along his formidable shoulder, then up over his withers and back, which caused him to twitch as though tickled. She laughed and continued along his hindquarters. "Hey buddy, you look great," she whispered, hugging his neck. "How about we go have a little work out, you and me, huh?" John Courage wrapped his head and neck around Josie's body, hugging her right back. She offered him another treat.

Josie reached outside the stall door for Johnnie's halter and was caught off guard at the sight of Ramon standing in the aisle, waiting to be noticed. He was a small but solid man, humble in demeanor, and handsome.

"Hey Ramon! How are you my friend? I've missed you." They moved together, back toward the gelding's stall. "He looks great, Ramon. He's been a winner down here, huh?" Josie knew Ramon was her point man for John Courage. Josie slipped the halter over Johnnie's head. "I'm gonna give him a little workout on the flat; you wanna give him a twirl for me first? Let him punch out a few bucks on the lunge line?"

"He's been real good, Miss Josie. Champion, 'cept for last week he put Miss Addie right in the dirt. She deserve it; out all night partying, showing up still half hot. She thinks nobody knows what she and that boyfriend were up to, but Ramon sees all. She deserve it and he let her know. This horse is loco, but smarter than you think." Ramon shook his head. "Let me tell you, Miss Josie, this horse, he is your horse. I saw you go in his stall just now. He does that for no one, I'm tell you, no one 'cept you. He's mean son of a bitch most of the time, too tough. He loves you. He respect you. Caballo loco." Ramon took over and led the horse to the grooming stall in the middle of the aisle. He fed the horse a peppermint candy, gave him a pat on the neck, and began to get him ready. "Caballo loco." He laughed. Josie knew that secretly John Courage was Ramon's favorite. Every groom liked to have the winner in his charge.

"I'll come watch you lunge him. Meet you out there," Josie said and left to scout out the cantina. She was ready for a breakfast sandwich, still one of her favorite indulgences.

"He's feeling his oats after that week off, huh, Ramon?" Josie called to the groom as she pulled up to the fence line in a Clover Field golf cart and pushed hard on the parking brake, causing a loud snap. Johnnie took full advantage of the distraction and threw his head down, firing his hind legs up into a prize-winning buck. Ramon put two hands on the line and pulled to steady the horse, bringing him back to the trot. This was no new trick to the experienced groom.

Ramon made Johnnie canter for awhile in both directions while Josie watched, then said, "He be good for you now, Miss Josie. He get his buck out. He's ready."

"Great, see you back at the barn, Ramon. Thanks."

"Good thing we're close in size," Josie said to Kenna, back at the tent. "You sure you don't mind sharing?"

"Go for it, give that spinner a work out. He needs to be champion this week. I'm putting it in your hands," her friend and boss kidded her. Josie zipped into Kenna's chaps and popped her helmet on. She took the reins and Ramon gave her a leg up, then helped her adjust the stirrups.

"Meet you up at the hunter ring," Josie said, tightening the girth. Then she called over her shoulder to Kenna, just for a laugh, "You know what Cleve says, he spins or he wins, this one!"

"I'm counting on the latter, my friend," Kenna called back. *I'm counting on the latter*, she said again to herself.

Josie walked Johnnie with a loose rein up to one of the schooling areas for hunters. She parked herself near the in-gate to the show ring, so that she and Johnnie could watch some of the day's competition. She spotted Charlie Weaver and Martha Sifton and made a mental note to tell Cleve. After the young gun Scott Stewart accepted the blue ribbon with a stunning bay stallion, Josie turned her horse and encouraged him forward.

"OK fella, let's get you ready to win Saturday." She asked for the trot and he moved as though happy to have her on his back. She could sense people watching as he floated around the schooling area in perfect form.

After some good work on the flat, Josie looked around for Ramon. He was already setting a jump for her. Josie jumped Johnnie back and forth over it a few times, Ramon gradually raising the height to match what Addie would have to jump in the junior hunter classes.

OK, concentrate, Josie said to herself, shortening her grip on the reins and cantering toward the now substantial jump. Arriving at the perfect take-off spot, John Courage powered off the ground with an overabundance of energy, jumping a foot higher than he needed to.

"Shit," Josie mumbled. She lost contact completely with the saddle, but managed to keep her balance, and with her feet remaining in the stirrups, recovered her position before he had all four feet firmly planted on the other side of the jump.

Johnnie, so proud of his prank, threw his head down between his front legs and tried to fire up a big buck. Josie was too quick for him and pulled up on the reins, lifting his head to thwart his attempt. "You cocky brat, you almost had me," she scolded the horse, half laughing at his mischievous behavior. "Can you believe that, Ramon? He almost jumped me off! Little bastard."

"He testing you, Miss Josie. Just wants to be sure you are paying attention." Ramon shook his head and laughed. "He be OK now, go again. I put the jump down a couple holes."

Josie cantered Johnnie around the ring while Ramon adjusted the jump. She pulled his head in close to his chest and made him work for his stride. She pushed hard against him with one leg, then hard against him with the other, demanding that he pay close attention. Then she gave him a breather.

"You want me to pay attention? Well I want you to do the same, you brat."

When Ramon was ready, Josie pushed her heels down hard and headed to the jump again. She jumped it in both directions several times; this time John Courage performed like a rock star. Perfect every time.

"OK, Ramon, let's put the rails up higher again, I want to be sure he's got no tricks up his sleeve. Let's lay your towel over the middle of the top rail too, just as a little teaser. If he jumps it fine twice, then we are good to go for today." Ramon moved in to adjust the jump and left his grooming rag dangling over the top rail, billowing lightly in the breeze.

Josie cantered Johnnie out of the corner and she knew immediately that he saw the towel on the jump. His whole body sucked back and Josie felt him hold his breath, but she was ready for him. She dug her spurs into his side, urging him forward. She knew he wasn't afraid, he was just being a jerk. It was exactly what she was hoping he would do.

"Don't even think about it, Johnnie," she said out loud to him as she got within four strides of the jump. He turned one ear back for just a second, then forward again. He relaxed, lengthened his stride and jumped in good form, cantering straight away on the landing side. Josie patted him on the neck, cantered around the ring and right back to the jump again. Johnnie jumped it with no nonsense. Josie cantered to the jump from the opposite direction and he was equally well behaved.

She slowed to a trot and let him move around the ring a few times on a loose rein, before pulling up to the walk.

"That's good for today, Ramon, don't you think? I'll walk him back." Ramon nodded, grabbed his towel, and reset the jump.

Josie followed the dusty path that wound through the horse show ground back to the stabling area. Johnnie was tired and hot, so she loosened the girth and let him walk on a loose rein. They crossed over the main dirt road, and Josie exchanged hellos with the traffic guard. She laughed thinking how the smell of the cantina made her feel hungry again. A hose-water lemonade sure would be great right about now.

As they passed the row of green port-o-johns, she reflected on the day long ago when she'd caught Tessa and Alan during their teenage rebel behavior. She smiled and looked up at the sky.

Shine your light on Tessa, Mama, she said silently. *She needs some family right now and I'm her family. She needs a little bit of magic, and you're her magic.* Then Josie thought about Cleve again. She missed him. No, she ached for him.

They made one last turn and meandered along until she came to the Clover Field set-up. She dismounted, hitched up her stirrups, and pulled the reins over Johnnie's head. To take her mind off Cleve, she whispered to Johnnie, holding his mouth and nose in her hands, "Thanks to you, you brat. Thanks to you I have so much." She gave him a kiss, and a molasses treat from her back pocket, then passed the reins to Ramon.

"Let's go," Kenna pressed Josie. "Girls' night out and I'm starving!"

39

The next day flew by. Josie rode Johnnie for an hour in the morning, and he was as prepared as he could be when Addie got a leg up and headed toward the schooling area Friday afternoon. Kenna and Josie rode up in a golf cart, Ramon cruised ahead on his dirt bike, and the whole team met at the grand hunter ring. Jack Sawyer just happened to show up there too. Kenna frowned in Josie's direction.

Addie gave Johnnie a light workout on the flat. Josie sat in the cart, watching. She looked over at Jack, and the two acknowledged one another with smiles. *He's a cute boy,* thought Josie, and she had a momentary flashback to a sixteen-year-old Alan Harmon, standing at the side of the ring watching beautiful, leggy Tessa ride, years ago.

"Now listen," said Kenna, standing in the ring next to one of the practice jumps. She spoke firmly and seriously to Addie. "You have got to let this horse know who is boss. He was ticked off at you two weeks ago. He tried to get the best of Josie yesterday, but she put him in his place. He's had a break so he's a little fresh. Take the upper hand right away and keep it. He needs to know you are as committed as he is. If you want to win, so does he. It's not complicated. OK, get this jump off the left lead first." Kenna pointed to the end of the ring, then drew an imaginary line to the jump. Addie picked up the canter. Josie sat silently in the golf cart, her fingers crossed. She watched as the chestnut horse made the turn and sighted in on the jump.

"C'mon you varmint, behave," she whispered aloud to no one. John Courage cantered quietly and left the ground in front of the jump like he was bored and uninterested, but when he landed on the far side he pulled his hind end up under him and scooted away, catching Addie off guard with reins that were too long. She grabbed them up fast and was able to negotiate the end of the ring, but not before Kenna had seen what had happened.

"Damn it, Addie, c'mon! I told you, take the upper hand. Don't give him the benefit of the doubt until he knows you are the boss. He's testing you, damn it. Left lead, again." Kenna motioned toward the jump with a flailing arm, aggravated.

Addie was aggravated, too. She was embarrassed to be admonished in front of Jack. Her adrenaline was pumping now and she got her head into the zone. She picked up the canter, stayed quietly focused, and in exemplary position, they jumped the next jump perfectly. She hoped there would be no more reprimand from her trainer.

"Better, better, thank God. OK, now give him a pat. Get that jump three more times like that and you're good. Right lead this time. Just keep that feel but let him go his way." Kenna was the one who was crossing her fingers now. *Fucker*, she thought.

Ending the lesson on a good note, Addie uncharacteristically asked Ramon to walk Johnnie back to the tent.

"I'm going with Jack," she announced definitively, almost defiantly. "See you guys later." Addie slid onto the back of Jack's dirt bike, wrapped her arms around his waist, and the two took off, headed who knew where.

Kenna glared over at Josie with disapproval. Josie shrugged her shoulders, caught in thought somewhere between concern and glee. She loved that kid, and she knew exactly where that young girl's head and heart were focused right now. Kenna, on the other hand, had a difficult time letting anything get in the way of winning.

Chuck and Harold's was a long trek from Wellington—just beyond the Breakers Hotel in Palm Beach—but so worth it. The food was delicious; stone crabs were in season, and Pamela insisted they all have some.

"This mustard horseradish is absolutely to die for!" she squealed at her first bite, chasing her crab claw with a sip of her chardonnay.

The four girls chatted and laughed incessantly as creatively presented entrées were delivered to the table. After her second glass of wine, Pam couldn't keep herself from asking, "How's that handsome man of yours, Josie? He certainly has stolen Addie's heart, hasn't he, Addie? Has he stolen yours, Josie? Did he give you something spectacular for Christmas? C'mon, do tell."

"Mom, stop." Addie scolded her mother, embarrassed. Josie detected the sharpness in Addie's delivery.

"Oh it's fine, Addie." Josie winked as she tapped Addie on the forearm. "He's pretty amazing, thanks for asking. We really are cut from the same cloth, which makes everything so great. We've known one another for a long time but somehow ten or twelve years snuck by us. That's a long story for another time." Josie looked down briefly, then continued. "We've been having a great time though, ever since he walked into Clover Field that day last fall. It's funny, you know, he always credits Johnnie with bringing us back together."

"Ooh, that almost makes it sound like I can take credit for matchmaking," Pamela said playfully. She sipped her wine.

"You and Doc Thurman," Josie added. "But Cleve believes all the credit goes to John Courage." The girls all giggled. They sipped more wine and chit-chatted about horses and houses and people.

As Addie's brownie sundae was delivered to the table, along with four spoons, Pamela's voice took on a more serious tone.

"Layton and I are confident that Addie will be starting at Brown in the fall. Although not officially accepted yet, we have it on good authority that she will get in." Addie looked down, spinning her spoon in the hot fudge, silent. Kenna glanced at her, and in an attempt to lighten the moment, stuck her own spoon into the ice cream, stealing a scoop. Pam continued. "We are definitely committed to compete at Devon in May and the Hampton Classic in August as long as Addie thinks she can handle it having not ridden for almost three months." Pam tipped her wine glass again and dabbed her lips with her napkin.

Three months? Josie was confused. She looked up to pay closer attention. Kenna, equally confused, leaned in.

"As a graduation gift we have decided to take Addie to Europe for the summer, on a fabulous tour, covering several countries. We are very excited about it." Pam nervously picked up her napkin, folded it, and placed it back in her lap.

Josie wondered just exactly who Pam meant by "we."

Pam went on, "Unfortunately it means that Addie won't be able to ride after Devon until the middle or so of August. So, we've decided that all the horses should be put up for sale starting, like, now; the only hitch being that if someone wants Classified or John Courage, they aren't available until after Addie shows them at Devon." She looked up and around the restaurant, searching for a waitress's eye. She raised her hand to command one over to the table.

The silence was completely awkward. Josie was taken aback, Kenna was clearly caught off guard, and Addie, who had barely moved, had taken on a rather indignant expression. After what seemed a very long pause, Kenna spoke.

"I have to admit, Pam, I am surprised, and a bit confused by your decision. But I respect it of course. They are your horses. I hope you won't mind my saying that if either of the hunters were to be champion at Devon the sale price could definitely be higher, so you might consider waiting until then to put those two up for sale."

"That's something to think about, but it's not just about the money. As you well know, Kenna, it's not really ever about the money with us. It's about what works and about how Layton sees things, from a practical perspective. We know Classified will most likely be easier to sell than John Courage, and with your guidance we will price them accordingly." In her effort to explain how they had arrived at this decision, Pamela really wasn't making any sense. Layton Crawford rarely involved himself in any of the day-to-day decisions regarding the horses, and as far as Kenna had ever been able to tell, it was almost always about money with him. To Josie, the entire conversation seemed an aberration.

Is this the wine talking? she wondered.

The waitress finally came by and asked if anyone would like to have anything else. Pamela ordered black coffee, Josie and Kenna passed. Addie looked up from her dessert and jumped with voracity into the conversation.

"This has nothing to do with business or practicality, Mom, and you know it. In fact it has very little to do with Dad at all. This is about getting me away from Jack for the summer, and that's just wrong. Why are you so against him? He is driven and dedicated. So am I. I've really focused to get these horses qualified. It's my last year and Dad said I could go hard until it was time to go to college. He even said I could go to indoors if I wanted to, my freshman year. Now you're cutting off my entire last summer. You know damn well this is about Jack, it has nothing to do with anything else. What are you so damn afraid of? Are you are afraid I will run off with him? I'm not going to do that, Mom. He wants to become a professional, I want to go to college. But I want this summer. My last summer to ride. I don't want to go to fucking Europe, I want to ride."

Addie looked at Josie and Kenna and apologized.

"Sorry you guys, that probably makes me sound like a spoiled brat." She mimicked herself using a squeaky, whiny voice with a scrunched-up face, "I don't wanna go to Europe for six weeks and stay in the finest hotels in the world, or shop on the Via Condotti or tour the Chianti region of Tuscany." She laughed out loud at herself. "But it's true. What do you think, Mom? You think I'm going to run off with Jack Sawyer and not go to Brown?" she repeated. "That's totally ridiculous and you know it!"

Josie could think only of Tessa right now, and she smiled, musing to herself, *It's not that ridiculous actually.* But she said nothing. By her calculation, Addie was dead right in her assessment of the situation. She loved that kid, smart and sassy, and willing to stand up for herself. Josie liked Jack too, and wondered why Pamela was so afraid to let Addie have a little fun with him. *Oh well, not my business,* she thought.

Pamela continued, a little defensive now. "Well, it's the decision we have made and we are going to stick with it. There's just one other thing. While we are gone, we would like Josie to be the only person to ride John Courage other than for sales trials. We all know he is a very tricky horse, and Josie you seem to know how to deal with him when he pulls his hijinks. His reputation in that regard already precedes him and Layton and I feel he will be the toughest one to sell, despite the fact that he has won as much as he has." Again there was a long, uncomfortable pause.

"That is, of course, fine," Kenna responded after folding her napkin and placing it back where it had started. She put her hands in her lap. "I would have recommended that anyway. As long as it's OK with you Jos'." She gestured in Josie's direction, and went on. "We will want to keep him tuned for trials and in case Addie will be able to take the time to show at indoors."

Kenna apologized to Addie for talking about her, rather than to her. Addie smiled. She knew this was a shock for Josie and Kenna. It was shock enough for her, and she had prior knowledge. The family war over this seemingly contrived plan of Pamela's had taken place a few days ago, back at the Crawfords' home in Colts Neck. It had not been pretty. Layton had actually defended Addie. Ultimately, Pamela won out.

"If we still have the hunters, she can ride them at indoors; the jumpers, no. Addie's free time will be too limited to practice for that. But hopefully by then we won't have to worry about any of it," Pamela directed. Again, Josie wondered who Pam was talking about when she used the word "we."

"Well, OK, then," said Kenna. She changed the subject in an attempt to close out the dinner on a lighter, more positive note. She turned her focus to Addie. "All the more reason to ride well this weekend, kid. If you can seal the deal on the circuit championship with Johnnie, then both hunters will pretty much be assured spots at indoors. Go to Europe and live a little vicariously for all of us schlubs that will have to hang out in the summer dust. It's the same every year, you won't be missing much." No sooner had Kenna said that than Josie thought to herself, *Ooh, you just put your foot in your mouth girlfriend.*

"Jack," Addie retaliated, although her eyes were fixed on Pamela, not Kenna. "I will be missing Jack, and all my friends, and my horses. And two weeks of Lake Placid, the most fun horse show of the summer. This sucks. Excuse me." Addie got up from the table and walked away, in the direction of her mother's rented Jaguar.

"Well," Pamela said and paused. She looked up and flagged the waitress once again. "I think it's time for the check. I've got this, you two. Go on and git. Sorry the night ended like this. I had visions of us talking about Paris, and Vienna, and Rome." Perhaps just a tad embarrassed, she air kissed both of them as they stood up from the table to leave.

Not what I expected from Pam, not what I expected at all, thought Josie as she and Kenna walked silently to the car. *Wait 'til I tell Cleve about this. I don't think he will believe me.* Again she thought about Tessa and Alan, and she chuckled. *Wow, this has been a weird night for sure.*

After a few minutes of driving with the only sound coming from the radio, Josie spoke up.

"Wow, Kens', I really didn't expect that from Pamela. What the hell? I mean she's always been so super cool and enthusiastic about the horses for Addie. And she's so super flirty all the time, you know what I mean? Comfortable and positive about everything. I can't believe she has such a tough time dealing with Addie having a crush. OK, a boyfriend. Seems weird to me." Josie was truly challenged by this turn of events. "I'm sad for Addie, really."

"One thing I've learned over the years, Jos', you can be sure that you never know what you're going to get from people. The Crawfords are good folk. They've been totally supportive of anything I've asked of them these last few years. Addie is a great kid to train. Who really knows why they have decided to do it this way. It may have nothing to do with the horses, or Jack, or even Addie for that matter. It probably doesn't. Who knows? It's not for us to question. Believe me, it's really not for us to question. The less we know, the better."

Kenna's were words of wisdom, and Josie had to agree with her friend. She felt a little differently about the Crawfords though.

"You are absolutely right. Well said, Kens'. That's why you run the place. You are so damn steadfast. But I love the Crawfords and I really, really care about that kid." Josie smiled.

"I know you do and your relationship with them has been an illustration of the exception to the rule. One other thing I know," Kenna added, enthusiastically, "you've got yourself a horse to ride for a while."

Hearing Kenna say those words caused Josie to break out in a cold sweat. A chill ran up her spine. *Lars,* she said his name quietly to herself. *Lars. A horse of your own for a while.* She'd heard those words at another time in her life and it hadn't worked out so well. She wasn't optimistic about this working out so well either. Her heart ached a little and all of a sudden Josie wasn't quite sure she was excited to have John Courage all to herself. She'd have to think about this. So rather than say anything she might regret, Josie decided to keep it simple. "Lucky me," she said, responding belatedly. *Lucky me, yeah right,* she thought. She couldn't wait to get back to Kenna's so she could call to check on Tessa, and then call Cleve. She had so much to discuss with him.

CLOVER FIELD FARM

40

"Circuit champion with both your hunters! That's freakin' amazing, Addie. I'm so proud of you!" Cleve clapped his hands in the direction of the gem of a kid whom he'd adored since the night he'd met her. Something about her reminded him, every time he saw her, of Josie Parker as a young girl. Although it had been weeks since the Clover Field horses and riders had returned from Wellington, Cleve was still teasing Addie about her successful circuit. Today was no different. Addie adored Cleve right back. For Josie, this was as good as having a little sister.

"Well let's see what you can pull off at Devon next week, Ivy Leaguer," Cleve challenged the young rider as she walked John Courage around the sand ring at Clover Field. It was May, and Addie had received her official acceptance letter from Brown University. She and her parents were wheels up for Europe right after her graduation from Morningstar Academy in early June.

A huge willow tree just outside the ring bowed in the warm breeze. The cherry trees lining the long driveway were in full clarion bloom. Sparks the cat walked along the fence top like she was balancing on a tight rope.

"That cat follows Johnnie wherever he goes. They are such buds. I'm surprised she doesn't get crushed the way she sleeps in Johnnie's stall all the time," Addie laughed as she unclipped the strap on her helmet and came to a halt near Cleve. From his perch on the fence Cleve scratched the horse's face under his forelock. Johnnie's upper lip twitched.

Turning to Addie after resetting the last jump, Josie nodded at Johnnie. "He's good to go for sure. Just remember the Ferris wheel outside the far end of the Dixon Oval at Devon. It's done in a lot of good horses and riders. Keep his head down so he'll be a little distracted when you're moving in that direction. Be aware of the scary stuff. You know—big dogs, strollers, umbrellas. Those can be the kiss of death to a winning trip; they will give him every excuse to porpoise and spin. In the under saddle, keep to the inside so the judges see you every time around. The jumps will be the least of your worries, he will shine with that long stride. And please, please have a cream cheese and olive tea sandwich for me." Josie loved those little, crust-less, white bread, triangle-shaped sandwiches the Philadelphia Main Line ladies made for lunch at Devon. "Don't forget the sweet tea, either," she begged. "OK, finished. Over and out." She headed for the gate in the direction of the barn.

"Who are you? Her trainer? Her mother? Her sports psychologist? Now you're ordering vicarious take out?" Cleve teased. "She's ridden at Devon, like, how many times?" He looked at Addie, shrugging his shoulders. "You're a pain in the ass, Parker. She's got this, relax."

"Well, most importantly," Josie said, feigning ignorance of Cleve's playful insults, "his molasses treats are in your show trunk, as usual. We all know those molasses treats are why he really wins." They all laughed; Cleve gave Josie a playful push out of his way as they all walked back to the barn. The air was full of positive karma.

Josie loved that chestnut horse more than ever. Since he'd come home from Florida, their bond had grown even stronger, and everyone, the Crawfords included, knew that Josie and John Courage were quite the duo.

While Addie focused on finishing up strong at school, Josie had lots of time in the saddle with Johnnie, and she thrived on it. She hated thinking about him being sold, and secretly she was happy knowing it would not be an easy accomplishment. The few riders who tried him at the end of the WEF circuit had not fared well, more than one of them falling prey to Johnnie's antics. The shivers had not caused any major problems for the horse or his care during Addie's tenure with him, but it had made a few potential buyers decline to even bother trying him. This suited Josie just fine. He would need a committed owner, a sophisticated trainer, and knowledgeable caretakers.

Doc Thurman had checked in a week or so after Johnnie had returned from Florida, and even Frank Parker had come to finally meet the enigmatic chestnut gelding that his daughter had fallen so hard for.

"Dad, I wish I could figure out a way to make him really mine," she told him as they stood out at the paddock fence. "There is so much déjà vu in all of this, and even though I am older and wiser, I still can't help but think I somehow let Lars down way back when. I don't want to do that to Johnnie. But the Crawfords want a hundred thousand for him and that's not a possibility even in my dreams. I've been saving every penny so Cleve can repair the barn roof at the cottage. We figure once we fix it up, we can maybe board a few retired ones there, and make a little extra income, but a hundred thou' is just out of my realm. Call me nuts, Dad, but I even buy a lottery ticket every week, and I buy one for Johnnie too. If one ticket hits, we both win. Hell, if one ticket hits, we all win!"

"Ah, Rosebud, life is not about counting on winning the lottery, I don't need to tell you that. That's a pipe dream, and don't get me wrong, I'd never condemn the idea of having dreams and goals. But you know darn well you have to work for them—that's always been your style. Your precious life has seen its devastating moments for sure, but think of all the good there has been. You and Lars shared an unbelievable year. Dwell on that, not on the negative. We only have the time we are given. That's how I feel about your mama. If you get into bed at night and can say honestly that you did the best you could to treat others the way you'd have them treat you, if you put your best foot forward and your all into every task, then goodness will prevail. You taught Lars so much, you gave him all the love and care a horse could expect while he was your responsibility, and you've done the same for John Courage. This is your time with him. It may be all you are given. Just keep doing what you're doing. Whatever is going to happen will, like it or not."

"You're right, Dad. I get it. I'm just so attached to him. I wish there was something I could do."

There was one other monumental bit of advice Frank Parker had to offer his only child.

"Well," he said, "never forget the magic your mama left for you in that silver box you've got. Remember what I told you once, to let those pieces help you write your own story, let them help you bring something special into your life. They've been sitting there a long time now, Jos', just sort of reminding you of the past. Maybe they can somehow get your pipe dream moving in the right direction." He laughed at himself, rather surprised that he had just waxed philosophical about something as out there as the likes of destiny. "Well, think about it anyway." Frank wasn't exactly sure what he had said. He just hoped he had imparted some good advice and that Josie might read between the lines. *She could probably sell the jewelry and buy the damn horse,* he mused to himself. *But that's for her to figure out.*

Josie hugged her dad. She looked up at the rays of sun shining down through the clouds and into the paddock. *God's light,* she mused. *Mama's light. There must be something I can do. I can't lose that damn horse. Think, Josie Parker, think.*

Josie and Cleve were reveling in being young lovers. For the first time in their lives, there was no conflict between them. They spent all their spare time together, and they were happy. Springtime somehow had a way of making the world seem just a bit more romantic, and at the end of their long work days, the routine for them included curling up on the couch with the dogs, a bottle of wine, some thrown-together dinner, and the television tuned to the evening news. Although Cleve owned his own small house in Lincroft, he and Josie had agreed that he should probably rent it out. Everything important and necessary in his life had pretty much taken up residence at the Haskell cottage, including himself and Fraser. There were no immediate, definitive plans in place, but Josie and Cleve were on the same page. They knew they were destined to be together forever.

Cleve considered a run at veterinary school, but chose against the pursuit. Rather, he and Josie decided they would fix up the barn at the cottage, lease out the stalls, and save until they could afford to buy a bigger place, where they would run a lay-up farm for rehabbing horses, and maybe start a breeding business. Cleve was Doc Thurman's right-hand man; Doc appreciated and relied on Cleve's instinct and knowledge, and Cleve had learned so much from his mentor. He knew Doc would invest in him in every way when the time was right.

"Oh gosh Cleve, if you'd only known him," Josie gushed to Cleve while they sat on the couch one evening. "Lars was the coolest horse. He was huge and handsome and could jump the moon. He wasn't the best mover and he didn't have the personality that Johnnie does, but he knew that he was mine as much as I knew he was mine. I feel like I really let him down. Damn that Jack Berardi. Damn him. I mean, it's not like I ever could have kept him but I don't even know where the poor horse wound up. He could have just called Mike O'Hara. Mike would've taken him back, I'm sure. He'd be like seventeen by now, if he'd lived that is. Who knows, but Lars was my horse, Cleve, my horse."

"I'm sure he knew how much you loved him, Jos'. Your love permeates everything you touch," Cleve consoled her.

"What I nice thing to say, Cleve Gregory. I love *you*, that's for sure." She leaned across the couch and pressed her lips gently against his. The perfect fit, she thought, just as she thought every single time they kissed.

"And you, you are a beautiful girl, Josie-Rose Parker. I love you more than you could know. Have I ever told you that?" Cleve returned the gesture of the kiss and then pulled her in close to his strong, broad chest. He kissed her again and then stood, extending a hand to her, and gestured toward the bedroom. The dogs retreated to their beds, and the candle was left flickering on the coffee table until it burned its own way out. All talking ceased for the evening. Love was in the air at the Haskell cottage.

It was that evening that the idea for a great plan came into Cleve Gregory's head, and he couldn't wait to put it into motion. He tossed and turned all night thinking about it, anxious for the sun to show itself so he could get up and get going. *Man if you pull this one off, you are the magic,* he said to himself as he reached across and caressed the long strawberry blond locks of Josie's hair. She slept on. Unable to lie still any longer, he pulled back the covers and headed, in his boxers, toward the back door to let the four pups out for their morning perusal of the backyard.

There seemed to be even more good karma in the air when Addie came back from Devon victorious. Everyone seemed over the top with excitement. Everyone except for Addie. Josie knew something wasn't right with her young friend.

Classified, Addie's other hunter, had tripped and cut himself in the schooling area the day the horses had arrived at the show in Pennsylvania. The wound needed a few stitches, so they scratched him from the competition and sent him home. He was scheduled to leave Clover Field the following week, to go to his new owner, a young rider from Charlottesville, Virginia. Addie was disappointed, to say the least. But experienced competitor that she had become, she knew she had to look forward positively. Josie knew that wasn't what was bothering her young protégé.

The jumper Addie still owned won some good ribbons, but it was the funny-looking little red horse that brought home the loving cup trophy.

"Grand hunter champion? Best child rider? That's just over the moon, Addie Crawford," Cleve blasted down the aisle when he saw her on what happened to be her last day at the barn. Addie was sad, and not even Cleve's big bear hug seemed to ease the pain of saying good-bye to everyone. But Josie knew there was something more profound on her mind, she just wasn't sure what it was.

"My advice to you is kiss your horses and get the hell out of here fast," Josie guided Addie. "Hanging around will only make it worse. Don't forget to give Ramon a big hug too; he's been depressed all week thinking about you leaving. Now c'mon, chin up. You'll be in Paris in less than a week, how bad can things be?" Josie asked rhetorically, attempting to lighten the mood and leave an opening for Addie to spill her guts if she needed or wanted to.

"How bad? Like super bad, if you really want to know. Real bad. Jack broke up with me my last day at Devon, Josie. He wasn't a jerk or anything; he was just honest. He told me he couldn't deal with the reality of me being gone all summer, and then heading off to Rhode Island in the fall. He said we'd never see each other, so there was no point. He's going to turn professional in December. He's in it to win it and I don't fit into that plan." Addie looked off into the distance, then continued. "He's right you know, Josie, he's right. We are going in two different directions. I just wanted to have this summer. Whatever, it sucks. It sucks mostly because my mom is getting exactly what she wanted."

Surprised to hear that Addie still held so much anger toward her mom, Josie contemplated everything the young, emotional girl had said before responding. She'd always felt that Addie and Pam had a relationship that emulated what she and her mama had, and all this nonsense just didn't seem to fit the bill. Or maybe it did. How did Josie know what might have happened if Dorie Parker had disapproved of Josie's choice in boyfriends? *Mama died before she even knew how I felt about Cleve. What if she hadn't liked him? Wouldn't that have changed everything?* She thought about Kenna telling her not to make any assumptions about what made people, customers, act the way they did. She thought about Tessa and the dysfunctional relationship she had with her mother. Nothing was perfect. Josie loved Addie, but she loved Pamela Crawford too. So she proceeded with caution.

"The way I see it Ad', good mamas only do what they think is best for us. They're not always right, but they are always trying to do the right thing. Your mom loves you. I don't for one minute believe she is taking you to Europe to get you away from Jack. Jack's a fine guy and she knows that. I know she's not purposely trying to take you from the horses either. It's just time for that to happen, unfortunately. Maybe it's a little more her time than yours, but it is what it is. She's losing her baby girl to college in a couple of months. Is it unrealistic to think she just might selfishly want some quality time with you before you go? Who knows what her real motivation is. And sometimes timing just stinks." Josie wasn't sure any of what she was offering was sinking in, but she continued. "Do yourself a big favor. Don't question it. Don't question her dedication to giving you a great life. She's your mom, and she's the only mom you will ever have. Not to sound morbid, but you never know how long she'll be around, take it from me. Everything else is just minutia. She is doing what she needs to do. Take a breath, kiss your horses, give me a hug, and get yourself to Paris. Seriously kiddo. Trust me, Jack's not going anywhere fast. A girl as great as you doesn't come along too often."

"I will second that," said Cleve, who'd walked up at the tail end of Josie's soliloquy. "Besides, by this time next year he'll probably have realized he's gay anyway. You know what the rumor mill has to say about that, right?" Cleve raised his eyebrows and pointed at his own cheek, poking fun.

"Shut up, Cleve. I know Jack's not gay, OK?" Addie finally smiled as she defended her young love. Josie embraced Addie and squeezed her tightly.

"I love you, kid. Have a great time and get back here safe and sound. I am sure your chestnut horse will be here waiting for you. He's not anxious to go home with anybody else, as he's illustrated during his last two trials. He'll be here, hanging out with me and Ramon, and Sparks." Josie kissed her young comrade on the forehead and released her hold. "By the way, I really like Hermès scarves," Josie winked.

"I love you guys too. Even you, Cleve, you pain in my ass. Take care of this girl." Addie moved from Josie to Cleve and reached out for his embrace. "And my kooky little horse, too."

And just like Josie had instructed, Addie turned on her heels and was gone.

41

B y mid-August, Cleve had just about finished the job of repairing the cottage barn roof. Renovating the small barn in his spare time was all a part of his secret grand plan. A plan that, other than Doc, no one knew about. Josie Parker was clueless and Cleve was quite proud that his surreptitious efforts were holding the surprise tight. *Can't usually get a damn thing past that brainiac,* he thought as he headed into the cottage one afternoon to make some phone calls before Josie got home.

"Good afternoon," he spoke into the phone, "my name is Cleve Gregory. I work with Doctor Peter Thurman in Colts Neck, New Jersey. I was wondering if I've dialed the correct number. I'm trying to reach the RichRanch Horse Auction."

He spoke at length with the person on the other end of the line, taking notes, asking questions, asking the same questions again. After five or ten minutes he hung the phone up. He raised his arms up and pushed the hair back off his forehead with both his hands, exhaling a large, loud breath, seemingly of frustration. He picked up the phone receiver and dialed another number.

"Good afternoon, my name is Cleve Gregory. I work with Doctor Peter Thurman in Colts Neck, New Jersey. I'm trying to reach Mr. Langley. Do I have the correct number? OK. Yes, thanks, I will hold on. Thanks again."

As far as any competitive equestrian was concerned, The Hampton Classic Horse Show in Bridgehampton, New York, signified the end of another summer and the last chance to earn qualifying points for the upcoming indoor series. The Classic was fast becoming a huge social event; spectators and exhibitors included an eclectic mix of celebrities, international figures, and major players from every industry. Everyone who was anyone in the Hamptons wanted to see and be seen at the Hampton Classic, on or off a horse. This year's show came and went with no Addie Crawford, who, just back from Europe, was too busy gearing up for orientation at Brown University.

"Fortunately for Addie, out of sight and out of mind seems to have done the trick. I don't think Addie had any interest at all in the Hampton Classic or even in stopping by Clover Field before heading to school," Josie conveyed to Kenna as they unloaded the horses coming back from the show on the Sunday of Labor Day weekend. "I talked to her for a long while on the phone last night. She is in a really good place and ready for the next chapter in her life. She was really ready after Devon, just not quite steady on her feet about it. She had a super great trip, and she's talked to Jack Sawyer who—news flash—is not gay yet," she laughed. "Most importantly she and Pamela are in a great place. I just know she is psyched to get to Brown."

"Like you say, lucky for her. Most of the riders who know they are heading off to college are like that; they have a whole new universe in front of them. You can't blame her, she's so smart and has so much to offer the big, wide world. As for Pam, remember what I told you last spring. You never know what motivates people to do what they do. We probably won't ever know if there is more to the story than meets the eye. They were really wonderful customers, I know you agree. I hate to see them gone from the barn."

Nonetheless, Josie still had the delightful task of keeping John Courage fit and ready for trials. He was the only one of the Crawfords' horses not yet sold. They had not even had a single offer. In fact, almost every time someone came to try him, Johnnie would inevitably manage to spit the rider into the dirt; on more than one occasion Josie and Kenna had been lambasted with harsh parting comments from disgruntled potential buyers.

"I heard that horse had a screw loose but I was willing to try him, he's so talented." Or, "That horse is like a one-man dog, I don't ever recall seeing him do that to Addie Crawford. You must have some good tricks up your sleeve, Kenna." Kenna was as frustrated as a trainer could be, she only *wished* she had a trick or two up her sleeve that would help her get to the bottom of the quirky chestnut horse.

For Josie, Johnnie was perfect every time out and the conundrum baffled her as much as it did Kenna. She couldn't figure out how to get him to behave for strangers. He was so damn smart.

"Listen, you pain in the ass, you have got to start treating other people with some respect," Josie scolded Johnnie as she walked him in from the paddock one morning. "Ramon and I are not going with you when you find a new owner, and you need to find one soon. Someone who will take care of you like we do. So stop making things tough for yourself." She shook her head as she led the horse along, and continued her soliloquy.

"I'm buying lottery tickets for us every week, boy, but it's not looking good. I can't afford to keep you. You don't want the Crawfords to get sick of having to carry you. Who knows what might happen if they do. God, Johnnie, I don't ever want you ending up like Lars." Then, immediately feeling like she'd made a hurtful comment to a friend, she retorted, "That won't happen, I promise."

She gave the gelding a solid pat on his neck and strangely, he stopped defiantly in his tracks, turning his head indignantly, to stare at her as though he understood exactly what she had said.

"You get what I'm saying, don't you John Courage?" Josie asked rhetorically. "I'm sorry," she said. He shook his entire body, as though relieving himself of bad energy, though more likely to expel a biting fly from his back, and waited for her command to walk on. Josie reached into her pocket and pulled out a cube of sugar, feeling guilty about what she had insinuated. *You won't end up like Lars,* she said under her breath as the two headed into the barn. She couldn't help how she felt. *You just won't. The Crawfords wouldn't do that to you and I won't let it happen again. I will figure something out.*

The weekend arrived. Josie and Cleve had agreed to take two days off from work, a rarity. The timing was perfect for both of them; with a break in the show calendar, life would be manageable at the barn and Cleve's business would slow down except for routine maintenance and emergency calls. Rather than their usual routine of popping out of bed with the sunrise, the two slept in on Saturday, rolling around under the sheets playfully for hours. The dogs stayed curled up in their own beds, somehow knowing that this morning was an exception to the rule and they would just have to wait it out.

Eventually making their way to the kitchen, Josie and Cleve tag teamed to cook up a huge breakfast. They danced around the house to loud music, using utensils as faux instruments. They took long showers, dressed slowly, and decided that their most important mission of the weekend was to settle on a paint color for the barn. They took the dogs for a walk along the trails behind the cottage, and then got to work hanging the new stall doors.

Leaning against the doorframe while Cleve worked at tightening the last hinges, Josie contemplated all he had done to make the barn like new. Looking further out, surveying her property on this quintessential Indian summer afternoon, she admired the beauty in front of her. The garden, though still lazily blooming with sedum, goldenrod, and coneflower, was looking a little worn. *I've got some work to do out there tomorrow,* she thought to herself. Her scrutiny continued and her focus zeroed in on the chicken coop, one of Josie's favorite treasures. The crowing rooster, beckoning to his hens, somehow prompted her to turn her attention back to Cleve, who simultaneously called out, his voice commanding but exhibiting the quality of a very content man.

"Hey, Earth to Josie Parker."

She smiled and said, "Sorry, it's just that it's so amazing here, Cleve." She reached out to give him one of the screws she was holding in her hand.

She stared down at him, watching him work. He lay stretched out on the barn floor, his plaid shirt ruched up around his torso which, exposed and tan, resembled a washboard, wide at the chest and narrow at the waist. As he twisted the screw into the two by four, the muscles in his arms flexed and relaxed with each turn of the Phillips-head. Josie felt heat rising in her cheeks. In an attempt to distract herself from her rapidly increasing desire and her pounding heart, she spoke, really hating to break the beautiful silence of the moment, but caught off guard and self-conscious over her reaction to this incredibly handsome man's unknowing display of consummate masculinity.

"Gray with white trim," she instructed, with heavy breath, jumping into her role as "chief picker of paint color," as Cleve had dubbed her.

"Someday I want our stable colors to be gray and white, with a little brown thrown in somewhere. That will make for pretty coolers. It's so hard to pick colors that no other barn has, and I haven't seen that combo anywhere."

"Gray with white trim it will be then, Miss Parker," he said without looking up. "Now what do you say we drive over to Long Branch tomorrow to get our feet in the sand? We can bring the dogs. Tomorrow is supposed to be spectacular and there won't be too many beach days left since it's already the second week of September." Josie nodded in agreement as Cleve reached up to take another screw. He instantly noticed the flush in her cheeks and something about the look in her eyes. She cast an angelic, demure vibe, and his heart began to race. The mood changed. Cleve playfully but deliberately grabbed her extended arm and pulled her gently down to her knees. Affectionately he brushed at her hair, twisting a lock or two with his fingers. He kissed her mouth with his full, perfect lips.

"Beautiful." He spoke, definitive but tranquil. He coaxed her to rise with him, and swung her body gently back and forth. He kissed her again. It was a long, seductive kiss.

Utterly weak now, she allowed her head to drop as she arched her back, exposing her long neck to his mouth and he kissed her there, several times. He supported her entire weight with one arm behind her, lifting her up with the other, then carried her across the aisle to the small hay room, where he lay her down on the straw.

"Maybe before we think about the beach we should christen this barn," he said without any question in his delivery. "I'd be a liar if I said I haven't thought about doing this every single day since I started working on the damn place." He wasn't looking for a response, but if he had been, Josie's body language was enough to convey everything he needed to know.

42

By the time the middle of October rolled around, the perennial garden had all but faded, and the woods were starting to look bare, but the little four-stall barn at the Haskell cottage had a new roof, new stalls, feed bins, buckets, floor mats, and shiny new paint; the only thing missing now? Occupants.

"You did such an outstanding job on the barn, Cleve," Josie complimented her handy man as they walked the property one evening after dinner. She reached out and touched his cheek in a gesture of thanks. "The paddocks are still so lush and green. There are all those trails back behind us in the conservancy. We are ready. We need some animals in there. How will we find some boarders?" She was goading him a bit; she had an ulterior motive.

"One thing at a time," Cleve said, thinking about his secret plan, "one thing at a time. Be patient, beautiful. I will talk to Doc about finding some good potential customers for us. He always hears about folks looking for a place to board lay-ups or retired ones. Maybe even a brood mare. I'm not worried. I've got this. You just leave it up to me and focus on getting that John Courage ready for the indoor shows." He wrapped his arm up over her shoulders and around her neck, pulling her to face him, and kissed her authoritatively, then frivolously pushed her away, spinning her so that she walked forward ahead of him. "I got this."

Josie wasn't for one minute worried. She was worried, however, contemplating what he might say about the idea she had for Johnnie's fate. She figured now was as good a time as any to spring her plan.

"I wanna know what you think about something. I have an idea." She walked backwards in front of him for a few paces, until he caught up to her, then they continued on, shoulder to shoulder. Cleve took Josie's hand, sensing that whatever it was that she was about to say might somehow be difficult for her.

"Hit me," he encouraged her to go on.

"It's a crazy idea and most likely unattainable, but I've been thinking about it for a while, and with the indoor series looming, I think it's now or never.

"I talked to Addie on the phone a few nights ago and she has no interest in showing at indoors; she's totally out of practice and she's pledging a sorority or something like that. She told me that her parents aren't really thrilled about the idea of someone else riding Johnnie there, but they will go along with it if Kenna thinks it's paramount to him getting sold. I get the principle, but truthfully, I don't think anyone would be able to get him around, he's been out of the show ring for too long now. He'll be a total brat no matter how well Ramon and I prepare him." She shrugged her shoulders in a gesture of doubt. "I could be wrong, but I know that horse. It's just not my place to say anything like that to Kens' right now. She's trying to run a business. I'm sure she will discuss it with me at some point."

Cleve nodded in agreement. *He spins or he wins*, he thought to himself and chuckled. The four dogs went galloping by, onto the scent of a skunk or a possum. "Here!" Cleve yelled out in a half-hearted attempt to corral them. "I'm listening, Jos', keep going." He squeezed her hand once again and Josie continued.

"As of right now he's got one more sales trial, with a girl from California who is coming east to ride at indoors. If that doesn't work, I don't see the Crawfords having a shot at selling him without sending him to Florida again, and they're not gonna want to do that. Like Addie said, her folks are pretty much over carrying the expense of the horse. They haven't had any offers at all. But Layton Crawford still thinks he should be able to get a hundred for him. I'm so worried about the fate of John Courage. This is feeling more and more like a big, bad déjà vu."

Cleve could sense Josie heating up and getting off the point of her story, so he interrupted.

"Hit me with the idea, Jos'. I can't imagine what you are thinking. C'mon, tell me." Truth be told, he was beginning to get the picture. He smiled.

"Well," she took in a deep breath. "In a round about way it's actually a Frank Parker idea." She stopped moving forward and turned to stand in front of Cleve. The moonlight, shining from behind, framed her face against the dark woods. He reached out to touch her cheek, preoccupied for just a second with her beauty.

"Stop, Cleve, please listen to me." She was harsh in her delivery and instantly realizing this said, "Sorry, this idea gives me such angst and I just need to get it out."

"Sorry," he said. "Go on."

"Anyway, Dad planted the seed when he came to Clover Field to meet Johnnie. So," she took another obvious breath, preparing to get her idea out in one fell swoop, totally convinced that Cleve would think she had lost her mind. "So, I think if I kept Johnnie at the cottage barn, or if Kens' would give me a break in Clover Field board, which I think she would, then I could afford to maintain him. It's not like I would be taking him to any of the big shows, but maybe I could manage some of the more local stuff once in a while, which would be fun. It would be like old times if you'd come along as my groom sometimes, huh?" This small diversion from the heart of the conversation gave rise to momentary playfulness. Cleve gave Josie an affectionate shove as if to imply he wouldn't be caught dead grooming for her.

"Yeah, right. That was then and this is now." He smiled at her and winked.

Serious again, she went on. "It's really just a question of coming up with the money to buy him." *There*, she thought to herself, *it's out there*. "So, this is my idea. I'm going to have Mama's jewelry appraised, all of it, even the ring. Even the ring," she repeated, in an attempt to convince herself. "That's really the best piece. I think it's the most valuable, the most meaningful for sure. You know Mama used to—wait, never mind that. I think with the ring as part of the deal, it could all be worth some serious money." She got back to the matter at hand.

"I think the guy at The Gold Tinker jewelry shop would do an appraisal for me, and then I will ask him what he would actually give me for all of it." She stared down at the grass, as though looking for something on the ground to fortify her so she could actually utter the remaining words. "Then, I'm going to offer that amount to the Crawfords, and if they will agree to sell him to me for that, I'm selling the jewelry and buying Johnnie." She paused just for a second then said, "It's a crazy idea right? Completely stupid."

Josie was relieved that she had shared this ridiculous idea with someone, with Cleve. She was completely confident he would tell her it was unrealistic and, well, wrong. That jewelry was Mama's memory, he would say. That ring was meant to stay in the Caldwell family forever. He would surely tell her that no horse was worth giving that up. Then, thank God, this screwy notion would be behind her, and she could get it out of her head. *After all, I'm not in the horse rescue business,* she thought to herself as she began to realize just how ludicrous this idea, once vocalized, actually sounded.

The darkness had settled in. It was a crisp, clear evening. Having walked the entire property, Cleve now pulled out a chair for Josie at the small wrought iron table on the back patio, then sat down himself. He lit the candle in the hurricane lantern. She tugged on the zipper of her fleece, closing it up around her neck, feeling a chill. Cleve took both of Josie's hands in his. He held them there for just a minute, then, in absolute Cleve fashion, let go and twirled one of her braids. She stared at him in anticipation of his response. He said nothing. Rather, in silence, he pulled the small elastic off the end of the braid and slowly untwisted her hair from the plait it had been confined to all day. He did the same with the other braid. He tipped his head and stared now, at the strawberry blond waves cascading along each side of her angelic face. He loved her hair. He loved all of her. He knew how much she loved that horse, and more importantly, he knew Josie couldn't help but feel that she could redeem herself from Lars' ill-fated end, if she could somehow ensure that Johnnie's future was secure. This was her albatross. The whole situation was daunting for her and he was keenly aware of the anguish she experienced every time someone came to Clover Field to try the horse. He knew she was tortured by the prospect of someone buying him. Tortured by the prospect of no one wanting him. He pushed a few locks behind her shoulder, tucking them in behind her ear. He felt so protective of her, and he wanted to lift this weight from her shoulders. He also truly believed what he was about to say.

"You're not closing the door on your mama if you sell her jewelry, Josie." He paused and offered a smile, though she didn't see it. She stared down and moved her hand across Fraser, who had jumped into her lap and curled up. Cleve continued, leaning in and crossing his arms over the top of the table.

"You're not letting her down. Actually, if she's up there in that sky somewhere watching us and listening to this conversation, I believe wholeheartedly that she is cheering you on. I bet she's got her fingers crossed hoping she can somehow play a positive role in what we've got going on right here." Josie looked up and he nodded, pointing his chin out across the yard, over to the barn. "'Come on, Josie,' she's saying. 'Go for it; don't be afraid. You love that horse and you should fight for him. If there's a chance those small pieces of metal can help you realize your dream, then they have served a far better purpose than they would have just being jewelry.' Maybe you should dig out that letter your father wrote and reread it. This moment is exactly what he was talking about. I think it's a great idea, Josie Parker. No, I think it's a perfect idea. Who knows if it will work, and you do need to consider that, but if you don't at least try, you will always wonder. Great idea, Parker."

Cleve gave Josie's shoulder an affectionate little push, endeavoring to take the heaviness out of the air surrounding them.

"The Crawfords love you, Jos'. They know you and Johnnie are, OK, weird." He laughed. "And hell, Layton Crawford is a Wall Street guy, he might just be intrigued by your proposition and go for it. I know those trader types, they love the roll of the dice. An artful deal is so tempting for them. You owe it to yourself to go for it, too. Go on, Jos', give it a whirl." He rubbed her arm now, and dipped his head in to kiss her forehead. They sat, silent, for a minute or so, then Cleve stood up to give her some breathing room and headed into the house. Fraser jumped down and followed Cleve. Token stayed at Josie's side. She sat at the table a while longer, elbows on her knees, head supported by her hands, staring blankly down at her clogs. She really hadn't expected Cleve to think it was a good idea; she was hoping he might be her voice of reason. And now she was totally confused. Scared, actually petrified. She stared down, watching the little puddles her tears made disappear instantly as they hit the ground. She wasn't really sure why she was crying, but in some strange way it felt good. It felt cathartic.

What is the answer? What is really the right thing to do? Am I selfish to want this horse for my own? she asked herself. *Am I trying to manufacture my future at someone else's cost? Is that right to do?* So many thoughts traveled through her cluttered mind. *Mama, Johnnie, Lars. I let Lars down*, she thought. *I can't let Johnnie down.* Yet the thought of parting with the jewels—not as material possessions, but rather with what they had symbolized for all these years—made her feel, well, disloyal. Especially thinking about the sapphire and diamond ring. She'd planned in her own fairy tale, and essentially promised Mama, to pass that ring along to her own daughter some day in the future. That ring, which had been in the Caldwell family for generations. That history was a fundamental part of her future, a part of the story already written. As long as she had those jewels, she could fulfill her responsibility to connect her past to whatever future Mama had envisioned. As long as she had those jewels, her connection to Mama was secure. This was a fierce dilemma for Josie Parker and she was struggling to find the solution. *Why am I now questioning the decision I made?*

Wait, she thought, *isn't that it? That's exactly it.* That box of precious metal and stones kept her past connected to her future, whatever that might become. Right there, no further away than her bedside table, was a crystal ball that let her see back into the past, and forward into the future. What tangible connection would she have to the past if she gave up the contents of the silver box with Mama's monogram on it? How would she bring that past into the future if she didn't have the ring to pass on to the next generation of the Caldwell family? Wasn't that her troth after all? *Isn't that my responsibility to my family history?* It was the safe, selfless decision. *Keep the jewels and the past stays with me. I can't rewrite the future. I can't change what has already been planned. It wouldn't be right. Whatever happens to Johnnie, happens. How could I even think that a horse could be more important than fulfilling a family legacy?* How could she take that chance? And how could she let go of something that for more than a decade had allowed her to feel Mama's touch against her skin.

I was only sixteen years old when that fucking aneurysm took you from me, Mama. Sixteen. I don't want to lose you again, and at the same time I want to save that horse. No one else will want him, I know it. It won't end well for John Courage. How do I know what to do?

She knew she couldn't have it both ways. She asked herself one final time. Could she really part with the only palpable asset she had to perpetuate her mother's memory? Josie cried as hard as she had ever cried. Harder than the night she'd finally let go after Mama's funeral. Her grief tonight was as real as it was back then. She felt such pain in her heart. Her mind raced in a million directions. This was more far more complicated than the sad loss of Lars. She'd had no control over that. Now she was confronted with a decision that had to be made. She had to get past thinking there was a way to make Johnnie become hers, or she had to get past thinking she was disloyal if she sold the jewels. She couldn't have it both ways.

Even Tessa had told her once, "Josie, you can have everything you want in life, you just can't have it all at the same time."

Damn Tessa, always right, Josie thought.

Josie dug deep into her core. She raised her head and wiped away her tears. *This is ridiculous*, she thought. *It's not that complicated. Grow up. He isn't meant to be mine*, she said to herself. *He just isn't meant to be mine, and that ring is meant to stay in our family. That is my obligation. That is the future.*

She stood and walked to the edge of the patio, and looked into the clear night sky. With her arms wrapped over her torso to fend off the chill, she whispered out loud, as though to the moon.

"I know the right thing to do, Mama. I know what I am going to do. It's not about the horse. It's about who I am, and all that you gave me, all that you taught me. And it's about perpetuating that, the Caldwell history. I love you, Mama. I miss you everyday. You are infinitely in my heart."

Josie turned to walk back to the cottage, emotionally exhausted, but feeling quite steadfast in her resolve. Token, uncharacteristically not following at Josie's heels, remained at the edge of the patio and barked tenaciously, beckoning Josie to turn to face the dark night sky for just an instant more. Josie returned.

Token stood beside her, quiet now, and she seemed to look up at the darkness too. Josie felt compelled to speak.

"If...if you think I am making the wrong decision," she whispered, "help me, Mama. Shine your light on me." The words proved that Josie had simply made a decision. Truly in her heart, after all her soul searching and deliberation, she was still so very conflicted.

And in that instant, that very instant, as the words fell from her lips, something quite amazing happened. From no specific place that could be pinpointed in the darkness, an incredibly vivid shooting star, maybe it was even a comet, brilliantly blazed a long, arresting trail in slow motion across the universe, right in front of Josie Parker's disbelieving eyes.

"Oh!" she cried out, physically taking a step back, awestruck as the beacon of light disappeared into the woods, leaving behind a glowing aftermath that lasted for several seconds.

"Oh!" she gasped again, pointing up to the sky and looking around her as though to see if anyone else had noticed. The tears rolled down her face again. This time she knew exactly why they were there. In this magnificent instant she felt liberated, happy, and completely exorcised of her torment. It was as though the words she'd heard Mama say to her years back had just been written across the sky.

> *Go. Go to what you love. Love what you go to. Don't have it any other way. Don't ever compromise on doing what makes you happy. Ever. Not ever in your whole life. It keeps your heart big and full. Go on, git. See you later.*

And she knew undeniably what Mama would say to her now.

"See you later, Mama," she whispered. Joy and confidence overtook her and she laughed at the night sky, now serene and tranquil. She gave Token a pat. "Thanks, girl."

The moment was life defining for Josie Parker. And in that moment she realized that not everything needed to make perfect sense. She realized too, that she had been incredibly remiss in giving credit where credit was due. John Courage, as Cleve had so often reminded her, had in fact connected her past to her future. Her future was not in a box of jewelry, her future was with Cleve, and if she could make it happen, the funny little chestnut horse should rightly be there as well. He'd brought Cleve from her past into her present. Lars and Mama would still be right there with her too, always. She didn't need anything material to keep either one of them close to her now, or moving forward.

At first a paradox, she somehow knew that her life from here on would be much more straightforward. That shooting star had served as a harbinger, announcing the beginning of a new chapter in the story of Josie Parker. She felt calm and protected with the knowledge that whatever was to happen would be as it should; she would not be judged. Not by Mama, not by her dad, not by Cleve. Her future would be whatever it would be. She could not manufacture it, but she could attempt to shape it, and that would not be a betrayal, not to anyone or any horse. She also believed now that Mama would want her to fight for Johnnie.

Relieved, she stood quietly for just a minute more, remembering her dad's words: *Whatever time we are given with someone or something is a gift. At the same time, we are not entitled, we have to work to make good things happen.* She remembered his Christmas letter: *Allow these pieces to help you create your own story.*

She turned once again toward the cottage, content to leave the moon and the stars behind, completely self-assured that her decision, having finally, truly been made, was the right one. There was not an ounce of conflict in her heart now.

"I'm gonna do it!" she proclaimed as she walked through the back door of the cottage. "I'm going to talk to the Crawfords and see what they think. You won't believe what just happened out there." She pointed behind her as she flopped down next to Cleve on the couch. "Never mind about that." She waved her arms to dismiss the thought of trying to explain the shooting star to him right now. "I suppose I already knew the right thing to do, I just needed to sort out my own inner conflict. I guess I just needed to see the light." *That and a shooting star,* she thought to herself briefly. "Who knows what the Crawfords might say, but it doesn't matter. I need to try to make John Courage mine. If it works out, it works out. If it doesn't, well then at least I will have tried, like you said. Cleve, I'm goin' for it."

"Awesome, Jos'." There was no need for further discussion. He could see that she had come to a good resolve and that she was weary. "Let's call it a night," he suggested. "What do you say? I'm shot."

"Oh gosh, I hope no one else buys him between now and the end of indoors!" All of a sudden Josie needed that upcoming sales trial with the girl from the west coast to be over. Waiting out the next few weeks would be hell, but she didn't feel it was right to offer her proposal until the "legitimate buyers" had their chance. She would take the silver box that held her future in it to the Gold Tinker as soon as she returned from her upcoming visit to Tessa's, and once that California trial was over, she would speak to the Crawfords about her idea. Unless, of course, the trial went well. She had no intention of jinxing anyone or anything, either way, so she let the subject go.

"C'mon, let's go." Cleve encouraged his girl to rise from the couch. "We've had enough drama for one night."

43

The cold of November settled in, and everyone at Clover Field was ready for the much-needed break that came between Thanksgiving and Christmas. Kenna had opted not to send Johnnie to the indoor series after all. She agreed with Josie that John Courage could have unilaterally ruined his own chances of ever getting sold if he performed badly in front of all the top equestrian professionals in the country. Additionally, neither Pamela nor Kenna wanted to be deceptive about the quirky horse's idiosyncrasies, and if he had performed like a rock star, that in itself could almost be considered inauthentic.

The girl from California who was coming to try Johnnie was a great rider. She'd placed high in the Medal and Maclay finals this year, and she already owned a couple of winning hunters. Her trainer, Joe Hennis, the tops on the west coast, thought John Courage would round out her string for the coming winter season in Palm Springs. They had planned to watch and try Johnnie at indoors, but since the decision had been made to scratch him, Kenna made arrangements with Joe for the Californians to come to the barn in Colts Neck the day after the National was over.

Mother and daughter arrived at Clover Field Monday morning at about ten. A black town car with New York livery plates zipped up the long driveway at far too great a speed, coming to a sharp halt at the entrance to the barn. The back door opened and a smallish, dark-haired, slightly chubby girl stepped out, took a few steps forward and looked around. She turned back and bent down to look into the back seat.

"Are you coming, Mom? C'mon, let's go," she said impatiently.

A woman, who at first glance, appeared far too young to have a teenage daughter, emerged from the town car, purposely neglecting to close the door, staring at it over her shoulder, then glaring over toward the driver's door.

"Jesus H. Christ, Petra, cool your jets," she said, turning to her daughter. "They will wait for us, we're the customers. What is the goddamn rush? Do you have your stuff from the trunk? Petra?" the woman screeched. She smoothed her skin tight jeans down over her thighs, straightened her Chanel boucle jacket, and reached back into the car, returning with her arms full of fur—a tiny Yorkie with a huge pink bow in one arm and a stunning sable coat in the other.

The driver, out of the car now as well, listening as he walked around to close the open back door, hesitated by the trunk. The woman motioned, indicating to the driver in a most condescending manner, to open it.

"Petra! Do you have your stuff from the trunk?" the woman asked again. The girl turned and stomped her foot.

"Mom! My chaps and hat are here, in my backpack. Geez. Let's go. And Mom, really, do you need to bring that ridiculous coat?"

Kenna saw all of this commotion as she made her way towards them from the barn. She had never met mother or daughter, but she'd heard from her west coast pals that this duo was a force with which to be reckoned. It was a classic story, not unfamiliar to the equestrian community of the west coast, but a bit rarer in the east. The mother, no doubt a model-cum-actress type a dozen or so years ago, when she'd married a Hollywood producer twice her age, was clearly going to great lengths, along with a plastic surgeon's help, to keep youth on her side. Truth was, they were doing a pretty good job. She was still gorgeous, except maybe for her neck, which pretty much gave her away. Granted, the skin tight jeans, Prada stilettos, and Chanel jacket could be considered maybe just a tiny bit overdressed for Clover Field Farm on a Monday morning in November, but she did look damn good. Her personality, as Frank Parker would say, stuck out all over, mostly out of her blouse.

The daughter, Petra deChenault, rumored to be spoiled and entitled, seemed genuinely curious and excited to be at the farm.

"Hi, I know you're Kenna. I've read about you in the *Chronicle* and I always see you at indoors. I know a bunch of your students, too. I wanted to say hello at Washington, but you were so busy. You're such an amazing equitation coach. Your riders always win!" she offered as she walked briskly up to Kenna, extending a hand. "I'm Petra, thanks for letting us come today. That's my mom, Olivia." She pointed in the direction of the Chanel, albeit a bit mortified. "She's coming. She's just getting her dog, Paris." Petra rolled her eyes as she mentioned the dog's name, and laughed, which caused Kenna to laugh as well. She quickly decided she liked this kid.

"Yup, I'm Kenna, nice to meet you, Petra. Joe has told me a lot about you. He's been your trainer for a long time, right? Congratulations by the way, you had a fantastic indoors. Well then, c'mon let's get going. Did you bring a saddle? No worries if you didn't. You can use one of ours. Why don't you head straight on in and I will wait for your mom." Kenna pointed down the aisle to where John Courage waited on the crossties. No way would she show off that horse's stall behavior if she didn't have to. Of course she would tell them that he could be a little cranky, but they didn't have to actually see just how cranky.

"Hi there, Kenna Mahon, I hope your trip here wasn't too tough, I know you guys must be exhausted. You've been out east a while now I imagine, no? Ready to head home I'm sure." Kenna referenced how well Petra had done at the National Horse Show, then turned in the direction of the barn. "Petra's already gone up, we can go this way to the ring if you like." Kenna pointed at the brick walkway. "Might be easier for you." She glanced down at the woman's Pradas. Olivia deChenault acknowledged the blunder and laughed.

"You know," she said as she shook Kenna's hand, "I got so excited about coming east that I packed all my 'New Yorkie' clothes. I didn't think about being out in the boonies. I'd have been much better off in a pair of boots today, I know. What the fuck was I thinking? You should have seen me trying to get around at Harrisburg in Manolos!"

Kenna wasn't sure if she should be insulted or not. *Was that comment for real? The "boonies"? And c'mon, her daughter has how many horses and she doesn't own a pair of muck boots?* She asked herself, *Is this woman as dumb as a jump standard or am I just totally unsophisticated?* She told herself her money would be on the latter, and she quietly giggled. The two women, sans the sable coat, made their way to where Petra would be riding Johnnie. Kenna walked out into the middle of the ring, Olivia stopped where the dirt began.

"I'm good right here." She pointed down to the solid footing, smiling. "Someone is going to video this, right?"

Joe Hennis hadn't been able to come with the deChenaults, so Kenna had suggested that they video tape the trial, then Petra could take it back to California to show her trainer.

"Yes, definitely, Ramon is going to do it. He's a pro. Here they come now." Kenna pointed toward the end of the ring.

Petra, in the saddle, directed Johnnie into the ring from the barn, Josie cautiously maintaining a light grip on the reins as she walked alongside them. Ramon walked out into the center of the ring and readied the video camera. Josie fed a treat to Johnnie and let go of the reins. She settled into the portal to watch. She'd heard this kid was a sharp, scrappy rider, and that's pretty much what John Courage needed. She hated the thought though, of losing him to the west coast. *OK, let's see how this goes*, she mumbled to herself, checking to be sure she had a few more molasses treats in her back pocket.

Ramon followed the chestnut horse around the ring through the lens of his camcorder as the young rider put the horse through his paces. Petra deChenault got right down to business, working him methodically on the flat, and John Courage responded like a champ. Josie chewed on a fingernail as she watched from a distance, as proud as she could be, and anxiety ridden at the same time; he was perfect.

"OK, Petra, how about you jump this little brush box a few times?" Kenna asked, directing the girl's attention to the single jump midway across the ring and motioning to Ramon that he should focus in on it. He headed in the direction of the jump, mumbling to himself.

"La Madre Santa, hace por favor, que este caballo se comporta. OK Johnnie my boy, let's get this done."

Petra picked up the right lead and cantered out of the turn toward the brush box jump. Josie could see Johnnie's ears were pricked forward, he was zoned in on the task put before him. Petra rode beautifully and the chestnut horse snapped his knees up and jumped a perfect jump. He cantered away without incident.

Kenna looked over at Josie for an instant, nodding a sign of relief. Josie remained frozen in her stare, not wanting to tip anyone off that they were both grateful that the horse had behaved. Petra jumped the jump perfectly two more times in each direction then pulled up to a walk and looked to Kenna for instruction. Petra gave Johnnie a pat on the neck, and he swished his tail in response.

Oh shit, Josie thought to herself when she saw that tail flip through the air. Just as she was thinking how much she liked this kid and that Johnnie seemed to as well, he raised the damn red warning flag. A signal Josie knew all too well. *Trouble ahead.* Josie crossed her fingers. *C'mon Johnnie, don't do it.*

From the center of the ring, Ramon, who also knew the significance of the swished tail, mumbled, "Cagado, la cola, problema esta viniendo. Shit, the tail, trouble is coming."

This would be the last straw for John Courage. Josie cringed as she watched Johnnie spit Petra, like a lawn dart, into the dirt of the indoor ring. He had successfully fooled the experienced rider into believing she could relax her leg away from the girth and let him float to the jump. One of his best tricks. It had taken Addie quite a while to stop falling for that one. Fortunately Petra was fine, both the first time he dumped her and the second, but her mother thought twice was quite enough and the deChenaults were gone in a flash, Olivia politely offering that she thought he was just a bit too much horse for Petra, but very talented just the same. Secretly, Josie uncrossed her fingers as soon as the two Californians and the Yorkie with the pink bow were in the town car and on their way. She knew that the challenge was now hers, and for just a second, she crossed them again. She would take the jewelry box to the Gold Tinker before she left for Tessa's on Wednesday. *Here goes nothing,* she said to herself as she turned back to the chores of the day.

44

On Tuesday morning, Cleve meandered around the house, killing time to be sure Josie left before he did. Josie kissed him good-bye and walked out the front door, carrying the silver jewelry box in a canvas duffle. Her plan was to drop it off at the Gold Tinker, so that by the time she returned from Florida, the appraisal would be done. Cleve watched discreetly from a front window in the cottage until her truck was far down the driveway. He let Fraser out into the backyard, poured himself a second cup of coffee, then turned to the kitchen phone. He dialed a number and stretched out the cord so he could sit down at the small dining table.

"Good morning, this is Cleve Gregory calling for Mr. Crawford please. Sure, I'll hold. Thanks." Cleve nervously tapped the end of his pencil against his yellow pad and waited. Within just a minute or two, he heard the sounds of someone fumbling to pick up the phone on the other end of the line.

"Don't tell me you're ready to give up the horse nonsense and come back to the wonderful world of finance, Mr. Gregory?" Layton Crawford did not begin with a typical greeting.

"No sir, not a chance. I'll take outdoors in the fresh air over a monitor on the floor any day of the week. I can lament about the compensation, but lucky for me, those few years at Randolph Brothers were fruitful, and I'm not doing so badly investing on my own. I do, however, have a trade proposition I would like to discuss with you. Is this a good time? Have you a got a few minutes to hear me out before the morning bell?"

"You bet, and why does my gut tell me this is going to have something to do with that pain in the ass chestnut horse my daughter can't seem to unload?"

"Funny sir, we all seem to preface any reference to that horse these days with the same colloquialism. Yes, you are right, I would like to talk with you about John Courage."

"Well, since we are speaking in colloquialisms, if the horseshoe fits, then wear it. What idea have you got up your sleeve, kid?"

The two men spoke at length, mostly about the trade proposal Cleve had to offer, but also about life, finance, horses, and of course, family. Layton and Cleve were only acquaintances, their paths had not crossed too many times since the night they had met at the National Horse Show. But as luck would have it, they were simpatico. Two men bonded over the love of some very special women woven into their lives. As Cleve placed the phone back in its cradle, he thought to himself, *Now there's a guy with credibility and integrity, unlike the asshole I had for a father. He's not out to impress or screw anyone and he does what he does because he loves it. More importantly, he loves his family. He really does. His wife, his daughter. They are his priority. And, he loves Josie too. That part definitely worked in my favor.*

Now that he was square with Layton Crawford, he needed to make yet another call, focusing back on the plan he'd been working on for months. Christmas would be here before he could count to ten and he needed to work out a few more details. He let Fraser back in, then picked up the phone and dialed again.

"Hey, Mike. Cleve Gregory, how are you? I'm just calling to make sure we are all set for next week. I know you've got a big weekend coming up with your Thanksgiving Day Hunt. I wish Josie and I could make it to the Hunt Ball on Saturday night, but I'm on call that whole weekend and Josie's flying down to Florida tomorrow to visit Tessa and Alan and the new baby for a few days. They had a healthy, hefty boy in August, you know. So great after the scare they had in the spring. Josie's been chomping at the bit to get down there and this is really the first shot she's had. Are we all good? Anything you need me to do between now and then?"

Cleve listened intently as Mike talked on the other end of the line. He took several notes and doodled a bit as the long-winded Irishman rambled on about the hunt, even bringing up the kennel at Hidden Green that had been Cleve's unfinished project of long ago. Ultimately he assured Cleve that everything that been had asked of him was good to go, and he wished Cleve, Josie, and their families a happy Thanksgiving.

"Okay, great, same back to you. I will check in with you in about two weeks. Thanks again for all your help. I couldn't have put this all into place without you. Really, I mean that. If all goes as planned, I will see you just before Christmas. Thanks Mike, I'll be talking to ya."

One more call to make. Again Cleve picked up the phone and dialed, this time connecting to the Gold Tinker Jewelry Shop in Rumson.

"Joe, hey brotha', what's happening?" Cleve didn't need to announce himself, his voice was completely familiar to the person on the other end of the line. "Haven't seen you in ages, man. Long time since our days on the baseball diamond at Parson Prep. Listen, you are about to pay me back for that favor I did for you junior year, remember?"

"Hey, Gregory, fuck you. You did me no favor, OK?" Joe Serocci's voice was laden with humor. Cleve laughed heartily at his old friend's reaction.

"Well, let's just say we helped each other through a tough time then, alright? But seriously man, I got a little covert action going on here and you are unknowingly right in the middle. I really need your help."

"You got it bro', anything for you. Just don't tell me you're getting married and you want a discount on a huge diamond. I get those calls every day of the week. That's boring shit. At least make it interesting bro'."

"Oh you have no idea how interesting and convoluted this is going to be. You remember Josie Parker, right?" Cleve began his saga and half an hour later he hung up from his last phone call of the morning, satisfied that everything was in place just as he needed it to be.

Smooth sailing now until Christmas, he hoped.

He grabbed his jacket, gloves and hat, and whistled to Fraser who followed obediently. He opened the front door and felt an emotional chill run through his body as he stepped out into the first snowfall of the season. He thought back to just a year ago when he'd stood on that front porch with Josie for the first time.

"It's snowing," she had whispered.

"You're beautiful," he'd replied.

Josie steeled herself as she stared into the bathroom mirror. Back from a great visit with Tessa, today she would make her call to Pamela Crawford.

Even though Josie was planning to talk with Pamela by way of a phone conversation, she felt compelled to dress as though she were participating in an interview. Somehow putting on her favorite white cotton blouse and the newly purchased navy, cashmere Ralph Lauren sweater gave her a sense of confidence. She pulled on her favorite jeans and secured them around her waist, sliding the Hermès scarf Addie had brought back from Paris through the belt loops and tying a knot at her hip. Instead of paddock boots, she slipped into her ankle-high suede boots with fringe around the top edge. *There*, she thought, *at least I look professional.*

She had already let Kenna know that she was going to be late to the barn. She slid her chair tightly up to the desk in her family room and put her hand on the phone; she knew the number by memory. She dialed and hoped she could hear above the din of her own pounding heart. Josie had full conviction about her decision, but she was still a nervous wreck. What if they said yes to her offer? What if they said no? The "what ifs" were a mile long in her brain and she just needed someone to answer on the other end, in a hurry.

"Hello, Crawford residence," the housekeeper answered.

"Lasanne, hi this is Josie, how are you? Happy holidays. Is Mrs. Crawford available to speak with me this morning?"

"One moment, I will check for you. Thank you, Miss Josie. I am fine. Happy holidays to you too."

"Hello Josie!" Pamela Crawford's voice came exuberantly through the receiver a minute later. "Are you calling to tell me that someone wants to buy that pain in the ass chestnut of ours? If not then you better be calling to tell me you are getting married or something that would be equally exciting to hear. I have no interest in bad news this morning, sweetie." *Wow*, thought Josie, *she's got some imagination.*

"Well, actually, there is someone who would like to make you an offer for John Courage." Josie took in a deep breath. "That someone would be me." The pause on the other end of the line seemed to last forever.

"I'm not sure I understand. You say you know someone who would like to make an offer?" Pamela seemed to be confused. Josie tried again.

"Well, actually, I would like to make an offer. I would like to buy Johnnie from you. I don't want to offend you or Layton in any way, but I would like to make a proposition. Do you have time to listen? Would now be an okay time? I could call back later." Josie was so anxiety ridden.

"Okay, sure. I still don't quite understand but try me. This is, of course, very important. Of course I have the time."

Josie talked a little about the jewelry box, and the letter from her father, and about how her parents and her grandmother had always encouraged her to allow the contents to help her create a life that encompassed all that was meaningful to her. Pamela knew much of the story, as she had listened to Josie talk often about her mama, and she remembered admiring some of the beautiful pieces when Josie had worn them to Madison Square Garden last November. Pam always felt a bit sad when Josie would talk about how she sometimes lived vicariously watching Addie and her interact.

"Well, after much deliberation, and well, frankly, an encounter with a shooting star, I took the jewelry box and the entirety of its contents to a reputable jeweler and had everything appraised. The jeweler is willing to give me sixty-five thousand dollars in exchange for all of it. I know that's not the number you are looking for, but I am hoping you will consider it. So, I'd like to make you an offer of sixty-five thousand dollars. You know how much I love him, Pam, and you know he would always have a good home with me. I'm not sure I could keep him at Clover Field, but Cleve and I have really fixed up the barn at my cottage, and he would be perfectly comfortable there. Anyway, I'd like to ask if you will discuss it with Layton and let me know. I hope more than anything that I haven't offended you with my conservative offer. You know that would never be my intention." Josie thought she just might cry. This was one of the most emotionally wrought moments of her life. The culmination of so many events, people, horses, situations. She wasn't sure what to think now, and she figured in all likelihood things probably wouldn't go in her favor, so she just breathed, and waited to hear Pamela's reaction.

"Josie, I'm actually, for possibly the first time in my life, quite speechless," Pamela Crawford confessed. "I'm so touched to the core by your offer, that I don't quite know what to say. What a beautiful proposition, and I know how personally important your mother's possessions are to you. The notion that you are willing to part with them in order to have John Courage become yours is overwhelming. You might not believe me but I understand the profound journey you must be on right now." Pamela's voice was weak and she found herself fighting back tears. She couldn't believe the gesture this wonderfully compassionate girl had just made. She sat down in the club chair she'd been standing next to and contemplated what to say next. It was Josie who spoke first.

"Well, I want you to know this is a well thought-out decision, nothing fly by night, and I'm not trying to take advantage in any way. I'd just really like to own him and this was the best I could come up with. I know it's not even close to what you are hoping to get. Thanks for even hearing me out. Really." Josie wanted to get off the phone now and put the whole frightening concept out of her mind. It was on the table and out of her hands. She knew she would have to dig deep for patience, and just wait.

"Josie, I promise you I will speak to Layton right away and get back to you as soon as possible. I am going to let Addie discuss this with us too. She will be totally on your side, as am I. We will just have to see how the businessman handles it. I will try to catch him in the right mood," Pam giggled. "I'm sorry. I wish I could tell you what I think he might say. But I have no idea. He does have tremendous respect for you, I do know that much. Anyway sweetie, we will get back to you right away. And Josie, you are a very special girl. Thank you, sweetheart, for your call this morning. Bye-bye."

"Thank you, Pam, I will cross my fingers. Thanks again. Merry Christmas. Bye."

Josie thought she might be sick. Her entire body was trembling and she was petrified. *How is this going to go?* she asked herself, pushing up from her desk and heading for the back door, pulling on a jacket and almost tripping over Token. She was a wreck. She headed toward the chicken coop, but turned back when she realized she was a little overdressed to go traipsing around in that mess. She stared at her beautifully renovated barn and headed in that direction.

Today the barn somehow felt different. As she stood in the aisle Josie had an overpowering sensation of horses occupying the stalls; her imagination bequeathed her the smell of fresh hay stacked alongside the bedding straw, the smell of grain in the small wood-bin Cleve had built. Perhaps it was the spirit of the season, but she allowed her mind to float. Admiring the beautiful new stall doors, she fantasized about hanging a wreath, just like the one she had hung for Lars years ago, if Johnnie, by a stroke of luck, came to live at the Haskell cottage. If...

She returned to the present when she heard the phone ringing in the house. *Oh my God*, she panicked and ran as fast as she could. *How stupid was I to leave the house? What if it's Pam?*

45

With all the unprecedented activity of the last few weeks, including Josie's trip to Florida, the cottage was void of any Christmas decoration, inside and out. Cleve suggested that he and Josie go to Delicious Orchards together to pick out a tree. He pressed her to consider going today; Christmas was less than two weeks away. To say Josie's demeanor the last few days had been melancholy was an understatement. She'd heard nothing from the Crawfords since her call to them four days prior.

"C'mon, we'll take your truck and go after work. I'll meet you at Clover Field and we can go straight from there. If we don't go today, I'm afraid there won't be any good trees left. Besides, I have to go with you to make sure you don't come home with any more puppies," Cleve chided her playfully as they left the County Deli where they'd met up for lunch. "Plus, I want to make sure you buy some extra packages of those incredible chocolate chip cookies. I'm not waiting until Christmas for those!"

"OK, OK, let's do it today. I will be finished at the barn around five. I'm sorry if I seem stressed, Cleve. You know I'm totally on edge waiting to hear something back from the Crawfords. I'm sure it's not good news if I haven't heard by now. I know it wasn't even close to enough money. I just wish I would hear from them so I can put it behind me, and try to find a little Christmas spirit. I am hoping Dad and Aunt Gayle will come to the cottage for Christmas Eve. I was thinking maybe we could invite your mom this year too."

"Your dad and Gayle would probably love that. As for my mom, I don't see that working, you know she doesn't drive anymore, and getting her up and back would be tough. But you are an angel for even thinking about her. Tell you what though, maybe after the holidays we could take a trip down to Virginia. I would love to introduce you to Peter and Mary Lyle; I can't believe that hasn't happened yet, and he chides me about it every time we talk on the phone. We could check in on Mom and Hap then too. After the holidays," he said. "That will be better."

As promised, Cleve pulled into Clover Field at 5:00 p.m. sharp. The place was exquisitely decorated, the huge evergreen tree in the front courtyard fully cloaked in a sea of white lights and small, single white candles flickering in each of the barn's windows. The main barn doors boasted huge boxwood wreaths, adorned with silver balls and twigs of holly, and wrapped in red bows. Kenna had really outdone herself this year and the Clover Field Christmas party, to be held at her house, was planned for next Saturday night. Cleve and Josie were planning to attend, along with Doc Thurman and his wife, Debbie, and William Fells and his fiancée, Beth.

Fraser popped out the front door of Cleve's truck and took off in search of Token, Ralphie, and Shorty. Josie came out of the barn before Cleve made it in; he offered her a warm embrace, and they all piled into Josie's truck. They drove in silence. The dogs all snuggled in the back seat. As though it were pasted like a billboard across her forehead, Cleve knew what was going on in Josie's mind. She was tortured.

"Here's some Christmas spirit for you, girlfriend." He leaned in to turn up the volume on the radio and started to sing, poking and prodding at Josie until she, more annoyed than flattered, conceded. Laughing at first, she began to sing along with Bruce Springsteen and Cleve.

He's making a list, he's checking it twice, gonna find out who's naughty or nice, Santa Claus is coming to town, Santa Claus is coming to town. Clarence Clemons wailed away on his saxophone.

"There's the smile I've been missing for the last few days." He leaned over and kissed her cheek, then pointed to a car pulling out of a front-and-center parking space as Josie turned off Route 36, into the parking lot. Delicious Orchards was bustling with shoppers; trees, wreaths, garlands, and delectable holiday treats were being loaded into and on top of cars jammed into the lot. The Christmas Shoppe was packed, so Cleve took a gentle hold of Josie's arm as he directed her back to the Fraser firs. They fussed and debated over two or three, and eventually settled on one they both agreed had the perfect shape and height for the cottage family room. Cleve organized to have the trunk get a fresh cut. He handed the worker a five dollar bill, thanked him in advance for tossing the tree in the pickup, and wished him a Merry Christmas.

"C'mon, let's go get a wreath for the front door, we'll grab one for Frank as well." Cleve gestured toward the greenhouse, and the two of them headed in that direction. Snow started to fall.

"You know," Josie offered, feeling a tad more holiday spirit after rocking out to Springsteen and finding the perfect tree, "when I was a little girl, Mama used to tell me that falling snow meant Santa's elves were around, checking to see who was behaving and who wasn't. I totally bought into it and would study the back yard intently, hoping to catch a glimpse of just one little guy with curled up, pointed shoes. To this day, when it snows at Christmas time I tease myself pretending there might be elves around. Silly, huh?" Josie made a funny face. She actually got a kick out of telling Cleve something he didn't know about her childhood.

"Not so silly, really. Stories like that have an indelible effect on the people we become." Cleve pulled open the greenhouse door and Josie walked through first. "Hey, lookie there," he pointed to the far end of the first aisle, "the Crawfords. They must have had the same idea we did. C'mon we have to go say hello. Don't be nervous. It's OK." Josie stood, frozen. "It's OK, c'mon. I gotcha."

Josie immediately felt awkward. Intimidated. This wasn't going to be a comfortable meet-up, and she really hoped the matter wasn't going to be settled right here and now. She was definitely not mentally prepared. Maybe they would just tell her they were still considering her offer and that they would let her know soon. She crossed her fingers inside her mittens. *This is really awkward,* she thought.

"Addie, look!" Pamela Crawford squealed as she pointed and moved in the direction of Cleve and Josie. "Look who is here! Hey, Merry Christmas, you two, Merry Christmas! Layton, look! Cleve and Josie!" She seemed genuinely surprised to see her two friends.

Josie was, frankly, shocked to see Layton Crawford at a place like Delicious Orchards. She had never figured him for the kind of guy who would make the trip to pick out the family Christmas tree. She always assumed the Crawfords had "people" for that. At the same time she was pleased to see him. She was always happy to be proven wrong if she'd made an error in judgment about someone. Besides, who cared? She respected Layton Crawford immensely whether he picked out the family Christmas tree or not. She instinctively moved right away towards Addie.

"Hey you! Give me a hug. Gosh you look great, beautiful. You just keep getting more beautiful! I haven't seen you in forever! I can't believe you haven't come by the barn to say hello. How long have you been home? I haven't even talked to you on the phone in, like what, a month?" Josie was sincerely happy to embrace her young pal. They had lost touch in the last couple months and seeing Addie now made Josie realize she just couldn't ever let that happen. This precious girl was someone she cherished. Josie wanted Addie to always be an integral part of her life, horses or no horses.

"Hi! Hi! I just got home last night, and I was going to call you, I swear, actually later this evening. I want to come to the barn and over to the cottage to hang out with you while I'm home. I just finished exams and I'm exhausted. But I'm so excited to be home for a whole month now!" She squeezed Josie tightly and instantly all was as it always had been between them.

"Hey, what about me, I don't rate a hug?" Cleve teased Addie as he turned from his handshake with Layton and quick embrace with Pam. "Merry Christmas, Ivy Leaguer. You flunk out of that place yet?" A big bear hug ensued between the two.

"Oh boy, I have missed you, you pain in my ass," Addie responded, laughing at Cleve. "Merry Christmas." She planted a big kiss on his cheek.

"So what are you all doing here?" Cleve asked.

What do you think they're doing here? Josie silently queried, a little embarrassed by what seemed nosiness on Cleve's part.

"Is this where you get your tree every year?" he continued. "Have you ever tried the chocolate chip cookies they sell? Josie gets them for all the guys at Clover Field as presents, and let me tell you, they are incredible."

Josie noticed now that Cleve clearly seemed like he was making peculiar small talk and appeared, oddly, a bit disconcerted. It wasn't like him to talk about chocolate chip cookies to the likes of the Crawford family. *Wait, isn't it me who's supposed to feel self-conscious right now? This is getting weirder by the minute.*

"Well, actually," Addie was the first to respond, "actually we came to buy a wreath." She looked over at her mother and father, in a curious way as though signaling one of them to take over the conversation. Pamela spoke.

"Well yes, we came to buy a wreath, and we thought this one was quite nice. What do you think, Josie?" Pamela showed off the evergreen circle she held in her hands. "I think the big red bow is just beautiful, and these pinecones give it such an organic feel, don't you think?"

Josie was oddly suspect. *What exactly is going on here? This conversation is bizarre,* she thought. *These people are our friends and they are acting so strange, like they've been caught in some criminal act; talking so superficially, as though they have something to hide. Could it be that I totally offended them this week and they were not happy to bump into us? Are they afraid to just tell me the answer is no?* She looked over at Cleve, who had an expression on his face the likes of which she had never seen. *I can't believe I have screwed up my relationship with this family,* she mused.

Now, Layton Crawford, the intellectual of the group, sensed that everyone was in an offbeat place, so he stepped up, put a hand on Cleve's shoulder, and spoke.

"OK, here's the deal. We are buying this wreath for you, Josie. We planned to give it to you to hang on John Courage's stall door. His stall door at your barn, at your cottage—his new home." He stood silent now, allowing Josie to comprehend what he had just said.

Josie thought she might just faint. She looked at Cleve, standing there with Layton, and now understood that he must have had prior knowledge of what was happening. She looked at Addie, who was smiling ear-to-ear, arms across her torso as though holding her excitement at bay. She looked at Pamela, whose tears had caused her mascara to run in fuzzy black lines down her cheeks. She was doing her best to smile at Josie. She slipped her arm through her husband's, in an effort to steady herself.

"I don't even know what to say," Josie started, "I am caught so off guard, I'm almost dizzy. I just didn't expect this at all. I thought surely that since I hadn't heard from you, that your answer was going to be no. I thought, just now, that surely I must have offended you. You have all been acting *so* weird. I mean, I wouldn't have blamed you, the amount you wanted and the amount I can give after I sell the—"

"Stop right there," Layton interrupted Josie quite bluntly, out of character for this otherwise consummate gentleman. "As for your mother's jewels and the money, we have made the decision, as a family, that we have no interest in taking either of them from you." He glanced over at Cleve. "John Courage belongs with you, Josie. It is very apparent, and we want you to have him."

Did I just hear those words? 'It is apparent'? Josie did her best to stay in the moment, to pay attention. Layton was still talking.

"He is a gift to you, for all the goodness you have imparted on our daughter and on our family these last several years. We will take nothing from you in return, you have already given us so much." He stood very straight, obviously quite uncomfortable with the act of expressing any form of sentiment, yet proud that the efforts of his family would provide this special friend of theirs with a most joyful Christmas season.

"Merry Christmas, sweetie," Pamela spoke through her tears, her head tilted to one side, lips trembling as the corners of her mouth tried to turn up. This was quite a moment for her. She embraced Josie and then pushed back, holding onto Josie at arm's length. "You have been such a dear friend to us, and an incredible mentor to Addie. You may not believe this, but you have had a tremendous impact in shaping the woman she is becoming. She has written essays for school about her experiences with you and Johnnie, and, oh I don't know, all the other stuff. You have clearly been such a positive influence in her life. We, Layton and I, are forever grateful. We love you, Josie. Almost as much, if not more, than John Courage does."

Layton turned now to face Cleve, again putting a hand on his shoulder, but addressed Josie as he spoke. Cleve was feeling a bit confused himself at this point.

"I'm going to risk breaking a confidence here, but there is something you need to know about this outstanding young man, Josie. I'm not one for public displays of affection, I think you know that about me, but his act of chivalry needs to be acknowledged. Cleve had this whole thing plotted from the get-go. The minute you told him about your plan to sell your inheritance, he put in a call to me. He asked me to pretend to consider your request, but to ultimately turn you down. He offered to buy John Courage himself, at my full asking price, so long as I wouldn't tell you. He wanted to surprise you, a Christmas present I suppose. He asked me too, to keep the entire conversation just between us, so when you called Pamela and made your offer, she had no knowledge of what Cleve and I had discussed. I only yesterday told her and Addie the whole story.

"I know too, that he called his old Parson Prep baseball teammate, Joe Serocci, who happens to own the Gold Tinker. He asked Joe to tell you that your mother's jewelry was worth far less than it truly is. He wanted the number to be low enough so that when I theoretically refused your offer, you would think it was only because of that."

Josie was the one shedding tears now, and she couldn't take her eyes off of Cleve, the most handsome man—no, the most amazing man—she had ever known.

"Cleve, you and I are traders," Layton continued. "We both love the roll of the dice. Nothing gets my adrenaline going more than a good trade. Well, there may be one or two other things that do, but they're not for discussion in mixed company," he joked, as any man would. Cleve grinned and listened, curious to hear what Layton had to say.

"Your trade, the one you offered to make with me, was quite possibly setting up to be the worst trade I've ever come across. And you were willing to make that trade, solely out of love for this young girl. I have to say, man, it moved me." He chuckled at his admission. "Now I know why the guys at Randolph Brothers were less than thrilled when you left the firm to go be a horseman. You are the epitome of a brilliant trader. No wonder you made yourself such a killing on that desk.

"Look, I know you weren't trying to use reverse psychology or tricks of the trade to make this thing turn out the way it's going to; you know that I am a brilliant trader as well. I know that offer was sincere. But damn it, son, you trumped me. You actually almost brought a tear to my eye. A love story like this hasn't been written in a long, long time. I'm not taking your lousy hundred K. It would make me the Grinch, the heartless boor. You won this trade, Gregory, fair and square. Passion was your lure. My only vengeance," and here Layton smiled, "is that you are now stuck with that pain in the ass chestnut horse."

Everyone in the group laughed and Cleve embraced Layton in an act of gratitude.

"Somehow I think maybe you trumped me right back, my friend," Cleve said. "Thank you very much." He extended his arm and the two men shook hands.

All three girls were crying and trying to figure out exactly what had just taken place. There was a lot Cleve would have to explain, but one thing Josie Parker knew for sure: Delicious Orchards would never be the same to her again, as long as she lived.

All five of them were now a tad embarrassed that they were standing in the wreath aisle of the greenhouse, sobbing and laughing and hugging. People were beginning to stare.

"Well," Layton said, saving them all, "this seems to be enough entertainment for one holiday evening. What do you say you and I talk tomorrow, Cleve? Let's have a little Christmas lunch in the city next week, Keene's steak house maybe. I'd like to try like hell to get you to come work for me, you clever son of a bitch." Layton gave Cleve an affectionate slap on the back and spoke once again to Josie who was now standing with Addie, their arms around each other in an embrace full of glee.

"You make arrangements to get that horse over to your place as soon as you can. The sooner you get him out of Clover Field, the sooner my board bill ceases." He winked and continued, "Addie can come help you get him settled in, I know she's planning to spend some quality time with you while she's home. Maybe you'll trade us some of those fresh eggs I hear you've got out there. I like to put a raw egg in my orange juice every morning. Keeps me manly," he joked.

"Ewwwwwww, Dad that's disgusting," Addie moaned, cringing.

The girls walked together out to the parking lot while the men went to settle up at the cashier's desk. Pamela handed the wreath to Josie and embraced her one more time.

"Pamela, I just don't even know what to say. Truly, I feel like I'm caught in a deep, deep fog right now. I can't believe this has actually happened. Thank you so much. Thank you for letting me become the keeper of your wonderful, magical, talented horse, and thank you so much for your generosity regarding my mama's jewels. I just don't know what else to say."

"Say nothing, sweet Josie, it's not necessary." The snow was beginning to accumulate and it was time for all to get on the road, to get home safely.

Pamela and Addie headed for their car, Layton waved good night to Josie, and she and Cleve climbed into the blue pickup. Josie held the wreath with the big red bow and "organic pinecones" tight to her chest. Cleve drove. She closed her eyes and opened them several times, just to be sure she wasn't dreaming.

"Cleve, there is so much about what happened tonight that I don't understand at all, and I am so overwhelmed right now. There is a lot you are going to have to explain. I mean, for one thing, you've really never told me about your Wall Street career. We've always just skimmed over that period of time and clearly there is a story to tell. Someday soon I want to hear the whole thing. Honestly I don't even know where to start. You were willing to buy Johnnie for me with your own savings. I mean that just blows me away. And you set the whole thing up to save Mama's jewels. I can't even pretend to know where to go with that." She hugged the wreath tighter.

"Let's just leave any more conversation about it 'til tomorrow." He reached out and massaged her neck and shoulder. "Chalk it up to the fact that I love you, Josie Parker. Chalk it up to that funny-looking chestnut horse, John Courage. If you think for one minute I would ever have let him out of our grasp, then you don't know me well at all. I owe that horse everything, and I aim to give it to him. Now just relax, and go easy there girl, you're gonna crush those pinecones if you squeeze that thing any tighter."

The snowflakes fell on the windshield of Josie's truck as the wipers moved back and forth, the headlights guiding them up the snow-covered country road that led to the Haskell cottage. Josie and Cleve held hands and rode along in silence except for the sound of the pups snoring in the back seat. Although neither actually knew what the other was thinking, the fact is they were both thinking the same thing.

And Josie Parker couldn't wait until tomorrow.

"Damn it, we forgot the chocolate chip cookies!" Cleve lamented as he stood at the coffee machine, bare-chested, in nothing more than a pair of University of Virginia sweats, pouring coffee into his mug the next morning. "The one thing I really wanted to get at D.O." He winked at his over-the-moon-happy girlfriend. He handed her a mug and said, "Listen, Kenna knows all about this thing with Johnnie, and she figured you would want to use the two-horse trailer at some point today, so don't feel like you have a ton of explaining to do once you get to work. She'll probably greet you at the barn with a big hug. She was really excited by this whole deal, despite the fact that it meant no commission for her," he kidded. "She loves you, Jos'."

"What about Ramon, does Ramon know too?"

Cleve nodded.

"Geez, you all are amazing. Plotting the way you did! I still just can't believe this. I can't wait to get him here, Cleve. I can't wait."

They sat at the kitchen table this morning, taking breakfast at a pace a little more leisurely than the norm. Cleve eventually got up to let the dogs in the back door and to check that the fireplace flue was closed. He threw back the family room curtains to reveal a backyard covered in winter white.

"Definitely going to be a white Christmas this year," he proclaimed. He stuck a finger in the Christmas tree stand, to assess how much water the Fraser fir had sucked up since he'd brought it inside.

"I wasn't sure which stall you want to put him in; let me know and I will hang his wreath before I take off this morning. I won't be home until pretty late tonight; we've got a few pre-purchase exams to get done before the twenty-fourth. Lots of lucky little girls will be finding new ponies under their Christmas trees this year." Again he winked at Josie, and she smirked at his tongue-in-cheek humor.

"Ha-ha, very funny. Hey, are you planning to have that lunch with Layton next week? I think you should. He really likes you, Cleve. Why wouldn't you consider going back to Wall Street? I mean it sounds like you were really good at whatever it was you were doing there."

Cleve sensed in Josie a prickly tone. Truth was, she was wondering why he would want to be fixing barn roofs and assisting a veterinarian when he could be making hundreds of thousands, if not millions, in the sophisticated world of finance. He knew, whether she realized it or not, that she just needed a little reassurance. Uncharacteristic of this otherwise confident, self-sufficient, stunning woman—but a woman nonetheless. One who was coming down off a pretty enormous natural high from the night before.

"Well let's look at it this way. You were a really good nurse, weren't you? You could have gone anywhere you wanted and had a job in a snap, no? But you were drawn to be right where you are now. If someone asked you to explain what it is that brought you back here, you would probably use the same exact word I would, which is probably the same exact word Layton Crawford would use to describe why he does what he does. Passion."

Josie tilted her head a touch to the side and nodded. Cleve was absolutely right. She turned back to the dishes in the sink and continued to listen.

"Passion is not something that can be accurately defined, really. It's different for every individual. It's not something that can be dissected, nor can one person's passion necessarily be understood by another. Passion is compelling. Completely and overwhelmingly compelling. Nothing and no one can stand in the way of an individual in pursuit of what they are truly passionate about. And someone's passion should never be judged. Yeah, I will have lunch with Layton; he's a fantastic guy and I have tremendous respect for him, and I don't judge his passion for one minute. He won't judge mine, either. Of course, like I said, he won't understand it, but he won't judge it. We will have a great lunch. I'm actually psyched about Keene's, I haven't been there in years. Anyway, beautiful, where should I hang that wreath?" And that was all Cleve intended to say about the prospect of his returning to Wall Street.

He wrapped his broad shoulders and strong arms around Josie from behind and pushed her hair over to one side, exposing the back of her neck. She braced her hands against the kitchen counter as he kissed her several times, gently pushing the weight of his bare chest against hers.

"This is what I am passionate about, Josie Parker. This right here. This is what I have been passionate about for the better part of my life. Nothing, and no one, can stand in the way of my pursuit of you. And now," he whispered in the deepest, sexiest voice she'd ever heard, "now I'm going to show you just how passionate I am about this pursuit."

Cleve slowly spun Josie to face him and lifted her up off her feet. Like so many times before, Josie's core began to pulsate with desire. He carried her down the hall and into the bedroom. Only the dogs and Josie's robe remained in the kitchen.

46

"Cleve," Josie said, imploring him to listen as they sat in the family room drinking wine and feasting on cheese and crackers a few days before Christmas. "The Crawfords giving me Johnnie is just about the most unreal thing that has ever happened to me. I hold it right up there with you walking back into my life after ten years. I really want to do something special in return. I've been kind of stumped, but I think I have an idea."

"Oh shit," Cleve feigned panic, "your ideas seem to get me into big trouble lately." He laughed and reached across the table for the bottle of wine. "Hold on, let me brace myself with some cabernet." He filled his glass, then topped off hers.

"What do you think about the idea of me giving Addie a piece of the jewelry? Specifically, I mean the ring. I want to. Let's face it, I was willing to sell the whole thing to get the horse. They know that, and yet they wouldn't let me do it because they knew its significance to me. You wouldn't let me do it." She offered a nod of deserved credit to Cleve. "I've only ever given any of it to Tessa and baby Rosilyn. Those gifts, meager as they were, were gifts straight from my heart, as this would be. I think those things meant something special to Tess'. Do you think it would mean something to Addie? Do you think they would understand that it is the most profound gesture I feel I can make, to show how indebted I am to their kindness and generosity? I just don't know what else I could do that would have as much meaning. I feel like Addie is family to me now, in the way that Tessa and Rosie are. So it seems the right thing to do. It feels, really, like I would be passing the ring down to family after all."

"I think it's a stellar idea, Jos'. Pamela will flip at the gesture and Addie will no doubt be incredibly touched—no, beyond touched. I mean, how many girls her age have a ring like that? A ring with such an amazing story attached? How many girls her age have a friend like you? She loves you as much as you love her and she will be thrilled to go back to school in January with a story like this to write. Not to mention how special she will know it is that you wanted to share your mama's magic with her." Cleve leaned over and kissed her. "You're a remarkably selfless person, Josie Parker, as I've said a million times before. How lucky I am to be in your universe."

"Well ditto, and right back atcha, but I'm not sure that luck deserves all the credit." Josie smiled and canoodled with her man, thinking about that shooting star from a few weeks back. "This seems to be a story guided more and more by—and I know it's corny to say—but more and more by the concept of destiny. Doo, doo, doo, doo." She raised an eyebrow whimsically and hummed the theme to the Twilight Zone. *Malarkey,* she could hear Frank Parker say. Cleve laughed.

"Come on 'destiny,' let's go check on our new tenant out in the barn. He seems to be acclimating well, but he's got to be a little lonely out there. Very wise and a super nice gesture of Kenna to send Sparks along with him. The two of those creatures are so weirdly attached. Better a cat than a goat or a donkey, I suppose."

"Oh Cleve, a donkey! Wouldn't that be—"

"*No.* Absolutely not. *No way*, not happening. Niente. OK, seriously, bundle up and let's go." He whistled for the dogs and grabbed their jackets.

Josie and Cleve decided they would have a spontaneous cocktail party at the cottage on Christmas Eve. There was so much to celebrate this year and Josie was exhilarated by the prospect of surprising Addie with the Caldwell family heirloom. It gave her tremendous joy to think she might have a chance to make someone else feel as special as she was feeling this season. Frank Parker and Aunt Gayle were invited, along with Kenna, Ramon and his girlfriend, Doc Thurman and Debbie, William Fells and Beth, and of course the entire Crawford family. Everyone accepted the invitation.

The day before Christmas Eve, Cleve made an eleventh-hour suggestion that they invite Mike O'Hara to the party. Little did Josie know, Cleve had already invited him. He couldn't imagine her having any objection.

"That's a fantastic idea, Cleve." She was actually thrilled. "Funny, I've been thinking about him lately. I guess it's just part of all the generosity of spirit going around; I've been channeling a lot of Auld Lang Syne, and our Chinese dinner date in the Hidden Green van has been on top of the list. Great, great idea. Will you call him, or should I?" Josie looked up from some concoction she was mixing in a big bowl, preparing hors d'oeuvres for the party.

"I've got it covered, Jos'. I will call Mike. I'm almost one hundred percent sure he will come. I don't think the guy has much of a social life these days. Although I do believe he has worked things out with Libby O."

"OK, thanks. I'd rather not add one more thing to my to-do list. I'm starting to get freaked out! You won't forget to shovel the front walk one more time, right? And the path to the barn?"

"Babe, everything looks perfectly amazing, but yes, I will shovel again. And by the way, the hors d'oeuvres you've made so far are delicious."

"Cleve!" she yelled, scolding him for raiding her production. She'd been working feverishly on them all day. "Come on, they're for the party! Go on, git. Go check on Johnnie and then call Mike O'Hara. Leave me to my Christmas music and my work, or we will be up all night."

The sun had already set. The tree, twinkling brightly from the colored lights Josie had labored over to get just right, the garland on the mantel adorned with her fall collection of dried flowers and abandoned bird nests, and all of Josie's treasured decorations were perfectly in place for the party tomorrow night. The dogs all sported red and green plaid collars, although Shorty was clearly mortified by the idea. He'd been hiding behind one of the Christmas pillows on the family room couch all afternoon. Christmas tunes floated through the house from the radio, topping off the already festive atmosphere in the Haskell cottage.

Cleve whistled to the dogs, threw on his jacket, and headed for the barn.

Well, now the final part of the plan is in place, he comforted himself silently as he glanced up to the sky. *Shine your light on us tomorrow night, Dorie Parker. We're almost there, we're almost there.* He looped his scarf around his neck, pulled his hat down over his ears, and trudged across the patio, then across the path to the cottage barn.

Josie had not had the chance to ride Johnnie since he had come to live at the Haskell cottage. She was fine with that. She and Cleve had pretty much decided that they would let him winter "old-school style," and have the next few months off to just be a horse. His whiskers were getting long and his coat was growing out thick and fluffy; Josie compared it to a man not shaving while he was on vacation. Soon he would only need a light blanket even on the coldest of nights. William would stop by regularly to keep his feet in shape and Cleve would be able to handle all the standard veterinary maintenance.

A horse in the cottage barn required a new morning routine. Josie rose earlier than usual these days so she could muck Johnnie's stall, straighten his blankets, feed him, and turn him out in the paddock. Cleve felt it would be easier if the two of them could just worry about the end-of-day chores, and suggested that she ask the guys at Clover Field to keep an ear out for someone who might want a few extra dollars every week to come take care of the morning routine. She liked that idea just fine.

Right away Ramon put in a plug for his cousin, Mas, to be considered for the position. He organized for Mas and Josie to meet and the two hit it off right away. Since the holidays were a slow time at Clover Field, Josie could spend a little more time at home, and as such, wanted to care for Johnnie herself through December. So she scheduled Mas to start after the new year began.

Tonight, after establishing that all was well in the barn, Cleve gave John Courage a once over and a pat on the neck. He fastened an extra sheet over the gelding.

"Well, if all goes as planned we will all be even more connected after tomorrow, my friend. I've got a little more magic up my sleeve. Magic, which believe it or not, has nothing to do with you!" He patted the horse again and turned to head back to the house. John Courage nickered as Cleve walked down the barn aisle, and Cleve called to the horse over his shoulder, "Oh come on, man, it can't always be all about you." Cleve turned out the lights and closed the barn doors. He looked up to the night sky again as he walked the path.

"I'm goin' with magic," he said out loud, reprising his theory of a year ago.

"I'll be home for Christmas, you can count on me. Please have snow, and mistletoe, and presents 'round the tree." Josie, tidying up the kitchen, was swaying back and forth, singing along to Frank Sinatra as Cleve walked back into the cottage. He threw his hat and jacket on the couch and raised his arms into a position that suggested the two of them should dance. Josie smiled shyly, nodding. Hand in hand they sashayed their way closer to the glow of the Christmas tree, and danced the evening to a close.

Christmas Eve will find me, where the love light gleams. I'll be home for Christmas, and you'll be in my dreams...

Yup, thought Cleve as he switched off the house lights. *You got that right, Frank Sinatra.*

47

Finally Christmas Eve had arrived and the party was to begin in two hours. Josie and Cleve were conducting an early night check, and all seemed well in the little cottage barn.

"Ramon will not like seeing his horse like this," Cleve teased as he dumped Johnnie's evening feed into his grain bucket. "You are as furry as a buffalo," he said to the horse.

Josie gave Johnnie a hug and a molasses treat, then whispered to him, his nose held up to her face by her hands, "Merry Christmas, John Courage. Merry Christmas, magic man. I love you so much. See you tomorrow. I'm going to send Cleve to check on you later, I'm sure I'll be stuck doing dishes."

Sparks was already curled up in a corner of the stall and the barn felt comfortably warm. Johnnie's wreath was proudly displayed on his door, along with the stall plate Josie had made literally the day after he'd officially become hers. She'd gone to Lawe's supply store to purchase it, the same place her dad had purchased the one she'd had for Lars. In fact, she still had that keepsake, buried in a drawer somewhere. She thought for a second, about where exactly it might be. *Oh well, I'll bump into it somewhere in the cottage one of these days.* That stall plate was something she intended to save forever.

She closed the sliding barn door but left the aisle light and the outdoor flood on, just in case Addie or Pamela wanted to wander out for a visit. They walked silently back to the house, holding hands. Josie looked up at the dark, cold, star-filled sky. She smiled, thinking about how much she loved her horse, her cottage, her man, her life.

Josie and Cleve showered and dressed. Cleve hooked the German crystal bracelet around Josie's wrist and fastened the clasp to secure a strand of grey pearls around her neck. Josie twisted a multi-stone earring onto each earlobe. She left her fingers bare; the sapphire and diamond ring was in a small box she had wrapped festively, sitting under the Christmas tree in the family room. She glanced across the bedroom to

Cleve and thought he had never looked more irresistible. He'd had his hair cut a bit shorter than usual and had put some kind of hair product in it to hold his bangs off his forehead. The Hermès Christmas tie Josie had given him last year was striking against his crisp, white button-down shirt, peeking out from under his blue blazer. As always, his jeans were just tight enough in all the right places. She noticed that he had polished the sterling silver belt buckle that boasted his granddad's initials.

I hope he likes the one I got him for Christmas, Josie thought about the silver rodeo buckle she had found in an antique shop in Red Bank a month or so earlier. It sat wrapped under the tree, alongside the other gifts she'd collected for her family, and of course her gift for Addie Crawford. She walked over to Cleve and put her arms around his shoulders, hugging him from behind.

"It's almost a shame we have guests showing up in half an hour," she said coquettishly into his ear. "As handsome as you look, I think I'm more interested in a private party right now." Cleve slowly stepped into his Gucci loafers, then turned to respond to her provocative tease.

"Now that is quite an alluring flirtation ma'am." He fitted a hand over each of her hips. "I do believe, Miss Josie," he said in his best southern accent, "that ah absolutely share the same sentiment." He kissed her bare neck, her ear, her nose, and finally her lips, with those perfectly puffy lips of his own, sending that familiar, always enticing, amazing chill right up her spine. "You look radiant, and I already know that you are going to be the 'hostess with the mostest.' As for the private party—oh, don't worry, we shall have our own private Christmas party. You just have to wait awhile." They kissed again, slowly, and stared into one another's eyes, lingering for a few seconds.

Josie checked herself in the full-length mirror on the back of the bedroom door. She assessed that she looked just fine in her hunter green velvet sheath. Her bare arms were shapely and toned from her long workdays at Clover Field, and her hemline landed at the perfect place, exposing just the right amount of leg. She felt pretty, actually, and ready to host her family along with all of her favorite friends at her first party ever in the Haskell cottage.

"Well, here goes nothing," she said to Cleve. They headed down the hall towards the kitchen.

"How about we start out with a glass of champagne, just the two of us?" he suggested as he followed behind her.

"Perfect," she responded.

Frank and Aunt Gayle arrived first. Cleve took their coats and Aunt Gayle immediately volunteered to help in the kitchen.

"Did you preheat your oven, sweetheart? That way you'll be ready to just throw things in as soon as you want. Do you have a pile of dish towels within reach? Where are your pot holders, and let me find a spatula...hmmmmm, probably right here in this drawer, no?" She went straight to work.

"Believe it or not I did preheat the oven, Aunt Gayle. Don't underestimate how much you've taught me." Josie winked at her aunt, hoping to make Gayle feel good about all the kitchen tricks she'd shared with Josie over the course of so many years of family gatherings.

Frank and Cleve toasted the holiday, each holding a glass of whiskey up to the girls' champagne flutes, then they departed for the family room.

The Crawfords arrived and on their coattails, William Fells and Beth. A rush of adrenaline made its way through Josie's body as she hugged Addie, so assured was she in her decision to pass the ring on to this special friend; she couldn't wait to give it to her, and she would be sure to tell her it was as much a gift from Johnnie as it was from her.

Doc Thurman had called to say he and Debbie would be running late. He had an emergency call he needed to take care of. Cleve offered to meet him wherever he was headed, but Doc insisted that Cleve stay right where he was.

Kenna arrived along with her dog Clancy, who was also sporting a red and green Christmas collar. He bounded off to play with his barn buddies. Ramon had followed Kenna in his own truck. He introduced his beautiful girlfriend, Lola, to everyone. Josie was very moved that he had accepted her invitation. She considered him an important person in her life and wanted him to know how much she sincerely cared about him. She'd been worried that he might have been too shy to actually show up. She gave both him and Lola a holiday hug, and sent them in the direction of the makeshift bar.

"Why is Mike driving in here in his van, Cleve?" Josie asked when she noticed the large, high headlights glaring into the kitchen window.

"Oh yeah, sorry. He told me earlier today he would probably be driving it; he had to deliver a pony to someone on his way here. You know, one of those ponies from Santa, going under the tree for some lucky little girl. He said the delivery drop was close by and it would just make sense for him to do it that way. I forgot to tell you. I'll go out and help him get the truck situated so he can get out easily, especially since we are expecting more snow later on. Hey Frank, wanna walk out with me? Mike O'Hara is here, and I know you haven't seen him in a long while."

Cleve and Frank threw on their coats, hats, and gloves and exited through the front door. Josie continued with her hostess tasks, chatting with Pamela and Layton, and at the same time running back and forth between the kitchen and the dining table, making sure platters and glasses were full. She was having a blast being the hostess, but secretly she was glad to have Aunt Gayle there, who was proving to be a tremendous help.

Eventually Cleve, Frank, and Mike came through the front door and there were hugs and admittedly a few happy tears all the way around. The night seemed to have a special joie de vivre about it, something beyond just good ol' Christmas spirit. Doc and Debbie Thurman arrived more promptly than they'd thought they would, and with that the party was complete.

While Cleve and Frank took over the responsibility of making sure everyone had full glasses of cheer and libation, Aunt Gayle and Josie passed the hors d'oeuvres. Pamela and Kenna chatted up Mike O'Hara; the old Irishman could barely get a word in edgewise. Addie, Beth, and Debbie admired the ornaments on the tree and the creativity of the mantel decorations, while Doc Thurman and William Fells discussed a horse from another farm that they couldn't seem to get sound. Ramon listened in as Lola stood shyly by his side.

The pleasant, incessant chatter all but muted the sound of the Christmas carols broadcasting over the radio, until William's ear caught a note or two of "Winter Wonderland" and he began to sing out loud. Quite surprisingly, Layton Crawford was the next to join in, and spontaneously all the guests began caroling, dogs barking along. It was a joyful scene. Josie looked across the room to Cleve, who winked a sign of congratulations and admiration; the moment reminded her of days at Hidden Green, when she would look up from a chore and find him staring at her. Now, unlike then, she was confident in his love for her and able to hold his affectionate gaze long enough to wordlessly return his sentiment. In time, Cleve moved to stand alone in front of the fireplace and tinkled his glass with his signet ring, prompting the group's attention.

"Merry Christmas, everyone, and thanks so much for making the trek to the Haskell cottage to be with Josie and me this Christmas Eve. Josie, thanks for putting on such a great show here tonight, and Gayle, your effort has not gone unnoticed. Thanks." He moved his eyes slowly across the room. "You are our family, our best friends," he said to the gathering of people, "but you are truly so much more to us than simply that. You all in one way or another represent our past, our present, and our future. We are beholden to you for all of the kindness, example, and generosity you have shown the two of us over what has been quite a long stretch of time." He hesitated a moment, then continued. "I'm sure my gal will concur that our gratitude for your friendship runs deep. Merry Christmas to everyone, cheers." Glass edge met glass edge until everyone in the room had acknowledged one another, and then Pamela Crawford, peering out the window, excitedly offered that it was snowing again.

The Thurmans, William and Beth, and Mike O'Hara all decided they would depart together. Doc wanted to be sure Mike made it up the country road safely in the van, and William had a pretty long haul to get back to Little Silver.

As Ramon guided Lola out the front door, he asked Josie if it would be acceptable for him to take his girl out to see John Courage.

"Of course! If Lola can do it in those high heels! Johnnie would be ticked as hell if he knew you were here and didn't say hello," Josie teased. "Just let the lights stay on when you leave. Cleve and I will no doubt go out for a little night check later. Merry Christmas, you two. So nice to meet you, Lola. Love you, Ramon. Thanks so much for coming."

"Feliz Navidad, Miss Josie, love you too," Ramon called back. The two disappeared around the side of the house.

Kenna, Frank Parker, and Aunt Gayle were the next group to head out.

"See you tomorrow, Rosebud. Take your time getting over to the house, I'm sure you will be sleeping in a bit in the morning. Send that man of yours out for the morning chores. And here's a little nostalgia for you. I think you'll be able to find just the right place for it here in the cottage, you can open it later." Her dad handed her a flat box, wrapped in Christmas paper, with no bow. "You're a great girl, Rosebud. Love you." Frank then shook Cleve's hand, and embraced him. "See you tomorrow, son." Aunt Gayle offered hugs to all, as did Kenna, and the three maneuvered carefully down the now snow-covered front steps.

The Crawfords had been escorted by their private driver in a capable SUV, and as the others left, Layton signaled out to his man that his family would be along in just a bit.

"What a lovely evening this has been, thank you so much for including us, Josie." Pamela walked over to her, holding her champagne flute out to toast the hostess one more time. Addie closed in on the two of them, not wanting to be left out of the accolade, and handed Josie a gift, beautifully wrapped, and noticeably similar in size to the one Frank Parker had handed her just a few minutes before.

"You can open it tomorrow, it's just a photo." Pamela gave up the mystery.

"Mom!" Addie admonished the giveaway. "That dress is amazing, Josie. I'm definitely going to be borrowing it one of these days! Maybe even this New Year's Eve. I have a hot date with this really cool guy I met at Brown last month. We're going into the city, to the University Club's big black tie party." Addie looked over for her mother's reaction, and seeing that it was one of approval, she smiled proudly.

This seemed to be the perfect lead-in for Josie. She placed the two gifts she held in her hand under the tree and picked up the small box, which she couldn't wait any longer to deliver.

"Well, that brings me to the heart of why Cleve and I truly wanted to have this little get-together tonight. And actually, it's perfect that you all are the last to leave. Cleve said everything so eloquently in his toast; I'm not going to try to say it again. But I would like to give this one small gift to you, Addie. You gave something to me that held incredible significance to your being. Something you love very much and which, although clearly of great value, in the end you couldn't really put a price on.

"Your dad, as did mine, though each at a different time, reminded me that you can't necessarily write every chapter of your life; sometimes life just becomes apparent. Life doesn't always go the way we think it might, and for sure it doesn't always go the way we want it to. We can only do the best we can, and hope that in the end if we have used the good judgment our parents have taught us, if we have maintained our integrity, and if we have treated people the way we would like to be treated—something my mama reminded me to practice every day—then perhaps, good things will come our way.

"You, your mom, and your dad have become such an integral part of my life. John Courage has somehow unknowingly connected us all, somehow made us all related, and as such, I consider you family. So this is my Christmas gift to you, something I hope will remain in our family for a long time to come." Josie handed the small square box to Addie.

Addie looked at the box and then stared up to Josie, seeking more of an explanation. Josie had said all she had to say. Addie looked at her mother, who stood close to Addie's dad, her head tilted to one side, as clueless as Addie. But she nodded, encouraging her daughter to open her gift. Addie looked over to Cleve, who was seated on the couch with Fraser on his lap. He winked at the young girl, giving her the "go ahead, it won't bite" nod, and Addie walked over to sit down next to him.

"Josie you really didn't have to give me a present, I didn't expect this at all," Addie spewed nervously. "We were just so happy to be coming to your first party at the cottage. Ironically though, on the way here we were discussing precisely what you said just now. That you and Cleve are like a part of our family, and that John Courage really brought us all together."

Addie methodically peeled back the paper from the little box and sat with it, unopened on her lap, staring. She looked up again to her mother and father, who were smiling, but clearly mystified, wondering

306 | Mimi Tashjian

as much as Addie what might possibly be hiding inside.

Addie lifted the box top, which remained attached at the back to its bottom, so at first she was the only one in the room other than Cleve who could see what was inside. She tilted her head, as if to get a sneak peek, then opened it all the way. She fell back against the pillows behind her and tears began rolling down her cheeks as quickly as her mouth fell wide open. She reached out to grab Cleve's upper arm.

"No, Josie, no way. I cannot accept this. This is crazy. This is—"

"Yours." Josie finished her young friend's sentence. "I am so happy to give this ring to you, Addie. It is meant to be yours. It will bond us forever and there is nothing I want more than to stay connected to you and your awesome family. Come on now, let's see if it fits, please." Josie smiled through tears and scrunched onto the couch next to Addie. Pamela and Layton moved in closer to watch the ring slide onto Addie's finger. She held her hand out in front of her to admire the beautiful sapphire surrounded in diamonds, as Josie had done herself so many times before. Pamela Crawford gasped.

"Oh my God, Josie, no! This is your mama's ring. This is the ring you told us has been in your family for generations! You can't, Josie, you just can't!" Pamela Crawford stood, supported by Layton's hand at her back, shaking her head, a hand on each of her cheeks.

Josie and Addie wrapped their arms around one another and held their embrace for a very long moment in time. It was Layton, the intellect, who delivered his family's essence of gratitude.

"Josie, your gesture leaves me with no words to adequately express the magnitude of sentiment you have elicited from every member of the Crawford family right now. I, who am rarely at a loss for words," he laughed a sweet, humble laugh, "have no idea what to say to you. My daughter, my wife, and I are so fortunate that you think of us as family. I for one am honored. Thank you, Josie. This is a Christmas that this family," he said, repeating his sentence and emphasizing the word family, "this is a Christmas this *family* will never forget."

Hugs were offered all around the family room, and the ring on Addie's finger was admired by all. Errant dishes and glasses were carried into the kitchen, and Cleve went to the bedroom to collect the Crawfords' outerwear. The driver had pulled the SUV up as close to the front door as possible; the snow was really starting to accumulate.

"Josie, thank you again, so much." Addie hugged her friend yet one more time. "I want you to know that I will cherish it, wear it proudly, and hopefully someday in the near future..." she cleared her throat and looked over at Cleve, "be able to pass it on to your own daughter. Until then I will gladly be its guardian, as I know you will always be to John Courage." The family made their way towards the SUV. Addie called back, "Oh, and I plan to write the whole story for my spring creative writing class; I will send you a copy of the essay!"

Josie and Cleve stood coatless on the front porch, arms around one another as they attempted to stay warm, watching as the SUV tires began to roll forward slowly. They waved as their last guests began their trek down the driveway, bringing the party to a close. They were completely perplexed when they noticed the crimson glare of the SUV's brake lights. The back window slid down and half of Addie Crawford's body emerged. She yelled back to them through the whipping snowfall.

"Hey, one last thing I forgot to tell you! Jack Sawyer is gay! He's got an awesomely hot boyfriend from Germany! Some really good rider, Marcus something or other! You were right, Cleve, you pain in my ass! Bye! Love you! Merry Christmas!"

All but Addie's waving arm disappeared back into the SUV, and the car pulled away into the dark. Josie and Cleve laughed their way back into the cottage.

Fortunately, the graciousness of all their guests left Cleve and Josie with very little cleanup required. Josie was particularly grateful; she was exhausted.

"What do you say we leave everything just like it is until tomorrow and head out to check the barn before we call it a night?" Cleve suggested. "I can't believe it's almost midnight. Did Addie and Pam ever get out to see Johnnie?"

Cleve took off his blazer and tie while he talked, and opened the top button of his shirt. He exchanged the blazer for a sweater from the entry hall closet, along with his down jacket, the pockets of which he had pre-loaded with molasses treats and snapped carrots. They both put on their muck boots.

"I don't think they did get out there," Josie said. "Pam had on some pretty crazy shoes that would make it pretty tricky to mush through the slippery snow, and I don't think Addie ever gave it a thought. I do think she loved the ring though, don't you?" Josie pulled on her long wool coat, and grabbed her hat and mittens. Cleve nodded.

"Hey, pretty girl, I will wait for you if you want to get out of that dress," he offered. "Of course if you take that dress off in front of me we probably won't ever make it out to the barn tonight," he teased.

"I'm good." She smiled. "I figure if there's any dirty work to be done out there, I will leave it to you, Cleve Gregory." She grabbed hold of his hand and they charged out into what was turning into a real snowstorm, leaving the dogs safe and warm in the cottage.

"Wow, this is crazy!" Josie squealed with glee. "Good thing everyone left when they did. I think there's already four or five inches on the ground!" She dipped her mitten into the fallen snow to check. "I sure hope Santa can get all those ponies delivered to all the hopeful little girls out there tonight. Good thing Mike delivered the one he had on his way here instead of on his way home."

"Darn good thing," Cleve responded. *Darn good thing*, he thought to himself as they reached the barn.

"Wait, didn't we leave the barn lights on earlier?" Josie asked in a whisper as Cleve slid the door open in front of her.

"Yeah, I guess Ramon must have instinctively turned them out when he left. Here, wait, I will just turn on the little light in the feed room so we don't disturb Johnnie if he's lying down. It's so late, you know?" The feed room light provided just the romantic glow Cleve was hoping for. He returned to Josie, who was standing at the corner of Johnnie's stall, tickling his upper lip, which he kept pushing through the wrought iron bars.

"Hey fella," she whispered. She played with him a few seconds more and then moved toward his stall door, intending to go in to give him a

Christmas hug.

"Cleve, what is that down there on that stall door?" she asked placidly, pointing to the other end of the barn aisle. She'd noticed something that she couldn't quite make out from where she was standing.

"Well, I'd say it looks like a wreath," he answered in a gentle manner as he walked ahead, not wanting to disturb the wondrous aura hovering in the barn. "Yup, it's a wreath identical to the one Johnnie's got," he said nonchalantly as he looked into the stall. "Perfect," he said quietly, but not so quietly that Josie had not heard him.

"What did you say?" She walked over to stand next to him, and following Cleve's lead, peered curiously into the stall. She was instantly astonished. So astonished that she had to grab onto one of the iron bars.

Curled up in complete repose, chin resting gently against clean, yellow straw, and back against the stall boards, was a large chestnut horse. Though it was difficult to see in the shadows of the stall walls, the white blaze down the middle of his face was so prominent it couldn't be missed. His one leg that was visible boasted a white sock almost to the knee. He was not a young horse; clearly Cleve had found a retiree. The horse looked familiar to Josie, but she was completely bewildered. Cleve had not mentioned that he had found a boarder for them.

And how did this horse get here? she asked herself. Then suddenly, she remembered Mike O'Hara driving in with his six-horse van earlier that evening.

"Cleve, this horse came here with Mike tonight, didn't he? Or she?" she asked quizzically. Josie was not by any means upset; rather, she was thrilled that John Courage was going to have some company. But she wanted more detail. "What's the deal? Who does the horse belong to? Do you know anything about him? Her? How come you didn't mention this to me? Does this horse have a name?"

"Hey, easy Daisy, slow down, let's take a look." Cleve tilted the wreath that was covering much of the front of the stall door. "Looks to me like it says something right here. If you come this way, and stop blocking the light, maybe we'll be able to make it out."

"What are you talking about?" Josie moved from where she was, leaning over in an attempt to decipher what he was referring to.

There it was. Josie stepped back, as though pushed by an invisible force.

That's weird, she thought, totally baffled. There was the green and white stall plate she had just been thinking about earlier. But why was it...

"What does it say, Jos'?" Cleve interrupted her thought, feigning ignorance.

"It says, LARS, Josie Parker. But I don't get it. Why is this stall plate here? And this wreath? Cleve?"

Wait, she thought. It couldn't be. She looked into the stall again. *Oh my God, oh my God, it can't be.* She looked at Cleve. He opened the stall door for her.

The chestnut gelding made no attempt to get up. There was no restlessness about him; he was peaceful and comfortable in the corner of the stall. He wore no blanket, for he, like Johnnie, was as furry as a buffalo. He dozed, unthreatened; it seemed he innately knew he was safe here. Josie crouched down now, and put her hand out so he could smell her. He nickered, faintly.

"I'm sure he smelled you the second you walked into the barn, Jos'. I am surprised he didn't jump up at the sound of your voice. He would never, ever forget your smell or the sound of your voice. You know that, right?"

Cleve walked quietly over to his girl and crouched down beside her. "He's fine, Josie, he's just fine. Honest. He's home now, and he's never leaving you again. I promised him, and I promise you. He's your horse, just like John Courage. John Courage helped me find you. I just paid it forward and helped Lars find you too. They're yours to keep. Forever. Merry Christmas, Josie Parker."

The serenity that overcame Josie at this moment was like nothing she had ever experienced. She felt no tears coming, none of joy nor sorrow. She felt absolutely perfect.

Here I am, she thought as she laid her head against Lars' neck, stroking him. *Insignificant Josie Parker; no Michelle Pfeiffer, but not half bad either. Josie Parker, never destined to be the "it" girl; Josie Parker, who has everything she could ever imagine wanting.*

Josie turned to Cleve.

"This has been the most amazing year of my life. And this, right here? Well, it's overwhelming. I know you will tell me the whole story of how you found him and brought him home to me, and I will never be able to thank you enough. I am the luckiest girl in the universe. Right now I feel like I am in some kind of belladonic haze, yet I know I am not dreaming, because you, Cleve Gregory, are really here with me, and you have made *all* my dreams come true. There is nothing left for me to dream about. I love you more than you will ever know."

"Well, these two homely chestnuts are the luckiest guys I know. They have the love of the most beautiful, most kind, most generous girl in the whole world. And they get to keep you forever. What have they got that I don't?" Cleve teased his girl.

They stayed in the barn for an hour or more, until Josie was truly sure both her horses wished to be left alone. She and Cleve closed up the barn and made their way back to the cottage.

48

B y the next morning, there was half a foot of snow on the ground. At 8:00 a.m., the sun was shining brightly and already the icicles along the cottage roof were starting to drip. Cleve walked into the bedroom, fully dressed, carrying two mugs of coffee, which he set down on one of the nightstands. He stoked the fire he had started when he'd been awakened by a crowing rooster an hour or so earlier. Christmas tunes drifted faintly into the bedroom from the family room. He sat down on the edge of the bed and tickled Josie's face with a lock of her hair.

"Hey, beautiful Josie Parker. Merry Christmas, lazy girl. Wake up. You've got two horses, four dogs, and a man to feed. Get your butt out of bed, we're all hungry. Besides, there are presents for all of us under the tree. Hey, wake up." He kissed her cheek and she stirred. "Are you awake? It's Christmas."

"Yes, yes, I'm awake," she said in a sleepy, jokingly annoyed voice. Waving Cleve off, she propped herself up on an elbow and opened her eyes. "And what a perfect Christmas it is, to wake up and have you be the first sight I see."

Josie sat up and leaned against her headboard. She looked out the window to the paddock and imagined Lars and John Courage grazing out there come spring. She reached her arms out to feel the warmth of the logs crackling in the fireplace and then motioned to Cleve.

"Nice flannels, Frosty," he kidded about her pajamas as he pulled her up from the bed. She gave him her best evil eye.

"I have got to call Tessa," she said as she disappeared into the bathroom. "I have so much to tell her. They're probably in the middle of the Santa Claus thing right now. Will you remind me later?" Cleve tossed another log on the fire. "She will not believe that you found Lars," she called out, "I can't believe you found Lars." She returned to the bedroom and flopped back down on the bed, grabbing Cleve's hand and pulling him down with her. They rolled into a cozy embrace, and held one another's gaze. "Cleve, you found Lars. For me. How—"

"Hey, hold on," he interrupted her, pushing himself back and taking control of the conversation. "That's a long story. I will tell you over omelets. But let me ask you a kind of important question while you are still half asleep. It might yield me better odds at getting my preferred answer." He smiled at her and twisted the lock of hair he'd used to tickle her cheek.

"OK, shoot. I'm plenty awake, by the way, so don't try pulling the wool over this girl's eyes," she scolded him, giggling. "What's the question?"

"Well, you've had a pretty good take so far this Christmas. At the risk of sounding selfish, there's something I've been wishing for, and maybe, if it's not asking too much, you will oblige me my wish as a Christmas present. I mean, I know you have stuff for me out there under the tree. But there is one thing I really want, one thing that I am hoping I can keep forever, kind of like you get to keep those horses. It's definitely not under the tree, and besides, I need to ask your permission before I can have it. I'm actually hoping those horses give me some bargaining power."

"OK, I think. Keep going, I'm trying to figure this out." *What could he want? Another dog? A horseshoe pit? A tractor maybe? He's being so vague. Not another dog, please.*

Cleve let go of her hair and pushed himself up from the bed. He walked over to stand in front of the fireplace. He turned back to face her. He seemed serious if not apprehensive.

"OK, here's the thing. What I want forever, is you, Josie Parker. It's you I'd like to keep forever."

She smiled, now understanding what was happening here, and she was flattered by his jitters.

"Just so you know," he went on, "man of chivalry that I am, I've already asked your dad, and he is perfectly fine with the idea. So, it's all up to you; you can say yes, or you can say no, but what I'm really hoping for here is that you will consider saying yes sometime in the next thirty seconds. The two horses, four dogs, and this hungry man are really hoping you will say yes, really quickly, so we can all just get on with our day."

He was doing his best to play the comic. She'd never seen him quite

314 | Mimi Tashjian

this vulnerable. *Well,* she thought, *maybe I have.* Nevertheless, she found it incredibly sexy and adorable.

"So, what do you think?" he asked impatiently.

Josie didn't have to think for even a second. She knew what her answer would be, but before she could respond, Cleve spoke again, not nervously, but with confidence now.

"Oh and just one other thing. I was thinking, not that you are a girl who likes to wear a lot of jewelry, but just in the hope that you might say yes, like, right now, I asked my friend Joe to make this for me. Well, for you actually." He dangled a small, blue velvet box in the air for a second, and then set it up on the fireplace mantel.

Cleve walked back across the room to Josie, who stood up from where she'd been sitting on the bed, completely entranced by this romantic gesture but feeling a little underdressed for the occasion in her silly flannel Christmas pajamas. She put one hand out to stop him in his tracks.

"Really, Cleve?" She smiled and put her other hand on her hip. "Really?" She made her best sultry face and unbuttoned the first button of her pajama top. She took a step toward him. "You are asking me to marry you, when I am standing here in Frosty the Snowman pajamas? I haven't brushed my teeth or my hair, or washed my face. Really?" She held her smile and waited, knowing that he would come to her.

"Exactly." He moved in now and put one arm around her waist, drawing her into him so that her pelvis was pressed tightly against his. With the other hand, he pulled her loose, messy hair forward over each of her shoulders. He kissed each of her eyes and then used a finger to gently wipe the sleep from them. He released the next button of her pajama top, exposing more than a hint of cleavage. He tilted his head and raised his eyebrow, grinning.

"OK, that's better, really," he teased her back.

Then Cleve Gregory got serious. He kissed her, on her delicate rosebud lips, that kiss with intention.

"You're beautiful, Josie Parker, have I ever told you that? Now stop procrastinating and say yes already. Tell me you will marry me. I'm starting to feel like my luck might be waning." He held her close, with great sincerity in his eyes, waiting, hopelessly romantic, for her answer.

"Our luck is out in that barn," she said, as focused and serious as she could be, "and it goes by the name John Courage. But this, this is our life together, right here in front of us, and it is not waning. It has always been right in front of us; it just took us a while to catch up with it. Yes, I will marry you, Cleve Gregory, of course I will. I can't imagine my life without you in it, ever again. Yes, yes, yes," she said softly, definitively, joyfully. "Did I say yes? I meant to say absolutely, without any doubt, whenever you want. I can't wait to be married to you."

Josie Parker put her arms over Cleve Gregory's shoulders and kissed him back, a long, slow kiss, like his had been, with intention. She gently searched for the taste buds of his tongue and he reciprocated, searching for hers; as soon as they were found, it was just enough.

This kiss is the perfect kiss, she thought.

This kiss is the perfect kiss, he thought.

Cleve spun Josie away from him now, holding her hand as they danced a lighthearted southern shag around the bedroom, once again finding cheer in the sound of Bruce and Clarence's lively rendition of "Santa Claus is Coming to Town." After a few twirls, Cleve stopped at the fireplace, reached for the small box, and opened it. With the utmost chivalry, he removed the ring from the box and slid it onto the proper finger of Josie's left hand. The fit was perfect. The familiar chill ran up Josie's spine, and in her core, she felt the weakness he could so often elicit.

"Cleve." She reached to touch him. "What an incredibly beautiful ring. You are the most amazing man." In a voice barely audible she continued, "And you are the story of my life." The diamond, set in a horseshoe of sapphires, was as striking and as perfect as a ring could be. Josie knew right away that this would become a new heirloom, a Gregory family heirloom to span generations the way the Caldwell one had. She hugged her man with all her might, with all her heart.

"Merry Christmas, Cleve."

"Merry Christmas, my love."

Standing in front of her bedroom mirror, Josie took stock. Her beautiful engagement ring cast sparkles of the sun's reflection across the room as she twisted and turned her hair into a pair of braids. Her family, overnight, had grown immensely; she and Addie Crawford shared a bond that would never be broken. Her past was right there with her, waiting for morning hay out in the barn, sitting in an exquisite sterling silver box on her chest of drawers. Her present was everywhere around her, here at the Haskell cottage, there at Clover Field Farm. Her future was apparent, and she believed with all her heart that the future was bright.

She slipped the new Gucci belt Tessa had sent her for Christmas through the loops of her jeans, and pulled her navy cashmere sweater over a white camisole. She left her feet bare, knowing she'd be pulling on her muck boots imminently. She stood for a minute to admire the framed pictures she had been given last night by the Crawfords and her dad; Johnnie jumping in winning form with Addie in the stirrups at Devon, and Lars wrapping his neck around her the last Christmas day she'd spent with him, over ten years ago at Hidden Green Farm. She'd placed them up on the mantel, joining the photographs she cherished most.

"Merry Christmas, Mama, love you every day," she said out loud to the photo of the two girls Frank Parker had taken so many years ago. She gently dragged a finger down the side of the frame, then turned to exit the bedroom just as Cleve yelled in from the kitchen.

"Hey, Parker, in case you missed it the first time, or the second, you've got two homely-looking geldings, four dogs, and a happy, hungry man to feed. Get out of those snowman pajamas and get your ass out here!"

"Hey batta, batta, hold your horses. I'm on my way." And that she was.

ACKNOWLEDGMENTS

The fiction version of this story lived in my mind for several years before it began to come to life on my laptop. But this story in its true form began long ago. All of the characters have been developed based on a myriad of people, personalities, and circumstance that sculpted and colored my own youth.

In this regard there are so many individuals to thank, and I couldn't possibly name them all. There are a few whom I must recognize however, as my tale, no pun intended, could truly never have taken shape without them.

First and foremost I must recognize my childhood barn mate, Maryann Parkinson Minor, and her four-legged prize, John Courage. They inspired my imagination to write about the journey of a young woman whose passions paved the path of her destiny. Maryann and I lost touch when we were about fifteen, but when we reconnected after thirty or so years, I learned of her relationship with John Courage. From here I turned back in time and began to write this novel. Thank you, Maryann, for taking the time to tell me about him and about your own life story.

Thank you, Betty Moss, for reminding me that our mutual pal Laura Yorke is a literary representative and noted editor, and thank you, Laura, for the countless hours of support you offered as my friend, my editor, and as my agent. You gave me the confidence to get this story out there, and I know that is because you have, like so many young equestriennes, lived it yourself.

Scott Stewart and Ken Berkley, there are so many reasons for which to thank you both that I have dedicated this book to you. Here, I offer my gratitude for providing me with inspiring surroundings, the opportunity to ride so many quality horses, and for your enduring friendship, one of love and trust and an indescribable bond. I love you both unconditionally.

Kathy Russell, your incredible artistry with a camera lens and your patience with me and my million revisions resulted in a book cover that I cherish. More than that however, I cherish your friendship and I look forward to our next project together.

Terence Prunty and Paige Bellissimo, you truly brought Cleve and Josie to life for me; thank you for your enthusiasm, your time and your beauty. Samantha Darling, thank you for posing, and for your constant enthusiasm and support.

Cathy Zicherman, thank you for your encouragement and for being such a supportive force, and for taking care of my girl when I couldn't. Your positivity is infectious. You never let the negative break through. I love you and your whole family.

A most sincere thanks to all my pre-publication readers, Mimi and Sophie Gochman, Karen Long-Dwight, Alexa Weisman, Michael Doane, Patti Blank, Karen Strickland, and Eleanor Bright. Your comments and criticisms were so constructive and your love of this novel gave me the confidence to share Josie Parker's story with everyone.

To my publishing and editing team...Ingram Content Group and Scribe Freelance...this is as much your accomplishment as it is mine. John Ingram, thank you so much for making this happen. Daniel Middleton and Jill Holdsworth, your patience made this book exponentially better. Watching it transform from its initial form into the final manuscript was an incredible experience for me. Thank you, Craig Pollock and Kristen Williams, for literally making John Courage become a book.

John Fischer, it all started with your help at the Nantucket Atheneum. Thank you for your format tutoring. I could not have created John Courage without you. It would have been a long-hand nightmare if you had not shown me how to use Word.

Maryann, Patti, Mimi, Amy, Wendy, Connie, Lisa, Nancy, Mary... thanks for being such a profound and monumental part of my early equestrian life. You all inspired many of Josie's experiences.

To all my friends who share the passion of loving animals, especially horses, my own life is richer for your touching it; I am so grateful that horses brought us together, and as such that I was able to write this novel. I'm a lucky girl.

ABOUT THE AUTHOR

Mimi Tashjian grew up on the New Jersey shore, where she began riding real ponies, at the age of six, when her rocking horse collapsed. Since her teens she has been a competitive equestrienne on the national A-rated circuit and has garnered several national championships with her winning hunters. She raised her three children in Greenwich, Connecticut and these days divides her time mostly between the beaches of Nantucket, Massachusetts and the show rings of Wellington, Florida. Tashjian holds a degree from Hood College and has been writing for as long as she can remember. This is her first novel, from which a portion of the proceeds will be donated to the Equestrian Aid Foundation, among other equine related charities.

CPSIA information can be obtained at www.ICGtesting.com
Printed in the USA
LVOW11*0046170216

475404LV00004B/7/P